Praise for
Nebula Awards 20,
Edited by George Zebrowski

"A must-buy for the serious collection-builder, and certainly a rewarding piece of reading for anyone"
—*Fantasy & Science Fiction Review*

"Among the best fiction collections of any kind in the past year"—*Los Angeles Herald Examiner*

"A collection guaranteed to give you something to argue about, and a gift to make your friends eager to sample more of the varied entrees on the ever-growing science fiction menu"—*Christian Science Monitor*

"Superior writing—and imagination—in this book, all the way through"—COPLEY NEWS SERVICE

"The finest Nebula Award collection yet. . . . If you want to know where the cutting edge of the science fiction field is currently, buy *Nebula Awards 20.*"
—*Science Fiction Review*

"The best anthology of the year"—*Fantasy Review*

NEBULA
AWARDS 21

SFWA's Choices for the Best
Science Fiction and Fantasy
1985

EDITED BY
George Zebrowski

HARCOURT BRACE JOVANOVICH, PUBLISHERS

SAN DIEGO   NEW YORK   LONDON

The Library of Congress has cataloged this serial publication as follows:

The Nebula awards.—No. 21—San Diego [CA]: Harcourt Brace Jovanovich,
    Publishers, c1983-
    v.; 22 cm.
    Annual.
    Vols. for 1983-   published for the Science Fiction Writers of America.
    Continues: Nebula award stories (1982)
    ISSN 0741-5567 = The Nebula awards.
    1. Science fiction, American—Periodicals. I. Science Fiction Writers of
America.
    PS648.S3N38   83-647399
                            813'.0876'08—dc19
                                            AACR 2   MARC-S
    Library of Congress
    ISBN 0-15-164928-6
    ISBN 0-15-665478-4 (Harvest/HBJ:pbk.)
Designed by G. B. D. Smith
Printed in the United States of America
First edition

A B C D E

Permission acknowledgments appear on page 334, which constitutes a continuation
of the copyright page.

In Memory of

Frank Herbert 1920–1986
Thomas N. Scortia 1926–1986
Manly Wade Wellman 1903 1986

Contents

Introduction

GEORGE ZEBROWSKI

Throughout the year the members of the Science Fiction Writers of America read and recommend stories and novels for the annual Nebula Awards. These recommendations are recorded in a newsletter, and toward the end of the year the recommendations are counted. A preliminary ballot is then drawn up and circulated to the membership. The top five novels (40,000 words or more), novellas (17,500–39,999 words), novelettes (7,500–17,499 words), and short stories (fewer than 7,500 words) are placed on the final ballot, which is then sent to members for their votes. A Nebula Awards jury may add one additional nominee to each category.

The twenty-first annual Nebula Awards ballot was longer than usual, since a number of works tied in the preliminary voting. (Throughout the year, incidentally, recommendations for the preliminary ballot were very heavy.) The final ballot—with winners indicated here by asterisks—was:

For Novel

Blood Music by Greg Bear (Arbor House)
Dinner at Deviant's Palace by Tim Powers (Ace Books)
* *Ender's Game* by Orson Scott Card (Tor Books)
Helliconia Winter by Brian W. Aldiss (Atheneum)
The Postman by David Brin (Bantam Spectra Books)
The Remaking of Sigmund Freud by Barry N. Malzberg (Del Rey)
Schismatrix by Bruce Sterling (Arbor House)

For Novella

"24 Views of Mount Fuji, by Hokusai" by Roger Zelazny (*Isaac Asimov's Science Fiction Magazine*, July 1985)
"The Gorgon Field" by Kate Wilhelm (*Isaac Asimov's Science Fiction Magazine*, August 1985)
"Green Days in Brunei" by Bruce Sterling (*Isaac Asimov's Science Fiction Magazine*, October 1985)
"Green Mars" by Kim Stanley Robinson (*Isaac Asimov's Science Fiction Magazine*, September 1985)
"The Only Neat Thing to Do" by James Tiptree, Jr. (*The Magazine of Fantasy & Science Fiction*, October 1985)
* "Sailing to Byzantium" by Robert Silverberg (*Isaac Asimov's Science Fiction Magazine*, February 1985)

For Novelette

"Dogfight" by Michael Swanwick and William Gibson (*Omni*, July 1985)
"The Fringe" by Orson Scott Card (*The Magazine of Fantasy & Science Fiction*, October 1985)

"A Gift from the Graylanders" by Michael Bishop (*Isaac Asimov's Science Fiction Magazine*, September 1985)
"The Jaguar Hunter" by Lucius Shepard (*The Magazine of Fantasy & Science Fiction*, May 1985)
"Paladin of the Lost Hour" by Harlan Ellison (*Universe 15*, Doubleday; *The Twilight Zone Magazine*, December 1985)
* "Portraits of His Children" by George R. R. Martin (*Isaac Asimov's Science Fiction Magazine*, November 1985)
"Rockabye Baby" by S. C. Sykes (*Analog*, Mid-December, 1985)

For Short Story

"Flying Saucer Rock and Roll" by Howard Waldrop (*Omni*, January 1985)
"The Gods of Mars" by Gardner Dozois, Jack Dann, and Michael Swanwick (*Omni*, March 1985)
"Heirs of the Perisphere" by Howard Waldrop (*Playboy*, July 1985)
"Hong's Bluff" by William F. Wu (*Omni*, March 1985)
"More Than the Sum of His Parts" by Joe Haldeman (*Playboy*, May 1985)
* "Out of All Them Bright Stars" by Nancy Kress (*The Magazine of Fantasy & Science Fiction*, March 1985)
"Paper Dragons" by James P. Blaylock (*Imaginary Lands*, Ace Books)
"Snow" by John Crowley (*Omni*, November 1985)

The results were announced and the awards presented at the Nebula Awards Banquet, at the Claremont Hotel in Berkeley, California, on April 26, 1986.

A longer ballot gave the editor of this volume a greater variety of works to choose from, beyond the winners. A work by the author of the winning novel and the winning works in the three shorter forms must, of course, be included. As a caretaker of talent and not its master—a point editors should hire people to whisper in their ears at lunches—I sometimes wonder if my choices are a way of scolding, of emphasizing one set of qualities over others; but I answer always that no awards process can be perfect, and that the direction given to me by the process is greater than any purely personal judgments.

Nearly all awards have come under fire in recent years. The Pulitzer Prize for fiction is regarded by many as a guarantee of mediocrity, the American Book Awards have been judged as erratic in method of selection, the Nobel Prize for literature is perceived as political in its motives and increasingly inadequate as the list of greats who never received it grows embarrassingly large.

Complaints are just as vocal in the world of SF, the philosophical differences among critics just as irreconcilable. The Hugo is often described as a mere popularity contest, the Nebula as a bloody field of contention for Young Turks; the John W. Campbell Award, given by a jury, has been charged with being untrue to its namesake, and with purveying mandarin tastes. Awards will never please everyone, but a healthy awards process admits imperfection freely while celebrating the search for excellence.

I take pride in the fact that the Nebula Awards anthology can do what award results cannot do—present a field of contenders to readers, so that they may taste the greater solution from which the winning crystals precipitate. (A special feature of this year's anthology, by the way, is the nominees' comments in the headnotes preceding each piece.) But the chemical analogy breaks down, because any of these works might have won. No other SF awards process honors its contenders in quite this way.

Readers should always judge for themselves. They should not be guided by the malpractice of reviewers, or the bents of even great critics. Reading fiction is not a collective activity, nor is writing it; the individual voice is what we should prize most. I recommend the entire ballot to readers.*

The ballot is always the result of clashes of taste, of critical insistence, and of countless intangible pressures. It is a list for the thoughtful reader.

In an essay on the preceding Nebula Awards collection, Algis Budrys puts the problem into what I believe is a definitive perspective:

"These are our best in this given stripe of time, and if one doubts it to some extent, one cannot doubt that they at least *represent* our particular sorts of bestness in that given stripe of time. An undeniable sense of quality arises from reading this or any other Nebula Awards anthology, with its varied ingenious and elegant attacks on the problem of being excellent. This is because they are in fact almost certainly attacks, instead, on the problem of doing the best possible job on the story, and letting being excellent take care of itself."

Johnson City, New York
15 June 1986

---

*I recommend also *A History of the Hugo, Nebula, and International Fantasy Awards* by Donald Franson and Howard DeVore, Misfit Press, 1985. The book is updated periodically and is available from Howard DeVore, 4705 Weddel, Dearborn, Michigan 48125. The book's interest is in its listings of recommended works for the preliminary Nebula ballot and of the numbers of votes received. The sense of competition conveyed is striking. The list of works and where to find them is a unique and invaluable help to readers.

NEBULA
AWARDS 21

What Was 1985 That We Were Mindful of It?

ALGIS BUDRYS

Algis Budrys, the author of the classic novels *Rogue Moon, Who?* and *Some Will Not Die*, as well as the more recent, highly praised *Michaelmas*, is also the best American critic of SF now writing. His essays appear in *The Magazine of Fantasy & Science Fiction*. His collected criticism from *Galaxy* was recently published as *Benchmarks* and won the 1986 Locus Award for best nonfiction. The author of numerous works of short fiction, Budrys is a member of the SFWA Hall of Fame and was honored with a Special Award from the Mystery Writers of America. A nurturer of new talent, Budrys has been a teacher at the annual Clarion summer writing workshop at Michigan State University and serves as a judge and editor for the Writers of the Future program. He is working on a new novel.

The thing about a nebula is that it takes on more character and definition as one gets farther away from it. Sitting at the banquet where the

Nebulas for 1985 were awarded by the membership of the SFWA, I was struck by two facts: one, that it's high time the Science Fiction Writers of America became, more accurately, the Speculative Fiction Writers of Anywhere; and two, that I could not discern in what ways 1985 stemmed from 1984 and so was going to have a terrible time writing this essay. Now that some days have passed, matters with regard to the latter are a little easier. But not much.

Annual awards—prestigious annual awards, which over the years, with few exceptions, have, indeed, identified the most significant work of their time—such awards take on mystical meaning. It is not pleasant to be a nominee waiting for the final verdict, making small talk and trying to keep down one's dinner. But that ends. Happily, sadly, or ambiguously, the announcement is made, after what only seems an eternity, and then the results are recorded, and one is either a winner or not. But then come those, such as I, who attempt to divine some greater meaning from it all, and that sort of activity goes on forever.

Going on forever, and reaching fresh conclusions with each fresh go, these post-factum assessments are presumed to finally locate the *character* of a time—to explain what forces caused certain persons to write in certain ways at a certain time, and what then caused their peers at that time to nominate that work for an award and then single out sole winners, thus implying that there are stories which are exactly on the mark and others which only approach it. That leads to identifying the mark, and that done, we can all relax, but only until the next reassessment occurs. When it occurs, it may very well controvert what was seemingly irrefutable.

For example, SF expert Richard Lupoff once edited some very promising anthologies of stories which *should* have won awards, and although we are confronted in that case by only one man's opinion, it was at least as persuasive as that of any essayist. This very volume contains some non-winners which are, nevertheless, outstanding stories that George Zebrowski chose to put in. By some tests—the frequency of reprints in future years, for example—some of them may eventually be said to have proven "better" than those which won the trophy. That's hardly the only relevant test, but it is a process indicative of the fact that excellence is in some ways a transient thing. Some of it arises from absolute merit; some of it derives from where the observer was standing at the time.

Among the winners stands Robert Silverberg, for his ingenious novella, "Sailing to Byzantium." Silverberg, like all the category winners this time, began his career in the latter half of this century (in 1954, to be precise). In 1971, novelette category winner George R. R. Martin (for "Portraits of His Children") published his first professional story. Novel winner Orson Scott Card, with Ender's Game, is more recently arrived than that—too recent to be listed in most of the standard reference works on SF—and so, too, is Nancy Kress, who gained the Nebula for her short story, "Out of All Them Bright Stars" (and gave the most gracious, best thought-out acceptance speech I have ever heard from any winner of any award).

One would think this tendency toward youth might have been balanced by the Grand Master Award to Arthur C. Clarke. But even Clarke began with first sales in 1946, and while that's not yesterday, it's not back in the traditional "Golden Age," either. Seven Grand Master Awards have now been given; Clarke joins Andre Norton as the only other SF giant to have been so honored for work begun after World War II.

That is work begun in a different universe from the one in which it first became possible to think about newsstand-borne SF as a literature. In effect, a certain time of struggle ended in 1945 with the detonation of the atomic bomb—as it was then called, borrowing terminology from the days when science fiction was still "scientifiction" or "stf" (pronounced "stef"). Other times of other sorts of struggle were to follow, and we are doubtless in one now, and shall speak of it. But it certainly had become impossible for the larger world to ignore science fiction or dismiss its practitioners. This condition persists; it takes on various aspects, and some of those are happier than others for some of us. But it *is* better than what came before.

Those who bear scars from the 1950s may smile wryly, but it is better to be wounded over the question of how well one writes than it is to be told that what one does is not writing. And that's the difference. Before the world had to cope with the fact of the bomb—oh, and the jet plane, and radar, and guided missiles—science fiction was the raving of "visionaries" (i.e., sweaty, pop-eyed lunatics). In response to this, some of our number tried to assert artistic links that would make it as respectable as fantasy, with its well-known classical roots. As a tactic, this fell short of its objective. Science fiction presented as a special case of fantasy somehow did not acquire any solider virtues in the public's esteem.

This hunt for the public's esteem occupied much of our thinking at the time. We were in a difficult position; no matter how sensibly we were addressed by our loved ones, or how sensibly we ourselves assessed our situations, we couldn't stop doing SF, either as producers or consumers. I suppose the only choice was to hope we could convert the world to our orientation. The place to start, rationally enough, would be with the literary establishment, which at least in some cases praised "experimental" fiction and spoke of various needs for "new" literary domains. We had failed to notice—we still fail to notice—that the literary establishment is in fact solidly conservative. "Experimental" means "restricted" and "new" means "revived." The people who migrate to New York City from Iowa and get into the literary mainstream do not in truth leave behind the good, age-old thought canals that make the corn grow.

They simply adopt a new vocabulary. And, oh, we wanted so much to share in it!

Time passed. After the bomb, which made us scarily knowledgeable, we were writers. We were writers because we obviously all had technical educations and connections. That would entail some requirement for concocting reports and memos, and thus enable us to flange out some approximation of narrative prose. By 1950 or so there were even some people with *real*—that is, conventional—writing experience who were willing to come in from time to time and demonstrate how it ought to be done. You may not think so, and certainly I didn't think so at the time, which coincided with my noviliate, but that *is* better.

It is not, as noted, better if it is happening to you right then. What I had expected, as an increasingly sophisticated member of the SF community in the 1940s, was that when I became a professional writer in, say, 1952 at the age of twenty-one—which I did—the ghetto would welcome me. I would of course be despicable everywhere else, but I would have a secure place in SF. You may imagine my disgust when variously gentile people began knocking at the walls, and even more my anguish when some of us inside threw open the gates at every least provocation, dragged in some of these downy birds, and set them up as models and arbiters while uttering glad cries. It still hurts to leaf through one of the 1950s' prestigious Best SF of the Year volumes, for instance, and find it crammed full of editorial matter kissing the south porches of conventional icons which have mostly since vanished in puce pufflets of insincere vapor.

It was a difficult time. Most of us who broke in then— Philip K. Dick, Robert Sheckley, Michael Shaara, Walter Tevis—had in fact been headed for writing careers all along and getting college educations which tended in that direction. Our affinity for SF came from honest immersion in *Amazing Stories, Astounding, Planet,* and *Startling,* but our technical educations were, by and large, no more than what any other liberal arts major rubs up against. As for practical experience, Shaara had been a policeman, I had been a landscape gardener and a cook, Sheckley had played guitar in a dance band, Dick had been a classical disc jockey, and Tevis, one presumes, had been hanging out in pool halls. In school, we had read the approved works of the approved writers, perused the recommended anthologies, and could do "Thee of the bridge, Roberto," shtick ad libitum with the best of them while humming calypso melodies. We paced the streets of Greenwich Village in the warm summer evenings, impressing tourists with our manner. It hurt, and it baffled, to be told by the establishment that we were technocrat clods, while from among our own number anthologist Judith Merril characterized us as stultified because we weren't publishing in the *Kenyon Review* so she could have discovered us.

But we worked on it, and things were beginning to take shape. There was an SF boom on in the magazines, and we could make a living. We ignored the strangers, and they eventually went away, pretty much; none of them knew how to write a story around an unrelated cover painting for a Bob Lowndes magazine. We were the first wave of truly professional writers generated by SF as descended from the inspiration of Hugo Gernsback, and we had shaken down into doing good variations on the expectable. Then Milford happened.

Right about the middle 1950s, there was a world convention in New York City, a place located about a hundred miles east of Milford, Pennsylvania, where Damon Knight, James Blish, and Judith Merril all lived because it was cheap and it was rural for their children. Knight was the pioneering critical book-review writer on SF, and the author of some short stories and novelettes that were vastly admirable for technique as well as ideation; he had a lot of clout. So, too, did Judith Merril, and no one who had ever met Jim Blish ever thought him stupid or uncultured, in both of C. P. Snow's mistaken senses of that word. Knight told us in New York that he and his cohorts were throwing a writers' conference in Milford next week, and would we all come?

Much to our amazement—not understanding the thing that was driving us—most of us did. Milford, a town accustomed to strange visitors and not altogether straight itself, yawned. But we, in a quasi-abandoned house on the west bank of the sluggish Delaware, were galvanized. There had never been so many of us in one room with unobstructed sight lines before, and as we listened to each other, we discovered that while writing may be a lonely profession—and SF writing a species of outright ostracism—we were all lonely in pretty much the same way.

And then the editors arrived—book publishers' editors, sent out to scout around for material that would fuel the hoped-for SF boom in that medium. They were cautious: most of them had only the foggiest notion of what this new thing might be. They were soft-spoken; they were accustomed to dealing with writers of another stripe. We, on the other hand, were accustomed to dealing with editors of another stripe—pulp-trained magazine editors who owned us for about two cents per word, and even when not loud-voiced were knowledgeably cynical toward pretensions, having seen a lot of us monkeys come and go, and mostly being converted monkeys themselves. None of them showed up to set an example of animal training for their more naive brethren. And we ate those.

A funny thing had happened to us on crossing the Delaware. All our lives, we had been thinking of ourselves as isolated cases, occasionally bumping into each other in small groups at conventions, or now and then visiting one another, but being essentially single-handed. Suddenly we had found that there might be another way of looking at it.

There is a painting in my mind, not yet executed but historically inevitable. It is done in the style sometimes known as Soviet realism. It will show a room full of people: the common room of a Milford, PA, inn on an early fall afternoon. Pitchers that once held beer, and empty pizza plates, can be seen on the long tables. Previously seated at the tables are about fifty science fiction writers—one can recognize Knight, Blish, and Merril, Theodore Sturgeon, Cyril Kornbluth, Theodore L. Thomas, Shag Graetz, Theodore R. Cogswell, and others. They are now in the act of rising to their feet. Some stare at each other in dawning wonder and fierce joy. Some grope for weapons. Most have their eyes fixed in one direction—toward an increasingly apprehensive, cowering knot of individuals on the other side of the room.

It is obvious from the leather patches on their jackets and their horn-rimmed glasses, to say nothing of the blue pencils peeping from their pockets, who these victims are. Their arms and hands are rising in front of their recoiling bodies. It is a feeble, futile reflex of self-protection. The title of the painting is *Liberty Dawns upon the Stefnists.*

It really was that way, in a way, though Ted Thomas and half the other people in the room will resent the analogy to bolshevism. Something catalyzed at what had been billed as a convivial meet-the-editors gathering. What it was, was the years of being non-U, which we had all been feeling but having to live with, and so pushing to the backs of our minds. Knight had pushed it toward the front of his. Milford was billed as an opportunity to meet as craftspersons, and in later years there was, indeed, a lot of emphasis on workshopping. But what the *first* Milford was, was in essence a union-organizing convocation.

It was not the SFWA. In due course, after fits and starts

over the succeeding years, it led to the formation of the
SFWA, with Knight as its founding president. But what it
was at Milford was a nameless, proud thing; an often profoundly emotional sense that we were far more alike than
we were different from each other. Every writer feels a
broad and deep range of affronts in the course of evolving
from youth to attainment; science fiction writers of those
generations feel them in particular. It's an inevitable process, and some even consider it a virtue in disguise. (Per-
sonally, I could have done without.) But at Milford we
caught a glimpse of the future—editors who frankly knew
less about it than we did, and publishers who could be
negotiated with, not truckled to. We began, dimly, to grasp
what contract terms were. Most of us had never seen anything beyond a rubber-stamp clause on the back of a check;
endorse the check, and you sold the aforementioned rights,
which usually boiled down to all rights, forever. We began
to tell each other the story of how Street & Smith, owner
thus of all rights to Harry Bates's "Farewell to The Master," had delightedly accepted 20th Century-Fox's first offer for the film rights: $400.00. As a paternalistic corporation
with a code of ethics, S&S generously gave Bates half, which
more than covered the price of tickets and popcorn, and
perhaps a few fifths of something comforting, when *The
Day the Earth Stood Still* was released in 1951. We told it to
ourselves with keen-edged little promises to ourselves about
our own futures.

Some have been kept, some have been broken. But the
idea that we might be worthy of serious attention, and that
the work might not be ephemeral, took hold and stayed.
Literarily, that's of course the more important thing. But
not having its writers die broke or having them avoid years
of the mind-bending circumstantial despairs and mind-
numbing vices that money panic engenders, is also of some
importance to a literature. (The last time I saw Harry Bates
alive, he was standing on the southeast corner of Sixth

Avenue and Fourteenth Street, leaning against the Nedick's, dressed by the Salvation Army, and his face looked numb as he stared unblinking westward in the twilight. People were carefully walking around him.)

So we here in the States were feeling pretty good about things, and considered that things were as they ought to be except for some few housekeeping details. Then someone—Judy, actually—discovered the New Wave and named it, over its own fervent objections that it didn't exist and it was all a coincidence.

Having learned at least the rudiments of how to hold our own on the outside, we now bedeviled ourselves. The New Wave was to be our homegrown hair shirt. It seems that all the time John Campbell was evolving SF over in the States, things had been going on, silently but deeply, over across the water.

All of us over here knew there were just two kinds of English SF writers: those who wrote like Americans for the American market—Arthur C. Clarke, Eric Frank Russell, A. Bertram Chandler—and those who were probably all one indefatigable man probably not named Astron del Martia, who had yet to sell his first contribution to *Astounding*.

Little did we know. It seems that while all this was going on, people who had been attending liberal arts colleges over *there*, or at least hanging around them, had been paying no attention to John W. Campbell, Jr., at all . . . except to despise him and all his descendants. Furthermore, they were firing up to have a magazine of their own— *New Worlds* (or, as one number was called, *Novy Mir*).

It took a while for the western branch of SF to accommodate to all that. The onslaught presented by those people was founded on approved reading lists drawn up by a far different sort of professor, and it was propelled by the same sort of ferocity that had brought Lester del Rey raging out of St. Charles, Minnesota (and Harlan Ellison out of Shaker Heights, Ohio?). But it was a more articulate, more waspish, and in some cases, more mannered ferocity. Too, there was a certain sense that for some of these people, SF was not a dead-serious thing; it was a genre, and to be played with as a sign of intellectual dexterity, but not to be believed in, not to be home and warmth and hidey-hole in asperous times. That was a blow struck at the very fundamentals of some of the observers standing aghast. Tell you the truth, I still don't like that part.

Nor were things helped much at first when Kingsley Amis (A) unexpectedly lectured on SF as a visiting disquisitor at Princeton, and (B) flabbergastingly declared it to be primarily a vehicle for social commentary, and named Frederik Pohl, not Robert Heinlein or John W. Campbell, Jr.—not even Ray Bradbury—as its brightest light. Frederik Pohl? The former James McCreigh and occasional Dirk Wylie, the retired literary agent and sometime (obviously) junior collaborator with Cyril Kornbluth? What in the world had Pohl ever written on his own except for some obviously trivial, because unliteral, short pieces for *Galaxy* magazine. *Galaxy* was hardly the cultural bellwether of SF by then, if it had ever been. Frederik *Pohl?*

Well, Mr. Pohl has since served as president of the SFWA and has written one or two nice longer works, *and* there are plenty of New Wave elements in modern-day SF, and the sky has not fallen. But it was, please believe my recollection, a very near thing. And I still don't like that one part. But we managed to get on down the road to the next controversion, and as such things will, a common complaint brought the formerly divided sides together.

Not to put too fine a face upon it, not all of us were delighted by the influx of "Star Trek" aficionados. They flooded our community, took over our conventions, ran around with those ridiculous pointy ears on, and to this day there is an underground school of private writing in which certain lady writers create for each other tales in which Spock and Kirk are lovers, so pervasive has the influence been.

More interesting, literarily, is the fact that "Star Trek" scenarios are in the mode of "modern" science fiction, which in the prose literature is synonymous with the 1940s. So as readers, the Trekkies were out of sync with the field, but there were, and are, so many of them that a pseudo-"modern" SF, not all of it contained solely within the continuing "Star Trek" novel genre, continues to cater to them and to exist beside—one could not actually say adulterate—the line of progress which the prose literature evolved.

Too, there's the fact that the Trekkies, who have now settled down peacefully within our ranks—just as well, considering how many of them there are—were probably the first science fiction fans not made by still media. Certainly, in their hundreds of thousands, they represented the most significant "nonliterary" event in SF history. Until *Star Wars*, of course.

Up till then, SF films had come and gone, each turning a few people to or away from SF, none of major importance except to cult followers in or out of the SF community. What has happened since George Lucas took up where *Planet Stories* left off is better handled as an event than as a trilogy of films.

It has been known for a long time that there is a market for tales combining quasi-oriental mysticism with rocket ships, ray pistols, and swords. An early beneficiary of this truth was Edgar Rice Burroughs, who made a lot of money out of John Carter of Mars while making a lot more out of Tarzan. Probably our best, certainly our steadiest practitioner in the genre was Leigh Brackett, who then actually worked on the second *Wars* film. It was the least they could do for her, since the entire series—the good parts, at least—is pure unabashed Brackett.

Some of us loved it. Certainly I loved the idea, successfully conveyed in the first film. But what it meant was a vast new public convinced it now understood what this science fiction/fantasy stuff was, and a roaring demand for space opera, special effects even in films that were better off without them, and a general tendency, or stampede, toward sword-swinging adventure of every stripe. Where oriental legends ran out, Celtic ones would do. Where Princess Leia had trod, scores of other young ladies now took up the gonfalon in scores of hopeless causes, persevering bravely. If it wasn't *The Lord of the Rings* or *Star Wars*, or their imitations, it was some blend of the two. Whatever "modern" SF, or stateside postmodernism, or the New Wave, or even what the amalgam of all those things plus the Trekkies had settled into, the clash of armor and the clank of contrivance dashed them all offstage.

One could hardly stop to draw breath. Every time you looked at SF, it had changed. And today, just when we thought we were going to suffer death by crush from trilogies and tetralogies, we suddenly have the "cyberpunk" movement, with its short, crisp, ultratechnological mask behind which it tells its romantic stories and its authors who—except for the sharp contrast presented by the diffident demeanor of leading light William Gibson—have a marked tendency toward chutzpah, as if the world had never seen fauvism before.

But, no—that's not today. That was yesterday. Good old yesterday, as Steve McQueen muses in *The Blob*. Only yesterday we were vehement and nasty; today we are suddenly Nancy Kress. And although *Ender's Game* is a novel about a child trained to war, it is a profoundly humane piece of work, informed by the life and thought of a profoundly gentle man.

As I looked at them standing there for the group photo, holding their Nebulas, it struck me that every one of them was markedly soft-spoken, though undeniably tough under it. (Most good writers are tough.) My friend George R.

R. Martin, who has stood up to some very mean things, is as gentle as a lamb. And my friend Bob Silverberg, who can flay with the rise of an eyebrow, does so very, very softly, though with a not fully concealed grin. Come to think of it, George actually talks like a Rogers Park mugger. And Scott Card has yet to give anyone the impression that his good manners are anything but the manners of a man who feels responsible for many reserved abilities.

I must get to know Nancy Kress better, I think.

It was odd, sitting there in the Claremont Resort Hotel overlooking San Francisco Bay, sipping Old Deductible and contemplating the west bank of the Delaware, and another time that was really exactly like this time, and the next.

We shall meet again, I thought to myself, and hear other winners announced, and we shall call them excellent. (Or we shall flare up and rail against them, in a brief spasm before we recall that we are not children, nor the sort of *nouveaux riches* who are execrable to servants. That will not be of consequence.) We shall be a year farther along, we shall call things excellent that we would not have called excellent a year ago, or a year hence from next year.

But they shall all be excellent, nevertheless. I don't know how much excellence we really have in us when compared to some other community. But if you prick us, we bleed, and if you do not stifle us, we sing, we have sung, we shall sing.

Heirs of the
Perisphere

HOWARD WALDROP

Howard Waldrop won a
Nebula in 1980 for his novelette "The Ugly Chickens."
His short fiction has appeared in *Playboy*, *Omni*, *Universe*, *Light Years and Dark*, and *Afterlives*. Doubleday has
just published his collection *Howard Who?* About "Heirs
of the Perisphere" he writes:

*"I'd wanted to do this story since I was six years old and
first saw pictures of the Westinghouse time capsule in the 1939
World's Fair. The presumption of people sticking things in the
ground to tell folks five thousand years from now about what
we were like struck me as strange even when I was only six."*

Bruce McAllister observed that this story "recapitulates all of science fiction itself *and* American culture, and
does it beautifully."

Things had not been going
well at the factory for the past fifteen hundred years or so.

A rare thunderstorm, a soaking rain and a freak lightning bolt changed all that.

When the lightning hit, an emergency generator went

to work as it had been built to do a millennium and a half before. It cranked up and ran the assembly line for a few minutes before freezing up and shedding its brushes and armatures in a fine spray. It had run just long enough to finish up some work in the custom-design section.

The factory completed, hastily certified, and wrongly programmed the three products that had been on the assembly line fifteen centuries before. Then the place went dark again.

"Gawrsh," said one of them, "it shore is dark in here!"

"Well, huh-huh, we can always use the infrared they gave us."

"Wak, wak, wak!" said the third. "What's the big idea?"

The custom-order jobs were animato-mechanical simulacra. They were designed to speak and act like the famous cartoon creations of a multimillionaire artist who late in life, in the latter half of the twentieth century, had opened a series of gigantic amusement parks.

Once, these giant theme parks had employed persons in costumes to act as hosts. Then the corporation that had run things after the cartoonist's death had seen the wisdom of building robots.

The simulacra would be less expensive in the long run, would never be late for work, could be programmed to speak many languages and would never try to pick up the clean-cut boys and girls who visited the parks.

These three had been built to be host robots in the third and largest of the parks, the one separated by an ocean from the two others.

The tallest of them had started as a cartoon dog but had become upright and had acquired a set of baggy pants, balloon shoes, a sweatshirt, a black vest and white gloves. On his head was a miniature carpenter's hat; long ears hung from it. He had two prominent incisors in his muzzle. He stood almost two meters tall and answered to the name GUF.

The second, a little shorter, was a white duck with a bright orange bill and feet and a blue-and-white sailor's tunic and cap. He had large eyes with little cuts out of the upper right corners of the pupils. He was naked from the waist down and was the only one of the three without gloves. He answered to the name DUN.

The third and smallest, just over a meter, was a rodent. He wore a red-bibbed playsuit with two large gold buttons at the waistline. He was shirtless and had shoes like two pieces of bread dough. His tail was long and thin, like a whip. His bare arms, legs, and chest were black, his face a pinkish tan. His white gloves were especially prominent. His most striking feature was his ears, which rotated on a track, first one way, then the other, so that seen from any angle, they could look like featureless black circles.

His name was MIK. His eyes, like those of GUF, were large, and the pupils were big round dots. His nose ended in a perfect sphere of polished onyx.

"Well," said MIK, brushing dust from his body, "I guess we'd better, huh-huh, get to work."

"Uh-hyuk," said GUF. "Won't be many people at thuh park in weather like thiyus."

"Oh, boy! Oh, boy!" quacked DUN. "Rain! Wak, wak, wak!" He ran out through a huge crack in the factory wall through which streamed rain and mist.

MIK and GUF came behind, GUF ambling with his hands in his pockets. MIK followed him, ranging in the ultraviolet and infrared, getting the feel of the landscape through the rain. "You'd have thought, huh-huh, they might have sent a truck over or something," he said. "I guess we'll have to walk."

"I didn't notice anyone at thuh facktry," said GUF. "Even if it was a day off, yuh'd think some of thuh workers would give unceasingly of their time, because, after all, thuh means of produckshun must be kept in thuh hands of thuh workers, uh-hyuk!"

GUF's specialty was communicating with visitors from the large totalitarian countries to the west of the park. He was especially well versed in dialectical materialism and correct Mao thought.

As abruptly as it had started, the storm ended. Great ragged gouts broke in the clouds, revealing fast-moving cirrus, a bright blue sky, the glow of a warming sun.

MIK looked around, consulting his programming. "That way, guys!" he said, unsure of himself. There were no familiar landmarks. All around them was rubble, and far away in the other direction was a sluggish ocean.

It was getting dark. The three sat on a pile of concrete.

"Looks like thuh park is closed," said GUF.

MIK sat with his hands under his chin. "This just isn't right, guys," he said. "We were supposed to report to the programming hut to get our first day's instructions. Now we can't even find the park!"

"Well, uh-hyuk," said GUF, "I seem tuh remember we could get aholt of thuh satellite in a 'mergency."

"Sure!" said MIK, jumping to his feet and pounding his fist into his glove. "That's it! Let's see, what frequency was that?"

"Six point five oh four," said DUN. He looked eastward. "Maybe I'll go to the ocean."

"Better stay here whiles we find somethin' out," said GUF.

"Well, make it snappy," said DUN.

MIK tuned in the frequency and broadcast the park's call letters.

"Zzzzzz. What? HOOSAT?"

"Uh, this is MIK, a simulacrum at the park. We're trying to get hold of one of the other parks for, huh-huh, instructions."

"In what language do you wish to communicate?" asked the satellite.

"Oh, sorry, huh-huh. We speak Japanese to each other, but we'll switch over to Artran if that's easier for you." GUF and DUN tuned in also.

"It's been a very long while since anyone spoke with me from down there." The satellite's well-modulated voice snapped and popped. "If you must know," HOOSAT continued, "it's been a while since anyone contacted me from anywhere. I can't say much for the stability of my orbit, either. Once, I was forty thousand kilometers up, very stable. . . ."

"Could you put us through to one of the other parks or maybe the studio itself, if you can do that? We'd, huh-huh, like to find out where to report for work."

"I'll attempt it," said HOOSAT. There was a pause and some static. "Predictably, there's no answer at any of the locations."

"Where are thuh folks?" asked GUF.

"I don't know. We satellites and monitoring stations used to worry about that frequently. Something happened to them."

"What?" asked all three robots at once.

"Hard to comprehend," said HOOSAT. "Ten or fifteen centuries ago. Very noisy in all spectra, then silence. Most of the ground stations ceased functioning within a century of that."

Then there was a burst of fuzzy static.

"Hello? HOOSAT?" asked the satellite. "It's been a long time since anyone . . ."

"It's still us!" said MIK. "The simulacra from the park. We—"

"Oh, that's right. What can I do for you?"

"Tell us where the people went."

"I have no idea."

"Well, where can we find out?" asked MIK.

"You might try the library."

"Where's that?"

"Let me focus in. I can give you the coordinates. Do you have standard navigational programming?"

"Boy, do we!" said MIK.

"Well, here's what you do. . . ."

"I'm sure there used to be many books here," said MIK. "It all seems to have turned to powder, though, doesn't it?"

"Doggone wizoo-wazoo waste of time," said DUN. He sat on one of the piles of dirt in the large broken-down building of which only one massive wall still stood. The recent rain had turned the meter-deep powder on the floor into a papier-mâché sludge.

"I guess there's nothing to do but start looking," said MIK.

"Hey, MIK, looka this!" yelled GUF. He came running with a steel box. "I found this just over there."

The box was plain, unmarked. There was a heavy lock to which MIK applied various pressures.

"It's, huh-huh, stuck."

"Gimme that!" yelled DUN. He grabbed it. Soon he was muttering under his beak. "Doggone razzle-frazzin' dad-gum thing!" He pulled and pushed, his face and bill turning redder and redder. He gripped the box with both his feet and hands. "Doggone dad-gum!" he yelled.

Suddenly he grew teeth, his brow slammed down, his shoulders tensed and he went into a blurred fury of movement. *"Wak, wak, wak, wak, wak!"* he screamed.

The box broke open and flew into three parts. So did the book inside.

DUN was still tearing in his fury.

"Wait! Look out, DUN!" yelled MIK. "Wait!"

"Gawrsh!" said GUF, running after the pages blowing in the breeze. "Help me, MIK!"

DUN stood atop the rubble, parts of the box and the book gripped in each hand. He simulated hard breathing, the redness draining from his face.

"It's open," he said quietly.

"Well, from what we've got left," said MIK, "this is called *The Book of the Time Capsule*, and it says they buried a cylinder a very, very long time ago. They printed up five thousand copies of this book and sent it to places all around the world where they thought it would be safe. They printed this book on acid-free paper and stuff like that so it wouldn't fall apart.

"And they thought what they put in the time capsule itself could explain to later generations what people were like in their day. So I figure maybe it could explain something to us, too."

"Well, let's go," said DUN.

"Well, huh-huh," said MIK. "I checked with HOOSAT and gave him the coordinates and, huh-huh, it's quite a little ways away."

"How far?" asked DUN, his brow beetling.

"Oh, huh-huh, about eighteen thousand kilometers. Just about halfway around the world."

"Oh, my aching feet!" said DUN.

"That's not literally true," said GUF. He turned to MIK. "Yuh think we should go that far?"

"Well, I'm not sure what we'll find. Those pages were lost when DUN opened the box. . . ."

"I'm sorry," said DUN in a contrite, small voice.

"But the people of that time were sure that everything could be explained by what was in the capsule."

"And yuh think it's still there?" asked GUF.

MIK put a determined look on his face. "I figure the only thing for us to do is set our caps, start out and whistle a little tune," he said.

"Yuh don't have a cap, MIK," said GUF.

"Well, I can still whistle! Let's go, fellas," he said. "It's *this* way!"

He puckered his lips and blew a work song. DUN quacked a tune about boats and water. GUF hummed *The East Is Red*.

They set off in this way across what had been the bottom of the Sea of Japan.

They were having troubles. Three weeks before, they had come to the end of all the songs with which each had been programmed and had had to start repeating themselves.

Their lubricants were beginning to fail; their hastily wired circuitry was overworked. GUF had a troublesome extensor in his ankle that sometimes hung up. But he went along cheerfully, sometimes hopping and quickstepping to catch up with the others when the foot refused to flex.

The major problem was the cold. There was a vast difference between the climate they had been built for and the one they found themselves in. The landscape was rocky and empty, the wind blew fiercely and it had begun to snow.

The terrain was difficult and the maps HOOSAT had given them were outdated. Something drastic had changed the course of rivers, the land, the shore line of the ocean itself. They detoured frequently.

The cold worked hardest on DUN. He was poorly insulated, and they had to slow their pace to his. He would do anything to avoid a snowdrift and so expended even more energy.

They stopped in the middle of a raging blizzard.

"Uh, MIK?" said GUF. "I don't think DUN can go much farther in this weather. An' my leg is givin' me lots o' problems. Yuh think maybe we could find someplace to hole up fer a spell?"

MIK looked at the bleakness and the whipping snow around them. "I guess you're right. Warmer weather would do us all some good. We'd conserve both heat and energy. Let's find a good place."

"Hey, DUN," said GUF. "Let's find a hidey-hole!"

"Oh, goody gumdrops!" said DUN. "I'm so cold."

They eventually found a deep rock shelter with a low fault crevice at the back. MIK had them gather up what sparse vegetation there was and take it into the shelter. MIK talked to HOOSAT, then wriggled his way through the brush they had piled to the other two.

Inside, they could barely hear the wind and snow. It was only slightly warmer than outside, but it felt wonderful and safe.

"I told HOOSAT to wake us up when it got warmer," said MIK. "Then we'll get on to that time capsule and find out all about people."

"G'night, MIK," said GUF.

"Good night, DUN," said MIK.

"Sleep tight and don't let the bedbugs bite. Wak, wak, wak," said DUN.

They shut themselves off.

MIK woke up. It was dark in the rock shelter, but it was also much warmer.

The brush was all crumbled away. A meter of rock and dust covered the cave floor, the dust stirring in the warm wind.

"Hey, fellas!" said MIK. "Hey, wake up. Spring is here!"

They stirred themselves.

"Let's go thank HOOSAT and get our bearings and be on our way," said MIK.

They stepped outside.

The stars were in the wrong places.

"Uh-oh!" said GUF.

"Would you look at that?" said DUN.

"I think we overslept," said MIK. "Let's see what HOOSAT has to say."

"Huh? HOOSAT?"

"Hello. This is DUN and MIK and GUF."

HOOSAT's voice now sounded like a badger whistling through its teeth.

"Glad to see ya up," said the satellite.

"We asked you to wake us up as soon as it got warmer!" said MIK.

"It just *got* warmer."

"It did?" asked GUF.

"Shoulda seen it," said HOOSAT. "Ice everywhere. Big ol' glaciers. You still aimin' to dig up that capsule thing?"

"Yes," said MIK, "we are."

"Well, you got an easy trip from now on. No more mountains in the way."

"What about people?" asked MIK.

"I ain't heard from any. My friend the military satellite said he thought he saw some fires, little teeny ones, but his eyes weren't what they used to be. He's gone now, too."

"Thuh fires mighta been built by people?" asked GUF.

"It's sorta likely. Weather ain't been much for lightning," said HOOSAT. "Hey, bub, you still got all those coordinates I give you?"

"I think so," said MIK.

"Well, I better give you new ones off these new constellations. Hold still; my aim ain't so good anymore." He dumped a bunch of numbers into MIK's head. "I won't be talkin' to you much longer."

"Why not?" they all asked.

"Well, you know . . . my orbit. I feel better now than I have in centuries. Real spry. Must be the ionization. Started a couple o' weeks ago. Sure has been nice talkin' to you young fellers after so long a time. Sure am glad I remembered to wake you up. I wish y'all a lotta luck. Boy, this air has a punch like a mule. Be careful. Good-bye."

Across the unfamiliar stars overhead, a point of light blazed, streaked in a long arc, then died on the night.

"Well," said MIK, "we're on our own."

"Gawrsh, I feel all sad," said GUF.

The trip was uneventful for the next few months. They walked across the long land bridge down a valley between stumps of mountains with the white teeth of glaciers still on them. They crossed a low range and entered flat land, without topsoil, from which dry river courses ran to the south. Then there was a land where things were flowering after the long winter. New streams sprang up.

They saw fire once and detoured but found only a burnt patch of forest. Once, way off in the distance, they saw a speck of light but didn't go to investigate, thinking it only another prairie fire.

Within two hundred kilometers of their goal, the land changed again to a flat, sandy waste littered with huge rocks. Little vegetation grew. There were few insects and animals, mostly lizards, which DUN chased every chance he got. The warmth seemed to be doing him good.

GUF's leg worsened. The foot first stuck, then flopped and windmilled. GUF kept humming songs and raggedly marching along with the other two.

DUN stopped, turned and watched behind them.

"What's wrong?" asked MIK.

"I got a feeling we're being followed," said DUN, squatting down behind a rock.

All three watched for a few minutes, ranging up and down the spectrum.

"DUN, I think mebbe yer seein' things, uh-hyuk," said GUF.

They continued on, DUN stopping occasionally to watch their trail.

When they passed one of the last trees, MIK had them all take limbs from it. "Might come in handy for pushing and digging," he said.

They stood on a plain of sand and rough dirt. There were huge piles of rubble all around. Far off was another ocean and to the north, a long, curving patch of green.

"We'll go to the ocean, DUN," said MIK, "after we get through here."

He was walking around in a smaller and smaller circle. Then he stopped. "Well, huh-huh, here we are," he said. "Latitude forty degrees, forty-four minutes, thirty-four seconds, point oh eight nine north. Longitude seventy-three degrees, fifty minutes, forty-three seconds, point eight four two west, by the way they *used* to figure it. The capsule is straight down, twenty-eight meters below the original surface. We've got a long way to go, because there's no telling how much soil has drifted over that. It's in a concrete tube, and we'll have to dig to the very bottom to get at the capsule. Let's get working."

It was early morning when they started. Just after noon, they found the top of the tube with its bronze tablet.

"Here's where the hard work starts," said MIK.

It took almost a week of continuous effort. Slowly the tube was exposed as the hole around it grew larger. Since GUF could work better standing still, they had him dig all the time, while DUN and MIK both dug and pushed rock and dirt clear of the crater.

They found some long, flat iron rods partway down and threw away the worn tree limbs and used the metal to better effect.

On one of his trips to push dirt out of the hole, DUN came back looking puzzled.

"I'm *sure* I saw something moving out there," he said. "When I looked, it went away."

"There yuh go again," said GUF. "Here, DUN, help me lift this rock."

It was hard work. Their motors were taxed. It rained once, and for a while there was a dust storm.

"Thuh way I see it," said GUF, looking at their handiwork, "is that yuh treat it like a great ol' big tree made o' rock."

They stood at the bottom of a vast crater. Up from its center stood the concrete tube.

"We've reached twenty-six meters," said MIK. "The capsule itself should be in the last two point three eight one six meters. So we should chop it off," he quickly calculated, "about here!" He drew a line all around the tube with a piece of chalky rock.

They began to smash at the concrete with rocks and pieces of iron and steel.

"*Timber!*" yelled DUN.

The column above the line lurched and with a crash shattered itself against the side of the crater wall.

"Oh, boy! Oh, boy!"

"Come help me, GUF," said MIK.

Inside the jagged top of the remaining shaft, an eyebolt stood out of the core.

They climbed up on the edge, reached in and raised the gleaming Cupraloy time capsule from its resting place.

On its side was a message to the finders, and just below the eyebolt at the top was a line and the words Cut Here.

"Well," said MIK, shaking GUF's and DUN's hands, "we did it, by gum!"

He looked at it a moment.

"How're we gonna open it?" asked GUF. "That metal shore looks tough!"

"I think maybe we can abrade it around the cutting line with sandstone and, well . . . go get me a real big, sharp piece of iron, DUN."

When DUN brought it, MIK handed the iron to GUF and put his long tail over a big rock.

"Go ahead, GUF," he said. "Won't hurt me a bit."

GUF slammed the piece of iron down.

"Uh-hyuk!" he said. "Clean as a whistle!"

MIK took his severed tail, sat down cross-legged near the eyebolt, poured sand on the cutting line and began to rub it across the line with his tail.

It took a full day, turning the capsule every few hours.

They pulled off the eyebolt end. A dusty, waxy mess was revealed.

"That'll be what's left of the waterproof mastic," said MIK. "Help me, you two." They lifted the capsule. "Twist!" he said.

The metal groaned. "Now, pull!"

A long, thin inner core, two meters by a third of a meter, slid out.

"OK," said MIK, putting down the capsule shell and wiping away mastic. "This inner shell is threaded in two parts. Turn that way; I'll turn this."

They did. Inside was a shiny sealed glass tube through which they could dimly see shapes and colors.

"Wow!" said GUF. "Looka that!"

"Oh, boy! Oh, boy!" said DUN.

"That's Pyrex," said MIK. "When we break that, we'll be through."

"I'll do it," said DUN, picking up a rock.

"Careful!" said GUF.

The rock shattered the glass. There was a loud noise as the partial vacuum disappeared.

"Oh, boy!" said DUN.

"Let's do this carefully," said MIK. "It's all supposed to be in some kind of order."

The first things they found were the messages from four famous humans and another whole copy of *The Book of the Time Capsule*. GUF picked that up.

There was another book, with a black cover and a gold cross on it. Then they came to a section marked Articles of Common Use. The first small packet was labeled Contributing to Convenience, Comfort, Health and Safety. MIK opened it.

Inside were an alarm clock, bifocals, a camera, a pencil, a nail file, a padlock and keys, a toothbrush, tooth powder, a safety pin, a knife, a fork and a slide rule.

The next packet was labeled Pertaining to the Grooming and Vanity of Women. Inside were an Elizabeth Arden Cyclamen Color Harmony Box, a rhinestone clip and a woman's hat, style of autumn 1938, designed by Lilly Daché.

"Golly-wow!" said DUN and put the hat on over his.

The next packet was marked For the Pleasure, Use and Education of Children.

First out was a small spring-driven toy car, then a small doll and a set of alphabet blocks. Then MIK reached in and pulled out a small cup.

He stared at it a long time. On the side of the cup was a decal with the name of the man who had created them and a picture of MIK, waving his hand in greeting.

"Gawrsh, MIK," said GUF. "It's *you!*"

A tossed rock threw up a shower of dirt next to his foot.

They all looked up.

Around the crater edge stood men, women and children dressed in ragged skins. They had sharp sticks, rocks and ugly clubs.

"Oh, boy," said DUN. "People!" He started toward them.

"Hello!" he said. "We've been trying to find you for a long time. Do you know the way to the park? We want to learn all about you."

He was speaking to them in Japanese.

The mob hefted its weapons. DUN switched to another language.

"I said, we come in peace. Do you know the way to the park?" he asked in Swedish.

They started down the crater, rocks flying before them.

"What's the matter with you?" yelled DUN. *"Wak, wak, wak!"* He raised his fists.

"Wait!" said MIK in English. "We're friends!"

Some of the crowd veered off toward him.

"Uh-oh!" said GUF. He took off, clanking up the most sparsely defended side of the depression.

Then the ragged people yelled and charged.

They got the duck first.

He stood, fists out, jumping up and down on one foot, hopping mad. Several grabbed him, one by the beak. They smashed at him with clubs, pounded him with rocks. He injured three of them seriously before they smashed him into a white-blue-and-orange pile.

"Couldn't we, huh-huh, talk this over?" asked MIK. They stuck a sharp stick into his ear mechanism, jamming it. One of his gloved hands was mashed. He fought back with the other and kicked his feet. He hurt them, but he was small. A boulder trapped his legs; then they danced on him.

GUF made it out of the crater. He had picked the side with the most kids and they drew back, thinking he was attacking them. When they saw he was trying to escape, they gave gleeful chase, bouncing sticks and rocks off his hobbling form.

"Whoa!" he yelled as more people ran to intercept him and he skidded to a stop. He ran up a long, slanting pile of rubble. More humans poured out of the crater to get him.

He reached the end of the long, high mound above the crater rim. His attackers paused, throwing sticks and rocks, yelling at him.

"Halp!" GUF yelled. "Haaaaaaaaaalp!"

An arrow sailed into the chest of his nearest attacker.

GUF turned. Other humans, dressed in cloth, stood in a line around the far side of the crater. They had bows and arrows, metal-tipped spears and carried iron knives in their belts.

As GUF watched, the archers sent another flight of arrows into the people who had attacked the robots.

The skin-dressed band of humans screamed and fled up out of the crater, down from the mounds, leaving their wounded and the scattered contents of the time capsule behind them.

It took a while, but soon the human in command of the metal-using people and GUF made themselves understood to each other. The language was a very changed English-Spanish mixture.

"We're sorry we didn't know you were here sooner," the man said to GUF. "We rarely get out this far, and we heard you were here only this morning. Those *others*," he said with a grimace, "who followed you here from the Wastes won't bother you anymore."

He pointed to the patch of green to the north. "Our lands and village are there. We found this place twenty years ago. It's a good land, but others raid it as often as they can."

GUF looked down into the crater with its toppled column and debris. Cigarettes and tobacco drifted from the glass cylinder. The microfilm, with all its books and knowledge, was tangled all over the rocks. Samples of aluminum, hypernic and ferrovanadium gleamed in the dust. Razor blades, an airplane gear and glass wool were strewn up the sides of the slope.

The message from Grover Whalen opening the World's Fair and knowledge of how to build the microfilm reader were lost. The newsreel, with its pictures of Howard Hughes, Jesse Owens and Babe Ruth, bombings in China and a Miami Beach fashion show, was ripped and torn. The golf ball was in the hands of one of the fleeing children. Poker chips lay side by side with tungsten wire, combs, lipstick. GUF tried to guess what some of the items were.

"They destroyed one of your party," said the commander. "I think the other one is still alive."

"I'll tend to 'em," said GUF.

"We'll take you back to our village," said the man. "There are lots of things we'd like to know about you."

"That goes double fer us," said GUF. "Those other folks pretty much tore up what we came to find."

GUF picked up the small cup from the ground. He walked to where they had MIK propped up against a rock.

"Hello, GUF," he said. "Huh-huh, I'm not in such good shape." His glove hung uselessly on his left arm. His ears were bent and his nose was chipped. He gave off a noisy whir when he moved.

"Oh, hyuk-hyuk," said GUF. "We'll go back with these nice people, and yuh'll rest up and be right as rain, I guarantee."

"DUN didn't make it, did he, GUF?"

GUF was quiet a moment. "Nope, MIK, he didn't. I'm shore sorry it turned out this way. I'm gonna miss thuh ol' hothead."

"Me, too," said MIK. "Are we gonna take him with us?"

"Shore thing," said GUF. He waved to the nearby men.

The town was in a green valley watered by two streams full of fish. There were small fields of beans, tomatoes and corn in town, and cattle and sheep grazed on the hillsides, watched over by guards. There were a coppersmith's shop, a council hut and many houses of wood and stone.

GUF was walking up the hill to the house MIK was in.

They had been there a little more than two weeks, talking with the people of the village, telling them what they knew. GUF usually played with the children when he and MIK didn't have to be around the grown folks. But from the day after they had buried DUN up on the hill, MIK had been getting worse. His legs had quit altogether, and he could now see only in the infrared.

"Hello, GUF," said MIK.

"How yuh doin', pardner?"

"Not so good," said MIK. "Are they making any progress on the flume?"

Two days before, MIK had told them how to get water more efficiently from one of the streams up to the middle of the village.

"We've almost got it now," said GUF. "I'm sure they'll be up and thank yuh when they're finished."

"They don't need to do that," said MIK.

"I know, but these are real nice folks, MIK. And they've had it pretty bad, what with one thing and another. They like talkin' to yuh."

GUF noticed that some of the women and children sat outside the hut, waiting to see MIK.

"I won't stay very long," said GUF. "I gotta get back and organize the cadres into work teams and instructional teams and so forth, like they asked me to help with."

"Sure thing, GUF," said MIK. "I—"

There was a great whirring noise from MIK and the smell of burning silicon.

GUF looked away. "They just don't have thuh stuff

here," he said, "that I could use to fix yuh. Maybe I could find somethin' at thuh crater. . . ."

"Don't bother," said MIK. "I doubt . . ."

GUF looked at the village. "Oh," he said, reaching into the bag someone had made him. "I been meaning to give yuh this fer more'n a week and keep fergettin'." He handed MIK the cup from the time capsule with his picture on the side.

"I've been thinking about this since we found it," said MIK. He turned it in his good hand, barely able to see its outline. "I wonder what else we lost at the crater."

"Lots o' stuff," said GUF, "but we got to keep this."

"This was supposed to last a long time," said MIK, "and tell people what other people were like for future ages? Then the people who put this there must really have liked the man who thought us up!"

"That's fer shore," said GUF.

"And me, too, I wonder?"

"You probably most of all," said GUF.

MIK smiled. The smile froze. His eyes went white and a thin line of condensation rose up from the ear tracks. The hand gripped the cup tightly.

Outside, the people began to sing a real sad song.

It was a bright, sunny morning. GUF put flowers on MIK's and DUN's graves at the top of the hill. He patted the earth, stood up uncertainly.

He had replaced his frozen foot with a wood-wheeled cart with which he could skate along almost as easily as walking.

He stood up and thought of MIK. He sat his carpenter's cap forward on his head and whistled a little tune.

He picked up his wooden toolbox and started off down the hill to build the kids a swing set.

Out of All Them Bright Stars

NANCY KRESS

Nancy Kress has published short fiction in *Omni, Isaac Asimov's Science Fiction Magazine*, and *The Magazine of Fantasy & Science Fiction*. Her books include *The Prince of Morning Bells, The Golden Grove, The White Pipes*, and *Trinity and Other Stories* (the title story was a Nebula nominee last year). She lives in upstate New York.

About her winning short story, Kress writes:

"[It] is a story about people who are not at the center of the action. Science fiction tends to focus on serious movers and doers: starship captains, scientific or military geniuses, corporate or political spies, humans discovering alien races. But that does not describe most of us, who at the moment of first contact will have been at the dentist. This is therefore a story of someone whose life must cope with history, not cause it—like most humanity."

So I'm filling the catsup bottles at the end of the night, and I'm listening to the radio Charlie has stuck up on top of the movable panel in the ceiling, when the door opens and one of them walks in. I know right away it's one of them—no chance to make a mistake about *that*—even though it's got on a nice-cut suit and a brim hat like Humphrey Bogart used to wear in *Casablanca*. But there's nobody with it, no professor from the college or government men like on the TV show from the college or even any students. It's all alone. And we're a long way out on the highway from the college.

It stands in the doorway, blinking a little, with rain dripping off its hat. Kathy, who's supposed to be cleaning the coffee machine behind the counter, freezes and stares with one hand still holding the used filter up in the air like she's never going to move again. Just then Charlie calls out from the kitchen, "Hey, Kathy, you ask anybody who won the trifecta?" and she doesn't even answer him. Just goes on staring with her mouth open like she's thinking of screaming but forgot how. And the old couple in the corner booth, the only ones left from the crowd after the movie got out, stop chewing their chocolate cream pie and stare, too. Kathy closes her mouth and opens it again, and a noise comes out like "Uh—errrgh . . ."

Well, that made me annoyed. Maybe she tried to say "ugh" and maybe she didn't, but here it is standing in the doorway with rain falling around it in little drops and we're staring like it's a clothes dummy and not a customer. So I think that's not right and maybe we're even making it feel a little bad. *I* wouldn't like Kathy staring at me like that, and I dry my hands on my towel and go over.

"Yes, sir, can I help you?" I say.

"Table for one," it says, like Charlie's was some nice steak house in town. But I suppose that's the kind of place the government people mostly take them to. And besides, its voice is polite and easy to understand, with a sort of accent but not as bad as some we get from the college. I can tell what it's saying. I lead him to a booth in the corner opposite the old couple, who come in every Friday night and haven't left a tip yet.

He sits down slowly. I notice he keeps his hands on his lap, but I can't tell if that's because he doesn't know what to do with them or because he thinks I won't want to see them. But I've seen the close-ups on TV—they don't look so weird to me like they do to some. Charlie says they make his stomach turn, but I can't see it. You'd think he'd of seen worse meat in Vietnam. He talks enough like he did, on and on, and sometimes we even believe him.

I say, "Coffee, sir?"

He makes a sort of movement with his eyes. I can't tell what the movement means, but he says in that polite voice, "No, thank you. I am unable to drink coffee," and I think that's a good thing, because I suddenly remember that Kathy's got the filter out. But then he says, "May I have a green salad, please? With no dressing, please."

The rain is still dripping off his hat. I figure the government people never told him to take off his hat in a restaurant, and for some reason that tickles me and makes me feel real bold. This polite blue guy isn't going to bother anybody, and that fool Charlie was just spouting off his mouth again.

"The salad's not too fresh, sir," I say, experimental-like, just to see what he'll say next. And it's the truth—the salad is left over from yesterday. But the guy answers like I asked him something else.

"What is your name?" he says, so polite I know he's curious and not starting anything. And what could he start anyway, blue and with those hands? Still, you never know.

"Sally," I say. "Sally Gourley."

"I am John," he says, and makes that movement with his eyes again. All of a sudden it tickles me—"John!" For this blue guy! So I laugh, and right away I feel sorry, like I might have hurt his feelings or something. How could you tell?

"Hey, I'm sorry," I say, and he takes off his hat. He does it real slow, like taking off the hat is important and means something, but all there is underneath is a bald blue head. Nothing weird like with the hands.

"Do not apologize," John says. "I have another name, of course, but in my own language."

"What is it?" I say, bold as brass, because all of a sudden I picture myself telling all this to my sister Mary Ellen and her listening real hard.

John makes some noise with his mouth, and I feel my own mouth open because it's not like a word he says at all, it's a beautiful sound—like a birdcall, only sadder. It's just that I wasn't expecting it, that beautiful sound right here in Charlie's diner. It surprised me, coming out of that bald blue head. That's all it was: surprise.

I don't say anything. John looks at me and says, "It has a meaning that can be translated. It means—" But before he can say what it means, Charlie comes charging out of the kitchen, Kathy right behind him. He's still got the racing form in one hand, like he's been studying the trifecta, and he pushes right up against the booth and looks red and furious. Then I see the old couple scuttling out the door, their jackets clutched to their fronts, and the chocolate cream pie not half-eaten on their plates. I see they're going to stiff me for the check, but before I can stop them, Charlie grabs my arm and squeezes so hard his nails slice into my skin.

"What the hell do you think you're doing?" he says right to me. Not so much as a look at John, but Kathy can't stop looking and her fist is pushed up to her mouth.

I drag my arm away and rub it. Once I saw Charlie push his wife so hard she went down and hit her head and had to have four stitches. It was me that drove her to the emergency room.

Charlie says again, "What the hell do you think you're doing?"

"I'm serving my table. He wants a salad. Large." I can't remember if John'd said a large or a small salad, but I figure a large order would make Charlie feel better. But Charlie doesn't want to feel better.

"You get him out of here," Charlie hisses. He still doesn't look at John. "You hear me, Sally? You get him *out*. The government says I gotta serve spiks and niggers, but it don't say I gotta serve *him!*"

I look at John. He's putting on his hat, ramming it onto his bald head, and half-standing in the booth. He can't get out because Charlie and me are both in the way. I expect John to look mad or upset, but except that he's holding the muscles in his face in some different way, I can't see any change of expression. But I figure he's got to feel something bad, and all of a sudden I'm mad at Charlie, who's a bully and who's got the feelings of a scumbag. I open my mouth to tell him so, plus one or two other little things I been saving up, when the door flies open and in burst four men, and damn if they aren't *all* wearing hats like Humphrey Bogart in *Casablanca*. As soon as the first guy sees John, his walk changes and he comes over slower but more purposeful-like, and he's talking to John and to Charlie in a sincere voice like a TV anchorman giving out the news.

I see the situation now belongs to him, so I go back to the catsup bottles. I'm still plenty burned, though, about Charlie manhandling me and about Kathy rushing so stupid into the kitchen to get Charlie. She's a flake and always has been.

Charlie is scowling and nodding. The harder he scowls, the nicer the government guy's voice gets. Pretty soon the government man is smiling sweet as pie. Charlie slinks back into the kitchen, and the four men move toward the door with John in the middle of them like some high-school football huddle. Next to the real men, he looks stranger than he did before, and I see how really flat his face is. But then when the huddle's right opposite the table with my catsup bottles, John breaks away and comes over to me.

"I am sorry, Sally Gourley," he says. And then: "I seldom have the chance to show our friendliness to an ordinary Earth person. I make so little difference!"

Well, that throws me. His voice sounds so sad, and besides, I never thought of myself as an ordinary Earth person. Who would? So I just shrug and wipe off a catsup bottle with my towel. But then John does a weird thing. He just touches my arm where Charlie squeezed it, just touches it with the palm of those hands. And the palm's not slimy at all—dry, and sort of cool, and I don't jump or anything. Instead, I remember that beautiful noise when he said his other name. Then he goes out with three of the men, and the door bangs behind them on a gust of rain because Charlie never fixed the air-stop from when some kids horsing around broke it last spring.

The fourth man stays and questions me: What did the alien say, what did I say. I tell him, but then he starts over again, like he didn't believe me the first time, and that gets me mad. Also, he has this snotty voice, and I see how his eyebrows move when I slip once and accidentally say, "he don't." I might not know what John's muscles mean, but I sure the hell can read those eyebrows. So I get miffed, and pretty soon he leaves and the door bangs behind him.

I finish the catsup and mustard bottles, and Kathy finishes the coffee machine. The radio in the ceiling plays something instrumental, no words, real sad. Kathy and me start to wash down the booths with disinfectant, and because we're doing the same work together and nobody comes in, I finally say to her, "It's funny."

She says, "What's funny?"

"Charlie called that guy 'him' right off. 'I don't got to serve 'him,' he said. And I thought of him as 'it' at first, least until I had a name to use. But Charlie's the one who threw him out."

Kathy swipes at the back of her booth. "And Charlie's right. That thing scared me half to death, coming in here

like that. And where there's food being served, too." She
snorts and sprays on more disinfectant.

Well, she's a flake. Always has been.

"The *National Enquirer*," Kathy goes on, "told how they
have all this firepower up there in the big ship that hasn't
landed yet. My husband says they could blow us all to
smithereens, they're so powerful. I don't know why they
come here. *We* don't want them. I don't even know why
they came, all that way."

"They want to make a difference," I say, but Kathy
barrels on ahead, not listening.

"The Pentagon will hold them off, it doesn't matter what
weapons they got up there or how much they insist on
seeing about our defenses, the Pentagon won't let them
get any toeholds on Earth. That's what my husband says.
Blue bastards."

I say, "Will you please shut up?"

She gives me a dirty look and flounces off. I don't care.
None of it is anything to me. Only, standing there with
the disinfectant in my hand, looking at the dark windows
and listening to the music wordless and slow on the radio,
I remember that touch on my arm, so light and cool. And
I think they didn't come here with any firepower to blow
us all to smithereens. I just don't believe it. But then why
did they come? Why come all that way from another star
to walk into Charlie's diner and order a green salad with
no dressing from an ordinary Earth person?

Charlie comes out with his keys to unlock the cash reg-
ister and go over the tapes. I remember the old couple
who stiffed me and I curse to myself. Only pie and coffee,
but it still comes off my salary. The radio in the ceiling
starts playing something else, not the sad song, but nothing snappy neither. It's a love song, about some guy giving and giving and getting treated like dirt. I don't like it.

"Charlie," I say, "what did those government men say
to you?"

He looks up from his tapes and scowls, "What do you care?"

"I just want to know."

"And maybe I don't want you to know," he says, and smiles nasty-like. Me asking him has put him in a better mood, the creep. All of a sudden I remember what his wife said when she got the stitches, "The only way to get something from Charlie is to let him smack me around a little, and then ask him when I'm down. He'll give me anything when I'm down. He gives me shit if he thinks I'm on top."

I do the rest of the cleanup without saying anything. Charlie swears at the night's take—I know from my tips that it's not much. Kathy teases her hair in front of the mirror behind the doughnuts and pies, and I put down the breakfast menus. But all the time I'm thinking, and I don't much like my thoughts.

Charlie locks up and we all leave. Outside it's stopped raining, but it's still misty and soft, real pretty but too cold. I pull my sweater around myself and in the parking lot, after Kathy's gone, I say, "Charlie."

He stops walking toward his truck. "Yeah?"

I lick my lips. They're all of a sudden dry. It's an experiment, like, what I'm going to say. It's an experiment.

"Charlie. What if those government guys hadn't come just then and the . . . blue guy hadn't been willing to leave? What would you have done?"

"What do you care?"

I shrug. "I don't care. Just curious. It's *your* place."

"Damn right it's my place!" I could see him scowl, through the mist. "I'd of squashed him flat!"

"And then what? After you squashed him flat, what if the men came then and made a stink?"

"Too bad. It'd be too late by then, huh?" He laughs, and I can see how he's seeing it: the blue guy bleeding on the linoleum, and Charlie standing over him, dusting his hands together.

Charlie laughs again and goes off to his truck, whistling. He has a little bounce to his step. He's still seeing it all, almost like it really *had* happened. Over his shoulder he calls to me, "They're built like wimps. Or girls. All bone, no muscle. Even *you* must of seen that," and his voice is cheerful. It doesn't have any more anger in it, or hatred, or anything but a sort of friendliness. I hear him whistle some more, until the truck engine starts up and he peels out of the parking lot, laying rubber like a kid.

I unlock my Chevy. But before I get in, I look up at the sky. Which is really stupid because of course I can't see anything, with all the mists and clouds. No stars.

Maybe Kathy's husband is right. Maybe they do want to blow us all to smithereens. I don't think so, but what the hell difference does it ever make what I think? And all at once I'm furious at John, furiously mad, as furious as I've ever been in my life.

Why does he have to come here, with his birdcalls and his politeness? Why can't they all go someplace else besides here? There must be lots of other places they can go, out of all them bright stars up there behind the clouds. They don't need to come here, here where I need this job and that means I need Charlie. He's a bully, but I want to look at him and see nothing else but a bully. Nothing else but that. That's all I want to see in Charlie, in the government men—just small-time bullies, nothing special, not a mirror of anything, not a future of anything. Just Charlie. That's all. I won't see anything else.

I won't.

"I make so little difference," he says.

Yeah. Sure.

The Fringe

ORSON SCOTT CARD

Orson Scott Card won the John W. Campbell Memorial Award for best new writer in 1977. His short fiction has appeared in *Omni*, *Isaac Asimov's Science Fiction Magazine*, and *The Magazine of Fantasy & Science Fiction*. His novels include *Songmaster*, *Hart's Hope*, and *Speaker for the Dead*. He is this year's Nebula winner in the novel, and was a nominee in the novelette. He lives in North Carolina with his wife and three children.

About his winning novel, *Ender's Game* (which also won the 1985 Hugo Award for best novel), and his novelette, "The Fringe," Card writes: (*On* Ender's Game)
"I was a seventeen-year-old theater student in 1968, commuting from Orem, Utah, to Brigham Young University on the old river-bottom road in the back of my dad's Datsun when I first thought of the idea of null-gravity war games to train children to pilot military spacecraft. It was not until 1975 that I actually began to write the story, lying on the grass outside the Salt Palace in Salt Lake City waiting for a girlfriend who had taken her boss's kids to the circus. I wrote it straight through, one draft, the way I wrote my plays; not surprisingly, the story consisted largely of dialogue and stage directions, and I could

never keep straight whether Ender's last name was Wiggin or Wiggins.

"Flawed as it was, I could do no better at the time, so I sent it to Analog; *Ben Bova wrote back, urging me to cut it in half and suggesting a title change. I was so naive I thought this was a rejection, and sent it to another editor, who kept it five months and—after I pestered him by telephone—rejected it conclusively. By then Ben's call for revision looked a lot better, so I cut one battle and ten pages and sent it back. He published it with my title, and 'Ender's Game' was generously received. Years later, I sold a novel-length sequel,* Speaker for the Dead, *to Tom Doherty's new house, Tor, but in the process of writing it I realized that the novelette 'Ender's Game' did not adequately prepare for* Speaker. *At the ABA convention in Dallas I asked Tom Doherty if I could expand Ender into a novel. His handshake turned out to be better than any contract I had ever signed.*

"In writing the novel, I kept only one sentence from the original novelette—the first sentence I wrote: 'Remember, the enemy's gate is down.' I had the help of two fine editors— Kristine A. Card, who is a vital part of everything I write, and Tor editor Harriet McDougal. In the years since writing the novelette, I had changed a bit, too. Penury had made me a prolific writer, Ronald Reagan had made me a Democrat, and my family had given me the perspective to see Ender's tale as more than a lonely-child story or a war story. The book is dedicated to my son Geoffrey for good reason."

(On "The Fringe") "Years ago I worked out an outline for a musical play called Pageant Wagon, *which was to be scored by my longtime collaborator, composer Robert Stoddard. I never quite got to the play, but I have been haunted by the setting— a future in which heavy rains have refilled the Great Salt Lake and allowed the reclamation of the sagebrush deserts of Utah. (A map of prehistoric Lake Bonneville hangs on the wall in my office.)*

"When John Kessel and Mark Van Name invited me to take part in the Sycamore Hill Writers Workshop, I had not sold a short story in three years, or written one in two. But I arrived at the workshop with a couple of ideas—the Utah set-

ting, and my hopes and fears for the future of my youngest son Charlie, who was born with cerebral palsy. The result was 'The Fringe,' written on my PC junior in the basement of Mark Van Name's house near Durham. The ambient intelligence, talent, skill, and wisdom of the writers I lived with during those intense days in January became the catalyst for the writing of this story and its companion piece, 'Salvage.' "

LaVon's book report was drivel, of course. Carpenter knew it would be from the moment he called on the boy. After Carpenter's warning last week, he knew LaVon would have a book report— LaVon's father would never let the boy be suspended. But LaVon was too stubborn, too cocky, too much the leader of the other sixth-graders' constant rebellion against authority to let Carpenter have a complete victory.

"I really, truly loved *Little Men*," said LaVon. "It just gave me goose bumps."

The class laughed. Excellent comic timing, Carpenter said silently. But the only place that comedy is useful here in the New Soil country is with the gypsy pageant wagons. That's what you're preparing yourself for, LaVon, a career as a wandering parasite who lives by sucking laughter out of weary farmers.

"Everybody nice in this book has a name that starts with *D*. Demi is a sweet little boy who never does anything wrong. Daisy is so good that she could have seven children and still be a virgin."

He was pushing the limits now. A lot of people didn't like mention of sexual matters in the school, and if some pinheaded child decided to report this, the story could be twisted into something that could be used against Carpenter. Out here near the fringe, people were desperate for entertainment. A crusade to drive out a teacher for corrupting the morals of youth would be more fun than a traveling show, because everybody could feel righteous and safe when he was gone. Carpenter had seen it before. Not that he was afraid of it, the way most teachers were. *He* had a career no matter what. The university would take him back, eagerly; they thought he was crazy to go out and teach in the low schools. I'm safe, absolutely safe, he thought. They can't wreck my career. And I'm not going to get prissy about a perfectly good word like *virgin*.

"Dan looks like a big bad boy, but he has a heart of gold, even though he does say real bad words like *devil* sometimes." LaVon paused, waiting for Carpenter to react. So Carpenter did not react.

"The saddest thing is poor Nat, the street fiddler's boy. He tries hard to fit in, but he can never amount to anything in the book, because his name doesn't start with *D*."

The end. LaVon put the single paper on Carpenter's desk, then went back to his seat. He walked with the careful elegance of a spider, each long leg moving as if it were unconnected to the rest of his body, so that even walking did not disturb the perfect calm. The boy rides on his body the way I ride in my wheelchair, thought Carpenter. Smooth, unmoved by his own motion. But *he* is graceful and beautiful, fifteen years old and already a master at winning the devotion of the weakhearted children around him. *He* is the enemy, the torturer, the strong and beautiful man who must confirm his beauty by preying on the weak. I am not as weak as you think.

LaVon's book report was arrogant, far too short, and flagrantly rebellious. That much was deliberate, calculated to annoy Carpenter. Therefore Carpenter would not show the slightest trace of annoyance. The book report had also been clever, ironic, and funny. The boy, for all his mask of languor and stupidity, had brains. He was better than this farming town; he could do something that mattered in the world besides driving a tractor in endless contour patterns around the fields. But the way he always had the

Fisher girl hanging on him, he'd no doubt have a baby and a wife and stay here forever. Become a big shot like his father, maybe, but never leave a mark in the world to show he'd been here. Tragic, stupid waste.

But don't show the anger. The children will misunderstand, they'll think I'm angry because of LaVon's rebelliousness, and it will only make this boy more of a hero in their eyes. Children choose their heroes with unerring stupidity. Fourteen, fifteen, sixteen years old, all they know of life is cold and bookless classrooms interrupted now and then by a year or two of wrestling with this stony earth, always hating whatever adult it is who keeps them at their work, always adoring whatever fool gives them the illusion of being free. You children have no practice in surviving among the ruins of your own mistakes. We adults who knew the world before it fell, we feel the weight of the rubble on our backs.

They were waiting for Carpenter's answer. He reached out to the computer keyboard attached to his wheelchair. His hands struck like paws at the oversized keys. His fingers were too stupid for him to use them individually. They clenched when he tried to work them, tightened into a fist, a little hammer with which to strike, to break, to attack; he could not use them to grasp or even hold. Half the verbs of the world are impossible to me, he thought as he often thought. I learn them the way the blind learn words of seeing—by rote, with no hope of ever knowing truly what they mean.

The speech synthesizer droned out the words he keyed. "Brilliant essay, Mr. Jensen. The irony was powerful, the savagery was refreshing. Unfortunately, it also revealed the poverty of your soul. Alcott's title was ironic, for she wanted to show that despite their small size, the boys in her book were great-hearted. You, however, despite your large size, are very small of heart indeed."

LaVon looked at him through heavy-lidded eyes.

Hatred? Yes, it was there. Do hate me, child. Loathe me enough to show me that you can do anything I ask you to do. Then I'll own you, then I can get something decent out of you, and finally give you back to yourself as a human being who is worthy to be alive.

Carpenter pushed outward on both levers, and his wheelchair backed up. The day was nearly over, and tonight he knew something would change, painfully, in the life of the town of Reefrock. And because in a way the arrests would be his fault, and because the imprisonment of a father would cause upheaval in some of these children's families, he felt it his duty to prepare them as best he could to understand why it had to happen, why, in the larger view, it was good. It was too much to expect that they would actually understand, today; but they might remember, might forgive him someday for what they would soon find out he had done to them.

So he pawed at the keys again. "Economics," said the computer. "Since Mr. Jensen has made an end of literature for the day." A few more keys, and the lecture began. Carpenter entered all his lectures and stored them in memory, so that he could sit still as ice in his chair, making eye contact with each student in turn, daring them to be inattentive. There were advantages in letting a machine speak for him; he had learned many years ago that it frightened people to have a mechanical voice speak his words while his lips were motionless. It was monstrous, it made him seem dangerous and strange. Which he far preferred to the way he looked: weak as a worm, his skinny, twisted, palsied body rigid in his chair; his body looked strange but pathetic. Only when the synthesizer spoke his acid words did he earn respect from the people who always, always looked downward at him.

"Here in the settlements just behind the fringe," his voice went, "we do not have the luxury of a free economy. The rains sweep onto this ancient desert and find nothing here but a few plants growing in the sand. Thirty years ago nothing lived here; even the lizards had to stay where there was something for insects to eat, where there was water to drink. Then the fires we lit put a curtain in the sky, and the ice moved south, and the rains that had always passed north of us now raked and scoured the desert. It was opportunity."

LaVon smirked as Kippie made a great show of dozing off. Carpenter keyed an interruption in the lecture. "Kippie, how well will you sleep if I send you home now for an afternoon nap?"

Kippie sat bolt upright, pretending terrible fear. But the pretense was also a pretense; he *was* afraid, and so to conceal it he pretended to be pretending to be afraid. Very complex, the inner life of children, thought Carpenter.

"Even as the old settlements were slowly drowned under the rising Great Salt Lake, your fathers and mothers began to move out into the desert, to reclaim it. But not alone. We can do nothing alone here. The fringers plant their grass. The grass feeds the herds and puts roots into the sand. The roots become humus, rich in nitrogen. In three years the fringe has a thin lace of soil across it. If at any point a fringer fails to plant, if at any point the soil is broken, then the rains eat channels under it, and tear away the fringe on either side, and eat back into farmland behind it. So every fringer is responsible to every other fringer, and to us. How would you feel about a fringer who failed?"

"The way I feel about a fringer who succeeds," said Pope. He was the youngest of the sixth-graders, only thirteen years old, and he sucked up to LaVon disgracefully.

Carpenter punched four codes. "And how is that?" asked Carpenter's metal voice.

Pope's courage fled. "Sorry."

Carpenter did not let go. "What is it you call fringers?"

he asked. He looked from one child to the next, and they would not meet his gaze. Except LaVon.

"What do you call them?" he asked again.

"If I say it, I'll get kicked out of school," said LaVon. "You want me kicked out of school?"

"You accuse them of fornicating with cattle, yes?"

A few giggles.

"Yes, sir," said LaVon. "We call them cow-fornicators, sir."

Carpenter keyed in his response while they laughed. When the room was silent, he played it back. "The bread you eat grows in the soil they created, and the manure of their cattle is the strength of your bodies. Without fringers you would be eking out a miserable life on the shores of the Mormon Sea, eating fish and drinking sage tea, and don't forget it." He set the volume of the synthesizer steadily lower during the speech, so that at the end they were straining to hear.

Then he resumed his lecture. "After the fringers came your mothers and fathers, planting crops in a scientifically planned order: two rows of apple trees, then six meters of wheat, then six meters of corn, then six meters of cucumbers, and so on; year after year, moving six more meters out, following the fringers, making more land, more food. If you didn't plant what you were told, and harvest it on the right day, and work shoulder to shoulder in the fields whenever the need came, then the plants would die, the rain would wash them away. What do you think of the farmer who does not do his labor or take his work turn?"

"Scum," one child said. And another: "He's a wallow, that's what he is."

"If this land is to be truly alive, it must be planted in a careful plan for eighteen years. Only then will your family have the luxury of deciding what crop to plant. Only then will you be able to be lazy if you want to, or work extra hard and profit from it. Then some of you can get rich, and others can become poor. But now, today, we do everything together, equally, and so we share equally in the rewards of our work."

LaVon murmured something.

"Yes, LaVon?" asked Carpenter. He made the computer speak very loudly. It startled the children.

"Nothing," said LaVon.

"You said, 'Except teachers.' "

"What if I did?"

"You are correct," said Carpenter. "Teachers do not plow and plant in the fields with your parents. Teachers are given much more barren soil to work in, and most of the time the few seeds we plant are washed away with the first spring shower. You are living proof of the futility of our labor. But we try, Mr. Jensen, foolish as the effort is. May we continue?"

LaVon nodded. His face was flushed. Carpenter was satisfied. The boy was not hopeless—he could still feel shame at having attacked a man's livelihood.

"There are some among us," said the lecture, "who believe they should benefit more than others from the work of all. These are the ones who steal from the common storehouse and sell the crops that were raised by everyone's labor. The black market pays high prices for the stolen grain, and the thieves get rich. When they get rich enough, they move away from the fringe, back to the cities of the high valleys. Their wives will wear fine clothing, their sons will have watches, their daughters will own land and marry well. And in the meantime, their friends and neighbors, who trusted them, will have nothing, will stay on the fringe, growing the food that feeds the thieves. Tell me, what do you think of a black marketeer?"

He watched their faces. Yes, they knew. He could see how they glanced surreptitiously at Dick's new shoes, at Kippie's wristwatch. At Yutonna's new city-bought blouse.

At LaVon's jeans. They knew, but out of fear they had said nothing. Or perhaps it wasn't fear. Perhaps it was the hope that their own fathers would be clever enough to steal from the harvest, so they could move away instead of earning out their eighteen years.

"Some people think these thieves are clever. But I tell you they are exactly like the mobbers of the plains. They are the enemies of civilization."

"*This* is civilization?" asked LaVon.

"Yes." Carpenter keyed an answer. "We live in peace here, and you know that today's work brings tomorrow's bread. Out on the prairie they don't know that. Tomorrow a mobber will be eating their bread, if they haven't been killed. There's no trust in the world, except here. And the black marketeers feed on trust. Their neighbors' trust. When they've eaten it all, children, what will you live on then?"

They didn't understand, of course. When it was story problems about one truck approaching another truck at sixty kleeters and it takes an hour to meet, how far away were they?—the children could handle that, could figure it out laboriously with pencil and paper and prayers and curses. But the questions that mattered sailed past them like little dust devils, noticed but untouched by their feeble, self-centered little minds.

He tormented them with a pop quiz on history and thirty spelling words for their homework, then sent them out the door.

LaVon did not leave. He stood by the door, closed it, spoke. "It was a stupid book," he said.

Carpenter clicked the keyboard. "That explains why you wrote a stupid book report."

"It wasn't stupid. It was funny. I read the damn book, didn't I?"

"And I gave you a B."

LaVon was silent a moment, then said, "Do me no favors."

"I never will."

"And shut up with that goddamn machine voice. You can make a voice yourself. My cousin's got palsy and she howls to the moon."

"You may leave now, Mr. Jensen."

"I'm gonna hear you talk in your natural voice some-day, Mr. Machine."

"You had better go home now, Mr. Jensen."

LaVon opened the door to leave, then turned abruptly and strode the dozen steps to the head of the class. His legs now were tight and powerful as horses' legs, and his arms were light and strong. Carpenter watched him and felt the same old fear rise within him. If God was going to let him be born like this, he could at least keep him safe from the torturers.

"What do you want, Mr. Jensen?" But before the computer had finished speaking Carpenter's words, LaVon reached out and took Carpenter's wrists, held them tightly. Carpenter did not try to resist; if he did, he might go tight and twist around on the chair like a slug on a hot shovel. That would be more humiliation than he could bear, to have this boy see him writhe. His hands hung limp from LaVon's powerful fists.

"You just mind your business," LaVon said. "You only been here two years, you don't know nothin', you under-stand? You don't see nothin', you don't say nothin', you understand?"

So it wasn't the book report at all. LaVon had actually understood the lecture about civilization and the black market. And knew that it was LaVon's own father, more than anyone else in town, who was guilty. Nephi Delos Jensen, big shot foreman of Reefrock Farms. Have the marshals already taken your father? Best get home and see.

"Do you understand me?"

But Carpenter would not speak. Not without his com-puter. This boy would never hear how Carpenter's own voice sounded, the whining, baying sound, like a dog trying to curl its tongue into human speech. *You'll never hear my voice, boy.*

"Just try to expel me for this, Mr. Carpenter. I'll say it never happened. I'll say you had it in for me."

Then he let go of Carpenter's hands and stalked from the room. Only then did Carpenter's legs go rigid, lifting him on the chair so that only the computer over his lap kept him from sliding off. His arms pressed outward, his neck twisted, his jaw opened wide. It was what his body did with fear and rage; it was why he did his best never to feel those emotions. Or any others, for that matter. Dispassionate, that's what he was. He lived the life of the mind, since the life of the body was beyond him. He stretched across his wheelchair like a mocking crucifix, hating his body and pretending that he was merely waiting for it to calm, to relax.

And it did, of course. As soon as he had control of his hands again, he took the computer out of speech mode and called up the data he had sent on to Zarahemla yesterday morning—the crop estimates for three years, and the final weight of the harvested wheat and corn, cukes and berries, apples and beans. For the first two years, the estimates were within 2 percent of the final total. The third year the estimates were higher, but the harvest stayed the same. It was suspicious. Then the bishop's accounting records. It was a sick community. When the bishop was also seduced into this sort of thing, it meant the rottenness touched every corner of village life. Reefrock Farms looked no different from the hundred other villages just this side of the fringe, but it was diseased. Did Kippie know that even his father was in on the black-marketeering? If you couldn't trust the bishop, who was left?

The words of his own thoughts tasted sour in his mouth. Diseased. *They aren't so sick, Carpenter,* he told himself. *Civilization has always had its parasites and survived. But* it survived because it rooted them out from time to time, cast them away and cleansed the body. Yet they made heroes out of the thieves and despised those who reported them. There's no thanks in what I've done. It isn't love I'm earning. It isn't love I feel. Can I pretend that I'm not just a sick and twisted body taking vengeance on those healthy enough to have families, healthy enough to want to get every possible advantage for them?

He pushed the levers inward, and the chair rolled forward. He skillfully maneuvered between the chairs, but it still took nearly a full minute to get to the door. I'm a snail. A worm living in a metal carapace, a water snail creeping along the edge of the aquarium glass, trying to keep it clean from the filth of the fish. I'm the loathsome one; they're the golden ones that shine in the sparkling water. They're the ones whose death is mourned. But without me they'd die. I'm as responsible for their beauty as they are. More, because I work to sustain it, and they simply—are.

It came out this way whenever he tried to reason out an excuse for his own life. He rolled down the corridor to the front door of the school. He knew, intellectually, that his work in crop rotation and timing had been the key to opening up the vast New Soil Lands here in the eastern Utah desert. Hadn't they invented a civilian medal for him, and then, for good measure, given him the same medal they gave to the freedom riders who went out and brought immigrant trains safely into the mountains? I was a hero, they said, this worm in his wheelchair house. But Governor Monson had looked at him with those distant, pitying eyes. He, too, saw the worm; Carpenter might be a hero, but he was still Carpenter.

They had built a concrete ramp for his chair after the second time the students knocked over the wooden ramp and forced him to summon help through the computer airlink network. He remembered sitting on the lip of the porch, looking out toward the cabins of the village. If anyone saw him, then they consented to his imprisonment, because they didn't come to help him. But Carpenter understood. Fear of the strange, the unknown. It wasn't *comfortable* for them, to be near Mr. Carpenter with the mechanical voice and the electric rolling chair. He understood, he really did, he was human, too, wasn't he? He even agreed with them. Pretend Carpenter isn't there, and maybe he'll go away.

The helicopter came as he rolled out onto the asphalt of the street. It landed in the circle, between the storehouse and the chapel. Four marshals came out of the gash in its side and spread out through the town.

It happened that Carpenter was rolling in front of Bishop Anderson's house when the marshal knocked on the door. He hadn't expected them to make the arrests while he was still going down the street. His first impulse was to speed up, to get away from the arrest. He didn't want to see. He liked Bishop Anderson. Used to, anyway. He didn't wish him ill. If the bishop had kept his hands out of the harvest, if he hadn't betrayed his trust, he wouldn't have been afraid to hear the knock on the door and see the badge in the marshal's hand.

Carpenter could hear Sister Anderson crying as they led her husband away. Was Kippie there, watching? Did he notice Mr. Carpenter passing by on the road? Carpenter knew what it would cost these families. Not just the shame, though it would be intense. Far worse would be the loss of their father for years, the extra labor for the children. To break up a family was a terrible thing to do, for the innocent would pay as great a cost as their guilty father, and it wasn't fair, for they had done no wrong. But it was the stern necessity, if civilization was to survive.

Carpenter slowed down his wheelchair, forcing himself to hear the weeping from the bishop's house, to let them look at him with hatred if they knew what he had done. And they would know: He had specifically refused to be anonymous. If I can inflict stern necessity on them, then I must not run from the consequences of my own actions. I will bear what I must bear, as well—the grief, the resentment, and the rage of the few families I have harmed for the sake of all the rest.

The helicopter had taken off again before Carpenter's chair took him home. It sputtered overhead and disappeared into the low clouds. Rain again tomorrow, of course. Three days dry, three days wet; it had been the weather pattern all spring. The rain would come pounding tonight. Four hours till dark. Maybe the rain wouldn't come until dark.

He looked up from his book. He *had* heard footsteps outside his house. And whispers. He rolled to the window and looked out. The sky was a little darker. The computer said it was 4:30. The wind was coming up. But the sounds he heard hadn't been the wind. It had been 3:30 when the marshals came. Four-thirty now, and footsteps and whispers outside his house. He felt the stiffening in his arms and legs. Wait, he told himself. There's nothing to fear. Relax. Quiet. Yes. His body eased. His heart pounded, but it was slowing down.

The door crashed open. He was rigid at once. He couldn't even bring his hands down to touch the levers so he could turn to see who it was. He just spread there helplessly in his chair as the heavy footfalls came closer.

"There he is." The voice was Kippie's.

Hands seized his arms, pulled on him; the chair rocked as they tugged him to one side. He could not relax. "Son of a bitch is stiff as a statue." Pope's voice. Get out of here, little boy, said Carpenter, you're in something too deep for you. But of course they did not hear him, since his fingers couldn't reach the keyboard where he kept his voice.

"Maybe this is what he does when he isn't at school. Just sits here and makes statues at the window." Kippie laughed.

"He's scared stiff, that's what he is."

"Just bring him out, and fast." LaVon's voice carried authority.

They tried to lift him out of the chair, but his body was too rigid; they hurt him, though, trying, for his thighs pressed up against the computer with cruel force, and they wrung at his arms.

"Just carry the whole chair," said LaVon.

They picked up the chair and pulled him toward the door. His arms smacked against the corners and the door-frame. "It's like he's dead or something," said Kippie. "He don't say nothin'."

He was shouting at them in his mind, however. What are you doing here? Getting some sort of vengeance? Do you think punishing me will bring your fathers back, you fools?

They pulled and pushed the chair into the van they had parked in front. The bishop's van—Kippie wouldn't have the use of *that* much longer. How much of the stolen grain was carried in here?

"He's going to roll around back here," said Kippie.

"Tip him over," said LaVon.

Carpenter felt the chair fly under him; by chance he landed in such a way that his left arm was not caught behind the chair. It would have broken then. As it was, the impact with the floor bent his arm forcibly against the strength of his spasmed muscles; he felt something tear, and his throat made a sound in spite of his effort to bear it silently.

"Did you hear that?" said Pope. "He's got a voice."

"Not for much longer," said LaVon.

For the first time Carpenter realized that it wasn't just pain that he had to fear. Now, only an hour after their fathers had been taken, long before time could cool their rage, these boys had murder in their hearts.

The road was smooth enough in town, but soon it became rough and painful. From that, Carpenter knew they were headed toward the fringe. He could feel the cold metal of the van's corrugated floor against his face; the pain in his arm was settling down to a steady throb. Relax, quiet, calm, he told himself. How many times in your life have you wished to die? Death means nothing to you, fool— you decided that years ago—death is nothing but a release from this corpse. So what are you afraid of? Calm, quiet. His arms bent, his legs relaxed.

"He's getting soft again," reported Pope. From the front of the van, Kippie guffawed. "Little and squirmy. Mr. Bug. We always call you that, you hear me, Mr. Bug? There was always two of you. Mr. Machine and Mr. Bug. Mr. Machine was mean and tough and smart, but Mr. Bug was weak and squishy and gross, with wiggly legs. Made us want to puke, looking at Mr. Bug."

I've been tormented by master torturers in my childhood, Pope Griffith. You are only a pathetic echo of their talent. Carpenter's words were silent, until his hands found the keys. His left hand was almost too weak to use, after the fall, so he coded the words clumsily with his right hand alone. "If I disappear the day of your father's arrest, Mr. Griffith, don't you think they'll guess who took me?"

"Keep his hands away from the keys!" shouted LaVon. "Don't let him touch the computer."

Almost immediately the van lurched and took a savage bounce as it left the roadway. Now it was clattering over rough, unfinished ground. Carpenter's head banged against the metal floor, again and again. The pain of it made him go rigid; fortunately, spasms always carried his head upward to the right, so that his rigidity kept him from having his head beaten to unconsciousness.

Soon the bouncing stopped. The engine died. Carpenter could hear the wind whispering over the open desert land. They were beyond the fields and orchards, out past the grassland of the fringe. The van doors opened. LaVon and Kippie reached in and pulled him out, chair and all. They dragged the chair to the top of a wash. There was no water in it yet.

"Let's just throw him down," said Kippie. "Break his spastic little neck." Carpenter had not guessed that anger could burn so hot in these languid, mocking boys.

But LaVon showed no fire. He was cold and smooth as snow. "I don't want to kill him yet. I want to hear him talk first."

Carpenter reached out to code an answer. LaVon slapped his hands away, gripped the computer, braced a foot on the wheelchair, and tore the computer off its mounting. He threw it across the arroyo; it smacked against the far side and tumbled down into the dry wash. Probably it wasn't damaged, but it wasn't the computer Carpenter was frightened for. Until now Carpenter had been able to cling to a hope that they just meant to frighten him. But it was unthinkable to treat precious electronic equipment that way, not if civilization still had any hold on LaVon.

"With your *voice*, Mr. Carpenter. Not the machine, your own voice."

Not for you, Mr. Jensen. I don't humiliate myself for you.

"Come on," said Pope. "You know what we said. We just take him down into the wash and leave him there."

"We'll send him down the quick way," said Kippie. He shoved at the wheelchair, teetering it toward the brink.

"We'll *take* him down!" shouted Pope. "We aren't going to kill him! You promised!"

"Lot of difference it makes," said Kippie. "As soon as it rains in the mountains, this sucker's gonna fill up with water and give him the swim of his life."

"We don't kill him," insisted Pope.

"Come on," said LaVon. "Let's get him down into the wash."

Carpenter concentrated on not going rigid as they

wrestled the chair down the slope. The walls of the wash weren't sheer, but they were steep enough that the climb down wasn't easy. Carpenter tried to concentrate on mathematics problems so he wouldn't panic and writhe for them again. Finally the chair came to rest at the bottom of the wash.

"You think you can come here and decide who's good and who's bad, right?" said LaVon. "You think you can sit on your little throne and decide whose father's going to jail, is that it?"

Carpenter's hands rested on the twisted mountings that used to hold his computer. He felt naked, defenseless without his stinging, frightening voice to whip them into line. LaVon was smart to take away his voice. LaVon knew what Carpenter could do with words.

"Everybody does it," said Kippie. "You're the only one who doesn't black the harvest, and that's only because you can't."

"It's easy to be straight when you can't get anything on the side, anyway," said Pope.

Nothing's easy, Mr. Griffith. Not even virtue.

"My father's a good man!" shouted Kippie. "He's the bishop, for Christ's sake! And you sent him to jail!"

"If he ain't shot," said Pope.

"They don't shoot you for blacking anymore," said LaVon. "That was in the old days."

The old days. Only five years ago. But those were the old days for these children. Children are innocent in the eyes of God, Carpenter reminded himself. He tried to believe that these boys didn't know what they were doing to him.

Kippie and Pope started up the side of the wash. "Come on," said Pope. "Come on, LaVon."

"Minute," said LaVon. He leaned close to Carpenter and spoke softly, intensely, his breath hot and foul, his spittle like sparks from a cookfire on Carpenter's face. "Just ask me," he said. "Just open your mouth and beg me, little man, and I'll carry you back up to the van. They'll let you live if I tell them to, you know that."

He knew it. But he also knew that LaVon would never tell them to spare his life.

"Beg me, Mr. Carpenter. Ask me please to let you live, and you'll live. Look. I'll even save your little talk box for you." He scooped up the computer from the sandy bottom and heaved it up out of the wash. It sailed over Kippie's head just as he was emerging from the arroyo.

"What the hell was that, you trying to kill me?"

LaVon whispered again. "You know how many times you made me crawl? And now I gotta crawl forever; my father's a jailbird thanks to you; I got little brothers and sisters—even if you hate me, what've you got against them, huh?"

A drop of rain struck Carpenter in the face. There were a few more drops.

"Feel that?" said LaVon. "The rain in the mountains makes this wash flood every time. You crawl for me, Carpenter, and I'll take you up."

Carpenter didn't feel particularly brave as he kept his mouth shut and made no sound. If he actually believed LaVon might keep his promise, he would swallow his pride and beg. But LaVon was lying. He couldn't afford to save Carpenter's life now, even if he wanted to. It had gone too far, the consequences would be too great. Carpenter had to die, accidentally drowned, no witnesses, such a sad thing, such a great man, and no one the wiser about the three boys who carried him to his dying place.

If he begged and whined in his hound voice, his cat voice, his bestial monster voice, then LaVon would smirk at him in triumph and whisper, "Sucker." Carpenter knew the boy too well. Tomorrow LaVon would have second thoughts, of course, but right now there'd be no softening. He only wanted his triumph to be complete, that's why he held out a hope. He wanted to watch Carpenter twist like a worm and bay like a hound before he died. It was a victory, then, to keep silence. Let him remember me in his nightmares of guilt, let him remember I had courage enough not to whimper.

LaVon spat at him; the spittle struck him in the chest. "I can't even get it in your ugly little worm face," he said. Then he shoved the wheelchair and scrambled up the bank of the wash.

For a moment the chair hung in the balance; then it tipped over. This time Carpenter relaxed during the fall and rolled out of the chair without further injury. His back was to the side of the wash they had climbed; he couldn't see if they were watching him or not. So he held still, except for a slight twitching of his hurt left arm. After a while the van drove away.

Only then did he begin to reach out his arms and paw at the sand of the arroyo bottom. His legs were completely useless, dragging behind him. But he was not totally helpless without his chair. He could control his arms, and by reaching them out and then pulling his body onto his elbows, he could make good progress across the sand. How did they think he got from his wheelchair to bed, or to the toilet? Hadn't they seen him use his hands and arms? Of course they saw, but they assumed that because his arms were weak, they were useless.

Then he got to the arroyo wall and realized that they *were* useless. As soon as there was any slope to climb, his left arm began to hurt badly. And the bank was steep. Without being able to use his fingers to clutch at one of the sagebrushes or tree starts, there was no hope he could climb out.

The lightning was flashing in the distance, and he could hear the thunder. The rain here was a steady *plick plick plick* on the sand, a tiny slapping sound on the few leaves.

It would already be raining heavily in the mountains. Soon the water would be here.

He dragged himself another meter up the slope despite the pain. The sand scraped his elbows as he dug with them to pull himself along. The rain fell steadily now, many large drops, but still not a downpour. It was little comfort to Carpenter. Water was beginning to dribble down the sides of the wash and form puddles in the streambed.

With bitter humor he imagined himself telling Dean Wintz, "On second thought, I don't want to go out and teach sixth grade. I'll just go right on teaching them here, when they come off the farm. Just the few who want to learn something beyond sixth grade, who want a university education. The ones who love books and numbers and languages, the ones who understand civilization and want to keep it alive. Give me the children who *want* to learn, instead of these poor sandscrapers who go to school only because the law commands that six years out of their first fifteen years have to be spent as captives in the prison of learning."

Why do the fire-eaters go out searching for the old missile sites and risk their lives disarming them? To preserve civilization. Why do the freedom riders leave their safe homes and go out to bring the frightened, lonely refugees in to the safety of the mountains? To preserve civilization.

And why had Timothy Carpenter informed the marshals about the black-marketeering he had discovered in Reefrock Farms? Was it, truly, to preserve civilization?

Yes, he insisted to himself.

The water was flowing now along the bottom of the wash. His feet were near the flow. He painfully pulled himself up another meter. He had to keep his body pointed straight toward the side of the wash, or he would not be able to stop himself from rolling to one side or the other.

He found that by kicking his legs in his spastic, uncontrolled fashion, he could root the toes of his shoes into the sand just enough that he could take some pressure off his arms, just for a moment.

No, he told himself. It was not just to preserve civilization. It was because of the swaggering way their children walked, in their stolen clothing, with their full bellies and healthy skin and hair, cocky as only security can make a child feel. Enough and to spare, that's what they had, while the poor suckers around them worried whether there'd be food enough for the winter, and if their mother was getting enough so the nursing baby wouldn't lack, and whether their shoes could last another summer. The thieves could take a wagon up the long road to Price or even to Zarahemla, the shining city on the Mormon Sea, while the children of honest men never saw anything but the dust and sand and ruddy mountains of the fringe.

Carpenter hated them for that, for all the differences in the world, for the children who had legs and walked nowhere that mattered, for the children who had voices and used them to speak stupidity, who had deft and clever fingers and used them to frighten and compel the weak. For all the inequalities in the world, he hated them and wanted them to pay for it. They couldn't go to jail for having obedient arms and legs and tongues, but they could damn well go for stealing the hard-earned harvest of trusting men and women. Whatever his own motives might be, that was reason enough to call it justice.

The water was rising many centimeters every minute. The current was tugging at his feet now. He released his elbows to reach them up for another, higher purchase on the bank, but no sooner had he reached out his arms than he slid downward and the current pulled harder at him. It took great effort just to return to where he started, and his left arm was on fire with the tearing muscles. Still, it was life, wasn't it? His left elbow rooted him in place while he reached with his right arm and climbed higher still, and again higher. He even tried to use his fingers to cling to the soil, to a branch, to a rock, but his fists stayed closed and hammered uselessly against the ground.

Am I vengeful, bitter, spiteful? Maybe I am. But whatever my motive was, they were thieves, and had no business remaining among the people they had betrayed. It was hard on the children, of course, cruelly hard on them, to have their fathers stripped away from them by the authorities. But how much worse would it be for the fathers to stay, and the children to learn that trust was for the stupid and honor for the weak? What kind of people would we be then, if the children could do their numbers and letters but couldn't hold someone else's plate and leave the food on it untouched?

The water was up to his waist. The current was rocking him slightly, pulling him downstream. His legs were floating behind him now, and water was trickling down the bank, making the earth looser under his elbows. So the children wanted him dead now, in their fury. He would die in a good cause, wouldn't he?

With the water rising faster, the current swifter, he decided that martyrdom was not all it was cracked up to be. Nor was life, when he came right down to it, something to be given up lightly because of a few inconveniences. He managed to squirm up a few more centimeters, but now a shelf of earth blocked him. Someone with hands could have reached over it easily and grabbed hold of the sagebrush just above it.

He clenched his mouth tight and lifted his arm up onto the shelf of dirt. He tried to scrape some purchase for his forearm, but the soil was slick. When he tried to place some weight on the arm, he slid down again.

This was it, this was his death, he could feel it; and in the sudden rush of fear, his body went rigid. Almost at once his feet caught on the rocky bed of the river and stopped him from sliding farther. Spastic, his legs were of some use to him. He swung his right arm up, scraped his fist on the sagebrush stem, trying to pry his clenched fingers open.

And, with agonizing effort, he did it. All but the smallest finger opened enough to hook the stem. Now the clenching was some help to him. He used his left arm mercilessly, ignoring the pain, to pull himself up a little farther, onto the shelf; his feet were still in the water, but his waist wasn't, and the current wasn't strong against him now.

It was a victory, but not much of one. The water wasn't even a meter deep yet, and the current wasn't yet strong enough to have carried away his wheelchair. But it was enough to kill him, if he hadn't come this far. Still, what was he really accomplishing? In storms like this, the water came up near the top; he'd have been dead for an hour before the water began to come down again.

He could hear, in the distance, a vehicle approaching on the road. Had they come back to watch him die? They couldn't be that stupid. How far was this wash from the highway? Not far—they hadn't driven that long on the rough ground to get here. But it meant nothing. No one would see him, or even the computer that lay among the tumbleweeds and sagebrush at the arroyo's edge.

They might hear him. It was possible. If their window was open—in a rainstorm? If their engine was quiet—but loud enough that he could hear them? Impossible, impossible. And it might be the boys again, come to hear him scream and whine for life; I'm not going to cry out now, after so many years of silence—

But the will to live, he discovered, was stronger than shame; his voice came unbidden to his throat. His lips and tongue and teeth that in childhood had so painstakingly practiced words that only his family could ever understand now formed a word again: "Help!" It was a difficult word; it almost closed his mouth, it made him too quiet to hear. So at last he simply howled, saying nothing except the terrible sound of his voice.

The brakes squealed, long and loud, and the vehicle rattled to a stop. The engine died. Carpenter howled again. Car doors slammed. "I tell you it's just a dog somewhere, somebody's old dog—"

Carpenter howled again.

"Dog or not, it's alive, isn't it?"

They ran along the edge of the arroyo, and someone saw him.

"A little kid!"

"What's he doing down there!"

"Come on, kid, you can climb up from there!"

I nearly killed myself climbing this far, you fool, if I *could* climb, don't you think I *would* have? Help me! He cried out again.

"It's not a little boy. He's got a beard—"

"Come on, hold on, we're coming down!"

"There's a wheelchair in the water—"

"He must be a cripple."

There were several voices, some of them women, but it was two strong men who reached him, splashing their feet in the water. They hooked him under the arms and carried him to the top.

"Can you stand up? Are you all right? Can you stand?"

Carpenter strained to squeeze out the word: "No."

The older woman took command. "He's got palsy, as any fool can see. Go back down there and get his wheelchair, Tom, no sense in making him wait till they can get him another one, go on down! It's not that bad down there, the flood isn't here yet!" Her voice was crisp and clear, perfect speech, almost foreign it was so precise. She and the young woman carried him to the truck. It was a big old flatbed truck from the old days, and on its back was a canvas-covered heap of odd shapes. On the canvas Carpenter read the words Sweetwater's Miracle Pageant. Traveling-show people, then, racing for town to get out of the rain, and through some miracle they had heard his call.

"Your poor arms," said the young woman, wiping off grit and sand that had sliced his elbows. "Did you climb that far out of there with just your arms?"

The young men came out of the arroyo muddy and cursing, but they had the wheelchair. They tied it quickly to the back of the truck; one of the men found the computer, too, and took it inside the cab. It was designed to be rugged, and to Carpenter's relief it still worked.

"Thank you," said his mechanical voice.

"I told them I heard something, and they said I was crazy," said the old woman. "You live in Reefrock?"

"Yes," said his voice.

"Amazing what those old machines can still do, even after being dumped there in the rain," said the old woman. "Well, you came close to death, there, but you're all right, it's the best we can ask for. We'll take you to the doctor."

"Just take me home. Please."

So they did, but insisted on helping him bathe and fixing him dinner. The rain was coming down in sheets when they were done. "All I have is a floor," he said, "but you can stay."

"Better than trying to pitch the tents in this." So they stayed the night.

Carpenter's arms ached too badly for him to sleep, even though he was exhausted. He lay awake thinking of the current pulling him, imagining what would have happened to him, how far he might have gone downstream before drowning, where his body might have ended up. Caught in a snag somewhere, dangling on some branch or rock as the water went down and left his slack body to dry in the sun. Far out in the desert somewhere, maybe. Or perhaps the floodwater might have carried him all the way to the Colorado and tumbled him head over heels down the rapids, through the canyons, past the ruins of the old dams, and finally into the Gulf of California. He'd pass through Navaho territory then, and the Hopi Protectorate, and into areas that the Chihuahua claimed and threatened to go to war to keep. He'd see more of the world than he had seen in his life.

I saw more of the world tonight, he thought, than I had ever thought to see. I saw death and how much I feared it.

And he looked into himself, wondering how much he had changed.

Late in the morning, when he finally awoke, the pageant people were gone. They had a show, of course, and had to do some kind of parade to let people know. School would let out early so they could put on the show without having to waste power on lights. There'd be no school this afternoon. But what about his morning classes? There must have been some question when he didn't show up; someone would have called, and if he didn't answer the phone, someone would have come by. Maybe the show people had still been here when they came. The word would have spread through school that he was still alive.

He tried to imagine LaVon and Kippie and Pope hearing that Mr. Machine, Mr. Bug, Mr. Carpenter was still alive. They'd be afraid, of course. Maybe defiant. Maybe they had even confessed. No, not that. LaVon would keep them quiet. Try to think of a way out. Maybe even plan an escape, though finding a place to go that wasn't under Utah authority would be a problem.

What am I doing? Trying to plan how my enemies can escape retribution? I should call the marshals again and tell them what happened. If someone hasn't called them already.

His wheelchair waited by his bed. The show people had shined it up for him, got rid of all the muck. Even straightened the computer mounts and tied the computer on; jury-rigged it, but it would do. Would the motor run, after being under water? He saw that they had even changed batteries and had the old one set aside. They were good people. Not at all what the stories said about show gypsies. Though there was no natural law that people who help cripples can't also seduce all the young girls in the village.

His arms hurt and his left arm was weak and trembly, but he managed to get into the chair. The pain brought back yesterday. I'm alive today, and yet today doesn't feel any different from last week, when I was also alive. Being on the brink of death wasn't enough; the only transformation is to die.

He ate lunch because it was nearly noon. Eldon Finch came by to see him, along with the sheriff. "I'm the new bishop," said Eldon.

"Didn't waste any time," said Carpenter.

"I gotta tell you, Brother Carpenter, things are in a tizzy today. Yesterday, too, of course, what with avenging angels dropping out of the sky and taking away people we all trusted. There's some says you shouldn't've told, and some says you did right, and some ain't sayin' nothin' 'cause they're afraid somethin'll get told on *them*. Ugly times, ugly times, when folks steal from their neighbors."

Sheriff Budd finally spoke up. "Almost as ugly as tryin' to drownd 'em."

The bishop nodded. " 'Course you know the reason we come, Sheriff Budd and me, we come to find out who done it."

"Done what?"

"Plunked you down that wash. You aren't gonna tell me you drove that little wheelie chair of yours out there past the fringe. What, was you speedin' so fast you lost control and spun out? Give me peace of heart, Brother

Carpenter, give me trust." The bishop and the sheriff both laughed at that. Quite a joke.

Now's the time, thought Carpenter. Name the names. The motive will be clear, justice will be done. They put you through the worst hell of your life, they made you cry out for help, they taught you the taste of death. Now even things up.

But he didn't key their names into the computer. He thought of Kippie's mother crying at the door. When the crying stopped, there'd be years ahead. They were a long way from proving out their land. Kippie was through with school, he'd never go on, never get out. The adult burden was on those boys now, years too young. Should their families suffer even more, with another generation gone to prison? Carpenter had nothing to gain, and many who were guiltless stood to lose too much.

"Brother Carpenter," said Sheriff Budd. "Who was it?"

He keyed in his answer. "I didn't get a look at them."

"Their voices, didn't you know them?"

"No."

The bishop looked steadily at him. "They tried to kill you, Brother Carpenter. That's no joke. You like to died, if those show people hadn't happened by. And I have my own ideas who it was, seein' who had reason to hate you unto death yesterday."

"As you said. A lot of people think an outsider like me should have kept his nose out of Reefrock's business."

The bishop frowned at him. "You scared they'll try again?"

"No."

"Nothin' I can do," said the sheriff. " I think you're a damn fool, Brother Carpenter, but nothin' I can do if you don't even care."

"Thanks for coming by."

He didn't go to church Sunday. But on Monday he went

to school, same time as usual. And there were LaVon and Kippie and Pope, right in their places. But not the same as usual. The wisecracks were over. When he called on them, they answered if they could and didn't if they couldn't. When he looked at them, they looked away.

He didn't know if it was shame or fear that he might someday tell; he didn't care. The mark was on them. They would marry someday, go out into even newer lands just behind the ever-advancing fringe, have babies, work until their bodies were exhausted, and then drop into a grave. But they'd remember that one day they had left a cripple to die. He had no idea what it would mean to them, but they would remember.

Within a few weeks LaVon and Kippie were out of school; with their fathers gone, there was too much field-work and school was a luxury their families couldn't afford for them. Pope had an older brother still at home, so he stayed out the year.

One time Pope almost talked to him. It was a windy day that spattered sand against the classroom window, and the storm coming out of the south looked to be a nasty one. When class was over, most of the kids ducked their heads and rushed outside, hurrying to get home before the downpour began. A few stayed, though, to talk with Carpenter about this and that. When the last one left, Carpenter saw that Pope was still there. His pencil was hovering over a piece of paper. He looked up at Carpenter, then set the pencil down, picked up his books, started for the door. He paused for a moment with his hand on the doorknob. Carpenter waited for him to speak. But the boy only opened the door and went on out.

Carpenter rolled over to the door and watched him as he walked away. The wind caught at his jacket. Like a kite, thought Carpenter, it's lifting him along.

But it wasn't true. The boy didn't rise and fly. And now Carpenter saw the wind like a current down the village street, sweeping Pope away. All the bodies in the world, caught in that same current, that same wind, blown down the same rivers, the same streets, and finally coming to rest on some snag, through some door, in some grave, God knows where or why.

Sailing to Byzantium

ROBERT SILVERBERG

Robert Silverberg was awarded his first Nebula in 1969 for his short story "Passengers." In 1971 he received two Nebulas, for his short story "Good News from the Vatican," and for the novel *A Time of Changes*; In 1974 he won for a novella, "Born With the Dead." This year he became the only author to have won the Nebula five times. His many novels include *Dying Inside*, *Lord Valentine's Castle*, *Gilgamesh the King*, and *Tom O' Bedlam*; his new novel is *Star of Gypsies*.

He writes about how he sailed to Byzantium:

"I have spent, in the aggregate, at least four or five years of my life as a tourist—two weeks here, three weeks there. It adds up after a while. My travels have taken me to Istanbul and Jerusalem, to Rome and Paris, to Sydney and Melbourne and Adelaide, to Nairobi and Tunis and Marrakesh. The first time I tasted Dover sole was in the airport at Nice; the first time I saw color television was in a motel in Evansville, Indiana. I have been to see a goodly chunk of this planet, in other words; and I am still working assiduously at seeing the rest of it. Always as a tourist, of course, a visitor dropping in from some distant world, a diligent sightseer who wanders around peering at cathedrals and museums and marketplaces. I never try to

delude myself, let alone anyone else, into thinking I am or could ever be a permanent resident of the places I visit.

"My travels have figured largely in the texture of my writing. (They would have been mere pointless amusement if they hadn't.) My characters tend to move freely and sometimes a little compulsively from place to place; they have a practiced familiarity with the complexities of hotels and airports; and when I describe some remote city of this world or even of another, it is with a sense of detail that comes from having looked closely at a great many exotic places.

"The notion for 'Sailing to Byzantium' came to me out of all this traveling. What if there were an entire society—an entire world—that lived in a state of perpetual tourism? What if no one had any true home, but everyone traveled an endless circuit from place to place around the world? And what if none of those places were real, but only elegant temporary mock-ups of past glories? 'That year the five cities were Chang-an, Asgard, New Chicago, Timbuctoo, Alexandria,' I found myself writing, and the rest began to take shape.

"Chang-an no longer exists, New Chicago does not yet exist, Asgard never existed. Timbuctoo and Alexandria are real enough, though their present-day incarnations are not nearly as spectacular as the simulations depicted in the story. I doubt that I'll live to see New Chicago, and I don't expect to visit Asgard. But the maps are unfolded, and this year's choice is in the process of being made. Athens? Lisbon? Senegal? Mali? Such a big planet—so little time—"

At dawn he arose and stepped out onto the patio for his first look at Alexandria, the one city he had not yet seen. That year the five cities were Chang-an, Asgard, New Chicago, Timbuctoo, Alexandria: the usual mix of eras, cultures, realities. He and Gioia, making the long flight from Asgard in the distant north the night before, had arrived late, well after sundown, and had gone straight to bed. Now, by the gentle

apricot-hued morning light, the fierce spires and battle-
ments of Asgard seemed merely something he had
dreamed.

The rumor was that Asgard's moment was finished,
anyway. In a little while, he had heard, they were going
to tear it down and replace it, elsewhere, with Mohenjo-
daro. Though there were never more than five cities, they
changed constantly. He could remember a time when they
had had Rome of the Caesars instead of Chang-an, and
Rio de Janeiro rather than Alexandria. These people saw
no point in keeping anything very long.

It was not easy for him to adjust to the sultry intensity
of Alexandria after the frozen splendors of Asgard. The
wind, coming off the water, was brisk and torrid both at
once. Soft turquoise wavelets lapped at the jetties. Strong
presences assailed his senses: the hot heavy sky, the stinging scent of the red lowland sand borne on the breeze, the
sullen swampy aroma of the nearby sea. Everything trembled and glimmered in the early light. Their hotel was
beautifully situated, high on the northern slope of the huge
artificial mound known as the Paneium that was sacred to
the goat-footed god. From here they had a total view of
the city: the wide noble boulevards, the soaring obelisks
and monuments, the palace of Hadrian just below the hill,
the stately and awesome Library, the temple of Poseidon,
the teeming marketplace, the royal lodge that Mark An-
tony had built after his defeat at Actium. And of course
the Lighthouse, the wondrous many-windowed Lighthouse, the seventh wonder of the world, that immense
pile of marble and limestone and reddish-purple Aswan
granite rising in majesty at the end of its mile-long causeway. Black smoke from the beacon-fire at its summit curled
lazily into the sky. The city was awakening. Some temporaries in short white kilts appeared and began to trim the
dense dark hedges that bordered the great public build-

ings. A few citizens wearing loose robes of vaguely Grecian style were strolling in the streets.

There were ghosts and chimeras and phantasies everywhere about. Two slim elegant centaurs, a male and a female, grazed on the hillside. A burly thick-thighed swordsman appeared on the porch of the temple of Poseidon holding a Gorgon's severed head; he waved it in a wide arc, grinning broadly. In the street below the hotel gate three small pink sphinxes, no bigger than housecats, stretched and yawned and began to prowl the curbside. A larger one, lion-sized, watched warily from an alleyway: their mother, surely. Even at this distance he could hear her loud purring.

Shading his eyes, he peered far out past the Lighthouse and across the water. He hoped to see the dim shores of Crete or Cyprus to the north, or perhaps the great dark curve of Anatolia. *Carry me toward that great Byzantium*, he thought. *Where all is ancient, singing at the oars.* But he beheld only the endless empty sea, sun-bright and blinding though the morning was just beginning. Nothing was ever where he expected it to be. The continents did not seem to be in their proper places any longer. Gioia, taking him aloft long ago in her little flitterflitter, had shown him that. The tip of South America was canted far out into the Pacific; Africa was weirdly foreshortened; a broad tongue of ocean separated Europe and Asia. Australia did not appear to exist at all. Perhaps they had dug it up and used it for other things. There was no trace of the world he once had known. This was the fiftieth century. "The fiftieth century after *what*?" he had asked several times, but no one seemed to know, or else they did not care to say.

"Is Alexandria very beautiful?" Gioia called from within.

"Come out and see."

Naked and sleepy-looking, she padded out onto the white-tiled patio and nestled up beside him. She fit neatly under his arm. "Oh, yes, yes!" she said softly. "So very beautiful, isn't it? Look, there, the palaces, the Library, the Lighthouse! Where will we go first? The Lighthouse, I think. Yes? And then the marketplace—I want to see the Egyptian magicians—and the stadium, the races—will they be having races today, do you think? Oh, Charles, I want to see everything!"

"Everything? All on the first day?"

"All on the first day, yes," she said. "Everything."

"But we have plenty of time, Gioia."

"Do we?"

He smiled and drew her tight against his side.

"Time enough," he said gently.

He loved her for her impatience, for her bright bubbling eagerness. Gioia was not much like the rest in that regard, though she seemed identical in all other ways. She was short, supple, slender, dark-eyed, olive-skinned, narrow-hipped, with wide shoulders and flat muscles. They were all like that, each one indistinguishable from the rest, like a horde of millions of brothers and sisters—a world of small, lithe, childlike Mediterraneans, built for juggling, for bull-dancing, for sweet white wine at midday and rough red wine at night. They had the same slim bodies, the same broad mouths, the same great glossy eyes. He had never seen anyone who appeared to be younger than twelve or older than twenty. Gioia was somehow a little different, although he did not quite know how; but he knew that it was for that imperceptible but significant difference that he loved her. And probably that was why she loved him also.

He let his gaze drift from west to east, from the Gate of the Moon down broad Canopus Street and out to the harbor, and off to the tomb of Cleopatra at the tip of long slender Cape Lochias. Everything was here and all of it perfect, the obelisks, the statues and marble colonnades, the courtyards and shrines and groves, great Alexander himself in his coffin of crystal and gold: a splendid gleaming pagan city. But there were oddities—an unmistakable mosque near the public gardens, and what seemed to be a Christian church not far from the Library. And those ships in the harbor, with all those red sails and bristling masts—surely they were medieval, and late medieval at that. He had seen such anachronisms in other places before. Doubtless these people found them amusing. Life was a game for them. They played at it unceasingly. Rome, Alexandria, Timbuctoo—why not? Create an Asgard of translucent bridges and shimmering ice-girt palaces, then grow weary of it and take it away? Replace it with Mohenjo-daro? Why not? It seemed to him a great pity to destroy those lofty Nordic feasting-halls for the sake of building a squat, brutal, sun-baked city of brown brick; but these people did not look at things the way he did. Their cities were only temporary. Someone in Asgard had said that Timbuctoo would be the next to go, with Byzantium rising in its place. Well, why not? Why not? They could have anything they liked. This was the fiftieth century, after all. The only rule was that there could be no more than five cities at once. "Limits," Gioia had informed him solemnly when they first began to travel together, "are very important." But she did not know why, or did not care to say.

He stared out once more toward the sea.

He imagined a newborn city congealing suddenly out of mists, far across the water: shining towers, great domed palaces, golden mosaics. That would be no great effort for them. They could just summon it forth whole out of time, the Emperor on his throne and the Emperor's drunken soldiery roistering in the streets, the brazen clangor of the cathedral gong rolling through the Grand Bazaar, dolphins leaping beyond the shoreside pavilions. Why not? They had Timbuctoo. They had Alexandria. Do you crave Constantinople? Then behold Constantinople! Or Avalon, or Lyonnesse, or Atlantis. They could have anything they liked. It is pure Schopenhauer here: the world as will and imagination. Yes! These slender dark-eyed people journeying tirelessly from miracle to miracle. Why not Byzantium next? Yes! Why not? *That is no country for old men*, he thought. *The young in one another's arms, the birds in the trees*— yes! Yes! Anything they liked. They even had him. Suddenly he felt frightened. Questions he had not asked for a long time burst through into his consciousness. *Why am I? Why am I here? Who is this woman beside me?*

"You're so quiet all of a sudden, Charles," said Gioia, who could not abide silence for very long. "Will you talk to me? I want you to talk to me. Tell me what you're looking for out there."

He shrugged. "Nothing."

"Nothing?"

"Nothing in particular."

"I could see you seeing something."

"Byzantium," he said. "I was imagining that I could look straight across the water to Byzantium. I was trying to get a glimpse of the walls of Constantinople."

"Oh, but you wouldn't be able to see as far as that from here. Not really."

"I know."

"And anyway Byzantium doesn't exist."

"Not yet. But it will. Its time comes later on."

"Does it?" she said. "Do you know that for a fact?"

"On good authority. I heard it in Asgard," he told her. "But even if I hadn't, Byzantium would be inevitable, don't you think? Its time would have to come. How could we not do Byzantium, Gioia? We certainly will do Byzantium, sooner or later. I know we will. It's only a matter of time. And we have all the time in the world."

A shadow crossed her face. "Do we? Do we?"

He knew very little about himself, but he knew that he was not one of them. That he knew. He knew that his name was Charles Phillips and that before he had come to live among these people he had lived in the year 1984, when there had been such things as computers and television sets and baseball and jet planes, and the world was full of cities, not merely five but thousands of them, New York and London and Johannesburg and Paris and Liverpool and Bangkok and San Francisco and Buenos Aires and a multitude of others, all at the same time. There had been four and a half billion people in the world then; now he doubted that there were as many as four and a half million. Nearly everything had changed beyond comprehension. The moon still seemed the same, and the sun; but at night he searched in vain for familiar constellations. He had no idea how they had brought him from then to now, or why. It did no good to ask. No one had any answers for him; no one so much as appeared to understand what it was that he was trying to learn. After a time he had stopped asking; after a time he had almost entirely ceased wanting to know.

He and Gioia were climbing the Lighthouse. She scampered ahead, in a hurry as always, and he came along behind her in his more stolid fashion. Scores of other tourists, mostly in groups of two or three, were making their way up the wide flagstone ramps, laughing, calling to one another. Some of them, seeing him, stopped a moment, stared, pointed. He was used to that. He was so much taller than any of them; he was plainly not one of them. When they pointed at him he smiled. Sometimes he nodded a little acknowledgment.

He could not find much of interest in the lowest level, a massive square structure two hundred feet high built of huge marble blocks: within its cool musty arcades were hundreds of small dark rooms, the offices of the Lighthouse's keepers and mechanics, the barracks of the garrison, the stables for the three hundred donkeys that carried the fuel to the lantern far above. None of that appeared inviting to him. He forged onward without halting until he emerged on the balcony that led to the next level. Here the Lighthouse grew narrower and became octagonal: its face, granite now and handsomely fluted, rose in a stunning sweep above him.

Gioia was waiting for him there. "This is for you," she said, holding out a nugget of meat on a wooden skewer. "Roast lamb. Absolutely delicious. I had one while I was waiting for you." She gave him a cup of some cool green sherbet also, and darted off to buy a pomegranate. Dozens of temporaries were roaming the balcony, selling refreshments of all kinds.

He nibbled at the meat. It was charred outside, nicely pink and moist within. While he ate, one of the temporaries came up to him and peered blandly into his face. It was a stocky swarthy male wearing nothing but a strip of red and yellow cloth about its waist. "I sell meat," it said. "Very fine roast lamb, only five drachmas."

Phillips indicated the piece he was eating. "I already have some," he said.

"It is excellent meat, very tender. It has been soaked for three days in the juices of—"

"Please," Phillips said. "I don't want to buy any meat. Do you mind moving along?"

The temporaries had confused and baffled him at first, and there was still much about them that was unclear to him. They were not machines—they looked like creatures of flesh and blood—but they did not seem to be human beings, either, and no one treated them as if they were. He supposed they were artificial constructs, products of a technology so consummate that it was invisible. Some appeared to be more intelligent than others, but all of them behaved as if they had no more autonomy than characters in a play, which was essentially what they were. There were untold numbers of them in each of the five cities, playing all manner of roles: shepherds and swineherds, street-sweepers, merchants, boatmen, vendors of grilled meats and cool drinks, hagglers in the marketplace, schoolchildren, charioteers, policemen, grooms, gladiators, monks, artisans, whores and cutpurses, sailors— whatever was needed to sustain the illusion of a thriving, populous urban center. The dark-eyed people, Gioia's people, never performed work. There were not enough of them to keep a city's functions going, and in any case they were strictly tourists, wandering with the wind, moving from city to city as the whim took them, Chang-an to New Chicago, New Chicago to Timbuctoo, Timbuctoo to Asgard, Asgard to Alexandria, onward, ever onward.

The temporary would not leave him alone. Phillips walked away and it followed him, cornering him against the balcony wall. When Gioia returned a few minutes later, lips prettily stained with pomegranate juice, the temporary was still hovering about him, trying with lunatic persistence to sell him a skewer of lamb. It stood much too close to him, almost nose to nose, great sad cowlike eyes peering intently into his as it extolled with mournful mooing urgency the quality of its wares. It seemed to him that he had had trouble like this with temporaries on one or two earlier occasions. Gioia touched the creature's elbow lightly and said, in a short sharp tone Phillips had never heard her use before, "He isn't interested. Get away from him." It went at once. To Phillips she said, "You have to be firm with them."

"I was trying. It wouldn't listen to me."

"You ordered it to go away, and it refused?"

"I asked it to go away. Politely. Too politely, maybe."

"Even so," she said. "It should have obeyed a human, regardless."

"Maybe it didn't think I was human," Phillips suggested. "Because of the way I look. My height, the color of my eyes. It might have thought I was some kind of temporary myself."

"No," Gioia said, frowning. "A temporary won't solicit another temporary. But it won't ever disobey a citizen, either. There's a very clear boundary. There isn't ever any confusion. I can't understand why it went on bothering you." He was surprised at how troubled she seemed: far more so, he thought, than the incident warranted. A stupid device, perhaps miscalibrated in some way, overenthusiastically pushing its wares—what of it? What of it? Gioia, after a moment, appeared to come to the same conclusion. Shrugging, she said, "It's defective, I suppose. Probably such things are more common than we suspect, don't you think?" There was something forced about her tone that bothered him. She smiled and handed him her pomegranate. "Here. Have a bite, Charles. It's wonderfully sweet. They used to be extinct, you know. Shall we go on upward?"

The octagonal midsection of the Lighthouse must have been several hundred feet in height, a grim claustrophobic tube almost entirely filled by the two broad spiraling ramps that wound around the huge building's central well. The ascent was slow: a donkey team was a little way ahead of them on the ramp, plodding along laden with bundles of kindling for the lantern. But at last, just as Phillips was growing winded and dizzy, he and Gioia came out onto the second balcony, the one marking the transition between the octagonal section and the Lighthouse's uppermost storey, which was cylindrical and very slender.

She leaned far out over the balustrade. "Oh, Charles, look at the view! Look at it!"

It was amazing. From one side they could see the entire city, and swampy Lake Mareotis and the dusty Egyptian plain beyond it, and from the other they peered far out into the gray and choppy Mediterranean. He gestured toward the innumerable reefs and shallows that infested the waters leading to the harbor entrance. "No wonder they needed a lighthouse here," he said. "Without some kind of gigantic landmark they'd never have found their way in from the open sea."

A blast of sound, a ferocious snort, erupted just above him. He looked up, startled. Immense statues of trumpet-wielding Tritons jutted from the corners of the Lighthouse at this level; that great blurting sound had come from the nearest of them. A signal, he thought. A warning to the ships negotiating that troubled passage. The sound was produced by some kind of steam-powered mechanism, he realized, operated by teams of sweating temporaries clustered about bonfires at the base of each Triton.

Once again he found himself swept by admiration for the clever way these people carried out their reproductions of antiquity. Or *were* they reproductions? he wondered. He still did not understand how they brought their cities into being. For all he knew, this place was the authentic Alexandria itself, pulled forward out of its proper time just as he himself had been. Perhaps this was the true and original Lighthouse, and not a copy. He had no idea which was the case, nor which would be the greater miracle.

"How do we get to the top?" Gioia asked.

"Over there, I think. That doorway."

The spiraling donkey-ramps ended here. The loads of lantern fuel went higher via a dumb-waiter in the central shaft. Visitors continued by way of a cramped staircase, so narrow at its upper end that it was impossible to turn around while climbing. Gioia, tireless, sprinted ahead. He clung to the rail and labored up and up, keeping count of the tiny window-slits to ease the boredom of the ascent. The count was nearing a hundred when finally he stumbled into the vestibule of the beacon chamber. A dozen or so visitors were crowded into it. Gioia was at the far side, by the wall that was open to the sea.

It seemed to him he could feel the building swaying in the winds, up here. How high were they? Five hundred feet, six hundred, seven? The beacon chamber was tall and narrow, divided by a catwalk into upper and lower sections. Down below, relays of temporaries carried wood from the dumb-waiter and tossed it on the blazing fire. He felt its intense heat from where he stood, at the rim of the platform on which the giant mirror of polished metal was hung. Tongues of flame leaped upward and danced before the mirror, which hurled its dazzling beam far out to sea. Smoke rose through a vent. At the very top was a colossal statue of Poseidon, austere, ferocious, looming above the lantern.

Gioia sidled along the catwalk until she was at his side. "The guide was talking before you came," she said, pointing. "Do you see that place over there, under the mirror? Someone standing there and looking into the mirror gets a view of ships at sea that can't be seen from here by the naked eye. The mirror magnifies things."

"Do you believe that?"

She nodded toward the guide. "It said so. And it also told us that if you look in a certain way, you can see right across the water into the city of Constantinople."

She is like a child, he thought. They all are. He said, "You told me yourself this very morning that it isn't possible to see that far. Besides, Constantinople doesn't exist right now."

"It will," she replied. "*You* said that to me, this very morning. And when it does, it'll be reflected in the Lighthouse mirror. That's the truth. I'm absolutely certain of it." She swung about abruptly toward the entrance of the beacon chamber. "Oh, look, Charles! Here come Nissandra and Aramayne! And there's Hawk! There's Stengard!" Gioia laughed and waved and called out names. "Oh, everyone's here! *Everyone!*"

They came jostling into the room, so many newcomers that some of those who had been there were forced to scramble down the steps on the far side. Gioia moved among them, hugging, kissing. Phillips could scarcely tell one from another—it was hard for him even to tell which were the men and which the women, dressed as they all were in the same sort of loose robes—but he recognized some of the names. These were her special friends, her set, with whom she had journeyed from city to city on an endless round of gaiety in the old days before he had come into her life. He had met a few of them before, in Asgard, in Rio, in Rome. The beacon-chamber guide, a squat wide-shouldered old temporary wearing a laurel wreath on its bald head, reappeared and began its potted speech, but no one listened to it; they were all too busy greeting one another, embracing, giggling. Some of them edged their way over to Phillips and reached up, standing on tiptoes, to touch their fingertips to his cheek in that odd hello of theirs. "Charles," they said gravely, making two syllables out of the name, as these people often did. "So good to see you again. Such a pleasure. You and Gioia—such a handsome couple. So well suited to each other."

Was that so? He supposed it was.

The chamber hummed with chatter. The guide could not be heard at all. Stengard and Nissandra had visited New Chicago for the water-dancing—Aramayne bore tales of a feast in Chang-an that had gone on for *days*—Hawk and Hekna had been to Timbuctoo to see the arrival of the salt caravan, and were going back there soon—a final party soon to celebrate the end of Asgard that absolutely should not be missed—the plans for the new city, Mohenjo-daro—we have reservations for the opening, we wouldn't pass it up for anything—and, yes, they were definitely going to do Constantinople after that, the planners were already deep into their Byzantium research—so good to see you, you look so beautiful all the time—have you been to the Library yet? The zoo? To the temple of Serapis?—

To Phillips they said, "What do you think of our Alexandria, Charles? Of course you must have known it well in your day. Does it look the way you remember it?" They were always asking things like that. They did not seem to comprehend that the Alexandria of the Lighthouse and the Library was long lost and legendary by his time. To them, he suspected, all the places they had brought back into existence were more or less contemporary. Rome of the Caesars, Alexandria of the Ptolemies, Venice of the Doges, Chang-an of the T'angs, Asgard of the Aesir, none any less real than the next nor any less unreal, each one simply a facet of the distant past, the fantastic immemorial past, a plum plucked from that dark backward and abysm of time. They had no contexts for separating one era from another. To them all the past was one borderless timeless realm. Why then should he not have seen the Lighthouse before, he who had leaped into this era from the New York of 1984? He had never been able to explain it to them. Julius Caesar and Hannibal, Helen of Troy and Charlemagne, Rome of the gladiators and New York of the Yankees and Mets, Gilgamesh and Tristan and Othello and Robin Hood and George Washington and Queen Victoria—to them, all equally real and unreal, none of them any more than bright figures moving about on a painted canvas. The past, the past, the elusive and fluid past—to them it was a single place of infinite accessibility and infinite connectivity. Of course they would think he had seen the Lighthouse before. He knew better than to try again to explain things. "No," he said simply. "This is my first time in Alexandria."

They stayed there all winter long, and possibly some of the spring. Alexandria was not a place where one was sharply aware of the change of seasons, nor did the passage of time itself make itself very evident when one was living one's entire life as a tourist.

During the day there was always something new to see. The zoological garden, for instance: a wondrous park, miraculously green and lush in this hot dry climate, where astounding animals roamed in enclosures so generous that they did not seem like enclosures at all. Here were camels, rhinoceroses, gazelles, ostriches, lions, wild asses; and here too, casually adjacent to those familiar African beasts, were hippogriffs, unicorns, basilisks, and fire-snorting dragons with rainbow scales. Had the original zoo of Alexandria had dragons and unicorns? Phillips doubted it. But this one did; evidently it was no harder for the backstage craftsmen to manufacture mythic beasts than it was for them to turn out camels and gazelles. To Gioia and her friends all of them were equally mythical, anyway. They were just as awed by the rhinoceros as by the hippogriff. One was no more strange—nor any less—than the other. So far as Phillips had been able to discover, none of the mammals or birds of his era had survived into this one except for a few cats and dogs, though many had been reconstructed.

And then the Library! All those lost treasures, re-claimed from the jaws of time! Stupendous columned mar-ble walls, airy high-vaulted reading-rooms, dark coiling stacks stretching away to infinity. The ivory handles of seven hundred thousand papyrus scrolls bristling on the shelves. Scholars and librarians gliding quietly about, smil-ing faint scholarly smiles but plainly preoccupied with se-rious matters of the mind. They were all temporaries, Phillips realized. Mere props, part of the illusion. But were the scrolls illusions too? "Here we have the complete dra-mas of Sophocles," said the guide with a blithe wave of its hand, indicating shelf upon shelf of texts. Only seven of his hundred twenty-three plays had survived the succes-sive burnings of the library in ancient times by Romans, Christians, Arabs: were the lost ones here, the *Triptolemus*, the *Nausicaa*, the *Jason*, and all the rest? And would he find here too, miraculously restored to being, the other van-ished treasures of ancient literature—the memoirs of Odysseus, Cato's history of Rome, Thucydides' life of Pericles, the missing volumes of Livy? But when he asked if he might explore the stacks, the guide smiled apologetically and said that all the librarians were busy just now. Another time, perhaps? Perhaps, said the guide. It made no difference, Phillips decided. Even if these people somehow had brought back those lost masterpieces of antiquity, how would he read them? He knew no Greek.

The life of the city buzzed and throbbed about him. It was a dazzlingly beautiful place: the vast bay thick with sails, the great avenues running rigidly east-west, north-south, the sunlight rebounding almost audibly from the bright walls of the palaces of kings and gods. They have done this very well, Phillips thought: very well indeed. In the marketplace hard-eyed traders squabbled in half a dozen mysterious languages over the price of ebony, Arabian incense, jade, panther-skins. Gioia bought a dram of pale musky Egyptian perfume in a delicate tapering glass flask. Magicians and jugglers and scribes called out stridently to passersby, begging for a few moments of attention and a handful of coins for their labor. Strapping slaves, black and tawny and some that might have been Chinese, were put up for auction, made to flex their muscles, to bare their teeth, to bare their breasts and thighs to prospective buyers. In the gymnasium naked athletes hurled javelins and discuses, and wrestled with terrifying zeal. Gioia's friend Stengard came rushing up with a gift for her, a golden necklace that would not have embarrassed Cleopatra. An hour later she had lost it, or perhaps had given it away while Phillips was looking elsewhere. She bought another, even finer, the next day. Anyone could have all the money he wanted, simply by asking: it was as easy to come by as air, for these people.

Being here was much like going to the movies, Phillips told himself. A different show every day: not much plot, but the special effects were magnificent and the detail-work could hardly have been surpassed. A megamovie, a vast entertainment that went on all the time and was being played out by the whole population of Earth. And it was all so effortless, so spontaneous: just as when he had gone to a movie he had never troubled to think about the myriad technicians behind the scenes, the cameramen and the costume designers and the set-builders and the electricians and the model-makers and the boom operators, so too here he chose not to question the means by which Alexandria had been set before him. It felt real. It *was* real. When he drank the strong red wine it gave him a pleasant buzz. If he leaped from the beacon chamber of the Lighthouse he suspected he would die, though perhaps he would not stay dead for long: doubtless they had some way of restoring him as often as was necessary. Death did not seem to be a factor in these people's lives.

By day they saw sights. By night he and Gioia went to parties, in their hotel, in seaside villas, in the palaces of the high nobility. The usual people were there all the time, Hawk and Hekna, Aramayne, Stengard and Shelimir, Nissandra, Asoka, Afonso, Protay. At the parties there were five or ten temporaries for every citizen, some as mere servants, others as entertainers or even surrogate guests, mingling freely and a little daringly. But everyone knew, all the time, who was a citizen and who just a temporary. Phillips began to think his own status lay somewhere between. Certainly they treated him with a courtesy that no one ever would give a temporary, and yet there was a condescension to their manner that told him not simply that he was not one of them but that he was someone or something of an altogether different order of existence. That he was Gioia's lover gave him some standing in their eyes, but not a great deal: obviously he was always going to be an outsider, a primitive, ancient and quaint. For that matter he noticed that Gioia herself, though unquestionably a member of the set, seemed to be regarded as something of an outsider, like a tradesman's great-granddaughter in a gathering of Plantagenets. She did not always find out about the best parties in time to attend; her friends did not always reciprocate her effusive greetings with the same degree of warmth; sometimes he noticed her straining to hear some bit of gossip that was not quite being shared with her. Was it because she had taken him for her lover? Or was it the other way around: that she had chosen to be his lover precisely because she was *not* a full member of their caste?

Being a primitive gave him, at least, something to talk about at their parties. "Tell us about war," they said. "Tell us about elections. About money. About disease." They wanted to know everything, though they did not seem to pay close attention: their eyes were quick to glaze. Still, they asked. He described traffic jams to them, and politics, and deodorants, and vitamin pills. He told them about cigarettes, newspapers, subways, telephone directories, credit cards, and basketball.

"Which was your city?" they asked. New York, he told them. "And when was it? The seventh century, did you say?" The twentieth, he told them. They exchanged glances and nodded. "We will have to do it," they said. "The World Trade Center, the Empire State Building, the Citicorp Center, the Cathedral of St. John the Divine: how fascinating! Yankee Stadium. The Verrazzano Bridge. We will do it all. But first must come Mohenjo-daro. And then, I think, Constantinople. Did your city have many people?" Seven million, he said. Just in the five boroughs alone. They nodded, smiling amiably, unfazed by the number.

Seven million, seventy million—it was all the same to them, he sensed. They would just bring forth the temporaries in whatever quantity was required. He wondered how well they would carry the job off. He was no real judge of Alexandrias and Asgards, after all. Here they could have unicorns and hippogriffs in the zoo, and live sphinxes prowling in the gutters, and it did not trouble him. Their fanciful Alexandria was as good as history's, or better. But how sad, how disillusioning it would be, if the New York that they conjured up had Greenwich Village uptown and Times Square in the Bronx, and the New Yorkers, gentle and polite, spoke with the honeyed accents of Savannah or New Orleans. Well, that was nothing he needed to brood about just now. Very likely they were only being courteous when they spoke of doing his New York. They had all the vastness of the past to choose from: Nineveh, Memphis of the Pharaohs, the London of Victoria or Shakespeare or Richard the Third, Florence of the Medici, the Paris of Abelard and Heloise or the Paris of Louis XIV, Moctezuma's Tenochtitlan and Atahuallpa's Cuzco; Damascus, St. Petersburg, Babylon, Troy. And then there were all the cities like New Chicago, out of time that was time yet unborn to him but ancient history to them. In such richness, such an infinity of choices, even mighty New York might have to wait a long while for its turn. Would he still be among them by the time they got around to it? By then, perhaps, they might have become bored with him and returned him to his own proper era. Or possibly he would simply have grown old and died. Even here, he supposed, he would eventually die, though no one else ever seemed to. He did not know. He realized that in fact he did not know anything.

The north wind blew all day long. Vast flocks of ibises appeared over the city, fleeing the heat of the interior, and screeched across the sky with their black necks and scrawny legs extended. The sacred birds, descending by the thousands, scuttered about in every crossroad, pouncing on spiders and beetles, on mice, on the debris of the meatshops and the bakeries. They were beautiful but annoyingly ubiquitous, and they splashed their dung over the marble buildings; each morning squadrons of temporaries carefully washed it off. Gioia said little to him now. She

seemed cool, withdrawn, depressed; and there was something almost intangible about her, as though she were
gradually becoming transparent. He felt it would be an in-
trusion upon her privacy to ask her what was wrong. Perhaps it was only restlessness. She became religious, and
presented costly offerings at the temples of Serapis, Isis,
Poseidon, Pan. She went to the necropolis west of the city
to lay wreaths on the tombs in the catacombs. In a single
day she climbed the Lighthouse three times without any
sign of fatigue. One afternoon he returned from a visit to
the Library and found her naked on the patio; she had
anointed herself all over with some aromatic green salve.
Abruptly she said, "I think it's time to leave Alexandria,
don't you?"

She wanted to go to Mohenjo-daro, but Mohenjo-daro was
not yet ready for visitors. Instead they flew eastward to
Chang-an, which they had not seen in years. It was Phillips's suggestion: he hoped that the cosmopolitan gaudi-
ness of the old T'ang capital would lift her mood.

They were to be guests of the Emperor this time: an
unusual privilege, which ordinarily had to be applied for
far in advance, but Phillips had told some of Gioia's highly
placed friends that she was unhappy, and they had quickly
arranged everything. Three endlessly bowing functionar-
ies in flowing yellow robes and purple sashes met them at
the Gate of Brilliant Virtue in the city's south wall and conducted them to their pavilion, close by the imperial palace
and the Forbidden Garden. It was a light, airy place, thin
walls of plastered brick braced by graceful columns of some
dark, aromatic wood. Fountains played on the roof of green
and yellow tiles, creating an unending cool rainfall of re-
circulating water. The balustrades were of carved marble,
the door-fittings were of gold.

There was a suite of private rooms for him, and another for her, though they would share the handsome da-

mask-draped bedroom at the heart of the pavilion. As soon as they arrived Gioia announced that she must go to her rooms to bathe and dress. "There will be a formal reception for us at the palace tonight," she said. "They say the imperial receptions are splendid beyond anything you could imagine. I want to be at my best." The Emperor and all his ministers, she told him, would receive them in the Hall of the Supreme Ultimate; there would be a banquet for a thousand people; Persian dancers would perform, and the celebrated jugglers of Chung-nan. Afterward everyone would be conducted into the fantastic landscape of the Forbidden Garden to view the dragon-races and the fireworks.

He went to his own rooms. Two delicate little maid servants undressed him and bathed him with fragrant sponges. The pavilion came equipped with eleven temporaries who were to be their servants: soft-voiced unobtrusive cat-like Chinese, done with perfect verisimilitude, straight black hair, glowing skin, epicanthic folds. Phillips often wondered what happened to a city's temporaries when the city's time was over. Were the towering Norse heroes of Asgard being recycled at this moment into wiry dark-skinned Dravidians for Mohenjo-daro? When Timbuctoo's day was done, would its brightly robed black warriors be converted into supple Byzantines to stock the arcades of Constantinople? Or did they simply discard the old temporaries like so many excess props, stash them in warehouses somewhere, and turn out the appropriate quantities of the new model? He did not know; and once when he had asked Gioia about it she had grown uncomfortable and vague. She did not like him to probe for information, and he suspected it was because she had very little to give. These people did not seem to question the workings of their own world; his curiosities were very twentieth-century of him, he was frequently told, in that gently patronizing way of theirs. As his two little maids patted him with their sponges he thought of asking them where they had served before Chang-an. Rio? Rome? Haroun al-Raschid's Baghdad? But these fragile girls, he knew, would only giggle and retreat if he tried to question them. Interrogating temporaries was not only improper, but pointless: it was like interrogating one's luggage.

When he was bathed and robed in rich red silks he wandered the pavilion for a little while, admiring the tinkling pendants of green jade dangling on the portico, the lustrous auburn pillars, the rainbow hues of the intricately interwoven girders and brackets that supported the roof. Then, wearying of his solitude, he approached the bamboo curtain at the entrance to Gioia's suite. A porter and one of the maids stood just within. They indicated that he should not enter; but he scowled at them and they melted from him like snowflakes. A trail of incense led him through the pavilion to Gioia's innermost dressing-room. There he halted, just outside the door.

Gioia sat naked with her back to him at an ornate dressing table of some rare flame-colored wood inlaid with bands of orange and green porcelain. She was studying herself intently in a mirror of polished bronze held by one of her maids: picking through her scalp with her fingernails, as a woman might do who was searching out her gray hairs.

But that seemed strange. Gray hair, on Gioia? On a citizen? A temporary might display some appearance of aging, perhaps, but surely not a citizen. Citizens remained forever young. Gioia looked like a girl. Her face was smooth and unlined, her flesh was firm, her hair was dark: that was true of all of them, every citizen he had seen. And yet there was no mistaking what Gioia was doing. She found a hair, frowned, drew it taut, nodded, plucked it. Another. Another. She pressed the tip of her finger to her cheek as if testing it for resilience. She tugged at the skin below her eyes, pulling it downward. Such familiar little gestures of vanity; but so odd here, he thought, in this world of the perpetually young. Gioia, worried about growing old? Had he simply failed to notice the signs of age on her? Or was it that she worked hard behind his back at concealing them? Perhaps that was it. Was he wrong about the citizens, then? Did they age even as the people of less blessed eras had always done, but simply have better ways of hiding it? How old was she, anyway? Thirty? Sixty? Three hundred?

Gioia appeared satisfied now. She waved the mirror away; she rose; she beckoned for her banquet robes. Phillips, standing unnoticed by the door, studied her with admiration: the small round buttocks, almost but not quite boyish, the elegant line of her spine, the surprising breadth of her shoulders. No, he thought, she is not aging at all. Her body is still like a girl's. She looks as young as on the day they first had met, however long ago that was—he could not say; it was hard to keep track of time here; but he was sure some years had passed since they had come together. Those gray hairs, those wrinkles and sags for which she had searched just now with such desperate intensity, must all be imaginary, mere artifacts of vanity. Even in this remote future epoch, then, vanity was not extinct. He wondered why she was so concerned with the fear of aging. An affectation? Did all these timeless people take some perverse pleasure in fretting over the possibility that they might be growing old? Or was it some private fear of Gioia's, another symptom of the mysterious depression that had come over her in Alexandria?

Not wanting her to think that he had been spying on her, when all he had really intended was to pay her a visit, he slipped silently away to dress for the evening. She came to him an hour later, gorgeously robed, swaddled from chin to ankles in a brocade of brilliant colors shot through with threads of gold, face painted, hair drawn up tightly and fastened with ivory combs: very much the lady of the court. His servants had made him splendid also, a lustrous black surplice embroidered with golden dragons over a sweeping floor-length gown of shining white silk, a necklace and pendant of red coral, a five-cornered gray felt hat that rose in tower upon tower like a ziggurat. Gioia, grinning, touched her fingertips to his cheek. "You look marvelous!" she told him. "Like a grand mandarin!"

"And you like an empress," he said. "Of some distant land: Persia, India. Here to pay a ceremonial visit on the Son of Heaven." An excess of love suffused his spirit, and, catching her lightly by the wrist, he drew her toward him, as close as he could manage it considering how elaborate their costumes were. But as he bent forward and downward, meaning to brush his lips lightly and affectionately against the tip of her nose, he perceived an unexpected strangeness, an anomaly: the coating of white paint that was her makeup seemed oddly to magnify rather than mask the contours of her skin, highlighting and revealing details he had never observed before. He saw a pattern of fine lines radiating from the corners of her eyes, and the unmistakable beginning of a quirk-mark in her cheek just to the left of her mouth, and perhaps the faint indentation of frown-lines in her flawless forehead. A shiver traveled along the nape of his neck. So it was not affectation, then, that had had her studying her mirror so fiercely. Age was in truth beginning to stake its claim on her, despite all that he had come to believe about these people's agelessness. But a moment later he was not so sure. Gioia turned and slid gently half a step back from him—she must have found his stare disturbing—and the lines he had thought he had seen were gone. He searched for them and saw only girlish smoothness once again. A trick of the light? A figment of an overwrought imagination? He was baffled.

"Come," she said. "We mustn't keep the Emperor waiting."

Five mustachioed warriors in armor of white quilting

and seven musicians playing cymbals and pipes escorted them to the Hall of the Supreme Ultimate. There they found the full court arrayed: princes and ministers, high officials, yellow-robed monks, a swarm of imperial concubines. In a place of honor to the right of the royal thrones, which rose like gilded scaffolds high above all else, was a little group of stern-faced men in foreign costumes, the ambassadors of Rome and Byzantium, of Arabia and Syria, of Korea, Japan, Tibet, Turkestan. Incense smouldered in enameled braziers. A poet sang a delicate twanging melody, accompanying himself on a small harp. Then the Emperor and Empress entered: two tiny aged people, like waxen images, moving with infinite slowness, taking steps no greater than a child's. There was the sound of trumpets as they ascended their thrones. When the little Emperor was seated—he looked like a doll up there, ancient, faded, shrunken, yet still somehow a figure of extraordinary power—he stretched forth both his hands, and enormous gongs began to sound. It was a scene of astonishing splendor, grand and overpowering.

These are all temporaries, Phillips realized suddenly. He saw only a handful of citizens—eight, ten, possibly as many as a dozen—scattered here and there about the vast room. He knew them by their eyes, dark, liquid, knowing. They were watching not only the imperial spectacle but also Gioia and him; and Gioia, smiling secretly, nodding almost imperceptibly to them, was acknowledging their presence and their interest. But those few were the only ones in here who were autonomous living beings. All the rest—the entire splendid court, the great mandarins and paladins, the officials, the giggling concubines, the haughty and resplendent ambassadors, the aged Emperor and Empress themselves, were simply part of the scenery. Had the world ever seen entertainment on so grand a scale before? All this pomp, all this pageantry, conjured up each night for the amusement of a dozen or so viewers?

At the banquet the little group of citizens sat together at a table apart, a round onyx slab draped with translucent green silk. There turned out to be seventeen of them in all, including Gioia; Gioia appeared to know all of them, though none, so far as he could tell, was a member of her set that he had met before. She did not attempt introductions. Nor was conversation at all possible during the meal: there was a constant astounding roaring din in the room. Three orchestras played at once and there were troupes of strolling musicians also, and a steady stream of monks and their attendants marched back and forth between the tables loudly chanting sutras and waving censers to the deafening accompaniment of drums and gongs. The Emperor did not descend from his throne to join the banquet; he seemed to be asleep, though now and then he waved his hand in time to the music. Gigantic half-naked brown slaves with broad cheekbones and mouths like gaping pockets brought forth the food, peacock tongues and breast of phoenix heaped on mounds of glowing saffron-colored rice, served on frail alabaster plates. For chopsticks they were given slender rods of dark jade. The wine, served in glistening crystal beakers, was thick and sweet, with an aftertaste of raisins, and no beaker was allowed to remain empty for more than a moment.

Phillips felt himself growing dizzy: when the Persian dancers emerged he could not tell whether there were five of them or fifty, and as they performed their intricate whirling routines it seemed to him that their slender muslin-veiled forms were blurring and merging one into another. He felt frightened by their proficiency, and wanted to look away, but he could not. The Chung-nan jugglers that followed them were equally skillful, equally alarming, filling the air with scythes, flaming torches, live animals, rare porcelain vases, pink jade hatchets, silver bells, gilded cups, wagon-wheels, bronze vessels, and never missing a catch. The citizens applauded politely but did not seem

impressed. After the jugglers, the dancers returned, performing this time on stilts; the waiters brought platters of
steaming meat of a pale lavender color, unfamiliar in taste
and texture: filet of camel, perhaps, or haunch of hippo-
potamus, or possibly some choice chop from a young
dragon. There was more wine. Feebly Phillips tried to wave
it away, but the servitors were implacable. This was a drier
sort, greenish-gold, austere, sharp on the tongue. With it
came a silver dish, chilled to a polar coldness, that held
shaved ice flavored with some potent smoky-flavored
brandy. The jugglers were doing a second turn, he noticed. He thought he was going to be ill. He looked helplessly toward Gioia, who seemed sober but fiercely
animated, almost manic, her eyes blazing like rubies. She
touched his cheek fondly.

A cool draft blew through the hall: they had opened
one entire wall, revealing the garden, the night, the stars.
Just outside was a colossal wheel of oiled paper stretched
on wooden struts. They must have erected it in the past
hour: it stood a hundred fifty feet high or even more, and
on it hung lanterns by the thousands, glimmering like giant
fireflies. The guests began to leave the hall. Phillips let
himself be swept along into the garden, where under a
yellow moon strange crook-armed trees with dense black
needles loomed ominously. Gioia slipped her arm through
his. They went down to a lake of bubbling crimson fluid
and watched scarlet flamingo-like birds ten feet tall fastid-
iously spearing angry-eyed turquoise eels. They stood in
awe before a fat-bellied Buddha of gleaming blue tilework,
seventy feet high. A horse with a golden mane came
prancing by, striking showers of brilliant red sparks wherever its hooves touched the ground. In a grove of lemon
trees that seemed to have the power to wave their slender
limbs about, Phillips came upon the Emperor, standing by
himself and rocking gently back and forth. The old man
seized Phillips by the hand and pressed something into his

palm, closing his fingers tight about it; when he opened his fist a few moments later he found his palm full of gray irregular pearls. Gioia took them from him and cast them into the air, and they burst like exploding firecrackers, giving off splashes of colored light. A little later, Phillips realized that he was no longer wearing his surplice or his white silken undergown. Gioia was naked too, and she drew him gently down into a carpet of moist blue moss, where they made love until dawn, fiercely at first, then slowly, languidly, dreamily. At sunrise he looked at her tenderly and saw that something was wrong.

"Gioia?" he said doubtfully.

She smiled. "Ah, no. Gioia is with Fenimon tonight. I am Belilala."

"With—Fenimon?"

"They are old friends. She had not seen him in years."

"Ah. I see. And you are—?"

"Belilala," she said again, touching her fingertips to his cheek.

It was not unusual, Belilala said. It happened all the time; the only unusual thing was that it had not happened to him before now. Couples formed, traveled together for a while, drifted apart, eventually reunited. It did not mean that Gioia had left him forever. It meant only that just now she chose to be with Fenimon. Gioia would return. In the meanwhile he would not be alone. "You and I met in New Chicago," Belilala told him. "And then we saw each other again in Timbuctoo. Have you forgotten? Oh, yes, I see that you have forgotten!" She laughed prettily; she did not seem at all offended.

She looked enough like Gioia to be her sister. But, then, all the citizens looked more or less alike to him. And apart from their physical resemblance, so he quickly came to realize, Belilala and Gioia were not really very similar. There was a calmness, a deep reservoir of serenity, in Belilala that Gioia, eager and volatile and ever impatient, did not seem to have. Strolling the swarming streets of Chang-an with Belilala, he did not perceive in her any of Gioia's restless feverish need always to know what lay beyond, and beyond, and beyond even that. When they toured the Hsing-ch'ing Palace, Belilala did not after five minutes begin—as Gioia surely would have done—to seek directions to the Fountain of Hsuan-tsung or the Wild Goose Pagoda. Curiosity did not consume Belilala as it did Gioia. Plainly she believed that there would always be enough time for her to see everything she cared to see. There were some days when Belilala chose not to go out at all, but was content merely to remain at their pavilion playing a solitary game with flat porcelain counters, or viewing the flowers of the garden.

He found, oddly, that he enjoyed the respite from Gioia's intense world-swallowing appetites; and yet he longed for her to return. Belilala—beautiful, gentle, tranquil, patient—was too perfect for him. She seemed unreal in her gleaming impeccability, much like one of those Sung celadon vases that appear too flawless to have been thrown and glazed by human hands. There was something a little soulless about her: an immaculate finish outside, emptiness within. Belilala might almost have been a temporary, he thought, though he knew she was not. He could explore the pavilions and palaces of Chang-an with her, he could make graceful conversation with her while they dined, he could certainly enjoy coupling with her; but he could not love her or even contemplate the possibility. It was hard to imagine Belilala worriedly studying herself in a mirror for wrinkles and gray hairs. Belilala would never be any older than she was at this moment; nor could Belilala ever have been any younger. Perfection does not move along an axis of time. But the perfection of Belilala's glossy surface made her inner being impenetrable to him. Gioia was more vulnerable, more obviously flawed—her restlessness, her moodiness, her vanity, her fears—and therefore she was more accessible to his own highly imperfect twentieth-century sensibility.

Occasionally he saw Gioia as he roamed the city, or thought he did. He had a glimpse of her among the miracle-vendors in the Persian Bazaar, and outside the Zoroastrian temple, and again by the goldfish pond in the Serpentine Park. But he was never quite sure that the woman he saw was really Gioia, and he never could get close enough to her to be certain: she had a way of vanishing as he approached, like some mysterious Lorelei luring him onward and onward in a hopeless chase. After a while he came to realize that he was not going to find her until she was ready to be found.

He lost track of time. Weeks, months, years? He had no idea. In this city of exotic luxury, mystery, and magic all was in constant flux and transition and the days had a fitful, unstable quality. Buildings and even whole streets were torn down of an afternoon and re-erected, within days, far away. Grand new pagodas sprouted like toadstools in the night. Citizens came in from Asgard, Alexandria, Timbuctoo, New Chicago, stayed for a time, disappeared, returned. There was a constant round of court receptions, banquets, theatrical events, each one much like the one before. The festivals in honor of past emperors and empresses might have given some form to the year, but they seemed to occur in a random way, the ceremony marking the death of T'ai Tsung coming around twice the same year, so it seemed to him, once in a season of snow and again in high summer, and the one honoring the ascension of the Empress Wu being held twice in a single season. Perhaps he had misunderstood something. But he knew it was no use asking anyone.

One day Belilala said unexpectedly, "Shall we go to Mohenjo-daro?"

"I didn't know it was ready for visitors," he replied.

"Oh, yes. For quite some time now."

He hesitated. This had caught him unprepared. Cautiously he said, "Gioia and I were going to go there together, you know."

Belilala smiled amiably, as though the topic under discussion were nothing more than the choice of that evening's restaurant.

"Were you?" she asked.

"It was all arranged while we were still in Alexandria. To go with you instead—I don't know what to tell you, Belilala." Phillips sensed that he was growing terribly flustered. "You know that I'd like to go. With you. But on the other hand I can't help feeling that I shouldn't go there until I'm back with Gioia again. If I ever am." How foolish this sounds, he thought. How clumsy, how adolescent. He found that he was having trouble looking straight at her. Uneasily he said, with a kind of desperation in his voice, "I did promise her—there was a commitment, you understand—a firm agreement that we would go to Mohenjo-daro together—"

"Oh, but Gioia's already there!" said Belilala in the most casual way.

He gaped as though she had punched him.

"What?"

"She was one of the first to go, after it opened. Months and months ago. You didn't know?" she asked, sounding surprised, but not very. "You really didn't know?"

That astonished him. He felt bewildered, betrayed, furious. His cheeks grew hot, his mouth gaped. He shook his head again and again, trying to clear it of confusion. It was a moment before he could speak. "Already there?" he said at last. "Without waiting for me? After we had talked about going there together—after we had agreed—"

Belilala laughed. "But how could she resist seeing the newest city? You know how impatient Gioia is!"

"Yes. Yes."

He was stunned. He could barely think.

"Just like all short-timers," Belilala said. "She rushes here, she rushes there. She must have it all, now, now, right away, at once, instantly. You ought never expect her to wait for you for anything for very long: the fit seizes her, and off she goes. Surely you must know that about her by now."

"A short-timer?" He had not heard that term before.

"Yes. You knew that. You must have known that." Belilala flashed her sweetest smile. She showed no sign of comprehending his distress. With a brisk wave of her hand she said, "Well, then, shall we go, you and I? To Mohenjo-daro?"

"Of course," Phillips said bleakly.

"When would you like to leave?"

"Tonight," he said. He paused a moment. "What's a short-timer, Belilala?"

Color came to her cheeks. "Isn't it obvious?" she asked.

Had there ever been a more hideous place on the face of the earth than the city of Mohenjo-daro? Phillips found it difficult to imagine one. Nor could he understand why, out of all the cities that had ever been, these people had chosen to restore this one to existence. More than ever they seemed alien to him, unfathomable, incomprehensible.

From the terrace atop the many-towered citadel he peered down into grim claustrophobic Mohenjo-daro and shivered. The stark, bleak city looked like nothing so much as some prehistoric prison colony. In the manner of an uneasy tortoise it huddled, squat and compact, against the gray monotonous Indus River plain: miles of dark burnt-brick walls enclosing miles of terrifyingly orderly streets, laid out in an awesome, monstrous gridiron pattern of maniacal rigidity. The houses themselves were dismal and forbidding too, clusters of brick cells gathered about small airless courtyards. There were no windows, only small doors that opened not onto the main boulevards but onto the tiny mysterious lanes that ran between the buildings. Who had designed this horrifying metropolis? What harsh, sour souls they must have had, these frightening and frightened folk, creating for themselves in the lush fertile plains of India such a Supreme Soviet of a city!

"How lovely it is," Belilala murmured. "How fascinating!"

He stared at her in amazement.

"Fascinating? Yes," he said. "I suppose so. The same way that the smile of a cobra is fascinating."

"What's a cobra?"

"Poisonous predatory serpent," Phillips told her. "Probably extinct. Or formerly extinct, more likely. It wouldn't surprise me if you people had re-created a few and turned them loose in Mohenjo to make things livelier."

"You sound angry, Charles."

"Do I? That's not how I feel."

"How do you feel, then?"

"I don't know," he said after a long moment's pause. He shrugged. "Lost, I suppose. Very far from home."

"Poor Charles."

"Standing here in this ghastly barracks of a city, listening to you tell me how beautiful it is, I've never felt more alone in my life."

"You miss Gioia very much, don't you?"

He gave her another startled look.

"Gioia has nothing to do with it. She's probably been having ecstasies over the loveliness of Mohenjo just like you. Just like all of you. I suppose I'm the only one who can't find the beauty, the charm. I'm the only one who looks out there and sees only horror, and then wonders why nobody else sees it, why in fact people would set up a place like this for *entertainment*, for *pleasure*—"

Her eyes were gleaming. "Oh, you are angry! You really are!"

"Does that fascinate you too?" he snapped. "A demonstration of genuine primitive emotion? A typical quaint twentieth-century outburst?" He paced the rampart in short quick anguished steps. "Ah. Ah. I think I understand it now, Belilala. Of course: I'm part of your circus, the star of the sideshow. I'm the first experiment in setting up the next stage of it, in fact." Her eyes were wide. The sudden harshness and violence in his voice seemed to be alarming and exciting her at the same time. That angered him even more. Fiercely he went on, "Bringing whole cities back out of time was fun for a while, but it lacks a certain authenticity, eh? For some reason you couldn't bring the inhabitants too; you couldn't just grab a few million prehistorics out of Egypt or Greece or India and dump them down in this era, I suppose because you might have too much trouble controlling them, or because you'd have the problem of disposing of them once you were bored with them. So you had to settle for creating temporaries to populate your ancient cities. But now you've got me. I'm something more real than a temporary, and that's a terrific novelty for you, and novelty is the thing you people crave more than anything else: maybe the *only* thing you crave. And here I am, complicated, unpredictable, edgy, capable of anger, fear, sadness, love, and all those other formerly extinct things. Why settle for picturesque architecture when you can observe picturesque emotion, too? What fun I must be for all of you! And if you decide that I was really interesting, maybe you'll ship me back where I came from and check out a few other ancient types—a Roman gladiator, maybe, or a Renaissance pope, or even a Neanderthal or two—"

"Charles," she said tenderly. "Oh, Charles, Charles, Charles, how lonely you must be, how lost, how troubled! Will you ever forgive me? Will you ever forgive us all?"

Once more he was astounded by her. She sounded entirely sincere, altogether sympathetic. Was she? Was she, really? He was not sure he had ever had a sign of genuine caring from any of them before, not even Gioia. Nor could he bring himself to trust Belilala now. He was afraid of her, afraid of all of them, of their brittleness, their slyness, their elegance. He wished he could go to her and have her take him in her arms; but he felt too much the shaggy prehistoric just now to be able to risk asking that comfort of her.

He turned away and began to walk around the rim of the citadel's massive wall.

"Charles?"

"Let me alone for a little while," he said.

He walked on. His forehead throbbed and there was a pounding in his chest. All stress systems going full blast, he thought: secret glands dumping gallons of inflammatory substances into his bloodstream. The heat, the inner confusion, the repellent look of this place—

Try to understand, he thought. Relax. Look about you. Try to enjoy your holiday in Mohenjo-daro.

He leaned warily outward, over the edge of the wall. He had never seen a wall like this; it must be forty feet thick at the base, he guessed, perhaps even more, and every brick perfectly shaped, meticulously set. Beyond the great rampart, marshes ran almost to the edge of the city, although close by the wall the swamps had been dammed and drained for agriculture. He saw lithe brown farmers down there, busy with their wheat and barley and peas. Cattle and buffaloes grazed a little farther out. The air was heavy, dank, humid. All was still. From somewhere close at hand came the sound of a droning, whining stringed instrument and a steady insistent chanting.

Gradually a sort of peace pervaded him. His anger subsided. He felt himself beginning to grow calm again.

He looked back at the city, the rigid interlocking streets, the maze of inner lanes, the millions of courses of precise brickwork.

It is a miracle, he told himself, that this city is here in this place and at this time. And it is a miracle that I am here to see it.

Caught for a moment by the magic within the bleakness, he thought he began to understand Belilala's awe and delight, and he wished now that he had not spoken to her so sharply. The city was alive. Whether it was the actual Mohenjo-daro of thousands upon thousands of years ago, ripped from the past by some wondrous hook, or simply a cunning reproduction, did not matter at all. Real or not, this was the true Mohenjo-daro. It had been dead and now, for the moment, it was alive again. These people, these *citizens*, might be trivial, but reconstructing Mohenjo-daro was no trivial achievement. And that the city that had been reconstructed was oppressive and sinister-looking was unimportant. No one was compelled to live in Mohenjo-daro any more. Its time had come and gone, long ago; those little dark-skinned peasants and craftsmen and merchants down there were mere temporaries, mere inanimate things, conjured up like zombies to enhance the illusion. They did not need his pity. Nor did he need to pity himself. He knew that he should be grateful for the chance to behold these things. Someday, when this dream had ended and his hosts had returned him to the world of subways and computers and income tax and television networks, he would think of Mohenjo-daro as he had once beheld it, lofty walls of tightly woven dark brick under a heavy sky, and he would remember only its beauty.

Glancing back, he searched for Belilala and could not for a moment find her. Then he caught sight of her carefully descending a narrow staircase that angled down the inner face of the citadel wall.

"Belilala!" he called.

She paused and looked his way, shading her eyes from the sun with her hand. "Are you all right?"

"Where are you going?"

"To the baths," she said. "Do you want to come?"

He nodded. "Yes. Wait for me, will you? I'll be right there." He began to run toward her along the top of the wall.

The baths were attached to the citadel: a great open tank the size of a large swimming pool, lined with bricks set on edge in gypsum mortar and waterproofed with asphalt, and eight smaller tanks just north of it in a kind of covered arcade. He supposed that in ancient times the whole complex had had some ritual purpose, the large tank used by common folk and the small chambers set aside for the private ablutions of priests or nobles. Now the baths were maintained, it seemed, entirely for the pleasure of visiting citizens. As Phillips came up the passageway that led to the main bath he saw fifteen or twenty of them lolling in the water or padding languidly about, while temporaries of the dark-skinned Mohenjo-daro type served them drinks and pungent little morsels of spiced meat as though this were some sort of luxury resort. Which was, he realized, exactly what it was. The temporaries wore white cotton loincloths; the citizens were naked. In his former life he had encountered that sort of casual public nudity a few times on visits to California and the south of France, and it had made him mildly uneasy. But he was growing accustomed to it here.

The changing-rooms were tiny brick cubicles connected by rows of closely placed steps to the courtyard that surrounded the central tank. They entered one and Belilala swiftly slipped out of the loose cotton robe that she had worn since their arrival that morning. With arms folded she stood leaning against the wall, waiting for him. After a moment he dropped his own robe and followed her outside. He felt a little giddy, sauntering around naked in the open like this.

On the way to the main bathing area they passed the private baths. None of them seemed to be occupied. They were elegantly constructed chambers, with finely jointed brick floors and carefully designed runnels to drain excess water into the passageway that led to the primary drain. Phillips was struck with admiration for the cleverness of the prehistoric engineers. He peered into this chamber and that to see how the conduits and ventilating ducts were arranged, and when he came to the last room in the sequence he was surprised and embarrassed to discover that it was in use. A brawny grinning man, big-muscled, deep-chested, with exuberantly flowing shoulder-length red hair and a flamboyant, sharply tapering beard, was thrashing about merrily with two women in the small tank. Phillips had a quick glimpse of a lively tangle of arms, legs, breasts, buttocks.

"Sorry," he muttered. His cheeks reddened. Quickly he ducked out, blurting apologies as he went. "Didn't realize the room was occupied—no wish to intrude—"

Belilala had proceeded on down the passageway. Phillips hurried after her. From behind him came peals of cheerful raucous booming laughter and high-pitched giggling and the sound of splashing water. Probably they had not even noticed him.

He paused a moment, puzzled, playing back in his mind that one startling glimpse. Something was not right. Those women, he was fairly sure, were citizens: little slender elfin dark-haired girlish creatures, the standard model. But the man? That great curling sweep of red hair? Not a citizen. Citizens did not affect shoulder-length hair. And *red?* Nor had he ever seen a citizen so burly, so powerfully muscular. Or one with a beard. But he could hardly be a temporary, either. Phillips could conceive no reason why there would be so Anglo-Saxon-looking a temporary at Mohenjo-daro; and it was unthinkable for a temporary to be frolicking like that with citizens, anyway.

"Charles?"

He looked up ahead. Belilala stood at the end of the passageway, outlined in a nimbus of brilliant sunlight. "Charles?" she said again. "Did you lose your way?"

"I'm right here behind you," he said. "I'm coming."

"Who did you meet in there?"

"A man with a beard."

"With a what?"

"A beard," he said. "Red hair growing on his face. I wonder who he is."

"Nobody I know," said Belilala. "The only one I know with hair on his face is you. And yours is black, and you shave it off every day." She laughed. "Come along, now! I see some friends by the pool!"

He caught up with her and they went hand in hand out into the courtyard. Immediately a waiter glided up to them, an obsequious little temporary with a tray of drinks. Phillips waved it away and headed for the pool. He felt terribly exposed: he imagined that the citizens disporting themselves here were staring intently at him, studying his hairy primitive body as though he were some mythical creature, a Minotaur, a werewolf, summoned up for their amusement. Belilala drifted off to talk to someone and he slipped into the water, grateful for the concealment it offered. It was deep, warm, comforting. With swift powerful strokes he breast-stroked from one end to the other.

A citizen perched elegantly on the pool's rim smiled at him. "Ah, so you've come at last, Charles!" Char-less. Two syllables. Someone from Gioia's set: Stengard, Hawk, Aramayne? He could not remember which one. They were all so much alike.

Phillips returned the man's smile in a half-hearted, tentative way. He searched for something to say and finally asked, "Have you been here long?"

"Weeks. Perhaps months. What a splendid achievement this city is, eh, Charles? Such utter unity of mood—such a total statement of a uniquely single-minded esthetic—"

"Yes. Single-minded is the word," Phillips said dryly.

"Gioia's word, actually. Gioia's phrase. I was merely quoting."

Gioia. He felt as if he had been stabbed.

"You've spoken to Gioia lately?" he said.

"Actually, no. It was Hekna who saw her. You do remember Hekna, eh?" He nodded toward two naked women standing on the brick platform that bordered the pool, chatting, delicately nibbling morsels of meat. They could have been twins. "There is Hekna, with your Belilala." Hekna, yes. So this must be Hawk, Phillips thought, unless there has been some recent shift of couples. "How sweet she is, your Belilala," Hawk said. "Gioia chose very wisely when she picked her for you."

Another stab: a much deeper one. "Is that how it was?" he said. "Gioia *picked* Belilala for me?"

"Why, of course!" Hawk seemed surprised. It went without saying, evidently. "What did you think? That Gioia would merely go off and leave you to fend for yourself?"

"Hardly. Not Gioia."

"She's very tender, very gentle, isn't she?"

"You mean Belilala? Yes, very," said Phillips carefully. "A dear woman, a wonderful woman. But of course I hope to get together with Gioia again soon." He paused. "They say she's been in Mohenjo-daro almost since it opened."

"She was here, yes."

"*Was?*"

"Oh, you know Gioia," Hawk said lightly. "She's moved along by now, naturally."

Phillips leaned forward. "Naturally," he said. Tension thickened his voice. "Where has she gone this time?"

"Timbuctoo, I think. Or New Chicago. I forget which one it was. She was telling us that she hoped to be in Timbuctoo for the closing-down party. But then Fenimon had some pressing reason for going to New Chicago. I can't remember what they decided to do." Hawk gestured sadly. "Either way, a pity that she left Mohenjo before the new visitor came. She had such a rewarding time with you, after all: I'm sure she'd have found much to learn from him also."

The unfamiliar term twanged an alarm deep in Phillips's consciousness. *"Visitor?"* he said, angling his head sharply toward Hawk. "What visitor do you mean?"

"You haven't met him yet? Oh, of course, you've only just arrived."

Phillips moistened his lips. "I think I may have seen him. Long red hair? Beard like this?"

"That's the one! Willoughby, he's called. He's—what?— a Viking, a pirate, something like that. Tremendous vigor and force. Remarkable person. We should have many more visitors, I think. They're far superior to temporaries, everyone agrees. Talking with a temporary is a little like talking to one's self, wouldn't you say? They give you no significant illumination. But a visitor—someone like this Willoughby—or like you, Charles—a visitor can be truly enlightening, a visitor can transform one's view of reality—"

"Excuse me," Phillips said. A throbbing began behind his forehead. "Perhaps we can continue this conversation later, yes?" He put the flats of his hands against the hot brick of the platform and hoisted himself swiftly from the pool. "At dinner, maybe—or afterward—yes? All right?" He set off at a quick half-trot back toward the passageway that led to the private baths.

———

As he entered the roofed part of the structure his throat grew dry, his breath suddenly came short. He padded quickly up the hall and peered into the little bath-chamber. The bearded man was still there, sitting up in the tank, breast-high above the water, with one arm around each of the women. His eyes gleamed with fiery intensity in the dimness. He was grinning in marvelous self-satisfaction; he seemed to brim with intensity, confidence, gusto.

Let him be what I think he is, Phillips prayed. I have been alone among these people long enough.

"May I come in?" he asked.

"Aye, fellow!" cried the man in the tub thunderously. "By my troth, come ye in, and bring your lass as well! God's teeth, I wot there's room aplenty for more folk in this tub than we!"

At that great uproarious outcry Phillips felt a powerful surge of joy. What a joyous rowdy voice! How rich, how lusty, how totally uncitizenlike!

And those oddly archaic words! *God's teeth? By my troth?* What sort of talk was that? What else but the good pure sonorous Elizabethan diction! Certainly it had something of the roll and fervor of Shakespeare about it. And spoken with—an Irish brogue, was it? No, not quite: it was English, but English spoken in no manner Phillips had ever heard.

Citizens did not speak that way. But a *visitor* might.

So it was true. Relief flooded Phillips's soul. Not alone, then! Another relict of a former age—another wanderer—a companion in chaos, a brother in adversity—a fellow voyager, tossed even farther than he had been by the tempests of time—

The bearded man grinned heartily and beckoned to Phillips with a toss of his head. "Well, join us, join us, man! 'Tis good to see an English face again, amidst all these Moors and rogue Portugals! But what have ye done with thy lass? One can never have enough wenches, d'ye not agree?"

The force and vigor of him were extraordinary: almost too much so. He roared, he bellowed, he boomed. He was so very much what he ought to be that he seemed more a character out of some old pirate movie than anything else, so blustering, so real, that he seemed unreal. A stage-Elizabethan, larger than life, a boisterous young Falstaff without the belly.

Hoarsely, Phillips said, "Who are you?"

"Why, Ned Willoughby's son Francis am I, of Plymouth. Late of the service of Her Most Protestant Majesty, but most foully abducted by the powers of darkness and cast away among these blackamoor Hindus, or whatever they be. And thyself?"

"Charles Phillips." After a moment's uncertainty he added, "I'm from New York."

"*New* York? What place is that? In faith, man, I know it not!"

"A city in America."

"A city in America, forsooth! What a fine fancy that is! In America, you say, and not on the Moon, or perchance underneath the sea?" To the women Willoughby said, "D'ye hear him? He comes from a city in America! With the face of an Englishman, though not the manner of one, and not quite the proper sort of speech. A city in America! A *city.* God's blood, what will I hear next?"

Phillips trembled. Awe was beginning to take hold of him. This man had walked the streets of Shakespeare's London, perhaps. He had clinked canisters with Marlowe or Essex or Walter Raleigh; he had watched the ships of the Armada wallowing in the Channel. It strained Phillips's spirit to think of it. This strange dream in which he found himself was compounding its strangeness now. He felt like a weary swimmer assailed by heavy surf, winded, dazed. The hot close atmosphere of the baths was driving him toward vertigo. There could be no doubt of it any longer. He was not the only primitive—the only *visitor*—who was wandering loose in this fiftieth century. They were conducting other experiments as well. He gripped the sides of the door to steady himself and said, "When you speak of Her Most Protestant Majesty, it's Elizabeth the First you mean, is that not so?"

"Elizabeth, aye! As to the First, that is true enough, but why trouble to name her thus? There is but one. First and Last, I do trow, and God save her, there is no other!"

Phillips studied the other man warily. He knew that he must proceed with care. A misstep at this point and he would forfeit any chance that Willoughby would take him seriously. How much metaphysical bewilderment, after all, could this man absorb? What did he know, what had any-one of his time known, of past and present and future and the notion that one might somehow move from one to the other as readily as one would go from Surrey to Kent? That was a twentieth-century idea, late nineteenth at best, a fantastical speculation that very likely no one had even considered before Wells had sent his time traveler off to stare at the reddened sun of the earth's last twilight. Willoughby's world was a world of Protestants and Catholics, of kings and queens, of tiny sailing vessels, of swords at the hip and ox-carts on the road: that world seemed to Phillips far more alien and distant than was this world of citizens and temporaries. The risk that Willoughby would not begin to understand him was great.

But this man and he were natural allies against a world they had never made. Phillips chose to take the risk.

"Elizabeth the First is the queen you serve," he said. "There will be another of her name in England, in due time. Has already been, in fact."

Willoughby shook his head like a puzzled lion. "An-other Elizabeth, d'ye say?"

"A second one, and not much like the first. Long after your Virgin Queen, this one. She will reign in what you think of as the days to come. That I know without doubt."

The Englishman peered at him and frowned. "You see the future? Are you a soothsayer, then? A necromancer, mayhap? Or one of the very demons that brought me to this place?"

"Not at all," Phillips said gently. "Only a lost soul, like yourself." He stepped into the little room and crouched by the side of the tank. The two citizen-women were staring at him in bland fascination. He ignored them. To Willoughby he said, "Do you have any idea where you are?"

The Englishman had guessed, rightly enough, that he was in India: "I do believe these little brown Moorish folk are of the Hindu sort," he said. But that was as far as his comprehension of what had befallen him could go.

It had not occurred to him that he was no longer living in the sixteenth century. And of course he did not begin to suspect that this strange and somber brick city in which he found himself was a wanderer out of an era even more remote than his own. Was there any way, Phillips wondered, of explaining that to him?

He had been here only three days. He thought it was devils that had carried him off. "While I slept did they come for me," he said. "Mephistophilis Sathanas his henchmen seized me—God alone can say why—and swept me in a moment out to this torrid realm from England, where I had reposed among friends and family. For I was between one voyage and the next, you must understand, awaiting Drake and his ship—you know Drake, the glorious Francis? God's blood, there's a mariner for ye! We were to go to the Main again, he and I, but instead here I be in this other place—" Willoughby leaned close and said, "I ask you, soothsayer, how can it be, that a man go to sleep in Plymouth and wake up in India? It is passing strange, is it not?"

"That it is," Phillips said.

"But he that is in the dance must needs dance on, though he do but hop, eh? So do I believe." He gestured toward the two citizen-women. "And therefore to console myself in this pagan land I have found me some sport among these little Portugal women—"

"Portugal?" said Phillips.

"Why, what else can they be, but Portugals? Is it not the Portugals who control all these coasts of India? See, the people are of two sorts here, the blackamoors and the others, the fair-skinned ones, the lords and masters who lie here in these baths. If they be not Hindus, and I think they are not, then Portugals is what they must be." He laughed and pulled the women against himself and rubbed his hands over their breasts as though they were fruits on a vine. "Is that not what you are, you little naked shameless Papist wenches? A pair of Portugals, eh?"

They giggled, but did not answer.

"No," Phillips said. "This is India, but not the India you think you know. And these women are not Portuguese."

"Not Portuguese?" Willoughby said, baffled.

"No more so than you. I'm quite certain of that."

Willoughby stroked his beard. "I do admit I found them very odd, for Portugals. I have heard not a syllable of their Portugee speech on their lips. And it is strange also that they run naked as Adam and Eve in these baths, and allow me free plunder of their women, which is not the way of Portugals at home, God wot. But I thought me, this is India, they choose to live in another fashion here—"

"No," Phillips said. "I tell you, these are not Portuguese, nor any other people of Europe who are known to you."

"Prithee, who are they, then?"

Do it delicately, now, Phillips warned himself. *Delicately.*

He said, "It is not far wrong to think of them as spirits of some kind—demons, even. Or sorcerers who have magicked us out of our proper places in the world." He paused, groping for some means to share with Willoughby, in a way that Willoughby might grasp, this mystery that had enfolded them. He drew a deep breath. "They've taken us not only across the sea," he said, "but across the years as well. We have both been hauled, you and I, far into the days that are to come."

Willoughby gave him a look of blank bewilderment.

"Days that are to come? Times yet unborn, d'ye mean? Why, I comprehend none of that!"

"Try to understand. We're both castaways in the same boat, man! But there's no way we can help each other if I can't make you see—"

Shaking his head, Willoughby muttered, "In faith, good friend, I find your words the merest folly. Today is today, and tomorrow is tomorrow, and how can a man step from one to t'other until tomorrow be turned into today?"

"I have no idea," said Phillips. Struggle was apparent on Willoughby's face; but plainly he could perceive no more than the haziest outline of what Phillips was driving at, if that much. "But this I know," he went on, "that your world and all that was in it is dead and gone. And so is mine, though I was born four hundred years after you, in the time of the second Elizabeth."

Willoughby snorted scornfully. "Four hundred—"

"You must believe me!"

"Nay! Nay!"

"It's the truth. Your time is only history to me. And mine and yours are history to *them*—ancient history. They call us visitors, but what we are is captives." Phillips felt himself quivering in the intensity of his effort. He was aware how insane this must sound to Willoughby. It was beginning to sound insane to him. "They've stolen us out of our proper times—seizing us like gypsies in the night—"

"Fie, man! You rave with lunacy!"

Phillips shook his head. He reached out and seized Willoughby tightly by the wrist. "I beg you, listen to me!" The citizen-women were watching closely, whispering to one another behind their hands, laughing. "Ask them!" Phillips cried. "Make them tell you what century this is! The sixteenth, do you think? Ask them!"

"What century could it be, but the sixteenth of our Lord?"

"They will tell you it is the fiftieth."

Willoughby looked at him pityingly. "Man, man, what a sorry thing thou art! The fiftieth, indeed!" He laughed. "Fellow, listen to me, now. There is but one Elizabeth, safe upon her throne in Westminster. This is India. The year is Anno 1591. Come, let us you and I steal a ship from these Portugals, and make our way back to England, and peradventure you may get from there to your America—"

"There is no England."

"Ah, can you say that and not be mad?"

"The cities and nations we knew are gone. These people live like magicians, Francis." There was no use holding anything back now, Phillips thought leadenly. He knew that he had lost. "They conjure up places of long ago, and build them here and there to suit their fancy, and when they are bored with them they destroy them, and start anew. There is no England. Europe is empty, featureless, void. Do you know what cities there are? There are only five in all the world. There is Alexandria of Egypt. There is Timbuctoo in Africa. There is New Chicago in America. There is a great city in China—in Cathay, I suppose you would say. And there is this place, which they call Mohenjo-daro, and which is far more ancient than Greece, than Rome, than Babylon."

Quietly Willoughby said, "Nay. This is mere absurdity. You say we are in some far tomorrow, and then you tell me we are dwelling in some city of long ago."

"A conjuration, only," Phillips said in desperation. "A likeness of that city. Which these folks have fashioned somehow for their own amusement. Just as we are here, you and I: to amuse them. Only to amuse them."

"You are completely mad."

"Come with me, then. Talk with the citizens by the great pool. Ask them what year this is; ask them about England; ask them how you come to be here." Once again Phillips grasped Willoughby's wrist. "We should be allies. If we work together, perhaps we can discover some way to get ourselves out of this place, and—"

"Let me be, fellow."

"Please—"

"Let me be!" roared Willoughby, and pulled his arm free. His eyes were stark with rage. Rising in the tank, he looked about furiously as though searching for a weapon. The citizen-women shrank back from him, though at the same time they seemed captivated by the big man's fierce outburst. "Go to, get you to Bedlam! Let me be, madman! Let me be!"

Dismally Phillips roamed the dusty unpaved streets of Mohenjo-daro alone for hours. His failure with Willoughby had left him bleak-spirited and somber: he had hoped to stand back to back with the Elizabethan against the citizens, but he saw now that that was not to be. He had bungled things; or, more likely, it had been impossible ever to bring Willoughby to see the truth of their predicament.

In the stifling heat he went at random through the confusing congested lanes of flat-roofed, windowless houses and blank, featureless walls until he emerged into a broad marketplace. The life of the city swirled madly around him:

the pseudo-life, rather, the intricate interactions of the thousands of temporaries who were nothing more than wind-up dolls set in motion to provide the illusion that pre-Vedic India was still a going concern. Here vendors sold beautiful little carved stone seals portraying tigers and monkeys and strange humped cattle, and women bargained vociferously with craftsmen for ornaments of ivory, gold, copper, and bronze. Weary-looking women squatted behind immense mounds of newly made pottery, pinkish-red with black designs. No one paid any attention to him. He was the outsider here, neither citizen nor temporary. They belonged.

He went on, passing the huge granaries where workmen ceaselessly unloaded carts of wheat and others pounded grain on great circular brick platforms. He drifted into a public restaurant thronging with joyless silent people standing elbow to elbow at small brick counters, and was given a flat round piece of bread, a sort of tortilla or chapatti, in which was stuffed some spiced mincemeat that stung his lips like fire. Then he moved onward, down a wide, shallow, timbered staircase into the lower part of the city, where the peasantry lived in cell-like rooms packed together as though in hives.

It was an oppressive city, but not a squalid one. The intensity of the concern with sanitation amazed him: wells and fountains and public privies everywhere, and brick drains running from each building, leading to covered cesspools. There was none of the open sewage and pestilent gutters that he knew still could be found in the India of his own time. He wondered whether ancient Mohenjo-daro had in truth been so fastidious. Perhaps the citizens had redesigned the city to suit their own ideals of cleanliness. No: most likely what he saw was authentic, he decided, a function of the same obsessive discipline that had given the city its rigidity of form. If Mohenjo-daro had been a verminous filthy hole, the citizens probably would have re-created it in just that way, and loved it for its fascinating, reeking filth.

Not that he had ever noticed an excessive concern with authenticity on the part of the citizens; and Mohenjo-daro, like all the other restored cities he had visited, was full of the usual casual anachronisms. Phillips saw images of Shiva and Krishna here and there on the walls of buildings he took to be temples, and the benign face of the mother-goddess Kali loomed in the plazas. Surely those deities had arisen in India long after the collapse of the Mohenjo-daro civilization. Were the citizens indifferent to such matters of chronology? Or did they take a certain naughty pleasure in mixing the eras—a mosque and a church in Greek Alexandria, Hindu gods in prehistoric Mohenjo-daro? Perhaps their records of the past had become contaminated with errors over the thousands of years. He would not have been surprised to see banners bearing portraits of Gandhi and Nehru being carried in procession through the streets. And there were phantasms and chimeras at large here again too, as if the citizens were untroubled by the boundary between history and myth: little fat elephant-headed Ganeshas blithely plunging their trunks into water-fountains, a six-armed, three-headed woman sunning herself on a brick terrace. Why not? Surely that was the motto of these people: *Why not, why not, why not?* They could do as they pleased, and they did. Yet Gioia had said to him, long ago, "Limits are very important." In what, Phillips wondered, did they limit themselves, other than the number of their cities? Was there a quota, perhaps, on the number of "visitors" they allowed themselves to kidnap from the past? Until today he had thought he was the only one; now he knew there was at least one other; possibly there were more elsewhere, a step or two ahead or behind him, making the circuit with the citizens who traveled endlessly from New Chicago to Chang-an to Alexandria. We should join forces, he thought, and compel them to send us back to our rightful eras. *Compel?* How? File a class-action suit, maybe? Demonstrate in the streets? Sadly he thought of his failure to make common cause with Willoughby. We are natural allies, he thought. Together perhaps we might have won some compassion from these people. But to Willoughby it must be literally unthinkable that Good Queen Bess and her subjects were sealed away on the far side of a barrier hundreds of centuries thick. He would prefer to believe that England was just a few months' voyage away around the Cape of Good Hope, and that all he need do was commandeer a ship and set sail for home. Poor Willoughby: probably he would never see his home again.

The thought came to Phillips suddenly:

Neither will you.

And then, after it:

If you could go home, would you really want to?

One of the first things he had realized here was that he knew almost nothing substantial about his former existence. His mind was well stocked with details on life in twentieth-century New York, to be sure; but of himself he could say not much more than that he was Charles Phillips and had come from 1984. Profession? Age? Parents' names? Did he have a wife? Children? A cat, a dog, hobbies? No data: none. Possibly the citizens had stripped such things from him when they brought him here, to spare him from the pain of separation. They might be capable of that kindness. Knowing so little of what he had lost, could he truly say that he yearned for it? Willoughby seemed to remember much more of his former life, and longed for it all the more. He was spared that. Why not stay here, and go on and on from city to city, sightseeing all of time past as the citizens conjured it back into being? Why not? Why not? The chances were that he had no choice about it, anyway.

He made his way back up toward the citadel and to

the baths once more. He felt a little like a ghost, haunting a city of ghosts.

Belilala seemed unaware that he had been gone for most of the day. She sat by herself on the terrace of the baths, placidly sipping some thick milky beverage that had been sprinkled with a dark spice. He shook his head when she offered him some.

"Do you remember I mentioned that I saw a man with red hair and a beard this morning?" Phillips said. "He's a visitor. Hawk told me that."

"Is he?" Belilala asked.

"From a time about four hundred years before mine. I talked with him. He thinks he was brought here by demons." Phillips gave her a searching look. "I'm a visitor too, isn't that so?"

"Of course, love."

"And how was *I* brought here? By demons also?"

Belilala smiled indifferently. "You'd have to ask someone else. Hawk, perhaps. I haven't looked into these things very deeply."

"I see. Are there many visitors here, do you know?"

A languid shrug. "Not many, no, not really. I've only heard of three or four besides you. There may be others by now, I suppose." She rested her hand lightly on his. "Are you having a good time in Mohenjo, Charles?"

He let her question pass as though he had not heard it.

"I asked Hawk about Gioia," he said.

"Oh?"

"He told me that she's no longer here, that she's gone on to Timbuctoo or New Chicago, he wasn't sure which."

"That's quite likely. As everybody knows, Gioia rarely stays in the same place very long."

Phillips nodded. "You said the other day that Gioia is a short-timer. That means she's going to grow old and die, doesn't it?"

"I thought you understood that, Charles."

"Whereas you will not age? Nor Hawk, nor Stengard, nor any of the rest of your set?"

"We will live as long as we wish," she said. "But we will not age, no."

"What makes a person a short-timer?"

"They're born that way, I think. Some missing gene, some extra gene—I don't actually know. It's extremely uncommon. Nothing can be done to help them. It's very slow, the aging. But it can't be halted."

Phillips nodded. "That must be very disagreeable," he said. "To find yourself one of the few people growing old in a world where everyone stays young. No wonder Gioia is so impatient. No wonder she runs around from place to place. No wonder she attached herself so quickly to the barbaric hairy visitor from the twentieth century, who comes from a time when *everybody* was a short-timer. She and I have something in common, wouldn't you say?"

"In a manner of speaking, yes."

"We understand aging. We understand death. Tell me: is Gioia likely to die very soon, Belilala?"

"Soon? Soon?" She gave him a wide-eyed child-like stare. "What is soon? How can I say? What you think of as soon and what I think of as soon are not the same things, Charles." Then her manner changed: she seemed to be hearing what he was saying for the first time. Softly she said, "No, no, Charles. I don't think she will die very soon."

"When she left me in Chang-an, was it because she had become bored with me?"

Belilala shook her head. "She was simply restless. It had nothing to do with you. She was never bored with you."

"Then I'm going to go looking for her. Wherever she may be, Timbuctoo, New Chicago, I'll find her. Gioia and I belong together."

"Perhaps you do," said Belilala. "Yes. Yes, I think you

really do." She sounded altogether unperturbed, unre-
jected, unbereft. "By all means, Charles. Go to her. Follow
her. Find her. Wherever she may be."

They had already begun dismantling Timbuctoo when
Phillips got there. While he was still high overhead, his
flitterflitter hovering above the dusty tawny plain where
the River Niger met the sands of the Sahara, a surge of
keen excitement rose in him as he looked down at the
square gray flat-roofed mud brick buildings of the great
desert capital. But when he landed he found gleaming
metal-skinned robots swarming everywhere, a horde of
them scuttling about like giant shining insects, pulling the
place apart.

He had not known about the robots before. So that
was how all these miracles were carried out, Phillips realized: an army of obliging machines. He imagined them
bustling up out of the earth whenever their services were
needed, emerging from some sterile subterranean storehouse to put together Venice or Thebes or Knossos or
Houston or whatever place was required, down to the finest detail, and then at some later time returning to undo
everything that they had fashioned. He watched them now,
diligently pulling down the adobe walls, demolishing the
heavy metal-studded gates, bulldozing the amazing laby-
rinth of alleyways and thoroughfares, sweeping away the
market. On his last visit to Timbuctoo that market had been
crowded with a horde of veiled Tuaregs and swaggering
Moors, black Sudanese, shrewd-faced Syrian traders, all of
them busily dickering for camels, horses, donkeys, slabs
of salt, huge green melons, silver bracelets, splendid vel-
lum Korans. They were all gone now, that picturesque
crowd of swarthy temporaries. Nor were there any citizens
to be seen. The dust of destruction choked the air. One of
the robots came up to Phillips and said in a dry crackling
insect-voice, "You ought not to be here. This city is closed."

He stared at the flashing, buzzing band of scanners and sensors across the creature's glittering tapered snout. "I'm trying to find someone, a citizen who may have been here recently. Her name is—"

"This city is closed," the robot repeated inexorably.

They would not let him stay as much as an hour. There is no food here, the robot said, no water, no shelter. This is not a place any longer. You may not stay. You may not stay. You may not stay.

This is not a place any longer.

Perhaps he could find her in New Chicago, then. He took to the air again, soaring northward and westward over the vast emptiness. The land below him curved away into the hazy horizon, bare, sterile. What had they done with the vestiges of the world that had gone before? Had they turned their gleaming metal beetles loose to clean everything away? Were there no ruins of genuine antiquity anywhere? No scrap of Rome, no shard of Jerusalem, no stump of Fifth Avenue? It was all so barren down there: an empty stage, waiting for its next set to be built. He flew on a great arc across the jutting hump of Africa and on into what he supposed was southern Europe: the little vehicle did all the work, leaving him to doze or stare as he wished. Now and again he saw another flitterflitter pass by, far away, a dark distant winged teardrop outlined against the hard clarity of the sky. He wished there was some way of making radio contact with them, but he had no idea how to go about it. Not that he had anything he wanted to say; he wanted only to hear a human voice. He was utterly isolated. He might just as well have been the last living man on Earth. He closed his eyes and thought of Gioia.

"Like this?" Phillips asked. In an ivory-paneled oval room sixty stories above the softly glowing streets of New Chicago he touched a small cool plastic canister to his upper lip and pressed the stud at his base. He heard a foaming sound; and then blue vapor rose to his nostrils.

"Yes," Cantilena said. "That's right."

He detected a faint aroma of cinnamon, cloves, and something that might almost have been broiled lobster. Then a spasm of dizziness hit him and visions rushed through his head: Gothic cathedrals, the Pyramids, Central Park under fresh snow, the harsh brick warrens of Mohenjo-daro, and fifty thousand other places all at once, a wild roller-coaster ride through space and time. It seemed to go on for centuries. But finally his head cleared and he looked about, blinking, realizing that the whole thing had taken only a moment. Cantilena still stood at his elbow. The other citizens in the room—fifteen, twenty of them—had scarcely moved. The strange little man with the celadon skin over by the far wall continued to stare at him.

"Well?" Cantilena asked. "What did you think?"

"Incredible."

"And very authentic. It's an actual New Chicagoan drug. The exact formula. Would you like another?"

"Not just yet," Phillips said uneasily. He swayed and had to struggle for his balance. Sniffing that stuff might not have been such a wise idea, he thought.

He had been in New Chicago a week, or perhaps it was two, and he was still suffering from the peculiar disorientation that the city always aroused in him. This was the fourth time that he had come here, and it had been the same every time. New Chicago was the only one of the reconstructed cities of this world that in its original incarnation had existed *after* his own era. To him it was an outpost of the incomprehensible future; to the citizens it was a quaint simulacrum of the archaeological past. That paradox left him aswirl with impossible confusions and tensions.

What had happened to *old* Chicago was of course impossible for him to discover. Vanished without a trace, that was clear: no Water Tower, no Marina City, no Hancock Center, no Tribune building, not a fragment, not an atom. But it was hopeless to ask any of the million-plus inhabitants of New Chicago about their city's predecessor. They were only temporaries; they knew no more than they had to know, and all that they had to know was how to go through the motions of whatever it was that they did by way of creating the illusion that this was a real city. They had no need of knowing ancient history.

Nor was he likely to find out anything from a citizen, of course. Citizens did not seem to bother much about scholarly matters. Phillips had no reason to think that the world was anything other than an amusement park to them. Somewhere, certainly, there had to be those who specialized in the serious study of the lost civilizations of the past— for how, otherwise, would these uncanny reconstructed cities be brought into being? "The planners," he had once heard Nissandra or Aramayne say, "are already deep into their Byzantium research." But who were the planners? He had no idea. For all he knew, they were the robots. Perhaps the robots were the real masters of this whole era, who created the cities not primarily for the sake of amusing the citizens but in their own diligent attempt to comprehend the life of the world that had passed away. A wild speculation, yes; but not without some plausibility, he thought.

He felt oppressed by the party gaiety all about him. "I need some air," he said to Cantilena, and headed toward the window. It was the merest crescent, but a breeze came through. He looked out at the strange city below.

New Chicago had nothing in common with the old one but its name. They had built it, at least, along the western shore of a large inland lake that might even be Lake Michigan, although when he had flown over it had seemed broader and less elongated than the lake he remembered.

The city itself was a lacy fantasy of slender pastel-hued buildings rising at odd angles and linked by a webwork of gently undulating aerial bridges. The streets were long parentheses that touched the lake at their northern and southern ends and arched gracefully westward in the middle. Between each of the great boulevards ran a track for public transportation—sleek aquamarine bubble-vehicles gliding on soundless wheels—and flanking each of the tracks were lush strips of park. It was beautiful, astonishingly so, but insubstantial. The whole thing seemed to have been contrived from sunbeams and silk.

A soft voice beside him said, "Are you becoming ill?"

Phillips glanced around. The celadon man stood beside him: a compact, precise person, vaguely Oriental in appearance. His skin was of a curious gray-green hue like no skin Phillips had ever seen, and it was extraordinarily smooth in texture, as though he were made of fine porcelain.

He shook his head. "Just a little queasy," he said. "This city always scrambles me."

"I suppose it can be disconcerting," the little man replied. His tone was furry and veiled, the inflection strange. There was something feline about him. He seemed sinewy, unyielding, almost menacing. "Visitor, are you?"

Phillips studied him a moment. "Yes," he said.

"So am I, of course."

"Are you?"

"Indeed." The little man smiled. "What's your locus? Twentieth century? Twenty-first at the latest, I'd say."

"I'm from 1984. 1984 A.D."

Another smile, a self-satisfied one. "Not a bad guess, then." A brisk tilt of the head. "Y'ang-Yeovil."

"Pardon me?" Phillips said.

"Y'ang-Yeovil. It is my name. Formerly Colonel Y'ang-Yeovil of the Third Septentriad."

"Is that on some other planet?" asked Phillips, feeling a bit dazed.

"Oh, no, not at all," Y'ang-Yeovil said pleasantly. "This very world, I assure you. I am quite of human origin. Citizen of the Republic of Upper Han, native of the city of Port Ssu. And you—forgive me—your name—?"

"I'm sorry. Phillips. Charles Phillips. From New York City, once upon a time."

"Ah, New York!" Y'ang-Yeovil's face lit with a glimmer of recognition that quickly faded. "New York—New York—it was very famous, that I know—"

This is very strange, Phillips thought. He felt greater compassion for poor bewildered Francis Willoughby now. This man comes from a time so far beyond my own that he barely knows of New York—he must be a contemporary of the real New Chicago, in fact; I wonder whether he finds this version authentic—and yet to the citizens this Y'ang-Yeovil too is just a primitive, a curio out of antiquity—

"New York was the largest city of the United States of America," Phillips said.

"Of course. Yes. Very famous."

"But virtually forgotten by the time the Republic of Upper Han came into existence, I gather."

Y'ang-Yeovil said, looking uncomfortable, "There were disturbances between your time and mine. But by no means should you take from my words the impression that your city was—"

Sudden laughter resounded across the room. Five or six newcomers had arrived at the party. Phillips stared, gasped, gaped. Surely that was Stengard—and Aramayne beside him—and that other woman, half-hidden behind them—

"If you'll pardon me a moment—" Phillips said, turning abruptly away from Y'ang-Yeovil. "Please excuse me.

Someone just coming in—a person I've been trying to find ever since—"

He hurried toward her.

"Gioia?" he called. "Gioia, it's me! Wait! Wait!"

Stengard was in the way. Aramayne, turning to take a handful of the little vapor-sniffers from Cantilena, blocked him also. Phillips pushed through them as though they were not there. Gioia, halfway out the door, halted and looked toward him like a frightened deer.

"Don't go," he said. He took her hand in his.

He was startled by her appearance. How long had it been since their strange parting on that night of mysteries in Chang-an? A year? A year and a half? So he believed. Or had he lost all track of time? Were his perceptions of the passing of the months in this world that unreliable? She seemed at least ten or fifteen years older. Maybe she really was; maybe the years had been passing for him here as in a dream, and he had never known it. She looked strained, faded, worn. Out of a thinner and strangely altered face her eyes blazed at him almost defiantly, as though saying, *See*? *See how ugly I have become*?

He said, "I've been hunting for you for—I don't know how long it's been, Gioia. In Mohenjo, in Timbuctoo, now here. I want to be with you again."

"It isn't possible."

"Belilala explained everything to me in Mohenjo. I know that you're a short-timer—I know what that means, Gioia. But what of it? So you're beginning to age a little. So what? So you'll only have three or four hundred years, instead of forever. Don't you think I know what it means to be a short-timer? I'm just a simple ancient man of the twentieth century, remember? Sixty, seventy, eighty years is all we would get. You and I suffer from the same malady, Gioia. That's what drew you to me in the first place. I'm certain of that. That's why we belong with each other now. However much time we have, we can spend the rest of it together, don't you see?"

"You're the one who doesn't see, Charles," she said softly.

"Maybe. Maybe I still don't understand a damned thing about this place. Except that you and I—that I love you—that I think you love me—"

"I love you, yes. But you don't understand. It's precisely because I love you that you and I—you and I can't—"

With a despairing sigh she slid her hand free of his grasp. He reached for her again, but she shook him off and backed up quickly into the corridor.

"Gioia?"

"Please," she said. "No. I would never have come here if I knew you were here. Don't come after me. Please. Please."

She turned and fled.

He stood looking after her for a long moment. Cantilena and Aramayne appeared, and smiled at him as if nothing at all had happened. Cantilena offered him a vial of some sparkling amber fluid. He refused with a brusque gesture. Where do I go now? he wondered. What do I do? He wandered back into the party.

Y'ang-Yeovil glided to his side. "You are in great distress," the little man murmured.

Phillips glared. "Let me be."

"Perhaps I could be of some help."

"There's no help possible," said Phillips. He swung about and plucked one of the vials from a tray and gulped its contents. It made him feel as if there were two of him, standing on either side of Y'ang-Yeovil. He gulped another. Now there were four of him. "I'm in love with a citizen," he blurted. It seemed to him that he was speaking in chorus.

"Love. Ah. And does she love you?"

"So I thought. So I think. But she's a short-timer. Do you know what that means? She's not immortal like the others. She ages. She's beginning to look old. And so she's been running away from me. She doesn't want me to see her changing. She thinks it'll disgust me, I suppose. I tried to remind her just now that I'm not immortal either, that she and I could grow old together, but she—"

"Oh, no," Y'ang-Yeovil said quietly. "Why do you think you will age? Have you grown any older in all the time you have been here?"

Phillips was nonplussed. "Of course I have. I—I—"

"Have you?" Y'ang-Yeovil smiled. "Here. Look at yourself." He did something intricate with his fingers and a shimmering zone of mirrorlike light appeared between them. Phillips stared at his reflection. A youthful face stared back at him. It was true, then. He had simply not thought about it. How many years had he spent in this world? The time had simply slipped by: a great deal of time, though he could not calculate how much. They did not seem to keep close count of it here, nor had he. But it must have been many years, he thought. All that endless travel up and down the globe—so many cities had come and gone— Rio, Rome, Asgard, those were the first three that came to mind—and there were others; he could hardly remember every one. Years. His face had not changed at all. Time had worked its harshness on Gioia, yes, but not on him.

"I don't understand," he said. "Why am I not aging?"

"Because you are not real," said Y'ang-Yeovil. "Are you unaware of that?"

Phillips blinked. "Not—real?"

"Did you think you were lifted bodily out of your own time?" the little man asked. "Ah, no, no, there is no way for them to do such a thing. We are not actual time travelers: not you, not I, not any of the visitors. I thought you were aware of that. But perhaps your era is too early for a proper understanding of these things. We are very cleverly done, my friend. We are ingenious constructs, marvelously stuffed with the thoughts and attitudes and events of our own times. We are their finest achievement, you know: far more complex even than one of these cities. We are a step beyond the temporaries—more than a step, a great deal more. They do only what they are instructed to do, and their range is very narrow. They are nothing but machines, really. Whereas we are autonomous. We move about by our own will; we think, we talk, we even, so it seems, fall in love. But we will not age. How could we age? We are not real. We are mere artificial webworks of mental responses. We are mere illusions, done so well that we deceive even ourselves. You did not know that? Indeed, you did not know?"

He was airborne, touching destination buttons at random. Somehow he found himself heading back toward Timbuctoo. *This city is closed. This is not a place any longer.* It did not matter to him. Why should anything matter?

Fury and a choking sense of despair rose within him. I am software, Phillips thought. I am nothing but software.

Not real. Very cleverly done. An ingenious construct. A mere illusion.

No trace of Timbuctoo was visible from the air. He landed anyway. The gray sandy earth was smooth, unturned, as though there had never been anything there. A few robots were still about, handling whatever final chores were required in the shutting-down of a city. Two of them scuttled up to him. Huge bland gleaming silver-skinned insects, not friendly.

"There is no city here," they said. "This is not a permissible place."

"Permissible by whom?"

"There is no reason for you to be here."

"There's no reason for me to be anywhere," Phillips said. The robots stirred, made uneasy humming sounds and ominous clicks, waved their antennae about. They seem troubled, he thought. They seem to dislike my attitude. Perhaps I run some risk of being taken off to the home for unruly software for debugging. "I'm leaving now," he told them. "Thank you. Thank you very much." He backed away from them and climbed into his flitterflitter. He touched more destination buttons.

We move about by our own will. We think, we talk, we even fall in love.

He landed in Chang-an. This time there was no reception committee waiting for him at the Gate of Brilliant Virtue. The city seemed larger and more resplendent: new pagodas, new palaces. It felt like winter: a chilly cutting wind was blowing. The sky was cloudless and dazzlingly bright. At the steps of the Silver Terrace he encountered Francis Willoughby, a great hulking figure in magnificent brocaded robes, with two dainty little temporaries, pretty as jade statuettes, engulfed in his arms. "Miracles and wonders! The silly lunatic fellow is here too!" Willoughby roared. "Look, look, we are come to far Cathay, you and I!"

We are nowhere, Phillips thought. *We are mere illusions, done so well that we deceive even ourselves.*

To Willoughby he said, "You look like an emperor in those robes, Francis."

"Aye, like Prester John!" Willoughby cried. "Like Tamburlaine himself! Aye, am I not majestic?" He slapped Phillips gaily on the shoulder, a rough playful poke that spun him halfway about, coughing and wheezing. "We flew in the air, as the eagles do, as the demons do, as the angels do! Soared like angels! Like angels!" He came close, looming over Phillips. "I would have gone to England, but the wench Belilala said there was an enchantment on me that would keep me from England just now; and so we voyaged to Cathay. Tell me this, fellow, will you go witness for me when we see England again? Swear that all that has befallen us did in truth befall? For I fear they will say I am as mad as Marco Polo, when I tell them of flying to Cathay."

"One madman backing another?" Phillips asked. "What can I tell you? You still think you'll reach England, do you?" Rage rose to the surface in him, bubbling hot. "Ah, Francis, Francis, do you know your Shakespeare? Did you go to the plays? We aren't real. *We aren't real.* We are such stuff as dreams are made on, the two of us. That's all we are. O brave new world! What England? Where? There's no England. There's no Francis Willoughby. There's no Charles Phillips. What we are is—"

"Let him be, Charles," a cool voice cut in.

He turned. Belilala, in the robes of an empress, coming down the steps of the Silver Terrace.

"I know the truth," he said bitterly. "Y'ang-Yeovil told me. The visitor from the twenty-fifth century. I saw him in New Chicago."

"Did you see Gioia there too?" Belilala asked.

"Briefly. She looks much older."

"Yes, I know. She was here recently."

"And has gone on, I suppose?"

"To Mohenjo again, yes. Go after her, Charles. Leave poor Francis alone. I told her to wait for you. I told her that she needs you, and you need her."

"Very kind of you. But what good is it, Belilala? I don't even exist. And she's going to die."

"You exist. How can you doubt that you exist? You feel, don't you? You suffer. You love. You love Gioia: is that not so? And you are loved by Gioia. Would Gioia love what is not real?"

"You think she loves me?"

"I know she does. Go to her, Charles. Go. I told her to wait for you in Mohenjo."

Phillips nodded numbly. What was there to lose?

"Go to her," said Belilala again. "Now."

"Yes," Phillips said. "I'll go now." He turned to Willoughby. "If ever we meet in London, friend, I'll testify for you. Fear nothing. All will be well, Francis."

He left them and set his course for Mohenjo-daro, half expecting to find the robots already tearing it down. Mohenjo-daro was still there, no lovelier than before. He went to the baths, thinking he might find Gioia there. She was not; but he came upon Nissandra, Stengard, Fenimon. "She has gone to Alexandria," Fenimon told him. "She wants to see it one last time, before they close it."

"They're almost ready to open Constantinople," Stengard explained. "The capital of Byzantium, you know, the great city by the Golden Horn. They'll take Alexandria away, you understand, when Byzantium opens. They say it's going to be marvelous. We'll see you there for the opening, naturally?"

"Naturally," Phillips said.

He flew to Alexandria. He felt lost and weary. All this is hopeless folly, he told himself. I am nothing but a puppet jerking about on its strings. But somewhere above the shining breast of the Arabian Sea the deeper implications of something that Belilala had said to him started to sink in, and he felt his bitterness, his rage, his despair, all suddenly beginning to leave him. *You exist. How can you doubt that you exist? Would Gioia love what is not real?* Of course. Of course. Y'ang-Yeovil had been wrong: visitors were something more than mere illusions. Indeed Y'ang-Yeovil had voiced the truth of their condition without understanding what he was really saying: *We think, we talk, we fall in love.* Yes. That was the heart of the situation. The visitors might be artificial, but they were not unreal. Belilala had been trying to tell him that just the other night. *You suffer. You love. You love Gioia. Would Gioia love what is not real?* Surely he was real, or at any rate real enough.

What he was was something strange, something that would probably have been all but incomprehensible to the twentieth-century people whom he had been designed to simulate. But that did not mean that he was unreal. Did one have to be of woman born to be real? No. No. No. His kind of reality was a sufficient reality. He had no need to be ashamed of it. And, understanding that, he understood that Gioia did not need to grow old and die. There was a way by which she could be saved, if only she would embrace it. If only she would.

When he landed in Alexandria he went immediately to the hotel on the slopes of the Paneium where they had stayed on their first visit, so very long ago; and there she was, sitting quietly on a patio with a view of the harbor and the Lighthouse. There was something calm and resigned about the way she sat. She had given up. She did not even have the strength to flee from him any longer.

"Gioia," he said gently.

She looked older than she had in New Chicago. Her face was drawn and sallow and her eyes seemed sunken; and she was not even bothering these days to deal with the white strands that stood out in stark contrast against the darkness of her hair. He sat down beside her and put his hand over hers, and looked out toward the obelisks, the palaces, the temples, the Lighthouse. At length he said, "I know what I really am, now."

"Do you, Charles?" She sounded very far away.

"In my era we called it software. All I am is a set of commands, responses, cross-references, operating some sort of artificial body. It's infinitely better software than we could have imagined. But we were only just beginning to learn how, after all. They pumped me full of twentieth-century reflexes. The right moods, the right appetites, the right irrationalities, the right sort of combativeness. Somebody knows a lot about what it was like to be a twentieth-century man. They did a good job with Willoughby, too, all that Elizabethan rhetoric and swagger. And I suppose they got Y'ang-Yeovil right. *He* seems to think so: who better to judge? The twenty-fifth century, the Republic of Upper Han, people with gray-green skin, half Chinese and half Martian for all I know. *Somebody* knows. Somebody here is very good at programming, Gioia."

She was not looking at him.

"I feel frightened, Charles," she said in that same distant way.

"Of me? Of the things I'm saying?"

"No, not of you. Don't you see what has happened to me?"

"I see you. There are changes."

"I lived a long time wondering when the changes would begin. I thought maybe they wouldn't, not really. Who wants to believe they'll get old? But it started when we were in Alexandria that first time. In Chang-an it got much worse. And now—now—"

He said abruptly, "Stengard tells me they'll be opening Constantinople very soon."

"So?"

"Don't you want to be there when it opens?"

"I'm becoming old and ugly, Charles."

"We'll go to Constantinople together. We'll leave tomorrow, eh? What do you say? We'll charter a boat. It's a quick little hop, right across the Mediterranean. Sailing to Byzantium! There was a poem, you know, in my time. Not forgotten, I guess, because they've programmed it into me. All these thousands of years, and someone still remembers old Yeats. *The young in one another's arms, birds in the trees.* Come with me to Byzantium, Gioia."

She shrugged. "Looking like this? Getting more hideous every hour? While *they* stay young forever? While *you*—" She faltered; her voice cracked; she fell silent.

"Finish the sentence, Gioia."

"Please. Let me alone."

"You were going to say, 'While *you* stay young forever too, Charles,' isn't that it? You knew all along that I was never going to change. I didn't know that, but you did."

"Yes. I knew. I pretended that it wasn't true—that as I aged, you'd age too. It was very foolish of me. In Chang-an, when I first began to see the real signs of it—that was when I realized I couldn't stay with you any longer. Because I'd look at you, always young, always remaining the same age, and I'd look at myself, and—" She gestured, palms upward. "So I gave you to Belilala and ran away."

"All so unnecessary, Gioia."

"I didn't think it was."

"But you don't have to grow old. Not if you don't want to!"

"Don't be cruel, Charles," she said tonelessly. "There's no way of escaping what I have."

"But there is," he said.

"You know nothing about these things."

"Not very much, no," he said. "But I see how it can be done. Maybe it's a primitive simple-minded twentieth-century sort of solution, but I think it ought to work. I've been playing with the idea ever since I left Mohenjo. Tell me this, Gioia: Why can't you go to them, to the program-mers, to the artificers, the planners, whoever they are, the ones who create the cities and the temporaries and the vis-itors. And have yourself made into something like me!"

She looked up, startled. "What are you saying?"

"They can cobble up a twentieth-century man out of nothing more than fragmentary records and make him plausible, can't they? Or an Elizabethan, or anyone else of any era at all, and he's authentic, he's convincing. So why couldn't they do an even better job with you? Produce a Gioia so real that even Gioia can't tell the difference? But a Gioia that will never age—a Gioia-construct, a Gioia-pro-gram, a visitor-Gioia! Why not? Tell me why not, Gioia."

She was trembling. "I've never heard of doing any such thing!"

"But don't you think it's possible?"

"How would I know?"

"Of course it's possible. If they can create visitors, they can take a citizen and duplicate her in such a way that—"

"It's never been done. I'm sure of it. I can't imagine any citizen agreeing to any such thing. To give up the body—to let yourself be turned into—into—"

She shook her head, but it seemed to be a gesture of astonishment as much as of negation.

He said, "Sure. To give up the body. Your natural body, your aging, shrinking, deteriorating short-timer body. What's so awful about that?"

She was very pale. "This is craziness, Charles. I don't want to talk about it any more."

"It doesn't sound crazy to me."

"You can't possibly understand."

"Can't I? I can certainly understand being afraid to die. I don't have a lot of trouble understanding what it's like to be one of the few aging people in a world where nobody grows old. What I can't understand is why you aren't even willing to consider the possibility that—"

"No," she said. "I tell you, it's crazy. They'd laugh at me."

"Who?"

"All of my friends. Hawk, Stengard, Aramayne—" Once again she would not look at him. "They can be very cruel, without even realizing it. They despise anything that seems ungraceful to them, anything sweaty and desperate and cowardly. Citizens don't do sweaty things, Charles. And that's how this will seem. Assuming it can be done at all. They'll be terribly patronizing. Oh, they'll be sweet to me, yes, dear Gioia, how wonderful for you, Gioia, but when I turn my back they'll laugh. They'll say the most wicked things about me. I couldn't bear that."

"They can afford to laugh," Phillips said. "It's easy to be brave and cool about dying when you know you're going to live forever. How very fine for them; but why should you be the only one to grow old and die? And they won't laugh, anyway. They're not as cruel as you think. Shallow, maybe, but not cruel. They'll be glad that you've found a way to save yourself. At the very least, they won't have to feel guilty about you any longer, and that's bound to please them. You can—"

"Stop it," she said.

She rose, walked to the railing of the patio, stared out toward the sea. He came up behind her. Red sails in the harbor, sunlight glittering along the sides of the Lighthouse, the palaces of the Ptolemies stark white against the sky. Lightly he rested his hand on her shoulder. She twitched as if to pull away from him, but remained where she was.

"Then I have another idea," he said quietly. "If you won't go to the planners, *I* will. Reprogram me, I'll say. Fix things so that I start to age at the same rate you do. It'll be more authentic, anyway, if I'm supposed to be playing the part of a twentieth-century man. Over the years I'll very gradually get some lines in my face, my hair will turn gray, I'll walk a little more slowly—we'll grow old together, Gioia. To hell with your lovely immortal friends. We'll have each other. We won't need them."

She swung around. Her eyes were wide with horror.

"Are you serious, Charles?"

"Of course."

"No," she murmured. "No. Everything you've said to me today is monstrous nonsense. Don't you realize that?"

He reached for her hand and enclosed her fingertips in his. "All I'm trying to do is find some way for you and me to—"

"Don't say any more," she said. "Please." Quickly, as though drawing back from a suddenly flaring flame, she tugged her fingers free of his and put her hand behind her. Though his face was just inches from hers he felt an immense chasm opening between them. They stared at one another for a moment; then she moved deftly to his left, darted around him, and ran from the patio.

Stunned, he watched her go, down the long marble corridor and out of sight. It was folly to give pursuit, he thought. She was lost to him: that was clear, that was beyond any question. She was terrified of him. Why cause her even more anguish? But somehow he found himself running through the halls of the hotel, along the winding garden path, into the cool green groves of the Paneium. He thought he saw her on the portico of Hadrian's palace, but when he got there the echoing stone halls were empty. To a temporary that was sweeping the steps he said, "Did you see a woman come this way?" A blank sullen stare was his only answer.

Phillips cursed and turned away.

"Gioia?" he called. "Wait! Come back!"

Was that her, going into the Library? He rushed past the startled mumbling librarians and sped through the stacks, peering beyond the mounds of double-handled scrolls into the shadowy corridors. "Gioia? *Gioia!*" It was a desecration, bellowing like that in this quiet place. He scarcely cared.

Emerging by a side door, he loped down to the harbor. The Lighthouse! Terror enfolded him. She might already be a hundred steps up that ramp, heading for the parapet from which she meant to fling herself into the sea. Scattering citizens and temporaries as if they were straws, he ran within. Up he went, never pausing for breath, though his synthetic lungs were screaming for respite, his ingeniously designed heart was desperately pounding. On the first balcony he imagined he caught a glimpse of her, but he circled it without finding her. Onward, upward. He went to the top, to the beacon chamber itself: no Gioia. Had she jumped? Had she gone down one ramp while he was ascending the other? He clung to the rim and looked out, down, searching the base of the Lighthouse, the rocks offshore, the causeway. No Gioia. I will find her somewhere, he thought. I will keep going until I find her. He went running down the ramp, calling her name. He reached ground level and sprinted back toward the center of town. Where next? The temple of Poseidon? The tomb of Cleopatra?

He paused in the middle of Canopus Street, groggy and dazed.

"Charles?" she said.

"Where are you?"

"Right here. Beside you." She seemed to materialize from the air. Her face was unflushed, her robe bore no trace of perspiration. Had he been chasing a phantom through the city? She came to him and took his hand, and said, softly, tenderly, "Were you really serious, about having them make you age?"

"If there's no other way, yes."

"The other way is so frightening, Charles."

"Is it?"

"You can't understand how much."

"More frightening than growing old? Than dying?"

"I don't know," she said. "I suppose not. The only thing I'm sure of is that I don't want you to get old, Charles."

"But I won't have to. Will I?" He stared at her.

"No," she said. "You won't have to. Neither of us will."

Phillips smiled. "We should get away from here," he said after a while. "Let's go across to Byzantium, yes, Gioia? We'll show up in Constantinople for the opening. Your friends will be there. We'll tell them what you've decided to do. They'll know how to arrange it. Someone will."

"It sounds so strange," said Gioia. "To turn myself into—into a visitor? A visitor in my own world?"

"That's what you've always been, though."

"I suppose. In a way. But at least I've been *real* up to now."

"Whereas I'm not?"

"Are you, Charles?"

"Yes. Just as real as you. I was angry at first, when I found out the truth about myself. But I came to accept it. Somewhere between Mohenjo and here, I came to see that it was all right to be what I am: that I perceive things, I form ideas, I draw conclusions. I am very well designed, Gioia. I can't tell the difference between being what I am and being completely alive, and to me that's being real enough. I think, I feel, I experience joy and pain. I'm as real as I need to be. And you will be too. You'll never stop being Gioia, you know. It's only your body that you'll cast away, the body that played such a terrible joke on you anyway." He brushed her cheek with his hand. "It was all said for us before, long ago:

> *Once out of nature I shall never take*
> *My bodily form from any natural thing,*
> *But such a form as Grecian goldsmiths make*
> *Of hammered gold and gold enamelling*
> *To keep a drowsy Emperor awake—*"

"Is that the same poem?" she asked.

"The same poem, yes. The ancient poem that isn't quite forgotten yet."

"Finish it, Charles."

> —"*Or set upon a golden bough to sing*
> *To lords and ladies of Byzantium*
> *Of what is past, or passing, or to come.*"

"How beautiful. What does it mean?"

"That it isn't necessary to be mortal. That we can allow

ourselves to be gathered into the artifice of eternity, that we can be transformed, that we can move on beyond the flesh. Yeats didn't mean it in quite the way I do—he wouldn't have begun to comprehend what we're talking about, not a word of it—and yet, and yet—the underlying truth is the same. Live, Gioia! With me!" He turned to her and saw color coming into her pallid cheeks. "It does make sense, what I'm suggesting, doesn't it? You'll attempt it, won't you? Whoever makes the visitors can be induced to remake you. Right? What do you think: can they, Gioia?"

She nodded in a barely perceptible way. "I think so," she said faintly. "It's very strange. But I think it ought to be possible. Why not, Charles? Why not?"

"Yes," he said. "Why not?"

In the morning they hired a vessel in the harbor, a low sleek pirogue with a blood-red sail, skippered by a rascally-looking temporary whose smile was irresistible. Phillips shaded his eyes and peered northward across the sea. He thought he could almost make out the shape of the great city sprawling on its seven hills, Constantine's New Rome beside the Golden Horn, the mighty dome of Hagia Sophia, the somber walls of the citadel, the palaces and churches, the Hippodrome, Christ in glory rising above all else in brilliant mosaic streaming with light.

"Byzantium," Phillips said. "Take us there the shortest and quickest way."

"It is my pleasure," said the boatman with unexpected grace.

Gioia smiled. He had not seen her looking so vibrantly alive since the night of the imperial feast in Chang-an. He reached for her hand—her slender fingers were quivering lightly—and helped her into the boat.

More Than the Sum of His Parts

JOE HALDEMAN

Joe Haldeman received a Nebula in 1975 for his first science fiction novel, *The Forever War*. He is also the winner of the Hugo, Ditmar, Galaxy, and Rhysling awards. His books include *Worlds, Worlds Apart, All My Sins Remembered, War Year, Infinite Dreams,* and *Dealing in Futures*. He teaches writing at the Massachusetts Institute of Technology and divides his time between the Boston area and his home in Florida.

About his nominated short story, he writes:
"This story pretty neatly demonstrated to me the truth that we rarely do know (or let ourselves know, perhaps) exactly where our stories come from. I thought I had this one nailed down, but I was wrong, wrong.

"The story was a 'where do you get your crazy ideas?' demonstration for my students at MIT—they gave me a random topic (cyborgs), and I chose a structure to pastiche ("Flowers for Algernon"). I told them one could write a perfectly good original story under those restrictions. It turned out to be a grisly tale of pain and madness centered around the surgical replacement of a man's genitals after a traumatic accident. I liked the story quite a lot, and so did Alice Turner at Playboy. *It became my favorite example of where stories come from: any-*

*where and nowhere; if you write every day they just drift down
and find you.*

*"A year later, teaching another fiction workshop at MIT,
we got to talking about pain in fiction. Surgery, specifically. I
told them I could write the book about it, after a Vietnam booby
trap that gave me injuries requiring more than a hundred stitches
to the genitals and a long and trying hospitalization. A lot of
nerve endings down there. 'Oh,' one of the students said; 'that's
where that* Playboy *story came from.'*

*"He was right, obviously. But it had never occurred to
me. Go figure."*

I think the most striking aspects of this story are its
uncompromising, bitter integrity and its chilling lines
about humanity's treatment of the animal world.

21 AUGUST 2058

They say I am to keep a de-
tailed record of my feelings, my perceptions, as I grow accustomed to the new parts. To that end, they gave me an
apparatus that blind people use for writing, like a tablet
with guide wires. It is somewhat awkward. But a recorder
would be useless, since I will not have a mouth for some
time and I can't type blind with only one hand.

Woke up free from pain. Interesting. Surprising to find
that it has been only five days since the accident. For the
record, I am, or was, Dr. Wilson Cheetham, senior engineer (quality control) for U.S. Steel's Skyfac station, a high-
orbit facility that produces foam steel and vapor-deposi-
tion materials for use in the cislunar community. But if
you are reading this, you must know all that.

Five days ago, I was inspecting the aluminum-deposi-
tion facility and had a bad accident. There was a glitch in
my jet-seat controls, and I suddenly flew straight into the

wide beam of charged aluminum vapor. Very hot. They turned it off in a second, but there was still plenty of time for the beam to breach the suit and thoroughly roast three quarters of my body.

Apparently there was a rescue bubble right there. I was unconscious, of course. They tell me that my heart stopped with the shock, but they managed to save me. My left leg and arm are gone, as is my face. I have no lower jaw, nose or external ears. I can hear after a fashion, though, and will have eyes in a week or so. They claim they will craft for me testicles and a penis.

I must be pumped full of mood drugs. I feel too calm. If I were myself, whatever fraction of myself is left, perhaps I would resist the insult of being turned into a sexless half-machine.

Ah, well. This will be a machine that can turn itself off.

22 AUGUST 2058

For many days there was only sleep or pain. That was in the weightless ward at Mercy. They stripped the dead skin off me bit by bit. There are limits to anesthesia, unfortunately. I tried to scream but found I had no vocal cords. They finally decided not to try to salvage the arm and leg, which saved some pain.

When I was able to listen, they explained that U.S. Steel valued my services so much that it was willing to underwrite a state-of-the-art cyborg transformation. Half the cost will be absorbed by Interface Biotech on the moon. Everybody will deduct me from his taxes.

This, then, is the catalog: first, new arm and leg. That's fairly standard. (I once worked with a woman who had two cyborg arms. It took weeks before I could look at her without feeling pity and revulsion.) Then they will attempt to build me a working jaw and mouth, which has been done only rarely and imperfectly, and rebuild the trachea, vocal cords, esophagus. I will be able to speak and drink, though except for certain soft foods, I won't eat in a normal way: salivary glands are beyond their art. No mucous membranes of any kind. A drastic cure for my chronic sinusitis.

Surprisingly, to me at least, the reconstruction of a penis is a fairly straightforward procedure, for which they've had lots of practice. Men are forever sticking them into places where they don't belong. They are particularly excited about my case because of the challenge in restoring sensation as well as function. The prostate is intact, and they seem confident that they can hook up the complicated plumbing involved in ejaculation. Restoring the ability to urinate is trivially easy, they say.

(The biotechnician in charge of the urogenital phase of the project talked at me for more than an hour, going into unnecessarily grisly detail. It seems that this replacement had been done occasionally even before they had any kind of mechanical substitute by sawing off a short rib and transplanting it, covering it with a skin graft from elsewhere on the body. The recipient thus was blessed with a permanent erection, unfortunately rather strange-looking and short on sensation. My own prosthesis will look very much like the real, shall we say, thing, and new developments in tractor-field mechanics and bionic interfacing should give it realistic response patterns.)

I don't know how to feel about all this. I wish they would leave my blood chemistry alone, so I could have some honest grief or horror. Instead of this placid waiting.

4 SEPTEMBER 2058

Out cold for thirteen days and I wake up with eyes. The arm and leg are in place but not powered up yet. I wonder what the eyes look like. (They won't give me a mirror until I have a face.) They feel like wet glass.

Very fancy eyes. I have a box with two dials that I can use to override the default mode; that is, the ability to see only normally. One of them gives me conscious control over pupil dilation, so I can see in almost total darkness or, if for some reason I wanted to, look directly at the sun without discomfort. The other changes the frequency response, so I can see in either the infrared or the ultraviolet. This hospital room looks pretty much the same in ultraviolet, but in infrared, it takes on a whole new aspect. Most of the room's illumination, then, comes from bright bars on the walls, radiant heating. My real arm shows a pulsing tracery of arteries and veins. The other is, of course, not visible except by reflection and is dark blue.

(Later.) Strange I didn't realize I was on the moon. I thought it was a low-gravity ward in Mercy. While I was sleeping, they sent me down to Biotech. Should have figured that out.

5 SEPTEMBER 2058

They turned on the "social" arm and leg and began patterning exercises. I am told to think of a certain movement and do its mirror image with my right arm or leg while attempting to execute it with my left. The trainer helps the cyborg unit along, which generates something like pain, though actually it doesn't resemble any real muscular ache. Maybe it's the way circuits feel when they're overloaded.

By the end of the session, I was able to make a fist without help, though there is hardly enough grip to hold a pencil. I can't raise the leg yet but can make the toes move.

They removed some of the bandages today, from shoulder to hip, and the test-tube skin looks much more real than I had prepared myself for—hairless and somewhat glossy, but the color match is perfect. In infrared it looks different, more uniform in color than the "real" side. I suppose that's because it hasn't aged forty years.

While putting me through my paces, the technician waxed rhapsodic about how good this arm is going to be—this set of arms, actually. I'm exercising with the "social" one, which looks much more convincing than the ones my coworker displayed ten years ago (no doubt a matter of money rather than advancing technology). The "working" arm, which I haven't seen yet, will be all metal, capable of being worn on the outside of a space suit. Besides having the two arms, I'll be able to interface with various waldos tailored to specific functions.

Fortunately, I am more ambidextrous than the average person. I broke my right wrist in the second grade and kept rebreaking it through the third, and so learned to write with both hands. All my life, I have been able to print more clearly with the left.

They claim to be cutting down on my medication. If that's the truth, I seem to be adjusting fairly well. Then again, I have nothing in my past experience to use as a basis for comparison. Perhaps this calmness is only a mask for hysteria.

6 SEPTEMBER 2058

Today I was able to tie a simple knot. I can lightly sketch out the letters of the alphabet—a large and childish scrawl but recognizably my own.

I've begun walking after a fashion, supporting myself between parallel bars. (The lack of hand strength is a neural problem, not a muscular one; when rigid, the arm and the leg are as strong as metal crutches.) As I practice, it's amusing to watch the reactions of people who walk into the room—people who aren't paid to mask their horror at being studied by two cold lenses embedded in a swathe of bandages over a shape that is not a head.

Tomorrow they start building my face. I will be essentially unconscious for more than a week. The limb patterning will continue as I sleep, they say.

14 SEPTEMBER 2058

When I was a child, my mother dressed me in costume each Halloween and escorted me around the high-rise, so I could beg for candy. One occasion, I wore the mask of a child star then popular on the cube, a tightly fitting plastic affair that covered the head, squeezing my pudgy features into something more in line with some Platonic ideal of childish beauty.

This face is like that. It is undeniably my face, but the skin is taut and unresponsive. Any attempt at expression produces a grimace.

I have almost normal grip in the hand now, though it is still clumsy. As they hoped, the sensory feedback from the fingertips and the palms seems to be more finely tuned than in my "good" hand. Tracing my new forefinger across my right wrist, I can sense the individual pores, and there is a marked temperature gradient as I pass over tendon or vein. And yet the hand and arm will eventually be capable of superhuman strength.

Touching my new face, I do not feel pores. They have improved on nature in the business of heat exchange.

22 SEPTEMBER 2058

Another week of sleep while they installed the new plumbing. When the anesthetic wore off, I felt a definite *something*—not pain, but neither was it the normal somatic heft of genitalia. Everything was bedded in gauze and bandage, though, and catheterized, so it would feel strange even to a normal person.

(Later.) An aide came in and gingerly snipped away

the bandages. He blushed; I don't think fondling was in his job description. When the catheter came out, there was a small sting of pain and relief.

It's not much of a copy. To reconstruct the face, they could consult hundreds of pictures and cubes, but it had never occurred to me that one day it might be useful to have a gallery of pictures of my private parts in various stages of repose. The technicians had approached the problem by bringing me a stack of photos culled from urological texts and pornography and having me sort through them as to closeness of fit.

It was not a task for which I had been well trained, by experience or disposition. Strange as it may seem in this age of unfettered hedonism, I haven't seen another man naked, let alone rampant, since leaving high school, twenty-five years ago. (I was stationed on Farside for eighteen months and never went near a sex bar, preferring an audience of one, even if I had to hire her, as was usually the case.)

So this one is rather longer and thicker than its predecessor—would all men unconsciously exaggerate?—and has only approximately the same aspect when erect. A young man's rakish angle.

Distasteful but necessary to write about the matter of masturbation. At first, it didn't work. With my right hand, it felt like holding another man, which I have never had any desire to do. With the new hand, the process proceeded in the normal way, though I must admit to a voyeuristic aspect. The sensations were extremely acute—ejaculation more forceful than I can remember from youth.

It makes me wonder. In a book I recently read about brain chemistry, the author made a major point of the notion that it was a mistake to completely equate mind with brain. The brain, he said, is in a way only the thickest and most complex segment of the nervous system: it coordinates our consciousness, but the actual mind suffuses through the body in a network of ganglia. In fact, he used sexuality as an example. When a man ruefully observes that his penis has a mind of its own, he is stating part of a larger truth.

But I, in fact, do have actual brains embedded in my new parts: the biochips that process sensory data coming in and action commands going back. Are these brains part of my consciousness the way the rest of my nervous system is? The masturbation experience indicates that they may be in business for themselves.

This is premature speculation, so to speak. We'll see how it feels when I move into a more complex environment, where I'm not so self-absorbed.

23 SEPTEMBER 2058

During the night, something evidently clicked. I woke up this morning with full strength in my cyborg limbs. One rail of the bed was twisted out of shape where I must have unconsciously gripped it. I bent it back quite easily.

Some obscure impulse makes me want to keep this talent secret for the time being. The technicians thought I would be able to exert three or four times the normal person's grip; this is obviously much more than that.

But why keep it a secret? I don't know. Let *them* tell *me* why I've done it. After all, this is supposed to be a record of my psychological adjustment or maladjustment.

(Later.) The techs were astonished, ecstatic. I demonstrated a pull of 90 kilograms. I know if I'd actually given it a good yank, I could have pulled the stress machine out of the wall. I'll give them 110 tomorrow and inch my way up to 125.

Obviously, I must be careful with force vectors. If I put too much stress on the normal parts of my body, I could do permanent injury. With my metal fist, I could punch a hole through an air-lock door, but it would probably tear the prosthesis out of its socket. Newton's laws still apply. Other laws will have to be rewritten.

24 SEPTEMBER 2058

I got to work out with three waldos today. A fantastic experience!

The first one was a disembodied hand and arm attached to a stand, the setup they use to train normal people in the use of waldos. The difference is that I don't need a waldo sleeve to imperfectly transmit my wishes to the mechanical double. I can plug into it directly.

I've been using waldos in my work ever since graduate school, but it was never anything like this. Inside the waldo sleeve, you get a clumsy kind of feedback from striated pressor field generators embedded in the plastic. With my setup, the feedback is exactly the kind a normal person feels when he touches an object but much more sensitive. The first time they asked me to pick up an egg, I tossed it up and caught it (no great feat of coordination in lunar gravity, admittedly, but I could have done it as easily in Earth normal).

The next waldo was a large earthmover that Western Mining uses over at Grimaldi Station. That was interesting, not only because of its size but because of the slight communications lag. Grimaldi is only a few dozen kilometers away, but there aren't enough unused data channels between here and there for me to use the land line to communicate with the earthmover hand. I had to relay via Comsat, so there was about a ten-second delay between the thought and the action. It was a fine feeling of power but a little confusing: I would cup my hand and scoop downward and then, a split second too late, would feel the resistance of the regolith—and then casually hold in my palm several *tonnes* of rock and dirt. People were standing around watching; with a flick of my wrist, I could have buried them. Instead, I dutifully dumped it onto the belt to the converter.

But the waldo that most fascinated me was the micro. It had been in use for only a few months; I had heard of it but hadn't had a chance to see it in action. It is a fully articulated hand barely a tenth of a millimeter long. I used it in conjunction with a low-power scanning electron microscope, moving around on the surface of a microcircuit. At that magnification, it looked like a hand on a long stick wandering through the corridors of a building whose walls varied from rough stucco to brushed metal to blistered gray paint, all laced over with thick cables of gold. When necessary, I could bring in another hand, manipulated by my right from inside a waldo sleeve, to help with simple carpenter and machinist tasks that, in the real world, translated into fundamental changes in the quantumelectrodynamic properties of the circuit.

This was the real power: not crushing metal tubes or lifting *tonnes* of rock but pushing electrons around to do my bidding. My first doctorate was in electrical engineering; in a sudden epiphany, I realized that I am the first *actual* electrical engineer in history.

After two hours, they made me stop; said I was showing signs of strain. They put me into a wheelchair, and I did fall asleep on the way back to my room, dreaming dreams of microcosmic and infinite power.

25 SEPTEMBER 2058

The metal arm. I expected it to feel fundamentally different from the social one, but of course it doesn't, most of the time. Circuits are circuits. The difference comes under conditions of extreme exertion: the soft hand gives me signals similar to pain if I come close to the level of stress that would harm the fleshlike material. With the metal hand,

I can rip off a chunk of steel plate a centimeter thick and feel nothing beyond "muscular" strain. If I had two of them, I could work marvels.

The mechanical leg is not so gifted. It has governors to restrict its strength and range of motion to that of a normal leg, which is reasonable. Even a normal person finds himself brushing the ceiling occasionally in lunar gravity. I could stand up sharply and find myself with a concussion or worse.

I like the metal arm, though. When I'm stronger (hah!), they say, they'll let me go outside and try it with a space suit. Throw something over the horizon.

Starting today, I'm easing back into a semblance of normal life. I'll be staying at Biotech for another six or eight weeks, but I'm patched into my Skyfac office and have started clearing out the backlog of paperwork. Two hours in the morning and two in the afternoon. It's diverting, but I have to admit my heart isn't really in it. Rather be playing with the micro. (Have booked three hours on it tomorrow.)

26 SEPTEMBER 2058

They have threaded an optical fiber through the micro's little finger, so I can watch its progress on a screen without being limited to the field of an electron microscope. The picture is fuzzy while the waldo is in motion, but if I hold it still for a few seconds, the computer assist builds up quite a sharp image. I used it to roam all over my right arm and hand, which was fascinating: hairs a tangle of stiff, black stalks, the pores small, damp craters. And everywhere evidence of the skin's slow death: translucent sheaves of desquamated cells.

I've taken to wearing the metal arm rather than the

social one. People's stares don't bother me. The metal one will be more useful in my actual work, and I want to get as much practice as possible. There is also an undeniable feeling of power.

27 SEPTEMBER 2058

Today I went outside. It was clumsy getting around at first. For the past eleven years, I've used a suit only in zero g, so all of my reflexes are wrong. Still, not much serious can go wrong at a sixth of a g.

It was exhilarating but at the same time frustrating, since I couldn't reveal all of my strength. I did almost overdo it once, starting to tip over a large boulder. Before it tipped, I realized that my left boot had crunched through ten centimeters of regolith in reaction to the amount of force I was applying. So I backed off and discreetly shuffled my foot to fill the telltale hole.

I could, indeed, throw a rock over the horizon. With a sling, I might be able to put a small one into orbit—rent myself out as a lunar launching facility.

(Later.) Most interesting. A pretty nurse who has been on this project since the beginning came into my room after dinner and proposed the obvious experiment. It was wildly successful.

Although my new body starts out with the normal pattern of excitation-plateau-orgasm, the resemblance stops there. I have no refractory period; the process of erection is completely under conscious control. This could make me the most popular man on the moon.

The artificial skin of the penis is as sensitive to tactile differentiation as that of the cyborg fingers: suddenly, I know more about a woman's internal topography than any man who ever lived—more than any *woman!*

I think tomorrow I'll take a trip to Farside.

28 SEPTEMBER 2058

Farside has nine sex bars. I read the guidebook descriptions and then asked a few locals for their recommendations and wound up going to a place cleverly called The Juice Bar.

In fact, the name was not just an expression of coy eroticism. They served nothing but fruit and juices there, most of them fantastically expensive Earth imports. I spent a day's pay on a glass of pear nectar and sought out the most attractive woman in the room.

That in itself was a mistake. I was not physically attractive even before the accident, and the mechanics have faithfully restored my coarse features and slight paunch. I was rebuffed.

So I went to the opposite extreme and looked for the plainest woman. That would be a better test, anyway: before the accident, I always demanded, and paid for, physical perfection. If I could duplicate the performance of last night with a woman to whom I was not sexually attracted—and do it in public—then my independence from the autonomic nervous system would be proved beyond doubt.

Second mistake. I was never good at small talk, and when I located my paragon of plainness, I began talking about the accident and the singular talent that had resulted from it. She suddenly remembered an appointment elsewhere.

I was not so open with the next woman, also plain. She asked whether there was something wrong with my face, and I told her half of the truth. She was sweetly sympathetic, motherly, which did not endear her to me. It did make her a good subject for the experiment. We left the socializing section of the bar and went back to the so-called love room.

There was an acrid quality to the air that I suppose was

compounded of incense and sweat; but, of course, my dry nose was not capable of identifying actual smells. For the first time, I was grateful for that disability; the place probably had the aroma of a well-used locker room. Plus pheromones.

Under the muted lights, red and blue as well as white, more than a dozen couples were engaged more or less actively in various aspects of amorous behavior. A few were frankly staring at others, but most were either absorbed with their own affairs or furtive in their voyeurism. Most of them were on the floor, which was a warm, soft mat, but some were using tables and chairs in fairly ingenious ways. Several of the permutations would no doubt have been impossible or dangerous in Earth's gravity.

We undressed, and she complimented me on my evident spryness. A nearby spectator made a jealous observation. Her own body was rather flaccid, doughy, and under previous circumstances, I doubt that I would have been able to maintain enthusiasm. There was no problem, however; in fact, I rather enjoyed it. She required very little foreplay, and I was soon repeating the odd sensation of hypersensitized exploration—gynecological spelunking.

She was quite voluble in her pleasure, and although she lasted less than a hour, we did attract a certain amount of attention. When she, panting, regretfully declined further exercise, a woman who had been watching, a rather attractive young blonde, offered to share her various openings. I obliged her for a while; although the well was dry, the pump handle was unaffected.

During that performance, I became aware that the pleasure involved was not a sexual one in any normal sense. Sensual, yes, in the way that a fine meal is a sensual experience, but with a remote subtlety that I find difficult to describe. Perhaps there is a relation to epicurism that is more than metaphorical. Since I can no longer taste food, a large area of my brain is available for the evaluation of other experience. It may be that the brain is reorganizing itself in order to take fullest advantage of my new abilities.

By the time the blonde's energy began to flag, several other women had taken an interest in my satyriasis. I resisted the temptation to find out what this organ's limit was, if, indeed, a limit existed. My back ached and the right knee was protesting, so I threw the mental switch and deflated. I left with a minimum of socializing. (The first woman insisted on buying me something at the bar. I opted for a banana.)

29 SEPTEMBER 2058

Now that I have eyes and both hands, there's no reason to scratch this diary out with a pen, so I'm entering it into the computer. But I'm keeping two versions.

I copied everything up to this point and then went back and edited the versions that I will show to Biotech. It's very polite and will remain so. For instance, it does not contain the following:

After writing last night's entry, I found myself still full of energy, and so put into action a plan that has been forming in my mind.

About two in the morning, I went downstairs and broke into the waldo labs. The entrance is protected by a five-digit combination lock, but, of course, that was no obstacle. My hypersensitive fingers could feel the tumblers rattling into place.

I got the microwaldo set up and then detached my leg. I guided the waldo through the leg's circuitry and easily disabled the governors. The entire operation took less than twenty minutes.

I did have to use a certain amount of care in walking, at first. There was a tendency to rise into the air or to overcompensate by limping. It was under control by the time I got back to my room. So once more, they have proved to be mistaken as to the limits of my abilities.

Testing the strength of the leg with a halfhearted kick, I put a deep dent in the metal wall at the rear of my closet. I'll have to wait until I can be outside, alone, to see what full force can do.

A comparison kick with my flesh leg left no dent but did hurt my great toe.

30 SEPTEMBER 2058

It occurs to me that I feel better about my body than I have in the past twenty years. Who wouldn't? Literally eternal youth in these new limbs and organs; if a part shows signs of wear, it can simply be replaced.

I was angry at the Biotech evaluation board this morning. When I simply inquired as to the practicality of replacing the right arm and leg as well, all but one were horrified. One was amused. I will remember him.

I think the fools are going to order me to leave Nearside in a day or two and go back to Mercy for psychiatric "help." I will leave when I want to, on my own terms.

1 OCTOBER 2058

This is being voice recorded in the Environmental Control Center at Nearside. It is 10:32; they have less than ninety minutes to accede to my demands. Let me backtrack.

After writing last night's entry, I felt a sudden surge of sexual desire. I took the shuttle to Farside and went back to The Juice Bar.

The plain woman from the previous night was waiting, hoping that I would show up. She was delighted when I suggested that we save money (and whatever residue of modesty we had left) by keeping ourselves to each other back at my room.

I didn't mean to kill her. That was not in my mind at all. But I suppose in my passion, or abandon, I carelessly propped my strong leg against the wall and then thrust with too much strength. At any rate, there was a snap and a tearing sound. She gave a small cry, and the lower half of my body was suddenly awash in blood. I had snapped her spine and evidently at the same time caused considerable internal damage. She must have lost consciousness very quickly, though her heart did not stop beating for nearly a minute.

Disposing of the body was no great problem. In the laundry room, I found a bag large enough to hold her comfortably. Then I went back to the room and put her and the sheet she had besmirched into the bag.

Getting her to the recycler would have been a problem if it had been a normal hour. She looked like nothing so much as a body in a laundry bag. Fortunately, the corridor was deserted.

The lock on the recycler room was child's play. The furnace door was a problem, though: it was easy to unlock, but its diameter was only twenty-five centimeters.

So I had to disassemble her. To save cleaning up, I did the job inside the laundry bag, which was clumsy and made it difficult to see the fascinating process.

I was so absorbed in watching that I didn't hear the door slide open. But the man who walked in made a slight gurgling sound that I somehow did hear over the cracking of bones. I stepped over to him and killed him with one kick.

I have to admit to a lapse in judgment at that point. I locked the door and went back to the chore at hand. After the woman was completely recycled, I repeated the process with the man—which was much easier. The female's layer of subcutaneous fat made disassembly of the torso a more slippery business.

It really was wasted time (though I did spend part of

it thinking out the final touches of the plan I am now engaged upon). I might as well have left both bodies there on the floor. I had kicked the man with great force—enough to throw me to the ground in reaction and badly bruise my right hip—and had split him open from crotch to heart. This made a bad enough mess, even if he hadn't compounded the problem by striking the ceiling. I would never have been able to clean that up, and it's not the sort of thing that would escape notice for long.

At any rate, it was only twenty minutes wasted, and I gained more time than that by disabling the recycler-room lock. I cleaned up, changed clothes, stopped by the waldo lab for a few minutes and then took the slidewalk to the Environmental Control Center.

There was only one young man on duty at the E.C.C. at that hour. I exchanged a few pleasantries with him and then punched him in the heart, softly enough not to make a mess. I put his body where it wouldn't distract me and then attended to the problem of the door.

There's no actual door on the E.C.C., but there is an emergency wall that slides into place if there's a drop in pressure. I typed up a test program simulating an emergency, and the wall obeyed. Then I walked over and twisted a few flanges around. Nobody would be able to get into the center with anything short of a cutting torch.

Sitting was uncomfortable with the bruised hip, but I managed to ease into the console and spend an hour or so studying logic and wiring diagrams. Then I popped off an access plate and moved the microwaldo down the corridors of electronic thought. The intercom began buzzing incessantly, but I didn't let it interfere with my concentration.

Nearside is protected from meteorite strike or (far more likely) structural failure by a series of 128 bulkheads that, like the emergency wall here, can slide into place and isolate any area where there's a pressure drop. It's done automatically, of course, but can also be controlled from here.

What I did, in essence, was to tell each bulkhead that it was under repair and should not close under any circumstance. Then I moved the waldo over to the circuits that controlled the city's eight air locks. With some rather elegant microsurgery, I transferred control of all eight solely to the pressure switch I now hold in my left hand.

It is a negative-pressure button—a dead-man switch taken from a power saw. As long as I hold it down, the inner doors of the air locks will remain locked. If I let go, they will all iris open. The outer doors are already open, as are the ones that connect the air-lock chambers to the suiting-up rooms. No one will be able to make it to a space suit in time. Within thirty seconds, every corridor will be a vacuum. People behind airtight doors may choose between slow asphyxiation and explosive decompression.

My initial plan had been to wire the dead-man switch to my pulse, which would free my good hand and allow me to sleep. That will have to wait. The wiring completed, I turned on the intercom and announced that I would speak to the coordinator and no one else.

When I finally got to talk to him, I told him what I had done and invited him to verify it. That didn't take long. Then I presented my demands:

Surgery to replace the rest of my limbs, of course. The surgery would have to be done while I was conscious (a heartbeat dead-man switch could be subverted by a heart machine) and it would have to be done here, so that I could be assured that nobody had fooled with my circuit changes.

The doctors were called in, and they insisted that such profound surgery couldn't be done under local anesthetic. I knew they were lying, of course—amputation was a fairly routine procedure even before anesthetics were invented. Yes, but I would faint, they said. I told them that I would not, and at any rate, I was willing to take the chance, and no one else had any choice in the matter.

(I have not yet mentioned that the totality of my plan

involves replacing all of my internal organs as well as all of the limbs—or at least those organs whose failure could cause untimely death. I will be a true cyborg then, a human brain in an "artificial" body, with the prospect of thousands of years of life. With a few decades—or centuries!—of research, I could even do something about the brain's shortcomings. I would wind up interfaced to EarthNet, with all of human knowledge at my disposal and with my faculties for logic and memory no longer fettered by the slow pace of electrochemical synapse.)

A psychiatrist, talking from Earth, tried to convince me of the error of my ways. He said that the dreadful trauma had "obviously" unhinged me, and the cyborg augmentation, far from effecting a cure, had made my mental derangement worse. He demonstrated, at least to his own satisfaction, that my behavior followed some classical pattern of madness. All this had been taken into consideration, he said, and if I were to give myself up, I would be forgiven my crimes and manumitted into the loving arms of the psychiatric establishment.

I did take time to explain the fundamental errors in his way of thinking. He felt that I had literally lost my identity by losing my face and genitalia and that I was at bottom a "good" person whose essential humanity had been perverted by physical and existential estrangement. Wrong. By his terms, what I actually *am* is an "evil" person whose true nature was revealed to him by the lucky accident that released him from existential propinquity with the common herd.

And evil is the accurate word, not maladjusted or amoral or even criminal. I am as evil by human standards as a human is evil by the standards of an animal raised for food, and the analogy is accurate. I will sacrifice humans not only for my survival but for comfort, curiosity or entertainment. I will allow to live anyone who doesn't bother me and reward generously those who help.

Now they have only forty minutes. They know I am
(End of recording.)

EXCERPT FROM SUMMARY REPORT
1 OCTOBER 2058

I am Dr. Henry Janovski, head of the surgical team that
worked on the ill-fated cyborg augmentation of Dr. Wilson
Cheetham.

We were fortunate that Dr. Cheetham's insanity did
interfere with his normally painstaking, precise nature. If
he had spent more time in preparation, I have no doubt
that he would have put us in a very difficult fix.

He should have realized that the protecting wall that
shut him off from the rest of Nearside was made of steel,
an excellent conductor of electricity. If he had insulated
himself behind a good dielectric, he could have escaped
his fate.

Cheetham's waldo was a marvelous instrument, but
basically it was only a pseudointelligent servomechanism
that obeyed well-defined radio-frequency commands. All
we had to do was override the signals that were coming
from his own nervous system.

We hooked a powerful amplifier up to the steel wall,
making it, in effect, a huge radio transmitter. To generate
the signal we wanted amplified, I had a technician put on
a waldo sleeve that was holding a box similar to Cheetham's dead-man switch. We wired the hand closed, turned
up the power and had the technician strike himself on the
chin as hard as he could.

The technician struck himself so hard that he blacked
out for a few seconds. Cheetham's resonant action, perhaps one hundred times more powerful, drove the bones
of his chin up through the top of his skull.

Fortunately, the expensive arm itself was not damaged. It is not evil or insane by itself, of course, as I shall prove.

The experiments will continue, though of course we will be more selective as to subjects. It seems obvious, in retrospect, that we should not use as subjects people who have gone through the kind of trauma that Cheetham suffered. We must use willing volunteers—such as myself.

I am not young, and weakness and an occasional tremor in my hands limit the amount of surgery I can do—much less than my knowledge would allow or my nature desire. My failing left arm I shall have replaced with Cheetham's mechanical marvel, and I will go through training similar to his—but for the good of humanity, not for ill.

What miracles I will perform with the knife!

Portraits of His Children

GEORGE R. R. MARTIN

George R. R. Martin received the Nebula Award in 1979 for his novelette "Sandkings." His books include *Dying of the Light*, *The Armageddon Rag*, *Fevre Dream*, *Songs of Stars and Shadows*, *A Song for Lya*, and *Nightflyers*. He lives in New Mexico.

About this year's winning novelette, he writes:

"The truth of it is, writers do have peculiar relationships with their characters. They are our children in more senses than one. They are born of our imaginations, carry much of ourselves in them, and embody whatever dreams we dream of immortality.

"I can't claim to be an exception. Abner Marsh and Joshua York, Sandy and Maggy and Froggy, Vul One-Wing and half-faced Bretan Braith, Kenny with his monkey, poor wasted Melody, the improved model Melantha Jhirl, and the callous Simon Kress, and of course my lost Lya. When I type I can see their faces.

"This is a writer's story, yes, and more true than some of us would care to admit."

Richard Cantling found the package leaning up against his front door, one evening in late October when he was setting out for his walk. It annoyed him. He had told his postman repeatedly to ring the bell when delivering anything too big to fit through the mail slot, yet the man persisted in abandoning the packages on the porch, where any passerby could simply walk off with them. Although, to be fair, Cantling's house was rather isolated, sitting on the river bluffs at the end of a cul-de-sac, and the trees effectively screened it off from the street. Still, there was always the possibility of damage from rain or wind or snow.

Cantling's displeasure lasted only an instant. Wrapped in heavy brown paper and carefully sealed with tape, the package had a shape that told all. Obviously a painting. And the hand that had block-printed his address in heavy green marker was unmistakably Michelle's. Another self-portrait then. She must be feeling repentant.

He was more surprised than he cared to admit, even to himself. He had always been a stubborn man. He could hold grudges for years, even decades, and he had the greatest difficulty admitting any wrong. And Michelle, being his only child, seemed to take after him in all of that. He hadn't expected this kind of gesture from her. It was . . . well, sweet.

He set aside his walking stick to lug the package inside, where he could unwrap it out of the damp and the blustery October wind. It was about three feet tall, and unexpectedly heavy. He carried it awkwardly, shutting the door with his foot and struggling down the long foyer toward his den. The brown drapes were tightly closed; the room was dark, and heavy with the smell of dust. Cantling had to set down the package to fumble for the light.

He hadn't used his den much since that night, two months ago, when Michelle had gone storming out. Her self-portrait was still sitting up above the wide slate mantle. Below, the fireplace badly wanted cleaning, and on the built-in bookshelves his novels, all bound in handsome dark leather, stood dusty and disarrayed. Cantling looked at the old painting and felt a brief wash of anger return to him, followed by depression. It had been such a nasty thing for her to do. The portrait had been quite good, really. Much more to his taste than the tortured abstractions that Michelle liked to paint for her own pleasure, or the trite paperback covers she did to make her living. She had done it when she was twenty, as a birthday gift for him. He'd always been fond of it. It captured her as no photograph had ever done, not just the lines of her face, the high angular cheekbones and blue eyes and tangled ash-blond hair, but the personality inside. She looked so young and fresh and confident, and her smile reminded him so much of Helen, and the way she had smiled on their wedding day. He'd told Michelle more than once how much he'd liked that smile.

And so, of course, it had been the smile that she'd started on. She used an antique dagger from his collection, chopped out the mouth with four jagged slashes. She'd gouged out the wide blue eyes next, as if intent on blinding the portrait, and when he came bursting in after her, she'd been slicing the canvas into ribbons with long angry crooked cuts. Cantling couldn't forget the moment. So ugly. And to do something like that to her own work . . . he couldn't imagine it. He had tried to picture himself mutilating one of his books, tried to comprehend what might drive one to such an act, and he had failed utterly. It was unthinkable, beyond even imagination.

The mutilated portrait still hung in its place. He'd been too stubborn to take it down, and yet he could not bear to look at it. So he had taken to avoiding his den. It wasn't hard. The old house was a huge, rambling place, with more rooms than he could possibly need or want, living alone

as he did. It had been built a century ago, when Perrot
had been a thriving river town, and they said that a
succession of steamer captains had lived there. Certainly
the steamboat gothic architecture and all the gingerbread
called up visions of the glory days on the river, and he
had a fine view of the Mississippi from the third-story
windows and the widow's walk. After the incident, Cantling had moved his desk and his typewriter to one of the
unused bedrooms and settled in there, determined to let
the den remain as Michelle had left it until she came back
with an apology.

He had not expected that apology quite so soon, however, nor in quite this form. A tearful phone call, yes—but
not another portrait. Still, this was nicer somehow, more
personal. And it was a gesture, the first step toward a reconciliation. Richard Cantling knew too well that he was
incapable of taking that step himself, no matter how lonely
he might become. And he had been lonely, he did not try
to fool himself on that score. He had left all his New York
friends behind when he moved out to this Iowa river town,
and had formed no local friendships to replace them. That
was nothing new. He had never been an outgoing sort.
He had a certain shyness that kept him apart, even from
those few friends he did make. Even from his family, really.
Helen had often accused him of caring more for his characters than for real people, an accusation that Michelle had
picked up on by the time she was in her teens. Helen was
gone too. They'd divorced ten years ago, and she'd been
dead for five. Michelle, infuriating as she could be, was
really all he had left. He had missed her, missed even the
arguments.

He thought about Michelle as he tore open the plain
brown paper. He would call her, of course. He would call
her and tell her how good the new portrait was, how much
he liked it. He would tell her that he'd missed her, invite
her to come out for Thanksgiving. Yes, that would be the

way to handle it. No mention of their argument, he didn't want to start it all up again, and neither he nor Michelle was the kind to back down gracefully. A family trait, that stubborn willful pride, as ingrained as the high cheekbones and squarish jaw. The Cantling heritage.

It was an antique frame, he saw. Wooden, elaborately carved, very heavy, just the sort of thing he liked. It would mesh with his Victorian decor much better than the thin brass frame on the old portrait. Cantling pulled the wrapping paper away, eager to see what his daughter had done. She was nearly thirty now—or was she past thirty already? He never could keep track of her age, or even her birthdays. Anyway, she was a much better painter than she'd been at twenty. The new portrait ought to be striking. He ripped away the last of the wrappings and turned it around.

His first reaction was that it was a fine, fine piece of work, maybe the best thing that Michelle Cantling had ever done.

Then, belatedly, the admiration washed away, and was replaced by anger. It wasn't her. It wasn't Michelle. Which meant it wasn't a replacement for the portrait she had so willfully vandalized. It was . . . something else.

Someone else.

It was a face he had never before laid eyes on. But it was a face he recognized as readily as if he had looked on it a thousand times. Oh, yes.

The man in the portrait was young. Twenty, maybe even younger, though his curly brown hair was already well-streaked with gray. It was unruly hair, disarrayed as if the man had just come from sleep, falling forward into his eyes. Those eyes were a bright green, lazy eyes somehow, shining with some secret amusement. He had high Cantling cheekbones, but the jawline was all wrong for a relative. Beneath a wide, flat nose, he wore a sardonic smile; his whole posture was somehow insolent. The portrait showed him dressed in faded dungarees and a raveled WMCA Good Guy sweatshirt, with a half-eaten raw onion in one hand. The background was a brick wall covered with graffiti.

Cantling had created him.

Edward Donohue. Dunnahoo, that's what they'd called him, his friends and peers, the other characters in Richard Cantling's first novel, *Hangin' Out*. Dunnahoo had been the protagonist. A wise guy, a smart mouth, too damn bright for his own good. Looking down at the portrait, Cantling felt as if he'd known him for half his life. As indeed he had, in a way. Known him and, yes, cherished him, in the peculiar way a writer can cherish one of his characters.

Michelle had captured him true. Cantling stared at the painting and it all came back to him, all the events he had bled over so long ago, all the people he had fashioned and described with such loving care. He remembered Jocko, and the Squid, and Nancy, and Ricci's Pizzeria where so much of the book's action had taken place (he could see it vividly in his mind's eye), and the business with Arthur and the motorcycle, and the climactic pizza fight. And Dunnahoo. Dunnahoo especially. Smarting off, fooling around, hanging out, coming of age. "Fuck 'em if they can't take a joke," he said. A dozen times or so. It was the book's closing line.

For a moment, Richard Cantling felt a vast, strange affection well up inside him, as if he had just been reunited with an old, lost friend.

And then, almost as an afterthought, he remembered all the ugly words that he and Michelle had flung at each other that night, and suddenly it made sense. Cantling's face went hard. "Bitch," he said aloud. He turned away in fury, helpless without a target for his anger. "Bitch," he said again, as he slammed the door of the den behind him.

"Bitch," he had called her.

She turned around with the knife in her hand. Her eyes were raw and red from crying. She had the smile in her hand. She balled it up and threw it at him. "Here, you bastard, you like the damned smile so much, here it is."

It bounced off his cheek. His face was reddening. "You're just like your mother," he said. "She was always breaking things too."

"You gave her good reason, didn't you?"

Cantling ignored that. "What the hell is wrong with you? What the hell do you think you're going to accomplish with this stupid melodramatic gesture? That's all it is, you know. Bad melodrama. Who the hell do you think you are, some character in a Tennessee Williams play? Come off it, Michelle. If I wrote a scene like this in one of my books, they'd laugh at me."

"This isn't one of your goddamned books!" she screamed. "This is real life. *My* life. I'm a real person, you son of a bitch, not a character in some damned book." She whirled, raised the knife, slashed and slashed again.

Cantling folded his arms against his chest as he stood watching. "I hope you're enjoying this pointless exercise."

"I'm enjoying the hell out of it," Michelle yelled back.

"Good. I'd hate to think it was for nothing. This is all very revealing, you know. That's your own face you're working on. I didn't think you had that much self-hate in you."

"If I do, we know who put it there, don't we?" She was finished. She turned back to him, and threw down the knife. She had begun to cry again, and her breath was coming hard. "I'm leaving. Bastard. I hope you're ever so fucking happy here, really I do."

"I haven't done anything to deserve this," Cantling said awkwardly. It was not much of an apology, not much of a bridge back to understanding, but it was the best he could do. Apologies had never come easily to Richard Cantling.

"You deserve a thousand times worse," Michelle had screamed back at him. She was such a pretty girl, and she looked so ugly. All that nonsense about anger making people beautiful was a dreadful cliche, and wrong as well; Cantling was glad he'd never used it. "You're supposed to be my father," Michelle said. "You're supposed to love me. You're supposed to be my father, and you *raped* me, you bastard."

Cantling was a light sleeper. He woke in the middle of the night, and sat up in bed shivering, with the feeling that something was wrong.

The bedroom seemed dark and quiet. What was it? A noise? He was very sensitive to noise. Cantling slid out from under the covers and donned his slippers. The fire he'd enjoyed before retiring for the night had burned down to embers, and the room was chilly. He felt for his tartan robe, hanging from the foot of the big antique four-poster, slipped into it, cinched the belt, and moved quietly to the bedroom door. The door creaked a little at times, so he opened it very slowly, very cautiously. He listened.

Someone was downstairs. He could hear them moving around.

Fear coiled in the pit of his stomach. He had no gun up here, nothing like that. He didn't believe in that. Besides, he was supposed to be safe. This wasn't New York. He was supposed to be safe here in quaint old Perrot, Iowa. And now he had a prowler in his house, something he had never faced in all of his years in Manhattan. What the hell was he supposed to do?

The police, he thought. He'd lock the door and call the police. He moved back to the bedside, and reached for the phone.

It rang.

Richard Cantling stared at the telephone. He had two

lines; a business number hooked up to his recording machine, and an unlisted personal number that he gave only to very close friends. Both lights were lit. It was his private number ringing. He hesitated, then scooped up the receiver. "Hello."

"The man himself," the voice said. "Don't get weird on me, Dad. You were going to call the cops, right? Stupid. It's only me. Come down and talk."

Cantling's throat felt raw and constricted. He had never heard that voice before, but he knew it, he knew it. "Who is this?" he demanded.

"Silly question," the caller replied. "You know who it is."

He did. But he said, "Who?"

"Not who. Dunnahoo." Cantling had written that line. "You're not real."

"There were a couple of reviewers who said that too. I seem to remember how it pissed you off, back then."

"You're not *real*," Cantling insisted.

"I'm cut to the goddamned quick," Dunnahoo said. "If I'm not real, it's your fault. So quit getting on my case about it, OK? Just get your ass in gear and hustle it downstairs so we can hang out together." He hung up.

The lights went out on the telephone. Richard Cantling sat down on the edge of his bed, stunned. What was he supposed to make of this? A dream? It was no dream. What could he do?

He went downstairs.

Dunnahoo had built a fire in the living room fireplace, and was settled into Cantling's big leather recliner, drinking Pabst Blue Ribbon from a bottle. He smiled lazily when Cantling appeared under the entry arch. "The man," he said. "Well, don't you look half-dead. Want a beer?"

"Who the hell are you?" Cantling demanded.

"Hey, we been round that block already. Don't bore me. Grab a beer and park your ass by the fire."

"An actor," Cantling said. "You're some kind of god-damned actor. Michelle put you up to this, right?"

Dunnahoo grinned. "An actor? Well, that's fuckin' un-likely, ain't it? Tell me, would you stick something that weird in one of your novels? No way, José. You'd never do it yourself and if somebody else did it, in one of them workshops or a book you were reviewing, you'd rip his fuckin' liver out."

Richard Cantling moved slowly into the room, staring at the young man sprawled in his recliner. It was no actor. It was Dunnahoo, the kid from his book, the face from the portrait. Cantling settled into a high, overstuffed armchair, still staring. "This makes no sense," he said. "This is like something out of Dickens."

Dunnahoo laughed. "This ain't no fucking Christmas Carol, old man, and I sure ain't no ghost of Christmas past."

Cantling frowned; whoever he was, that line was out of character. "That's wrong," he snapped. "Dunnahoo didn't read Dickens. Batman and Robin, yes, but not Dickens."

"I saw the movie, Dad," Dunnahoo said. He raised the beer bottle to his lips and had a swallow.

"Why do you keep calling me Dad?" Cantling said. "That's wrong too. Anachronistic. Dunnahoo was a street kid, not a beatnik."

"You're telling me? Like I don't know or something?" He laughed. "Shit man, what the hell else should I call you?" He ran his fingers through his hair, pushing it back out of his eyes. "After all, I'm still your fuckin' first-born."

She wanted to name it Edward, if it turned out to be a boy. "Don't be ridiculous, Helen," he told her.

"I thought you liked the name Edward," she said.

He didn't know what she was doing in his office any-way. He was working, or trying to work. He'd told her never to come into his office when he was at the typewriter. When they were first married, Helen was very good about that, but there had been no dealing with her since she'd gotten pregnant. "I do like the name Edward," he told her, trying hard to keep his voice calm. He hated being interrupted. "I like the name Edward a lot. I love the god-damned name Edward. That's why I'm using it for my protagonist. Edward, that's his name. Edward Donohue. So we can't use it for the baby because I've already used it. How many times do I have to explain that?"

"But you never *call* him Edward in the book," Helen protested.

Cantling frowned. "Have you been reading the book again? Damn it, Helen, I *told* you I don't want you messing around with the manuscript until it's done."

She refused to be distracted. "You never call him Edward," she repeated.

"No," he said. "That's right. I never call him Edward. I call him Dunnahoo, because he's a street kid, and because that's his street name, and he doesn't like to be called Edward. Only it's still his name, you see. Edward is his name. He doesn't like it, but it's his fucking *name*, and at the end he tells someone that his name is Edward, and that's real damned important. So we can't name the kid Edward, because *he's* named Edward, and I'm tired of this discussion. If it's a boy, we can name it Lawrence, after my grandfather."

"But I don't *want* to name him Lawrence," she whined. "It's so old-fashioned, and then people will call him Larry, and I hate the name Larry. Why can't you call the character in your book Lawrence?"

"Because his name is Edward."

"This is our baby I'm carrying," she said. She put a hand on her swollen stomach, as if Cantling needed a visual reminder.

He was tired of arguing. He was tired of discussing.

He was tired of being interrupted. He leaned back in his chair. "How long have you been carrying the baby?"

Helen looked baffled. "You know. Seven months now. And a week."

Cantling leaned forward and slapped the stack of man-uscript pages piled up beside his typewriter. "Well, I've been carrying *this* baby for three damned years now. This is the fourth fucking draft, and the last one. He was named Edward on the first draft, and on the second draft, and on the third draft, and he's damn well going to be named Edward when the goddamned book comes out. He'd been named Edward for *years* before that night of fond memory when you decided to surprise me by throwing away your diaphragm, and thereby got yourself knocked up."

"It's not fair," she complained. "He's only a character. This is our baby."

"Fair? You want fair? OK. I'll make it fair. Our first-born son will get named Edward. How's that for fair?"

Helen's face softened. She smiled shyly.

He held up a hand before she had a chance to say any-thing. "Of course, I figure I'm only about a month away from finishing this damn thing, if you ever stop interrupt-ing me. You've got a little further to go. But that's as fair as I can make it. You pop before I type THE END and you got the name. Otherwise, my baby here—" he slapped the manuscript again "is—first-born."

"You can't," she started.

Cantling resumed his typing.

"My first-born," Richard Cantling said.

"In the flesh," Dunnahoo said. He raised his beer bot-tle in salute, and said, "To fathers and sons, hey!" He drained it with one long swallow and flipped the bottle across the room end over end. It smashed in the fireplace.

"This is a dream," Cantling said.

Dunnahoo gave him a raspberry. "Look, old man, face it, I'm here." He jumped to his feet. "The prodigal returns," he said, bowing. "So where the fuck is the fatted calf and all that shit? Least you coulda done was order a pizza."

"I'll play the game," Cantling said. "What do you want from me?"

Dunnahoo grinned. "What? Who, me? Who the fuck knows? I never knew what I wanted, you know that. Nobody in the whole fucking book knew what they wanted."

"That was the point," Cantling said.

"Oh, I get it," Dunnahoo said. "I'm not dumb. Old Dicky Cantling's boy is anything but dumb, right?" He wandered off toward the kitchen. "There's more beer in the fridge. Want one?"

"Why not?" Cantling asked. "It's not every day my oldest son comes to visit. Dos Equis with a slice of lime, please."

"Drinking fancy spic beer now, huh? Shit. What ever happened to Piels? You could suck up Piels with the best of them, once upon a time." He vanished through the kitchen door. When he returned he was carrying two bottles of Dos Equis, holding them by the necks with his fingers jammed down into the open mouths. In his other hand he had a raw onion. The bottles clanked together as he carried them. He gave one to Cantling. "Here. I'll suck up a little culture myself."

"You forgot the lime," Cantling said.

"Get your own fuckin' lime," Dunnahoo said. "Whatcha gonna do, cut off my allowance?" He grinned, tossed the onion lightly into the air, caught it, and took a big bite. "Onions," he said. "I owe you for that one, Dad. Bad enough I have to eat raw onions, I mean, shit, but you fixed it so I don't even *like* the fucking things. You even said so in the damned book."

"Of course," Cantling said. "The onion had a dual

function. On one level, you did it just to prove how tough
you were. It was something none of the others hanging
out at Ricci's could manage. It gave you a certain status.
But on a deeper level, when you bit into an onion you
were making a symbolic statement about your appetite for
life, your hunger for it all, the bitter and the sharp parts
as well as the sweet."

Dunnahoo took another bite of onion. "Horseshit," he
said. "I ought to make you eat a fucking onion, see how
you like it."

Cantling sipped at his beer. "I was young. It was my
first book. It seemed like a nice touch at the time."

"Eat it raw," Dunnahoo said. He finished the onion.

Richard Cantling decided this cozy domestic scene had
gone on long enough. "You know, Dunnahoo or whoever
you are," he said in a conversational tone, "you're not what
I expected."

"What did you expect, old man?"

Cantling shrugged. "I made you with my mind instead
of my sperm, so you've got more of me in you than any
child of my flesh could ever have. You're me."

"Hey," said Dunnahoo, "not fucking guilty. I wouldn't
be you on a bet."

"You have no choice. Your story was built from my
own adolescence. First novels are like that. Ricci's was really
Pompeii Pizza in Newark. Your friends were my friends.
And you were me."

"That so?" Dunnahoo replied, grinning.

Richard Cantling nodded.

Dunnahoo laughed. "You should be so fuckin' lucky,
Dad."

"What does that mean?" Cantling snapped.

"You live in a dream world, old man, you know that?
Maybe you like to pretend you were like me, but there
ain't no way it's true. I was the big man at Ricci's. At Pompeii, you were the four-eyes hanging out back by the pin-

ball machine. You had me balling my brains out at sixteen. You never even got bare tit till you were past twenty, off in that college of yours. It took you weeks to come up with the wisecracks you had me tossing off every fuckin' time I turned around. All those wild, crazy things I did in that book, some of them happened to Dutch and some of them happened to Joey and some of them never happened at all, but none of them happened to you, old man, so don't make me laugh."

Cantling flushed a little. "I was writing fiction. Yes, I was a bit of a misfit in my youth, but . . ."

"A nerd," Dunnahoo said. "Don't fancy it up."

"I was not a nerd," Cantling said, stung. *"Hangin' Out* told the truth. It made sense to use a protagonist who was more central to the action than I'd been in real life. Art draws on life but it has to shape it, rearrange it, give it structure, it can't simply replicate it. That's what I did."

"Nah. What *you* did was to suck off Dutch and Joey and the rest. You helped yourself to their lives, man, and took credit for it all yourself. You even got this weird fuckin' idea that I was based on you, and you been thinking that so long you believe it. You're a leech, Dad. You're a god-damned thief."

Richard Cantling was furious. "Get out of here!" he said.

Dunnahoo stood up, stretched. "I'm fuckin' wounded. Throwing your baby boy out into the cold Ioway night, old man? What's wrong? You liked me well enough when I was in your damn book, when you could control every-thing I did and said, right? Don't like it so well now that I'm real, though. That's your problem. You never did like real life half as well as you liked books."

"I like life just fine, thank you," Cantling snapped.

Dunnahoo smiled. Standing there, he suddenly looked washed out, insubstantial. "Yeah?" he said. His voice seemed weaker than it had been.

"Yeah!" Cantling replied.

Now Dunnahoo was fading visibly. All the color had drained from his body, and he looked almost transparent. "Prove it," he said. "Go into your kitchen, old man, and take a great big bite out of your fuckin' raw onion of life." He tossed back his hair, and laughed, and laughed, and laughed, until he was quite gone.

Richard Cantling stood staring at the place where he had been for a long time. Finally, very tired, he climbed upstairs to bed.

He made himself a big breakfast the next morning: orange juice and fresh-brewed coffee, English muffins with lots of butter and blackberry preserves, a cheese omelette, six strips of thick-sliced bacon. The cooking and the eating were supposed to distract him. It didn't work. He thought of Dunnahoo all the while. A dream, yes, some crazy sort of dream. He had no ready explanation for the broken glass in the fireplace or the empty beer bottles in his living room, but finally he found one. He had experienced some sort of insane, drunken, somnambulist episode, Cantling decided. It was the stress of the ongoing quarrel with Michelle, of course, triggered by the portrait she'd sent him. Perhaps he ought to see someone about it, a doctor or a psychologist or someone.

After breakfast, Cantling went straight to his den, determined to confront the problem directly and resolve it. Michelle's mutilated portrait still hung above the fireplace. A festering wound, he thought; it had infected him, and the time had come to get rid of it. Cantling built a fire. When it was going good, he took down the ruined painting, dismantled the metal frame—he was a thrifty man, after all—and burned the torn, disfigured canvas. The oily smoke made him feel clean again.

Next there was the portrait of Dunnahoo to deal with. Cantling turned to consider it. A good piece of work, really.

She had captured the character. He could burn it, but that would be playing Michelle's own destructive game. Art should never be destroyed. He had made his mark on the world by creation, not destruction, and he was too old to change. The portrait of Dunnahoo had been intended as a cruel taunt, but Cantling decided to throw it back in his daughter's teeth, to make a splendid celebration of it. He would hang it, and hang it prominently. He knew just the place for it.

Up at the top of the stairs was a long landing; an ornate wooden bannister overlooked the first floor foyer and entry hall. The landing was fifteen feet long, and the back wall was entirely blank. It would make a splendid portrait gallery, Cantling decided. The painting would be visible to anyone entering the house, and you would pass right by it on the way to any of the second floor rooms. He found a hammer and some nails and hung Dunnahoo in a place of honor. When Michelle came back to make peace, she would see him there, and no doubt leap to the conclusion that Cantling had totally missed the point of her gift. He'd have to remember to thank her effusively for it.

Richard Cantling was feeling much better. Last night's conversation was receding into a bad memory. He put it firmly out of his mind and spent the rest of the day writing letters to his agent and publisher. In the late afternoon, pleasantly weary, he enjoyed a cup of coffee and some butter streusel he'd hidden away in the refrigerator. Then he went out on his daily walk, and spent a good ninety minutes hiking along the river bluffs with a fresh, cold wind in his face.

When he returned, a large square package was waiting on his porch.

He leaned it up against an armchair, and settled into his recliner to study it. It made him uneasy. It had an effect, no doubt of it. He could feel an erection stirring against his leg, pressing uncomfortably against his trousers.

The portrait was . . . well, frankly erotic.

She was in bed, a big old antique four-poster, much like his own. She was naked. She was half-turned in the painting, looking back over her right shoulder; you saw the smooth line of her backbone, the curve of her right breast. It was a large, shapely, and very pretty breast; the aureole was a pale pink and very large, and her nipple was erect. She was clutching a rumpled sheet up to her chin, but it did little to conceal her. Her hair was red-gold, her eyes green, her smile playful. Her smooth young skin had a flush to it, as if she had just risen from a bout of lovemaking. She had a peace symbol tattooed high on the right cheek of her ass. She was obviously very young. Richard Cantling knew just how young: she was eighteen, a child-woman, caught in that precious time between innocence and experience when sex is just a wonderfully exciting new toy. Oh yes, he knew a lot about her. He knew her well.

Cissy.

He hung her portrait next to Dunnahoo.

Dead Flowers was Cantling's title for the book. His editor changed it to *Black Roses*; more evocative, he said, more romantic, more upbeat. Cantling fought the change on artistic grounds, and lost. Afterwards, when the novel made the bestseller lists, he managed to work up the grace to admit that he'd been wrong. He sent Brian a bottle of his favorite wine.

It was his fourth novel, and his last chance. *Hangin' Out* had gotten excellent reviews and had sold decently, but his next two books had been panned by the critics and ignored by the readers. He had to do something different, and he did. *Black Roses* turned out to be highly controversial. Some reviewers loved it, some loathed it. But it sold and sold and sold, and the paperback sale and the film option (they never made the movie) relieved him of financial worries for the first time in his life. They were finally able to afford a down payment on a house, transfer Michelle to a private school and get her those braces; the rest of the money Cantling invested as shrewdly as he was able. He was proud of *Black Roses* and pleased by its success. It made his reputation.

Helen hated the book with a passion.

On the day the novel finally fell off the last of the lists, she couldn't quite conceal her satisfaction. "I knew it wouldn't last forever," she said.

Cantling slapped down the newspaper angrily. "It lasted long enough. What the hell's wrong with you? You didn't like it before, when we were barely scraping by. The kid needs braces, the kid needs a better school, the kid shouldn't have to eat goddamn peanut butter and jelly sandwiches every day. Well, that's all behind us. And you're more pissed off than ever. Give me a little credit. Did you like being married to a failure?"

"I don't like being married to a pornographer," Helen snapped at him.

"Fuck you," Cantling said.

She gave him a nasty smile. "When? You haven't touched me in weeks. You'd rather be fucking your Cissy."

Cantling stared at her. "Are you crazy, or what? She's a character in a book I wrote. That's all."

"Oh, go to hell," Helen said furiously. "You treat me like I'm a goddamned idiot. You think I can't read? You think I don't know? I read your shitty book. I'm not stupid. The wife, Marsha, dull ignorant boring Marsha, cud-chewing mousy Marsha, that cow, that nag, that royal pain-in-the-ass, that's me. You think I can't tell? I can tell, and so can my friends. They're all very sorry for me. You love me as much as Richardson loved Marsha. Cissy's just a character, right, like hell, like bloody hell." She was crying now. "You're in love with her, damn you. She's your own little wet dream. If she walked in the door right now you'd dump me as fast as Richardson dumps good old Marsha. Deny it. Go on, deny it, I dare you!"

Cantling regarded his wife incredulously. "I don't believe you. You're jealous of a character in my book. You're jealous of someone who doesn't exist."

"She exists in your head, and that's the only place that matters with you. Of course your damned book was a big seller. You think it was because of your writing? It was on account of the sex, on account of *her!*"

"Sex is an important part of life," Cantling said defensively. "It's a perfectly legitimate subject for art. You want me to pull down a curtain every time my characters go to bed, is that it? Coming to terms with sexuality, that's what *Black Roses* is all about. Of course it had to be written explicitly. If you weren't such a damned prude you'd realize that."

"I'm not a prude!" Helen screamed at him. "Don't you dare call me one, either." She picked up one of the breakfast plates and threw it at him. Cantling ducked; the plate shattered on the wall behind him. "Just because I don't like your goddamned filthy book doesn't make me a prude."

"The novel has nothing to do with it," Cantling said. He folded his arms against his chest but kept his voice calm. "You're a prude because of the things you do in bed. Or should I say the things you won't do?" He smiled.

Helen's face was red; beet red, Cantling thought, and rejected it, too old, too trite. "Oh, yes, but she'll do them, won't she?" Her voice was pure acid. "Cissy, your cute little Cissy. She'll get a sexy little tattoo on her ass if you ask her to, right? She'll do it outdoors, she'll do it in all kinds of strange places, with people all around. She'll wear kinky underwear, she thinks it's fun. She's always ready and she doesn't have any stretch marks and she has eighteen-year-old tits, and she'll *always* have eighteen-year-old tits, won't she? How the hell do I compete with that, huh? How? *HOW?*"

Richard Cantling's own anger was a cold, controlled, sarcastic thing. He stood up in the face of her fury and smiled sweetly. "Read the book," he said. "Take notes."

He woke suddenly, in darkness, to the light touch of skin against his foot.

Cissy was perched on top of the footboard, a red satin sheet wrapped around her, a long slim leg exploring under his blankets. She was playing footsie with him, and smiling mischievously. "Hi, Daddy," she said.

Cantling had been afraid of this. It had been in his mind all evening. Sleep had not come easily. He pulled his foot away and struggled to a sitting position.

Cissy pouted. "Don't you want to play?" she asked.

"I," he said, "don't believe this. This can't be real."

"It can still be fun," she said.

"What the hell is Michelle doing to me? How can this be happening?"

She shrugged. The sheet slipped a little; one perfect pink-tipped eighteen-year-old breast peeked out.

"You still have eighteen-year-old tits," Cantling said numbly. "You'll always have eighteen-year-old tits."

Cissy laughed. "Sure. You can borrow them, if you like, Daddy. I'll bet you can think of something interesting to do with them."

"Stop calling me Daddy," Cantling said.

"Oh, but you *are* my Daddy," Cissy said in her little-girl voice.

"Stop that!" Cantling said.

"Why? You want to, Daddy, you want to play with your little girl, don't you?" She winked. "Vice is nice but incest is best. The families that play together stay together." She looked around. "I like four-posters. You want to tie me up, Daddy? I'd like that."

"No," Cantling said. He pushed back the covers, got out of bed, found his slippers and robe. His erection throbbed against his leg. He had to get away, he had to put some distance between him and Cissy, otherwise . . . he didn't want to think about otherwise. He busied himself making a fire.

"I like that," Cissy said when he got it going. "Fires are so romantic."

Cantling turned around to face her again. "Why you?" he asked, trying to stay calm. "Richardson was the protagonist of *Black Roses*, not you. And why skip to my fourth book? Why not somebody from *Family Tree* or *Rain?*"

"Those gobblers?" Cissy said. "Nobody real there. You didn't really want Richardson, did you? I'm a lot more fun." She stood up and let go of the satin sheet. It puddled about her ankles, the flames reflected off its shiny folds. Her body was soft and sweet and young. She kicked free of the sheet and padded toward him.

"Cut it out, Cissy," Cantling barked.

"I won't bite," Cissy said. She giggled. "Unless you want me to. Maybe I should tie *you* up, huh?" She put her arms around him, gave him a hug, turned up her face for a kiss.

"Let go of me," he said, weakly. Her arms felt good. She felt good as she pressed up against him. It had been a long time since Richard Cantling had held a woman in his arms; he didn't like to think about how long. And he had never had a woman like Cissy, never, never. But he was frightened. "I can't do this," he said. "I can't. I don't want to."

Cissy reached through the folds of his robe, shoved her hand inside his briefs, squeezed him gently. "Liar," she said. "You want me. You've always wanted me. I'll bet you used to stop and jack off when you were writing the sex scenes."

"No," Cantling said. "Never."

"Never?" She pouted. Her hand moved up and down. "Well, I bet you wanted to. I bet you got hard, anyway. I bet you got hard every time you described me."

"I," he said. The denial would not come. "Cissy, please."

"Please," she murmured. Her hand was busy. "Yes, please." She tugged at his briefs and they fluttered to the floor. "Please," she said. She untied his robe and helped him out of it. "Please." Her hand moved along his side, played with his nipples; she stepped closer, and her breasts pressed lightly against his chest. "Please," she said, and she looked up at him. Her tongue moved between her lips.

Richard Cantling groaned and took her in his trembling arms.

She was like no woman he had ever had. Her touch was fire and satin, electric, and her secret places were sweet as honey.

In the morning she was gone.

Cantling woke late, too exhausted to make himself breakfast. Instead he dressed and walked into town, to a small cafe in a quaint hundred-year-old brick building at the foot of the bluffs. He tried to sort things out over coffee and blueberry pancakes.

None of it made any sense. It could not be happening, but it was; denial accomplished nothing. Cantling forked down a mouthful of homemade blueberry pancake, but the only taste in his mouth was fear. He was afraid for his sanity. He was afraid because he did not understand, did not want to understand. And there was another, deeper, more basic fear.

He was afraid of what would come next. Richard Cantling had published nine novels.

He thought of Michelle. He could phone her, beg her to call it off before he went mad. She was his daughter, his flesh and blood, surely she would listen to him. She loved him. Of course she did. And he loved her too, no matter what she might think. Cantling knew his faults. He had examined himself countless times, under various guises, in the pages of his books. He was impossibly stubborn, willful, opinionated. He could be rigid and unbending. He could be cold. Still, he thought of himself as a decent man. Michelle . . . she had inherited some of his perversity, she was furious at him, hate was so very close to love, but surely she did not mean to do him serious harm.

Yes, he could phone Michelle, ask her to stop. Would she? If he begged her forgiveness, perhaps. That day, that terrible day, she'd told him that she would never forgive him, never, but she couldn't have meant that. She was his only child. The only child of his flesh, at any rate.

Cantling pushed away his empty plate and sat back. His mouth was set in a hard rigid line. Beg for mercy? He did not like that. What had he done, after all? Why couldn't they understand? Helen had never understood and Michelle was as blind as her mother. A writer must live for his work. What had he done that was so terrible? What had he done that required forgiveness? Michelle ought to be the one phoning him.

The hell with it, Cantling thought. He refused to be cowed. He was right; she was wrong. Let Michelle call him if she wanted a rapprochement. She was not going to terrify him into submission. What was he so afraid of, anyway? Let her send her portraits, all the portraits she wanted to paint. He'd hang them up on his walls, display the paintings proudly (they were really an *hommage* to his work, after all), and if the damned things came alive at night and prowled through his house, so be it. He'd enjoy their visits. Cantling smiled. He'd certainly enjoyed Cissy, no doubt of that. Part of him hoped she'd come back. And even

Dunnahoo, well, he was an insolent kid, but there was no real harm in him, he just liked to mouth off.

Why, now that he stopped to consider it, Cantling found that the possibilities had a certain intoxicating charm. He was uniquely privileged. Scott Fitzgerald never attended one of Gatsby's fabulous parties, Conan Doyle could never really sit down with Holmes and Watson, Nabokov never actually tumbled Lolita. What would they have said to the idea?

The more he considered things, the more cheerful he became. Michelle was trying to rebuke him, to frighten him, but she was really giving him a delicious experience. He could play chess with Sergei Tederenko, the cynical emigré hustler from *En Passant*. He could argue politics with Frank Corwin, the union organizer from his Depression novel, *Times Are Hard*. He might flirt with beautiful Beth McKenzie, go dancing with crazy old Miss Aggie, seduce the Danzinger twins and fulfill the one sexual fantasy that Cissy had left untouched, yes, certainly, what the hell had he been afraid of? They were his own creations, his characters, his friends and family.

Of course, there was the new book to consider. Cantling frowned. That was a disturbing thought. But Michelle was his daughter, she loved him, surely she wouldn't go that far. No, of course not. He put the idea firmly aside and picked up his check.

He expected it. He was almost looking forward to it. And when he returned from his evening constitutional, his cheeks red from the wind, his heart beating just a little faster in anticipation, it was there waiting for him, the familiar rectangle wrapped in plain brown paper. Richard Cantling carried it inside carefully. He made himself a cup of coffee before he unwrapped it, deliberately prolonging the suspense to savor the moment, delighting in the thought of how deftly he'd turned Michelle's cruel little plan on its head.

He drank his coffee, poured a refill, drank that. The package stood a few feet away. Cantling played a little game with himself, trying to guess whose portrait might be within. Cissy had said something about none of the characters from *Family Tree* or *Rain* being real enough. Cantling mentally reviewed his life's work, trying to decide which characters seemed most real. It was a pleasant speculation, but he could reach no firm conclusions. Finally he shoved his coffee cup aside and moved to undo the wrappings. And there it was.

Barry Leighton.

Again, the painting itself was superb. Leighton was seated in a newspaper city room, his elbow resting on the gray metal case of an old manual typewriter. He wore a rumpled brown suit and his white shirt was open at the collar and plastered to his body by perspiration. His nose had been broken more than once, and was spread all across his wide, homely, somehow comfortable face. His eyes were sleepy. Leighton was overweight and jowly and rapidly losing his hair. He'd given up smoking but not cigarettes; an unlit Camel dangled from one corner of his mouth. "As long as you don't light the damned things, you're safe," he'd said more than once in Cantling's novel *ByeLine*.

The book hadn't done very well. It was a depressing book, all about the last week of a grand old newspaper that had fallen on bad times. It was more than that, though. Cantling was interested in people, not newspapers; he had used the failing paper as a metaphor for failing lives. His editor had wanted to work in some kind of strong, sensational subplot, have Leighton and the others on the trail of some huge story that offered the promise of redemption, but Cantling had rejected that idea. He wanted to tell a story about small people being ground down inexorably by time and age, about the inevitability of loneliness and defeat. He produced a novel as gray and brittle as newsprint. He was very proud of it.

No one read it.

Cantling lifted the portrait and carried it upstairs, to hang beside those of Dunnahoo and Cissy. Tonight should be interesting, he thought. Barry Leighton was no kid, like the others; he was a man of Cantling's own years. Very intelligent, mature. There was a bitterness in Leighton, Cantling knew very well; a disappointment that life had, after all, yielded so little, that all his bylines and big stories were forgotten the day after they ran. But the reporter kept his sense of humor through all of it, kept off the demons with nothing but a mordant wit and an unlit Camel. Cantling admired him, would enjoy talking to him. Tonight, he decided, he wouldn't bother going to bed. He'd make a big pot of strong black coffee, lay in some Seagram's, and wait.

It was past midnight and Cantling was rereading the leatherbound copy of *ByeLine* when he heard ice cubes clinking together in the kitchen. "Help yourself, Barry," he called out.

Leighton came through the swinging door, tumbler in hand. "I did," he said. He looked at Cantling through heavily lidded eyes, and gave a little snort. "You look old enough to be my father," he said. "I didn't think anybody could look *that* old."

Cantling closed the book and set it aside. "Sit down," he said. "As I recall, your feet hurt."

"My feet always hurt," Leighton said. He settled himself into an armchair and swallowed a mouthful of whisky. "Ah," he said, "that's better."

Cantling tapped the novel with a fingertip. "My eighth book," he said. "Michelle skipped right over three novels. A pity. I would have liked to meet some of those people."

"Maybe she wants to get to the point," Leighton suggested.

"And what is the point?"

Leighton shrugged. "Damned if I know. I'm only a newspaperman. Five Ws and an H. You're the novelist. You tell me the point."

"My ninth novel," Cantling suggested. "The new one."

"The last one?" said Leighton.

"Of course not. Only the most recent. I'm working on something new right now."

Leighton smiled. "That's not what my sources tell me."

"Oh? What do your sources say?"

"That you're an old man waiting to die," Leighton said. "And that you're going to die alone."

"I'm fifty-two," Cantling said crisply. "Hardly old."

"When your birthday cake has got more candles than you can blow out, you're old," said Leighton dryly. "Helen was younger than you, and she died five years ago. It's in the mind, Cantling. I've seen young octogenarians and old adolescents. And you, you had liver spots on your brain before you had hair on your balls."

"That's unfair," Cantling protested.

Leighton drank his Seagram's. "Fair?" he said. "You're too old to believe in fair, Cantling. Young people live life. Old people sit and watch it. You were born old. You're a watcher, not a liver." He frowned. "Not a liver, jeez, what a figure of speech. Better a liver than a gall bladder, I guess. You were never a gall bladder either. You've been full of piss for years, but you don't have any gall at all. Maybe you're a kidney."

"You're reaching, Barry," Cantling said. "I'm a writer. I've always been a writer. That's my life. Writers observe life, they report on life. It's in the job description. You ought to know."

"I do know," Leighton said. "I'm a reporter, remember? I've spent a lot of long gray years writing up other people's stories. I've got no story of my own. You know that, Cantling. Look what you did to me in *ByeLine*. The *Courier* croaks and I decide to write my memoirs and what happens?"

Cantling remembered. "You blocked. You rewrote your old stories, twenty-year-old stories, thirty-year-old stories. You had that incredible memory. You could recall all the people you'd ever reported on, the dates, the details, the quotes. You could recite the first story you'd had bylined word for word, but you couldn't remember the name of the first girl you'd been to bed with, couldn't remember your ex-wife's phone number, you couldn't . . . you couldn't . . ." His voice failed.

"I couldn't remember my daughter's birthday," Leighton said. "Where do you get those crazy ideas, Cantling?"

Cantling was silent.

"From life, maybe?" Leighton said gently. "I was a good reporter. That was about all you could say about me. You, well, maybe you're a good novelist. That's for the critics to judge, and I'm just a sweaty newspaperman whose feet hurt. But even if you are a good novelist, even if you're one of the great ones, you were a lousy husband, and a miserable father."

"No," Cantling said. It was a weak protest.

Leighton swirled his tumbler; the ice cubes clinked and clattered. "When did Helen leave you?" he asked.

"I don't . . . ten years ago, something like that. I was in the middle of the final draft of *En Passant*."

"When was the divorce final?"

"Oh, a year later. We tried a reconciliation, but it didn't take. Michelle was in school, I remember. I was writing *Times Are Hard*."

"You remember her third grade play?"

"Was that the one I missed?"

"The one you missed? You sound like Nixon saying,

'Was that the time I lied?' That was the one Michelle had the lead in, Cantling."

"I couldn't help that," Cantling said. "I wanted to come. They were giving me an award. You don't skip the National Literary League dinner. You can't."

"Of course not," said Leighton. "When was it that Helen died?"

"I was writing *ByeLine*," Cantling said.

"Interesting system of dating you've got there. You ought to put out a calendar." He swallowed some whisky.

"All right," Cantling said. "I'm not going to deny that my work is important to me. Maybe too important, I don't know. Yes, the writing has been the biggest part of my life. But I'm a decent man, Leighton, and I've always done my best. It hasn't all been like you're implying. Helen and I had good years. We loved each other once. And Michelle . . . I loved Michelle. When she was a little girl, I used to write stories just for her. Funny animals, space pirates, silly poems. I'd write them up in my spare time and read them to her at bedtime. They were something I did just for Michelle, for love."

"Yeah," Leighton said cynically. "You never even thought about getting them published."

Cantling grimaced. "That . . . you're implying . . . that's a distortion. Michelle loved the stories so much, I thought maybe other kids might like them too. It was just an idea. I never did anything about it."

"Never?"

Cantling hesitated. "Look, Bert was my friend as well as my agent. He had a little girl of his own. I showed him the stories once. Once!"

"I can't be pregnant," Leighton said. "I only let him fuck me once. Once!"

"He didn't even like them," Cantling said.

"Pity," replied Leighton.

"You're laying this on me with a trowel, and I'm not guilty. No, I wasn't father of the year, but I wasn't an ogre either. I changed her diaper plenty of times. Before *Black Roses*, Helen had to work, and I took care of the baby every day, from nine to five."

"You hated it when she cried and you had to leave your typewriter."

"Yes," Cantling said. "Yes, I hated being interrupted, I've always hated being interrupted, I don't care if it was Helen or Michelle or my mother or my roommate in college, when I'm writing I don't like to be interrupted. Is that a fucking capital crime? Does that make me inhuman? When she cried, I went to her. I didn't like it, I hated it, I resented it, but I *went to her*."

"When you heard her," said Leighton. "When you weren't in bed with Cissy, dancing with Miss Aggie, beating up scabs with Frank Corwin, when your head wasn't full of their voices, yeah, sometimes you heard, and when you heard you went. Congratulations, Cantling."

"I taught her to read," Cantling said. "I read her *Treasure Island* and *Wind in the Willows* and *The Hobbit* and *Tom Sawyer*, all kinds of things."

"All books you wanted to reread anyway," said Leighton. "Helen did the real teaching, with Dick and Jane."

"*I hate Dick and Jane!*" Cantling shouted.

"So?"

"You don't know what you're talking about," Richard Cantling said. "You weren't there. Michelle was there. She loved me, she still loves me. Whenever she got hurt, scraped her knee or got her nose bloodied, whatever it was, it was me she'd run to, never Helen. She'd come crying to me, and I'd hug her and dry her tears and I'd tell her . . . I used to tell her . . ." But he couldn't go on. He was close to tears himself; he could feel them hiding the corners of his eyes.

"I know what you used to tell her," said Barry Leighton in a sad, gentle voice.

"She remembered it," Cantling said. "She remembered it all those years. Helen got custody, they moved away, I didn't see her much, but Michelle always remembered, and when she was all grown up, after Helen was gone and Michelle was on her own, there was this time she got hurt, and I . . . I . . . ."

"Yes," said Leighton. "I know."

The police were the ones that phoned him. Detective Joyce Brennan, that was her name, he would never forget that name. "Mister Cantling?" she said.

"Yes?"

"Mister Richard Cantling?"

"Yes," he said. "Richard Cantling the writer." He had gotten strange calls before. "What can I do for you?"

She identified herself. "You'll have to come down to the hospital," she said to him. "It's your daughter, Mister Cantling. I'm afraid she's been assaulted."

He hated evasion, hated euphemism. Cantling's characters never passed away, they died; they never broke wind, they farted. And Richard Cantling's daughter . . . "Assaulted?" he said. "Do you mean she's been assaulted or do you mean she's been raped?"

There was a silence on the other end of the line. "Raped," she said at last. "She's been raped, Mister Cantling."

"I'll be right down," he said.

She had in fact been raped repeatedly and brutally. Michelle had been as stubborn as Helen, as stubborn as Cantling himself. She wouldn't take his money, wouldn't take his advice, wouldn't take the help he offered her through his contacts in publishing. She was going to make it on her own. She waitressed in a coffeehouse in the Village, and lived in a large, drafty, and run-down warehouse loft down by the docks. It was a terrible neighborhood, a dangerous neighborhood, and Cantling had told her so a hundred times, but Michelle would not listen. She would not even let him pay to install good locks and a security system. It had been very bad. The man had broken in before dawn on a Friday morning. Michelle was alone. He had ripped the phone from the wall and held her prisoner there through Monday night. Finally one of the busboys from the coffeehouse had gotten worried and come by, and the rapist had left by the fire escape.

When they let him see her, her face was a huge purple bruise. She had burn marks all over her, where the man had used his cigarette, and three of her ribs were broken. She was far beyond hysteria. She screamed when they tried to touch her; doctors, nurses, it didn't matter, she screamed as soon as they got near. But she let Cantling sit on the edge of her bed, and take her in his arms, and hold her. She cried for hours, cried until there were no more tears in her. Once she called him "Daddy," in a choked sob. It was the only word she spoke; she seemed to have lost the capacity for speech. Finally they tranquilized her to get her to sleep.

Michelle was in the hospital for two weeks, in a deep state of shock. Her hysteria waned day by day, and she finally became docile, so they were able to fluff her pillows and lead her to the bathroom. But she still would not, or could not, speak. The psychologist told Cantling that she might never speak again. "I don't accept that," he said. He arranged Michelle's discharge. Simultaneously he decided to get them both out of this filthy hellhole of a city. She had always loved big old spooky houses, he remembered, and she used to love the water, the sea, the river, the lake. Cantling consulted realtors, considered a big place on the coast of Maine, and finally settled on an old steamboat gothic mansion high on the bluffs of Perrot, Iowa. He supervised every detail of the move.

Little by little, recovery began.

She was like a small child again, curious, restless, full of sudden energy. She did not talk, but she explored everything, went everywhere. In spring she spent hours up on the widow's walk, watching the big towboats go by on the Mississippi far below. Every evening they would walk together on the bluffs, and she would hold his hand. One day she turned and kissed him suddenly, impulsively, on his cheek. "I love you, Daddy," she said, and she ran away from him, and as Cantling watched her run, he saw a lovely, wounded woman in her mid-twenties, and saw too the gangling, coltish tomboy she had been.

The dam was broken after that day. Michelle began to talk again. Short, childlike sentences at first, full of childish fears and childish naivete. But she matured rapidly, and in no time at all she was talking politics with him, talking books, talking art. They had many a fine conversation on their evening walks. She never talked about the rape, though; never once, not so much as a word.

In six months she was cooking, writing letters to friends back in New York, helping with the household chores, doing lovely things in the garden. In eight months she had started to paint again. That was very good for her; now she seemed to blossom daily, to grow more and more radiant. Richard Cantling didn't really understand the abstractions his daughter liked to paint, he preferred representational art, and best of all he loved the self-portrait she had done for him when she was still an art major in college. But he could feel the pain in these new canvases of hers, he could sense that she was engaged in an exorcism of sorts, trying to squeeze the pus from some wound deep inside, and he approved. His writing had been a balm for his own wounds more than once. He envied her now, in a way. Richard Cantling had not written a word for more than three years. The crashing commercial failure of *ByeLine*, his best novel, had left him blocked and impotent. He'd thought perhaps the change of scene might restore him as well as Michelle, but that had been a vain hope. At least one of them was busy.

Finally, late one night after Cantling had gone to bed, his door opened and Michelle came quietly into his bedroom and sat on the edge of his bed. She was barefoot, dressed in a flannel nightgown covered with tiny pink flowers. "Daddy," she said, in a slurred voice.

Cantling had woken when the door opened. He sat up and smiled for her. "Hi," he said. "You've been drinking."

Michelle nodded. "I'm going back," she said. "Needed some courage, so's I could tell you."

"Going back?" Cantling said. "You don't mean to New York? You can't be serious!"

"I got to," she said. "Don't be mad. I'm better now."

"Stay here. Stay with me. New York is uninhabitable, Michelle."

"I don't want to go back. It scares me. But I got to. My friends are there. My work is there. My life is back there, Daddy. My friend Jimmy, you remember Jimmy, he's art director for this little paperback house, he can get me some cover assignments, he says. He wrote. I won't have to wait tables anymore."

"I don't believe I'm hearing this," Richard Cantling said. "How can you go back to that damned city after what happened to you there?"

"That's why I have to go back," Michelle insisted. "That guy, what he did . . . what he did to me . . ." Her voice caught in her throat. She drew in her breath, got hold of herself. "If I don't go back, it's like he ran me out of town, took my whole life away from me, my friends, my art, everything. I can't let him get away with that, can't let him scare me off. I got to go back and take up what's mine, prove that I'm not afraid.''

Richard Cantling looked at his daughter helplessly. He reached out, gently touched her long, soft hair. She had finally said something that made sense in his terms. He would do the same thing, he knew. "I understand," he said. "It's going to be lonely here without you, but I understand, I do.''

"I'm scared," Michelle said. "I bought plane tickets. For tomorrow.''

"So soon?''

"I want to do it quickly, before I lose my nerve," she said. "I don't think I've ever been this scared. Not even . . . not even when it was happening. Funny, huh?''

"No," said Cantling. "It makes sense.''

"Daddy, hold me," Michelle said. She pressed herself into his arms. He hugged her and felt her body tremble.

"You're shaking," he said.

She wouldn't let go of him. "You remember, when I was real little, I used to have those nightmares, and I'd come bawling into your bedroom in the middle of the night and crawl into bed between you and Mommy.''

Cantling smiled. "I remember," he said.

"I want to stay here tonight," Michelle said, hugging him even more tightly. "Tomorrow I'll be back there, alone. I don't want to be alone tonight. Can I, Daddy?''

Cantling disengaged gently, looked her in the eyes. "Are you sure?''

She nodded; a tiny, quick, shy nod. A child's nod.

He threw back the covers and she crept in next to him. "Don't go away," she said. "Don't even go to the bathroom, okay? Just stay right here with me.''

"I'm here," he said. He put his arms around her, and Michelle curled up under the covers with her head on his shoulder. They lay together that way for a long time. He could feel her heart beating inside her chest. It was a soothing sound; soon Cantling began to drift back to sleep.

"Daddy?" she whispered against his chest.

He opened his eyes. "Michelle?"

"Daddy, I have to get rid of it. It's inside me and it's poison. I don't want to take it back with me. I have to get rid of it."

Cantling stroked her hair, long slow steady motions, saying nothing.

"When I was little, you remember, whenever I fell down or got in a fight, I'd come running to you, all teary, and show you my booboo. That's what I used to call it when I got hurt, remember, I'd say I had a booboo."

"I remember," Cantling said.

"And you, you'd always hug me and you'd say, 'Show me where it hurts,' and I would and you'd kiss it and make it better, you remember that? Show me where it hurts?"

Cantling nodded. "Yes," he said softly.

Michelle was crying quietly. He could feel the wetness soaking through the top of his pajamas. "I can't take it back with me, Daddy. I want to show you where it hurts. Please. Please."

He kissed the top of her head. "Go on."

She started at the beginning, in a halting whisper.

When dawn light broke through the bedroom windows, she was still talking. They never slept. She cried a lot, screamed once or twice, shivered frequently despite the weight of the blankets; Richard Cantling never let go of her, not once, not for a single moment. She showed him where it hurt.

Barry Leighton sighed. "It was a far, far better thing you did than you had ever done," he said. "Now if you'd only gone off to that far, far better rest right then and there, that very moment, everything would have been fine." He shook his head. "You never did know when to write Thirty, Cantling."

"Why?" Cantling demanded. "You're a good man, Leighton, tell me. Why is this happening. Why?"

The reporter shrugged. He was beginning to fade now. "That was the W that always gave me the most trouble," he said wearily. "Pick the story, and let me loose, and I could tell you the who and the what and the when and the where and even the how. But the *why* . . . ah, Cantling, you're the novelist, the whys are your province, not mine. The only Y that I ever really got on speaking terms with was the one goes with MCA."

Like the Cheshire cat, his smile lingered long after the rest of him was gone. Richard Cantling sat staring at the empty chair, at the abandoned tumbler, watching the whisky-soaked ice cubes melt slowly.

He did not remember falling asleep. He spent the night in the chair, and woke stiff and achy and cold. His dreams had been dark and shapeless and full of fear. He had slept well into the afternoon; half the day was gone. He made himself a tasteless breakfast in a kind of fog. He seemed distant from his own body, and every motion was slow and clumsy. When the coffee was ready, he poured a cup, picked it up, dropped it. The mug broke into a dozen pieces. Cantling stared down at it stupidly, watching rivulets of hot brown liquid run between the tiles. He did not have the energy to clean it up. He got a fresh mug, poured more coffee, managed to get down a few swallows.

The bacon was too salty; the eggs were runny, disgusting. Cantling pushed the meal away half-eaten, and drank more of the black, bitter coffee. He felt hung-over, but he knew that booze was not the problem.

Today, he thought. It will end today, one way or the other. She will not go back. *ByeLine* was his eighth novel, the next to last. Today the final portrait would arrive. A character from his ninth novel, his last novel. And then it would be over.

Or maybe just beginning.

How much did Michelle hate him? How badly had he wronged her? Cantling's hand shook; coffee slopped over the top of the mug, burning his fingers. He winced, cried out. Pain was so inarticulate. Burning. He thought of smoldering cigarettes, their tips like small red eyes. His stomach heaved. Cantling lurched to his feet, rushed to the bathroom. He got there just in time, gave his breakfast to the bowl. Afterwards he was too weak to move. He lay slumped against the cold white porcelain, his head swimming. He imagined somebody coming up behind him, taking him by the hair, forcing his face down into the water, flushing, flushing, laughing all the while, saying dirty, dirty, I'll get you clean, you're so dirty, flushing, flushing so the toilet ran and ran, holding his face down so the water and the vomit filled his mouth, his nostrils, until he could hardly breathe, until the world was almost black, until it was almost over, and then up again, laughing while he sucked in air, and then pushing him down again, flushing again, and again and again and again. But it was only his imagination. There was no one there. No one. Cantling was alone in the bathroom.

He forced himself to stand. In the mirror his face was gray and ancient, his hair filthy and unkempt. Behind him, leering over his shoulder, was another face. A man's face, pale and drawn, with black hair parted in the middle and slicked back. Behind a pair of small round glasses were eyes the color of dirty ice, eyes that moved constantly, frenetically, wild animals caught in a trap. They would chew off their own limbs to be free, those eyes. Cantling blinked and the face was gone. He turned on the cold tap, plunged his cupped hands under the stream, splashed water on his face. He could feel the stubble of his beard. He needed to shave. But there wasn't time, it wasn't important, he had to . . . he had to . . .

He had to do something. Get out of there. Get away,

get to someplace safe, somewhere his children couldn't find him.

But there was nowhere safe, he knew.

He had to reach Michelle, talk to her, explain, plead. She loved him. She *would* forgive him, she had to. She would call it off, she would tell him what to do.

Frantic, Cantling rushed back to the living room, snatched up the phone. He couldn't remember Michelle's number. He searched around, found his address book, flipped through it wildly. There, there; he punched in the numbers.

The phone rang four times. Then someone picked it up.

"Michelle—" he started.

"Hi," she said. "This is Michelle Cantling, but I'm not in right now. If you'll leave your name and number when you hear the tone, I'll get back to you, unless you're selling something."

The beep sounded. "Michelle, are you there?" Cantling said. "I know you hide behind the machine sometimes, when you don't want to talk. It's me. Please pick up. Please."

Nothing.

"Call me back, then," he said. He wanted to get it all in; his words tumbled over each other in their haste to get out. "I, you, you can't do it, please, let me explain, I never meant, I never meant, please . . ." There was the beep again, and then a dial tone. Cantling stared at the phone, hung up slowly. She would call him back. She had to, she was his daughter, they loved each other, she had to give him the chance to explain.

Of course, he had tried to explain before.

His doorbell was the old-fashioned kind, a brass key that projected out of the door. You had to turn it by hand, and when you did it produced a loud, impatient metallic rasp.

Someone was turning it furiously, turning it and turning it and turning it. Cantling rushed to the door, utterly baffled. He had never made friends easily, and it was even harder now that he had become so set in his ways. He had no real friends in Perrot, a few acquaintances perhaps, no one who would come calling so unexpectedly, and twist the bell with such energetic determination.

He undid his chain and flung the door open, wrenching the bell key out of Michelle's fingers.

She was dressed in a belted raincoat, a knitted ski cap, a matching scarf. The scarf and a few loose strands of hair were caught in the wind, moving restlessly. She was wearing high, fashionable boots and carrying a big leather shoulder bag. She looked good. It had been almost a year since Cantling had seen her, on his last Christmas visit to New York. It had been two years since she'd moved back east.

"Michelle," Cantling said. "I didn't . . . this is quite a surprise. All the way from New York and you didn't even tell me you were coming?"

"No," she snapped. There was something wrong with her voice, her eyes. "I didn't want to give you any warning, you bastard. You didn't give me any warning."

"You're upset," Cantling said. "Come in, let's talk."

"I'll come in all right." She pushed past him, kicked the door shut behind her with so much force that the buzzer sounded again. Out of the wind, her face got even harder. "You want to know why I came? I am going to tell you what I think of you. Then I'm going to turn around and leave, I'm going to walk right out of this house and out of your fucking life, just like Mom did. She was the smart one, not me. I was dumb enough to think you loved me, crazy enough to think you cared."

"Michelle, don't," Cantling said. "You don't understand. I do love you. You're my little girl, you—"

"Don't you *dare!*" she screamed at him. She reached

into her shoulder bag. "You call this *love*, you rotten bastard!" She pulled it out and flung it at him.

Cantling was not as quick as he'd been. He tried to duck, but it caught him on the side of his neck, and it hurt. Michelle had thrown it hard, and it was a big, thick, heavy hardcover, not some flimsy paperback. The pages fluttered as it tumbled to the carpet; Cantling stared down at his own photograph on the back of the dust-wrapper. "You're just like your mother," he said, rubbing his neck where the book had hit. "She always threw things too. Only you aim better." He smiled weakly.

"I'm not interested in your jokes," Michelle said. "I'll never forgive you. Never. Never ever. All I want to know is how you could do this to me, that's all. You tell me. You tell me now."

"I," Cantling said. He held his hands out helplessly. "Look, I . . . you're upset now, why don't we have some coffee or something, and talk about it when you calm down a little. I don't want a big fight."

"I don't give a fuck what you want," Michelle screamed. "I want to talk about it right now!" She kicked the fallen book.

Richard Cantling felt his own anger building. It wasn't right for her to yell at him like that, he didn't deserve this attack, he hadn't done anything. He tried not to say anything for fear of saying the wrong thing and escalating the situation. He knelt and picked up his book. Without thinking, he brushed it off, turned it over almost tenderly. The title glared up at him; stark, twisted red letters against a black background, the distorted face of a pretty young woman, mouth open in a scream. *Show Me Where It Hurts.*

"I was afraid you'd take it the wrong way," Cantling said.

"The *wrong way!*" Michelle said. A look of incredulity passed across her face. "Did you think I'd *like* it?"

"I, I wasn't sure," said Cantling. "I hoped . . . I mean,

I was uncertain of your reaction, and so I thought it would be better not to mention what I was working on, until, well . . .''

"Until the fucking thing was in the bookstore windows," Michelle finished for him.

Cantling flipped past the title page. "Look," he said, holding it out, "I dedicated it to you." He showed her:

To Michelle, who knew the pain.

Michelle swung at it, knocked it out of Cantling's hands. "You bastard," she said. "You think that makes it better? You think your stinking dedication excuses what you did? Nothing excuses it. I'll never forgive you."

Cantling edged back a step, retreating in the face of her fury. "I didn't do anything," he said stubbornly. "I wrote a book. A novel. Is that a crime?"

"You're my *father*," she shrieked. "You knew . . . you knew, you bastard, you knew I couldn't bear to talk about it, to talk about what happened. Not to my lovers or my friends or even my therapist. I can't, I just *can't*, I can't even think about it. You knew. I told you, I told only you, because you were my daddy and I trusted you and I had to get it out, and I told you, it was private, it was just between us, you knew, but what did you do? You wrote it all up in a goddamned book and *published* it for millions of people to read! Damn you, damn you. Were you planning to do that all along, you sonofabitch? Were you? That night in bed, were you memorizing every word?"

"I," said Cantling. "No, I didn't memorize anything, I just, well, I just remembered it. You're taking it all wrong, Michelle. The book's not about what happened to you. Yes, it's inspired by that, that was the starting point, but it's fiction, I changed things, it's just a novel."

"Oh yeah, Daddy, you changed things all right. Instead of Michelle Cantling it's all about Nicole Mitchell, and she's a fashion designer instead of an artist, and she's also kind of stupid, isn't she? Was that a change or is that what you think, that I was stupid to live there, stupid to let him in like that? It's all fiction, yeah. It's just a coincidence that it's about this girl that gets held prisoner and raped and tortured and terrorized and raped some more, and that you've got a daughter who was held prisoner and raped and tortured and terrorized and raped some more, right, just a fucking coincidence!"

"You don't understand," Cantling said helplessly.

"No, *you* don't understand. You don't understand what it's like. This is your biggest book in years, right? Number-one best-seller, you've never been number one before, haven't even been on the lists since *Times Are Hard*, or was it *Black Roses*? And why not, why not number one, this isn't no boring story about a has-been newspaper, this is *rape*, hey, what could be hotter? Lots of sex and violence, torture and fucking and terror, and doncha know, *it really happened*, yeah." Her mouth twisted and trembled. "It was the worst thing that ever happened to me. It was all the nightmares that have ever been. I still wake up screaming sometimes, but I was getting better, it was behind me. And now it's there in every bookstore window, and all my friends know, everybody knows, strangers come up to me at parties and tell me how sorry they are." She choked back a sob; she was halfway between anger and tears. "And I pick up your book, your fucking no-good book, and there it is again, in black and white, all written down. You're such a fucking *good* writer, Daddy, you make it all so real. A book you can't put down. Well, I put it down but it didn't help, it's all there, now it will always be there, won't it? Every day somebody in the world will pick up your book and read it and I'll get raped again. That's what you did. You finished the job for him, Daddy. You violated me, took me without my consent, just like he did. You raped me. You're my own father and you *raped* me!"

"You're not being fair," Cantling said. "I never meant to hurt you. The book . . . Nicole is strong and smart. It's the man who's the monster. He uses all those different names because fear has a thousand names, but only one face, you see. He's not just a man, he's the darkness made flesh, the mindless violence that waits out there for all of us, the gods that play with us like flies, he's a symbol of all—"

"He's the man who raped me! He's not a symbol!"

She screamed it so loudly that Richard Cantling had to retreat in the face of her fury. "No," he said. "He's just a character. He's . . . Michelle, I know it hurts, but what you went through, it's something people should know about, should think about, it's a part of life. Telling about life, making sense of it, that's the job of literature, that's my job. Someone had to tell your story. I tried to make it true, tried to do my—"

His daughter's face, red and wet with tears, seemed almost feral for a moment, unrecognizable, inhuman. Then a curious calm passed across her features. "You got one thing right," she said. "Nicole didn't have a father. When I was a little kid I'd come to you crying and my daddy would say show me where it hurts, and it was a private thing, a special thing, but in the book Nicole doesn't have a father, he says it, you gave it to him, he says show me where it hurts, he says it all the time. You're so ironic. You're so clever. The way he said it, it made him so real, more real than when he *was* real. And when you wrote it, you were right. That's what the monster says. Show me where it hurts. That's the monster's line. Nicole doesn't have a father, he's dead, yes, that was right too. I don't have a father. No I don't."

"Don't you talk to me like that," Richard Cantling said. It was terror inside him; it was shame. But it came out anger. "I won't have that, no matter what you've been through. I'm your father."

"No," Michelle said, grinning crazy now, backing away from him. "No, I don't have a father, and you don't have any children, no, unless it's in your books. Those are your children, your only children. Your books, your damned fucking books, those are your children, those are your children, those are your children." Then she turned and ran past him, down the foyer. She stopped at the door to his den. Cantling was afraid of what she might do. He ran after her.

When he reached the den, Michelle had already found the knife and set to work.

Richard Cantling sat by his silent phone and watched his grandfather clock tick off the hours toward darkness.

He tried Michelle's number at three o'clock, at four, at five. The machine, always the machine, speaking in a mockery of her voice. His messages grew more desperate. It was growing dim outside. His light was fading.

Cantling heard no steps on his porch, no knock on his door, no rasping summons from his old brass bell. It was an afternoon as silent as the grave. But by the time evening had fallen, he knew it was out there. A big square package, wrapped in brown paper, addressed in a hand he had known well. Inside a portrait.

He had not understood, not really, and so she was teaching him.

The clock ticked. The darkness grew thicker. The sense of a waiting presence beyond his door seemed to fill the house. His fear had been growing for hours. He sat in the armchair with his legs pulled up under him, his mouth hanging open, thinking, remembering. Heard cruel laughter. Saw the dim red tips of cigarettes in the shadows, moving, circling. Imagined their small hot kisses on his skin. Tasted urine, blood, tears. Knew violence, knew violation, of every sort there was. His hands, his voice, his face, his face, his face. The character with a dozen names, but fear had only a single face. The youngest of his children. His baby. His monstrous baby.

He had been blocked for so long, Cantling thought. If only he could make her understand. It was a kind of impotence, not writing. He had been a writer, but that was over. He had been a husband, but his wife was dead. He had been a father, but she got better, went back to New York. She left him alone, but that last night, wrapped in his arms, she told him the story, she showed him where it hurt, she gave him all that pain. What was he to do with it?

Afterwards he could not forget. He thought of it constantly. He began to reshape it in his head, began to grope for the words, the scenes, the symbols that would make sense of it. It was hideous, but it was life, raw strong life, the grist for Cantling's mill, the very thing he needed. She had showed him where it hurt; he could show them all. He did resist, he did try. He began a short story, an essay, finished some reviews. But it returned. It was with him every night. It would not be denied.

He wrote it.

"Guilty," Cantling said in the darkened room. And when he spoke the word, a kind of acceptance seemed to settle over him, banishing the terror. He was guilty. He had done it. He would accept the punishment, then. It was only right.

Richard Cantling stood and went to his door.

The package was there.

He lugged it inside, still wrapped, carried it up the stairs. He would hang him beside the others, beside Dunnahoo and Cissy and Barry Leighton, all in a row, yes. He went for his hammer, measured carefully, drove the nail. Only then did he unwrap the portrait, and look at the face within.

It captured her as no other artist had ever done, not just the lines of her face, the high angular cheekbones and blue eyes and tangled ash-blond hair, but the personality inside. She looked so young and fresh and confident, and he could see the strength there, the courage, the stubbornness. But best of all he liked her smile. It was a lovely smile, a smile that illuminated her whole face. The smile seemed to remind him of someone he had known once. He couldn't remember who.

Richard Cantling felt a strange, brief sense of relief, followed by an even greater sense of loss, a loss so terrible and final and total that he knew it was beyond the power of the words he worshiped.

Then the feeling was gone.

Cantling stepped back, folded his arms, studied the four portraits. Such excellent work; looking at the paintings, he could almost feel their presence in his house.

Dunnahoo, his first-born, the boy he wished he'd been.

Cissy, his true love.

Barry Leighton, his wise and tired alter ego.

Nicole, the daughter he'd never had.

His people. His characters. His children.

A week later, another, much smaller, package arrived. Inside the carton were copies of four of his novels, a bill, and a polite note from the artist inquiring if there would be any more commissions.

Richard Cantling said no, and paid the bill by check.

Poems

Once a year the members of the Science Fiction Poetry Association (many of whom also belong to the SFWA) present the Rhysling Awards for long and short poems. Named after the wandering blind poet of the spaceways created by Nebula Grand Master Robert A. Heinlein in his story "The Green Hills of Earth," the publication of the Rhysling winners has become something of a tradition in the Nebula anthology.

Bruce Boston, the winner in the short poem category, is the author of more than three hundred poems and some fifty short stories, appearing in *Twilight Zone*, *Isaac Asimov's Science Fiction Magazine*, *The New York Times Magazine*, and *Fiction*. *Alchemical Texts*, a collection of fantasy poems, is his most recent book. *Jackbird* is a collection of short stories published in 1976. He is a recipient of the Pushcart Prize for short fiction. He lives in Berkeley, California.

Siv Cedering is the bilingual (Swedish and English) author of two novels, four books for children, four books of poetry, plus several chapbooks. Her winning poem was first published in *Science 84* and is part of a group of astronomy poems in her latest book, *Letters from the Floating World: Selected and New Poems*. Her poetry has appeared in *Harper's, Ms., Paris Review, The New Republic, The Partisan Review,* and elsewhere. She has received prizes for her prose and photography as well as for her poetry. She also illustrates her books for children. She makes her home in Amagansett, New York.

BRUCE BOSTON

For Spacers Snarled in the Hair of Comets

If you've heard the stellar *vox humana*
the untuned ear takes for static,

if you've kissed the burning eyelids
of god and seized upon the moon's

reflection, disjointed and backwards,
in the choppy ink of some alien sea,

then you know how sleek and fleshy,
how treacherous, the stars can become.

While the universe falls with no boundary,
you and I sit in a cafe of a port city

on a planet whose name we've forgotten:
the vacuum is behind us and before us,

the spiced ale is cool and hallucinogenic.
Already the candle sparkles in our plates.

SIV CEDERING

Letter from Caroline Herschel (1750–1848)

for Carol

William is away, and I am minding
the heavens. I have discovered
eight new comets and three nebulae
never before seen by man,
and I am preparing an Index to
Flamsteed's observations, together with
a catalogue of 560 stars omitted from
the British Catalogue, plus a list of errata
in that publication. William says

I have a way with numbers, so I handle
all the necessary reductions and
calculations. I also plan
every night's observation
schedule, for he says my intuition
helps me turn the telescope to discover
star cluster after star cluster.

I have helped him polish the mirrors
and lenses of our new telescope. It is
the largest in existence. Can you imagine
the thrill of turning it to some new
corner of the heavens to see
something never before seen
from earth? I actually like
that he is busy with the Royal Society
and his club, for when I finish my other work
I can spend all night sweeping
the heavens.

Sometimes when I am alone
in the dark, and the universe reveals
yet another secret, I say the names

of my long-lost sisters, forgotten
in the books that record
our science—
    Aganice of Thessaly,
    Hyptia,
    Hildegard,
    Catherina Hevelius,
    Maria Agnesi
—as if the stars themselves could

remember. Did you know that Hildegard
proposed a heliocentric universe
300 years before Copernicus? that she
wrote of universal gravitation 500 years
before Newton? But who would listen
to her? She was just a nun, a woman.
What is our age, if that age was dark?

As for my name, it will also be
forgotten, but I am not accused
of being a sorceress, like Aganice,
and the Christians do not threaten to
drag me to church, to murder me, like they did
Hyptia of Alexandria, the eloquent young
woman who devised the instruments
used to accurately measure the position
and motion of

heavenly bodies.
However long we live, life is short, so I
work. And however important man becomes,
he is nothing compared to the stars.
There are secrets, dear sister, and it is
for us to reveal them. Your name, like mine,
is a song. Write soon,

                            Caroline

The Steam-powered Word Processor

ARTHUR C. CLARKE

The latest recipient of the Grand Master Nebula is one of the most distinguished writers ever to deserve the award. Born at Minehead, Somerset, England in 1917, Arthur C. Clarke went on to attend King's College, London, and graduated with first class honors in physics and mathematics. He served as chairman of the British Interplanetary Society and is a member of the Academy of Astronautics, the Royal Astronomical Society, and other scientific bodies. He served as an RAF officer in World War II and was in charge of the first radar talk-down system tests. His 1963 novel *Glide Path*, which he likes to describe as his only non–science fiction novel, is based on his experience with early radar. In fact the novel is a reverse kind of science fiction (it would have been SF if it had been published in 1940), written from hindsight, but with the same kinds of insights and prophetic passages contained in his works of foresight.

Clarke's fifty books have appeared in over thirty languages. His many awards include the UNESCO 1961 Kalinga Prize (previous winners have been Bertrand Russell and Julian Huxley); the AAAS-Westinghouse science writing prize; the Bradford Washburn Award; and the Hugo, Nebula, and John W. Campbell Awards—all three for the novel *Rendezvous with Rama*. Stanley Kubrick and he shared an Oscar nomination in 1968 for *2001: A Space Odyssey*. In 1981 Clarke received an Emmy for his contribution to satellite communications. *Arthur C. Clarke's Mysterious World*, a thirteen-part television series, has been seen in many countries. Clarke became a well-known television figure by joining Walter Cronkite during the CBS coverage of the Apollo lunar missions.

Clarke's invention, in 1945, of communications satellites earned him the 1982 Marconi International Fellowship; the gold medal of the Franklin Institute; the Vikram Sarabhai Professorship of the Physical Research Laboratory, Ahmedabad, India; and a King's College Fellowship, London. He is currently the Chancellor of the University of Moratuwa, near Colombo, Sri Lanka, where he makes his home.

Clarke's short fiction fills nine volumes to date. His best known novels are *Childhood's End, The City and the Stars, The Deep Range, Earthlight, Imperial Earth, 2001*, and *The Fountains of Paradise*. His most important works of nonfiction are *Profiles of the Future, The Promise of Space*, and *Ascent to Orbit*, a collection of his technical papers. *The Songs of Distant Earth* is his long-awaited new novel.

This man, whose influence on mass culture probably surpasses that of H. G. Wells, has been described as "a multifaceted, divided man, but this is illusion. Clarke is whole; it is our culture that is divided. More than any other SF writer, Clarke truly lives in the interzone between science and literature. His career has been a deliberate struggle to make this no-man's-land a place worth living and working in. And he has made both sides respect him on his own terms."

In response to his election as Grand Master, Clarke writes:

"The news that I'd been awarded a Grand Master Nebula was an unexpected and delightful surprise. Unexpected, because I never dreamed of receiving such an honor while still so young. Delightful, because—even though my modesty is second only to Isaac's—I like to be reminded from time to time that there's someone out there who actually reads my books.

"And I'm only half kidding about the age bit. I just can't get over the fact that the first magazine science fiction novel I ever read, circa 1931, was by a Grand Master who seems busier than ever these days. Hi, Jack—I still remember *The Green Girl*—and have stolen bits of it at least once.

"I'm also deeply appreciative of being the first Grand Master outside the United States. Although the US has been the spiritual home of SF for at least half a century, my countrymen Wells and Stapledon still remain the unapproached giants in our field—though I'm delighted to say they're now getting some hot competition from both sides of the Atlantic. People keep talking about the Golden Age of science fiction. It is here, it is here. . . . What we *thought* was gold was mostly gilt (though often the very best gilt).

"In thankfully accepting my Grandmastership (Masterdom?) I have but one twinge of regret. My interest in the future is hardly a well-kept secret—and now there seems nothing left for me to achieve. I honestly don't think that even the fabled summons from Stockholm would give me greater real pleasure than this tribute from my friends and peers.

"Much too cold there in December, anyway."

Clarke's acceptance message, dated 31 May 1986, arrived, very appropriately, via a computer-satellite data transmission from Sri Lanka, as part of regular modem data exchanges between Clarke and Gentry Lee, the Jet Propulsion Laboratories planetary scientist involved with the planned Galileo mission to Jupiter, with whom Clarke is working on a movie project.

The following short article, meticulously researched and documented, is a prime example of a Grand Master at play.

Foreword

Very little biographical material exists relating to the remarkable career of the now almost forgotten engineering genius, the Reverend Charles Cabbage (1815–188?), one-time vicar of St. Simians in the Parish of Far Tottering, Sussex. After several years of exhaustive research, however, I have discovered some new facts which, it seems to me, should be brought to a wider public.

I would like to express my thanks to Miss Drusilla Wollstonecraft Cabbage and the good ladies of the Far Tottering Historical Society, whose urgent wishes to disassociate themselves from many of my conclusions I fully understand.

As early as 1715 *The Spectator* refers to the Cabbage (or Cubage) family as a cadet branch of the de Coverleys (bar sinister, regrettably, though Sir Roger himself is not implicated). They quickly acquired great wealth, like many members of the British aristocracy, by judicious investment in the Slave Trade. By 1800 the Cabbages were the richest family in Sussex (some said in England), but as Charles was the youngest of eleven children he was forced to enter the Church and appeared unlikely to inherit much of the Cabbage wealth.

Before his thirtieth year, however, the incumbent of Far Tottering experienced a remarkable change of fortune, owing to the untimely demise of all his ten siblings in a series of tragic accidents. This turn of events, which contemporary writers were fond of calling "The Curse of the Cabbages," was closely connected with the vicar's unique collection of medieval weapons, oriental poisons, and venomous reptiles. Naturally, these unfortunate mishaps gave rise to much malicious gossip, and may be the reason why the Reverend Cabbage preferred to retain the protection of Holy Orders, at least until his abrupt departure from England.[1]

It may well be asked why a man of great wealth and minimal public duties should devote the most productive years of his life to building a machine of incredible complexity, whose purpose and operations only he could understand. Fortunately, the recent discovery of the Faraday-Cabbage correspondence in the archives of the Royal Institution now throws some light on this matter. Reading between the lines, it appears that the reverend gentleman resented the weekly chore of producing a two-hour sermon on basically the same themes, one hundred and four times a year. (He was also incumbent of Tottering-in-the-Marsh, pop. 73.) In a moment of inspiration which must have occurred around 1851—possibly after a visit to the Great Exhibition, that marvelous showpiece of confident Victorian know-how—he conceived a machine which would *automatically* reassemble masses of text in any desired order. Thus he could create any number of sermons from the same basic material.

This crude initial concept was later greatly refined. Although—as we shall see—the Reverend Cabbage was never able to complete the final version of his "Word Loom," he clearly envisaged a machine which would operate not only upon individual paragraphs but single lines of text. (The next stage—words and letters—he never attempted, though he mentions the possibility in his correspondence with Faraday, and recognized it as an ultimate objective.)

Once he had conceived the Word Loom, the inventive cleric immediately set out to build it. His unusual (some

---

[1] Ealing Studios deny the very plausible rumor that Alec Guinness's *Kind Hearts and Coronets* was inspired by these events. It is known, however, that at one time Peter Cushing was being considered for the role of the Reverend Cabbage.

would say deplorable) mechanical ability had already been amply demonstrated through the ingenious mantraps which protected his vast estates, and which had eliminated at least two other claimants to the family fortune.

At this point, the Reverend Cabbage made a mistake which may well have changed the course of technology— if not history. With the advantage of hindsight, it now seems obvious to us that his problems could only have been solved by the use of electricity. The Wheatstone telegraph had already been operating for years, and he was in correspondence with the genius who had discovered the basic laws of electromagnetism. How strange that he ignored the answer that was staring him in the face!

We must remember, however, that the gentle Faraday was now entering the decade of senility preceding his death in 1867. Much of the surviving correspondence concerns his eccentric faith (the now extinct religion of "Sandemanism") with which Cabbage could have had little patience.

Moreover, the vicar was in daily (or at least weekly) contact with a very advanced technology with over a thousand years of development behind it. The Far Tottering church was blessed with an excellent twenty-one-stop organ manufactured by the same Henry Willis whose 1875 masterpiece at North London's Alexandra Palace was proclaimed by Marcel Dupre as the finest concert organ in Europe.[2] Cabbage was himself no mean performer on this instrument, and had a complete understanding of its intricate mechanism. He was convinced that an assembly of pneumatic tubes, valves, and pumps could control all the operations of his projected Word Loom.

It was an understandable but fatal mistake. Cabbage had overlooked the fact that the sluggish velocity of sound—

[2]Since the 1970s my indefatigable brother Fred Clarke, with the help of such distinguished musicians as Sir Yehudi Menuhin (who has already conducted three performances of Handel's *Messiah* for this purpose), has spearheaded a campaign for the restoration of this magnificent instrument.

a miserable 330 meters a second—would reduce the machine's operating speed to a completely impracticable level. At best, the final version might have attained an information-handling rate of 0.1 Baud—so that the preparation of a single sermon would have required about ten weeks!

It was some years before the Reverend Cabbage realized this fundamental limitation: at first he believed that by merely increasing the available power he could speed up his machine indefinitely. The final version absorbed the entire output of a large steam-driven threshing machine—the clumsy ancestor of today's farm tractors and combine harvesters.

At this point, it may be as well to summarize what little is known about the actual mechanics of the Word Loom. For this, we must rely on garbled accounts in the *Far Tottering Gazette* (no complete runs of which exist for the essential years 1860–80) and occasional notes and sketches in the Reverend Cabbage's surviving correspondence. Ironically, considerable portions of the final machine were in existence as late as 1942. They were destroyed when one of the Luftwaffe's stray incendiary bombs reduced the ancestral home of Tottering Towers to a pile of ashes.[3]

The machine's "memory" was based—indeed, there was no practical alternative at the time—on the punched cards of a modified Jacquard Loom; Cabbage was fond of saying that he would weave thoughts as Jacquard wove tapestries. Each line of output consisted of twenty (later thirty) characters, displayed to the operator by letter wheels rotating behind small windows.

---

[3] A small portion—two or three gearwheels and what appears to be a pneumatic valve—are still in the possession of the local Historical Society. These pathetic relics reminded me irresistibly of another great technological might-have-been, the famous Anticythera Computer (see Derek de Solla Price, *Scientific American*, July 1959) which I last saw in 1965, ignominiously relegated to a cigar box in the basement of the Athens Museum. My suggestion that it was the museum's most important exhibit was not well received.

The principles of the machine's COS (Card Operating System) have not come down to us, and it appears—not surprisingly—that Cabbage's greatest problem involved the location, removal, and updating of the individual cards. Once text had been finalized, it was cast in type metal; the amazing clergyman had built a primitive Linotype at least a decade before Mergenthaler's 1886 patent!

Before the machine could be used, Cabbage was faced with the laborious task of punching not only the Bible but the whole of Cruden's Concordance on to Jacquard cards. He arranged for this to be done, at negligible expense, by the aged ladies of the Far Tottering Home for Relicts of Decayed Gentlefolk—now the local Disco and Breakdancing Club. This was another astonishing First, anticipating by a dozen years Hollerith's famed mechanization of the 1890 US Census.

But at this point, disaster struck. Hearing, yet again, strange rumors from the Parish of Far Tottering, no less a personage than the Archbishop of Canterbury descended upon the now obsessed vicar. Understandably appalled by discovering that the church organ had been unable to perform its original function for at least five years, Cantuar issued an ultimatum. Either the Word Loom must go—or the Reverend Cabbage must resign. (Preferably both: there were also hints of exorcism and reconsecration.)

This dilemma seems to have produced an emotional crisis in the already unbalanced clergyman. He attempted one final test of his enormous and unwieldy machine, which now occupied the entire western transcept of St. Simians. Over the protests of the local farmers (for it was now harvest time) the huge steam engine, its brassware gleaming, was trundled up to the church, and the belt drive connected (the stained-glass windows having long ago been removed to make this possible).

The reverend took his seat at the now unrecognizable console (I cannot forbear wondering if he booted the system with a foot pedal) and started to type. The letter-wheels rotated before his eyes as the sentences were slowly spelled out, one line at a time. In the vestry, the crucibles of molten lead awaited the commands that would be laboriously brought to them on puffs of air. . . .

Faster, faster! called the impatient vicar, as the workmen shoveled coal into the smoke-belching monster in the churchyard. The long belt, snaking through the narrow window, flapped furiously up and down, pumping horsepower upon horsepower into the straining mechanism of the Loom.

The result was inevitable. Somewhere, in the depths of the immense apparatus, something broke. Within seconds, the ill-fated machine tore itself into fragments. The vicar, according to eyewitnesses, was very lucky to escape with his life.

The next development was both abrupt and totally unexpected. Abandoning Church, wife, and thirteen children, the Reverend Cabbage eloped to Australia with his chief assistant, the village blacksmith.

To the class-conscious Victorians, such an association with a mere workman was beyond excuse (even an underfootman would have been more acceptable!)[4] The very name of Charles Cabbage was banished from polite society, and his ultimate fate is unknown, though there are reports that he later became chaplain of Botany Bay. The legend that he died in the outback when a sheepshearing machine he had invented ran amok is surely apocryphal.

---

[4] How D. H. Lawrence ever heard of this affair is still a mystery. As is now well known, he had originally planned to make the protagonist of his most famous novel not Lady Chatterley, but her husband; however, discretion prevailed, and the Cabbage Connection was revealed only when Lawrence foolishly mentioned it, in confidence, to Frank Harris, who promptly published it in the *Saturday Review*. Lawrence never spoke to Harris again; but then, no one ever did.

Afterword

The Rare Book section of the British Museum possesses the only known copy of the Reverend Cabbage's *Sermons in Steam*, long claimed by the family to have been manufactured by the Word Loom. Unfortunately, even a casual inspection reveals that this is not the case; with the exception of the last page (223–4), the volume was clearly printed on a normal flatbed press.

Page 223–4, however, is an obvious insert. The impression is very uneven, and the text is replete with spelling mistakes and typographical errors.

Is this indeed the only surviving production of perhaps the most remarkable—and misguided—technological effort of the Victorian Age? Or is it a deliberate fake, created to give the impression that the Word Loom actually operated at least once—however poorly?

We shall never know the truth, but as an Englishman I am proud of the fact that one of today's most important inventions was first conceived in the British Isles. Had matters turned out slightly differently, Charles Cabbage might now have been as famous as James Watt, George Stevenson—or even Isambard Kingdom Brunel.

Paper Dragons

JAMES P. BLAYLOCK

James P. Blaylock's novels include *The Elfin Ship, The Disappearing Dwarf, The Digging Leviathan, Homunculus,* and the recently completed *Land of Dreams.* His short fiction has appeared in *Unearth, TriQuarterly, Isaac Asimov's Science Fiction Magazine,* and various anthologies. He teaches part-time at Fullerton Community College in southern California.

About his haunting, reverie-filled fantasy Blaylock writes:

" 'Paper Dragons' is the rewrite of a story I wrote some five years ago—a story that hadn't worked so well and that had been sitting in the drawer waiting. What had to be done to it occurred to me in a sort of flash, appropriately, while I was wiring my remodeled service porch, and I dropped my pliers and wire strippers and went to work, rewriting the story, for the most part, in two days. It's partly about my love of northern California, partly about how things fall to bits, partly about how—in the midst of all the falling to bits—we catch random, shady, welcome glimpses of the beauty and mystery of a world too often veiled by the gray rhythms of day-to-day toil. The lights and outlets on the service porch worked, when I got back around to them. I hope the story did too."

238

Strange things are said to have happened in this world—some are said to be happening still—but half of them, if I'm any judge, are lies. There's no way to tell sometimes. The sky above the north coast has been flat gray for weeks—clouds thick overhead like carded wool not fifty feet above the ground, impaled on the treetops, on redwoods and alders and hemlocks. The air is heavy with mist that lies out over the harbor and the open ocean, drifting across the tip of the pier and breakwater now and again, both of them vanishing into the gray so that there's not a nickel's worth of difference between the sky and the sea. And when the tide drops, and the reefs running out toward the point appear through the fog, covered in the brown bladders and rubber leaves of kelp, the pink lace of algae, and the slippery sheets of sea lettuce and eel grass, it's a simple thing to imagine the dark bulk of the fish that lie in deepwater gardens and angle up toward the pale green of shallows to feed at dawn.

There's the possibility, of course, that winged things, their counterparts if you will, inhabit dens in the clouds, that in the valleys and caverns of the heavy, low skies live unguessed beasts. It occurs to me sometimes that if without warning a man could draw back that veil of cloud that obscures the heavens, snatch it back in an instant, he'd startle a world of oddities aloft in the skies: balloon things with hovering little wings like the fins of pufferfish, and spiny, leathery creatures, nothing but bones and teeth and with beaks half again as long as their ribby bodies.

There have been nights when I was certain I heard them, when the clouds hung in the treetops and foghorns moaned off the point and water dripped from the needles of hemlocks beyond the window onto the tin roof of Filby's garage. There were muffled shrieks and the airy flapping of distant wings. On one such night when I was out walking along the bluffs, the clouds parted for an instant and a spray of stars like a reeling carnival shone beyond, until, like a curtain slowly drawing shut, the clouds drifted up against each other and parted no more. I'm certain I glimpsed something—a shadow, the promise of a shadow—dimming the stars. It was the next morning that the business with the crabs began.

I awoke, late in the day, to the sound of Filby hammering at something in his garage—talons, I think it was, copper talons. Not that it makes much difference. It woke me up. I don't sleep until an hour or so before dawn. There's a certain bird, Lord knows what sort, that sings through the last hour of the night and shuts right up when the sun rises. Don't ask me why. Anyway, there was Filby smashing away some time before noon. I opened my left eye, and there atop the pillow was a bloodred hermit crab with eyes on stalks, giving me a look as if he were proud of himself, waving pincers like that. I leaped up. There was another, creeping into my shoe, and two more making away with my pocketwatch, dragging it along on its fob toward the bedroom door.

The window was open and the screen was torn. The beasts were clambering up onto the woodpile and hoisting themselves in through the open window to rummage through my personal effects while I slept. I pitched them out, but that evening there were more—dozens of them, bent beneath the weight of seashells, dragging toward the house with an eye to my pocketwatch.

It was a migration. Once every hundred years, Dr. Jensen tells me, every hermit crab in creation gets the wanderlust and hurries ashore. Jensen camped on the beach in the cove to study the things. They were all heading south like migratory birds. By the end of the week there was a tiresome lot of them afoot—millions of them to hear Jensen carry on—but they left my house alone. They dwindled as the next week wore out, and seemed to be straggling in from deeper water and were bigger and bigger: the size of a man's fist at first, then of his head, and then a giant, vast as a pig, chased Jensen into the lower branches of an oak. On Friday there were only two crabs, both of them bigger than cars. Jensen went home gibbering and drank himself into a stupor. He was there on Saturday though; you've got to give him credit for that. But nothing appeared. He speculates that somewhere off the coast, in a deepwater chasm a hundred fathoms below the last faded colors, is a monumental beast, blind and gnarled from spectacular pressures and wearing a seashell overcoat, feeling his way toward shore.

At night sometimes I hear the random echoes of far-off clacking, just the misty and muted suggestion of it, and I brace myself and stare into the pages of an open book, firelight glinting off the cut crystal of my glass, countless noises out in the foggy night among which is the occasional clack clack clack of what might be Jensen's impossible crab, creeping up to cast a shadow in the front porch lamplight, to demand my pocketwatch. It was the night after the sighting of the pig-sized crabs that one got into Filby's garage—forced the door apparently—and made a hash out of his dragon. I know what you're thinking. I thought it was a lie too. But things have since fallen out that make me suppose otherwise. He did, apparently, know Augustus Silver. Filby was an acolyte; Silver was his master. But the dragon business, they tell me, isn't merely a matter of mechanics. It's a matter of perspective. That was Filby's downfall.

There was a gypsy who came round in a cart last year. He couldn't speak, apparently. For a dollar he'd do the most amazing feats. He tore out his tongue, when he first arrived, and tossed it onto the road. Then he danced on it and shoved it back into his mouth, good as new. Then he pulled out his entrails—yards and yards of them like sausage out of a machine—then jammed them all back in and nipped shut the hole he'd torn in his abdomen. It made half the town sick, mind you, but they paid to see it. That's pretty much how I've always felt about dragons. I don't half believe in them, but I'd give a bit to see one fly, even if it were no more than a clever illusion.

But Filby's dragon, the one he was keeping for Silver, was a ruin. The crab—I suppose it was a crab—had shredded it, knocked the wadding out of it. It reminded me of one of those stuffed alligators that turns up in curiosity shops, all eaten to bits by bugs and looking sad and tired, with its tail bent sidewise and a clump of cotton stuffing shoved through a tear in its neck.

Filby was beside himself. It's not good for a grown man to carry on so. He picked up the shredded remnant of a dissected wing and flagellated himself with it. He scourged himself, called himself names. I didn't know him well at the time, and so watched the whole weird scene from my kitchen window: his garage door banging open and shut in the wind, Filby weeping and howling through the open door, storming back and forth, starting and stopping theatrically, the door slamming shut and slicing off the whole embarrassing business for thirty seconds or so and then sweeping open to betray a wailing Filby scrabbling among the debris on the garage floor—the remnants of what had once been a flesh and blood dragon, as it were, built by the ubiquitous Augustus Silver years before. Of course I had no idea at the time. Augustus *Silver*, after all. It almost justifies Filby's carrying on. And I've done a bit of carrying on myself since, although as I said, most of what prompted the whole business has begun to seem suspiciously like lies, and the whispers in the foggy night, the clacking and whirring and rush of wings, has begun to sound like thinly disguised laughter, growing fainter by the months and emanating from nowhere, from the clouds, from the wind and fog. Even the occasional letters from Silver himself have become suspect.

Filby is an eccentric. I could see that straightaway. How

he finances his endeavors is beyond me. Little odd jobs, I don't doubt—repairs and such. He has the hands of an archetypal mechanic: spatulate fingers, grime under the nails, nicks and cuts and scrapes that he can't identify. He has only to touch a heap of parts, wave his hands over them, and the faint rhythmic stirrings of order and pattern seem to shudder through the crossmembers of his workbench. And here an enormous crab had gotten in, and in a single night had clipped apart a masterpiece, a wonder, a thing that couldn't be tacked back together. Even Silver would have pitched it out. The cat wouldn't want it.

Filby was morose for days, but I knew he'd come out of it. He'd be mooning around the house in a slump, poking at yesterday's newspapers, and a glint of light off a copper wire would catch his eye. The wire would suggest something. That's how it works. He not only has the irritating ability to coexist with mechanical refuse; it speaks to him too, whispers possibilities.

He'd be hammering away some morning soon—damn all crabs—piecing together the ten thousand silver scales of a wing, assembling the jeweled bits of a faceted eye, peering through a glass at a spray of fine wire spun into a braid that would run up along the spinal column of a creature which, when released some misty night, might disappear within moments into the clouds and be gone. Or so Filby dreamed. And I'll admit it: I had complete faith in him, in the dragon that he dreamed of building.

In the early spring, such as it is, some few weeks after the hermit crab business, I was hoeing along out in the garden. Another frost was unlikely. My tomatoes had been in for a week, and an enormous green worm with spines had eaten the leaves off the plants. There was nothing left but stems, and they were smeared up with a sort of slime. Once when I was a child I was digging in the dirt a few days after a rain, and I unearthed a finger-sized worm with the face of a human being. I buried it. But this tomato worm had no such face. He was pleasant, in fact, with little piggy eyes and a smashed in sort of nose, as worm noses go. So I pitched him over the fence into Filby's yard. He'd climb back over—there was no doubting it. But he'd creep back from anywhere, from the moon. And since that was the case—if it was inevitable—then there seemed to be no reason to put him too far out of his way, if you follow me. But the plants were a wreck. I yanked them out by the roots and threw them into Filby's yard too, which is up in weeds anyway, but Filby himself had wandered up to the fence like a grinning gargoyle, and the clump of a half-dozen gnawed vines flew into his face like a squid. That's not the sort of thing to bother Filby though. He didn't mind. He had a letter from Silver mailed a month before from points south.

I was barely acquainted with the man's reputation then. I'd heard of him—who hasn't? And I could barely remember seeing photographs of a big, bearded man with wild hair and a look of passion in his eye, taken when Silver was involved in the mechano-vivisectionists' league in the days when they first learned the truth about the mutability of matter. He and three others at the university were responsible for the brief spate of unicorns, some few of which are said to roam the hills hereabouts, interesting mutants, certainly, but not the sort of wonder that would satisfy Augustus Silver. He appeared in the photograph to be the sort who would leap headlong into a cold pool at dawn and eat bulgar wheat and honey with a spoon.

And here was Filby, ridding himself of the remains of ravaged tomato plants, holding a letter in his hand, transported. A letter from the master! He'd been years in the tropics and had seen a thing or two. In the hills of the eastern jungles he'd sighted a dragon with what was quite apparently a bamboo ribcage. It flew with the xylophone clacking of windchimes, and had the head of an enormous lizard, the pronged tail of a devilfish, and clockwork wings

built of silver and string and the skins of carp. It had given
him certain ideas. The best dragons, he was sure, would
come from the sea. He was setting sail for San Francisco.
Things could be purchased in Chinatown—certain "neces-
saries," as he put it in his letter to Filby. There was mention of perpetual motion, of the building of an immortal
creature knitted together from parts of a dozen beasts.

I was still waiting for the issuance of that last crab, and
so was Jensen. He wrote a monograph, a paper of grave
scientific accuracy in which he postulated the correlation
between the dwindling number of the creatures and the
enormity of their size. He camped on the cliffs above the
sea with his son Bumby, squinting through the fog, his
eye screwed to the lens of a special telescope—one that
saw things, as he put it, particularly clearly—and waiting
for the first quivering claw of the behemoth to thrust up
out of the gray swells, cascading water, draped with weeds,
and the bearded face of the crab to follow, drawn along
south by a sort of migratory magnet toward heaven alone
knows what. Either the crab passed away down the coast
hidden by mists, or Jensen was wrong—there hasn't been
any last crab.

The letter from Augustus Silver gave Filby wings, as
they say, and he flew into the construction of his dragon,
sending off a letter east in which he enclosed forty dollars,
his unpaid dues in the Dragon Society. The tomato worm,
itself a wingless dragon, crept back into the garden four
days later and had a go at a half-dozen fresh plants, nibbling lacy arabesques across the leaves. Flinging it back
into Filby's yard would accomplish nothing. It was a worm
of monumental determination. I put him into a jar—a big,
gallon pickle jar, empty of pickles, of course—and I screwed
onto it a lid with holes punched in. He lived happily in a
little garden of leaves and dirt and sticks and polished
stones, nibbling on the occasional tomato leaf.

I spent more and more time with Filby, watching, in

those days after the arrival of the first letter, the mechanical bones and joints and organs of the dragon drawing together. Unlike his mentor, Filby had almost no knowledge of vivisection. He had an aversion to it, I believe, and as a consequence his creations were almost wholly mechanical—and almost wholly unlikely. But he had such an aura of certainty about him, such utter and uncompromising conviction that even the most unlikely project seemed inexplicably credible.

I remember one Saturday afternoon with particular clarity. The sun had shone for the first time in weeks. The grass hadn't been alive with slugs and snails the previous night—a sign, I supposed, that the weather was changing for the drier. But I was only half right. Saturday dawned clear. The sky was invisibly blue, dotted with the dark specks of what might have been sparrows or crows flying just above the treetops, or just as easily something else, something more vast—dragons, let's say, or the peculiar denizens of some very distant cloud world. Sunlight poured through the diamond panes of my bedroom window, and I swear I could hear the tomato plants and onions and snow peas in my garden unfurling, hastening skyward. But around noon great dark clouds roiled in over the Coast Range, their shadows creeping across the meadows and redwoods, picket fences, and chaparral. A spray of rain sailed on the freshening offshore breeze, and the sweet smell of ozone rose from the pavement of Filby's driveway, carrying on its first thin ghost an unidentifiable sort of promise and regret: the promise of wonders pending, regret for the bits and pieces of lost time that go trooping away like migratory hermit crabs, inexorably, irretrievably into the mists.

So it was a Saturday afternoon of rainbows and umbrellas, and Filby, still animated at the thought of Silver's approach, showed me some of his things. Filby's house was a marvel, given over entirely to his collections. Carven

heads whittled of soapstone and ivory and ironwood populated the rooms, the strange souvenirs of distant travel.
Aquaria bubbled away, thick with water plants and odd,
mottled creatures: spotted eels and leaf fish, gobies buried
to their noses in sand, flatfish with both eyes on the same
side of their heads, and darting anableps that had the
wonderful capacity to see above and below the surface of
the water simultaneously and so, unlike the mundane fish
that swam beneath, were inclined toward philosophy. I
suggested as much to Filby, but I'm not certain he understood. Books and pipes and curios filled a half-dozen cases,
and star charts hung on the walls. There were working
drawings of some of Silver's earliest accomplishments, intricate swirling sketches covered over with what were to
me utterly meaningless calculations and commentary.

On Monday another letter arrived from Silver. He'd
gone along east on the promise of something very rare in
the serpent line—an elephant trunk snake, he said, the
lungs of which ran the length of its body. But he was coming to the west coast, that much was sure, to San Francisco. He'd be here in a week, a month, he couldn't be
entirely sure. A message would come. Who could say
when? We agreed that I would drive the five hours south
on the coast road into the city to pick him up: I owned a
car.

Filby was in a sweat to have his creature built before
Silver's arrival. He wanted so badly to hear the master's
approval, to see in Silver's eyes the brief electricity of surprise and excitement. And I wouldn't doubt for a moment
that there was an element of envy involved. Filby, after
all, had languished for years at the university in Silver's
shadow, and now he was on the ragged edge of becoming
a master himself.

So there in Filby's garage, tilted against a wall of
roughcut fir studs and redwood shiplap, the shoulders,
neck, and right wing of the beast sat in silent repose, its

head a mass of faceted pastel crystals, piano wire, and bone clutched in the soft rubber grip of a bench vise. It was on Friday, the morning of the third letter, that Filby touched the bare ends of two microscopically thin copper rods, and the eyes of the dragon rotated on their axis, very slowly, blinking twice, surveying the cramped and dimly lit garage with an ancient, knowing look before the rods parted and life flickered out.

Filby was triumphant. He danced around the garage, shouting for joy, cutting little capers. But my suggestion that we take the afternoon off, perhaps drive up to Fort Bragg for lunch and a beer, was met with stolid refusal. Silver, it seemed, was on the horizon. I was to leave in the morning. I might, quite conceivably, have to spend a few nights waiting. One couldn't press Augustus Silver, of course. Filby himself would work on the dragon. It would be a night and day business, to be sure. I determined to take the tomato worm along for company, as it were, but the beast had dug himself into the dirt for a nap.

This business of my being an emissary of Filby struck me as dubious when I awoke on Saturday morning. I was a neighbor who had been ensnared in a web of peculiar enthusiasm. Here I was pulling on heavy socks and stumbling around the kitchen, tendrils of fog creeping in over the sill, the hemlocks ghostly beyond dripping panes, while Augustus Silver tossed on the dark Pacific swell somewhere off the Golden Gate, his hold full of dragon bones. What was I to say to him beyond, "Filby sent me." Or something more cryptic: "Greetings from Filby." Perhaps in these circles one merely winked or made a sign or wore a peculiar sort of cap with a foot-long visor and a pyramid-encased eye embroidered across the front. I felt like a fool, but I had promised Filby. His garage was alight at dawn, and I had been awakened once in the night by a shrill screech, cut off sharply and followed by Filby's cackling laughter and a short snatch of song.

I was to speak to an old Chinese named Wun Lo in a restaurant off Washington. Filby referred to him as "the connection." I was to introduce myself as a friend of Captain Augustus Silver and wait for orders. Orders—what in the devil sort of talk was that? In the dim glow of lamplight the preceding midnight such secret talk seemed sensible, even satisfactory; in the chilly dawn it was risible.

It was close to six hours into the city, winding along the tortuous road, bits and pieces of it having fallen into the sea on the back of winter rains. The fog rose out of rocky coves and clung to the hillsides, throwing a gray veil over dew-fed wildflowers and shore grasses. Silver fence-pickets loomed out of the murk with here and there the skull of a cow or a goat impaled atop, and then the quick passing of a half-score of mailboxes on posts, rusted and canted over toward the cliffs along with twisted cypresses that seemed on the verge of flinging themselves into the sea.

Now and again, without the least notice, the fog would disappear in a twinkling, and a clear mile of highway would appear, weirdly sharp and crystalline in contrast to its previous muted state. Or an avenue into the sky would suddenly appear, the remote end of which was dipped in opalescent blue and which seemed as distant and unattainable as the end of a rainbow. Across one such avenue, springing into clarity for perhaps three seconds, flapped the ungainly bulk of what might have been a great bird, laboring as if against a stiff, tumultuous wind just above the low-lying fog. It might as easily have been something else, much higher. A dragon? One of Silver's creations that nested in the dense emerald fog forests of the Coast Range? It was impossible to tell, but it seemed, as I said, to be struggling—perhaps it was old—and a bit of something, a fragment of a wing, fell clear of it and spun dizzily into the sea. Maybe what fell was just a stick being carried back to the nest of an ambitious heron. In an instant the fog closed, or rather the car sped out of the momentary clearing, and any opportunity to identify the beast, really to study it, was gone. For a moment I considered turning around, going back, but it was doubtful that I'd find that same bit of clarity, or that if I did, the creature would still be visible. So I drove on, rounding bends between redwood-covered hills that might have been clever paintings draped along the ghostly edge of Highway One, the hooks that secured them hidden just out of view in the mists above. Then almost without warning the damp asphalt issued out onto a broad highway and shortly thereafter onto the humming expanse of the Golden Gate Bridge.

Some few silent boats struggled against the tide below. Was one of them the ship of Augustus Silver, slanting in toward the Embarcadero? Probably not. They were fishing boats from the look of them, full of shrimp and squid and bug-eyed rock cod. I drove to the outskirts of Chinatown and parked, leaving the car and plunging into the crowd that swarmed down Grant and Jackson and into Portsmouth Square.

It was Chinese New Year. The streets were heavy with the smell of almond cookies and fog, barbecued duck and gunpowder, garlic and seaweed. Rockets burst overhead in showers of barely visible sparks, and one, teetering over onto the street as the fuse burned, sailed straightaway up Washington, whirling and glowing and fizzing into the wall of a curio shop, then dropping lifeless onto the sidewalk as if embarrassed at its own antics. The smoke and pop of firecrackers, the milling throng, and the nagging senselessness of my mission drove me along down Washington until I stumbled into the smoky open door of a narrow, three-story restaurant. Sam Wo it was called.

An assortment of white-garmented chefs chopped away at vegetables. Woks hissed. Preposterous bowls of white rice steamed on the counter. A fish head the size of a melon blinked at me out of a pan. And there, at a small table made of chromed steel and rubbed formica, sat my contact. It had to be him. Filby had been wonderfully accurate in his description. The man had a gray beard that wagged on the tabletop and a suit of similar color that was several sizes too large, and he spooned up clear broth in such a mechanical, purposeful manner that his eating was almost ceremonial. I approached him. There was nothing to do but brass it out. "I'm a friend of Captain Silver," I said, smiling and holding out a hand. He bowed, touched my hand with one limp finger, and rose. I followed him into the back of the restaurant.

It took only a scattering of moments for me to see quite clearly that my trip had been entirely in vain. Who could say where Augustus Silver was? Singapore? Ceylon? Bombay? He'd had certain herbs mailed east just two days earlier. I was struck at once with the foolishness of my position. What in the world was I doing in San Francisco? I had the uneasy feeling that the five chefs just outside the door were having a laugh at my expense, and that old Wun Lo, gazing out toward the street, was about to ask for money—a fiver, just until payday. I was a friend of Augustus Silver, wasn't I?

My worries were temporarily arrested by an old photograph that hung above a tile-faced hearth. It depicted a sort of weird shantytown somewhere on the north coast. There was a thin fog, just enough to veil the surrounding countryside, and the photograph had clearly been taken at dusk, for the long, deep shadows thrown by strange hovels slanted away landward into the trees. The tip of a lighthouse was just visible on the edge of the dark Pacific, and a scattering of small boats lay at anchor beneath. It was puzzling, to be sure—doubly so, because the lighthouse, the spit of land that swerved round toward it, the green bay amid cypress and eucalyptus was, I was certain, Point Reyes. But the shantytown, I was equally certain, didn't exist, couldn't exist.

The collection of hovels tumbled down to the edge of the bay, a long row of them that descended the hillside like a strange gothic stairway, and all of them, I swear it, were built in part of the ruins of dragons, of enormous winged reptiles—tin and copper, leather and bone. Some were stacked on end, tilted against each other like card houses. Some were perched atop oil drums or upended wooden pallets. Here was nothing but a broken wing throwing a sliver of shade; there was what appeared to be a tolerably complete creature, lacking, I suppose, whatever essential parts had once served to animate it. And standing alongside a cooking pot with a man who could quite possibly have been Wun Lo himself was Augustus Silver.

His beard was immense—the beard of a hill wanderer, of a prospector lately returned from years in unmapped goldfields, and that beard and broad-brimmed felt hat, his Oriental coat and the sharp glint of arcane knowledge that shone from his eyes, the odd harpoon he held loosely in his right hand, the breadth of his shoulders—all those bits and pieces seemed almost to deify him, as if he were an incarnation of Neptune just out of the bay, or a wandering Odin who had stopped to drink flower-petal tea in a queer shantytown along the coast. The very look of him abolished my indecision. I left Wun Lo nodding in a chair, apparently having forgotten my presence.

Smoke hung in the air of the street. Thousands of sounds—a cacophony of voices, explosions, whirring pinwheels, Oriental music—mingled into a strange sort of harmonious silence. Somewhere to the northwest lay a village built of the skins of dragons. If nothing else—if I discovered nothing of the arrival of Augustus Silver—I would at least have a look at the shantytown in the photograph. I pushed through the crowd down Washington, oblivious to the sparks and explosions. Then almost magically, like the Red Sea, the throng parted and a broad avenue of asphalt opened before me. Along either side of the suddenly clear street were grinning faces, frozen in anticipation. A vast cheering arose, a shouting, a banging on Chinese cymbals and tooting on reedy little horns. Rounding the corner and rushing along with the maniacal speed of an express train, careered the leering head of a paper dragon, lolling back and forth, a wild rainbow mane streaming behind it. The body of the thing was half a block long, and seemed to be built of a thousand layers of the thinnest sort of pastel-colored rice paper, sheets and sheets of it threatening to fly loose and dissolve in the fog. A dozen people crouched within, racing along the pavement, the whole lot of them yowling and chanting as the crowd closed behind and in a wave pressed along east toward Kearny, the tumult and color muting once again into silence.

The rest of the afternoon had an air of unreality to it, which, strangely, deepened my faith in Augustus Silver and his creations, even though all rational evidence seemed to point squarely in the opposite direction. I drove north out of the city, cutting off at San Rafael toward the coast, toward Point Reyes and Inverness, winding through the green hillsides as the sun traveled down the afternoon sky toward the sea. It was shortly before dark that I stopped for gasoline.

The swerve of shoreline before me was a close cousin of that in the photograph, and the collected bungalows on the hillside could have been the ghosts of the dragon shanties, if one squinted tightly enough to confuse the image through a foliage of eyelashes. Perhaps I've gotten that backward; I can't at all say anymore which of the two worlds had substance and which was the phantom.

A bank of fog had drifted shoreward. But for that, perhaps I could have made out the top of the lighthouse and completed the picture. As it was I could see only the gray veil of mist wisping in on a faint onshore breeze. At the gas station I inquired after a map. Surely, I thought, somewhere close by, perhaps within eyesight if it weren't for the fog, lay my village. The attendant, a tobacco-chewing lump of engine oil and blue paper towels, hadn't heard of it—the dragon village, that is. He glanced sideways at me. A map hung in the window. It cost nothing to look. So I wandered into a steel and glass cubicle, cold with rust and sea air, and studied the map. It told me little. It had been hung recently; the tape holding its corners hadn't yellowed or begun to peel. Through an open doorway to my right was the dim garage where a Chinese mechanic tinkered with the undercarriage of a car on a hoist.

I turned to leave just as the hovering fog swallowed the sun, casting the station into shadow. Over the dark Pacific swell the mists whirled in the seawind, a trailing wisp arching skyward in a rush, like surge-washed tidepool grasses or the waving tail of an enormous misty dragon, and for a scattering of seconds the last faint rays of the evening sun shone out of the tattered fog, illuminating the old gas pumps, the interior of the weathered office, the dark, tool-strewn garage.

The map in the window seemed to curl at the corners, the tape suddenly brown and dry. The white background tinted into shades of antique ivory and pale ocher, and what had been creases in the paper appeared, briefly, to be hitherto unseen roads winding out of the redwoods toward the sea.

It was the strange combination, I'm sure, of the evening, the dying sun, and the rising fog that for a moment made me unsure whether the mechanic was crouched in his overalls beneath some vast and finny automobile spawned of the peculiar architecture of the early sixties, or instead worked beneath the chrome and iron shell of a tilted dragon, frozen in flight above the greasy concrete floor, and framed by tiers of heater hoses and old dusty tires.

Then the sun was gone. Darkness fell within moments, and all was as it had been. I drove slowly north through the village. There was, of course, no shantytown

built of castaway dragons. There were nothing but warehouses and weedy vacant lots and the weathered concrete
and tin of an occasional industrial building. A tangle of
small streets comprised of odd, tumble-down shacks, some
few of them on stilts as if awaiting a flood of apocalyptic
proportions. But the shacks were built of clapboard and
asphalt shingles—there wasn't a hint of a dragon anywhere, not even the tip of a rusted wing in the jimson-
weed and mustard.

I determined not to spend the night in a motel, although I was tempted to, on the off chance that the fog
would dissipate and the watery coastal moonbeams would
wash the coastline clean of whatever it was—a trick of
sunlight or a trick of fog—that had confused me for an
instant at the gas station. But as I say, the day had, for the
most part, been unprofitable, and the thought of being
twenty dollars out of pocket for a motel room was intoler-
able.

It was late—almost midnight—when I arrived home,
exhausted. My tomato worm slept in his den. The light
still burned in Filby's garage, so I wandered out and peeked
through the door. Filby sat on a stool, his chin in his hands,
staring at the dismantled head of his beast. I suddenly re-
gretted having looked in; he'd demand news of Silver, and
I'd have nothing to tell him. The news—or rather the lack
of news—seemed to drain the lees of energy from him. He
hadn't slept in two days. Jensen had been round hours
earlier babbling about an amazingly high tide and of his
suspicion that the last of the crabs might yet put in an
appearance. Did Filby want to watch on the beach that
night? No, Filby didn't. Filby wanted only to assemble his
dragon. But there was something not quite right—some
wire or another that had gotten crossed, or a gem that had
been miscut—and the creature wouldn't respond. It was
so much junk.

I commiserated with him. Lock the door against Jensen's crab, I said, and wait until dawn. It sounded over-much like a platitude, but Filby, I think, was ready to grasp at any reason, no matter how shallow, to leave off his tink-ering.

The two of us sat up until the sun rose, drifting in and out of maudlin reminiscences and debating the merits of a stroll down to the bluffs to see how Jensen was faring. The high tide, apparently, was accompanied by a monumental surf, for in the spaces of meditative silence I could just hear the rush and thunder of long breakers collapsing on the beach. It seemed unlikely to me that there would be giant crabs afoot.

The days that followed saw no break in the weather. It continued dripping and dismal. No new letters arrived from Augustus Silver. Filby's dragon seemed to be in a state of perpetual decline. The trouble that plagued it receded deeper into it with the passing days, as if it were mocking Filby, who groped along in its wake, clutching at it, certain in the morning that he had the problem securely by the tail, morose that same afternoon that it had once again slipped away. The creature was a perfect wonder of sepa-rated parts. I'd had no notion of its complexity. Hundreds of those parts, by week's end, were laid out neatly on the garage floor, one after another in the order they'd been dismantled. Concentric circles of them expanded like rip-ples on a pond, and by Tuesday of the following week masses of them had been swept into coffee cans that sat here and there on the bench and floor. Filby was declin-ing, I could see that. That week he spent less time in the garage than he had been spending there in a single day during the previous weeks, and he slept instead long hours in the afternoon.

I still held out hope for a letter from Silver. He was, after all, out there somewhere. But I was plagued with the suspicion that such a letter might easily contribute to cer-tain of Filby's illusions—or to my own—and so prolong

what with each passing day promised to be the final defla-
tion of those same illusions. Better no hope, I thought,
than impossible hope, than ruined anticipation.

But late in the afternoon, when from my attic window
I could see Jensen picking his way along the bluffs, carrying with him a wood and brass telescope, while the orange
glow of a diffused sun radiated through the thinned fog
over the sea, I wondered where Silver was, what strange
seas he sailed, what rumored wonders were drawing him
along jungle paths that very evening.

One day he'd come, I was sure of it. There would be
patchy fog illuminated by ivory moonlight. The sound of
Eastern music, of Chinese banjos and copper gongs would
echo over the darkness of the open ocean. The fog would
swirl and part, revealing a universe of stars and planets
and the aurora borealis dancing in transparent color like
the thin rainbow light of paper lanterns hung in the wind-
swept sky. Then the fog would close, and out of the phantom mists, heaving on the groundswell, his ship would
sail into the mouth of the harbor, slowly, cutting the water
like a ghost, strange sea creatures visible in the phosphorescent wake, one by one dropping away and returning to
sea as if having accompanied the craft across ten thousand
miles of shrouded ocean. We'd drink a beer, the three of
us, in Filby's garage. We'd summon Jensen from his vigil.

But as I say, no letter came, and all anticipation was so
much air. Filby's beast was reduced to parts—a plate of
broken meats, as it were. The idea of it reminded me over-
much of the sad bony remains of a Thanksgiving turkey.
There was nothing to be done. Filby wouldn't be placated.
But the fog, finally, had lifted. The black oak in the yard
was leafing out and the tomato plants were knee-high and
luxuriant. My worm was still asleep, but I had hopes that
the spring weather would revive him. It wasn't, however,
doing a thing for Filby. He stared long hours at the salad
of debris, and when in one ill-inspired moment I jokingly

suggested he send to Detroit for a carburetor, he cast me such a savage look that I slipped out again and left him alone.

On Sunday afternoon a wind blew, slamming Filby's garage door until the noise grew tiresome. I peeked in, aghast. There was nothing in the heaped bits of scrap that suggested a dragon, save one dismantled wing, the silk and silver of which was covered with greasy hand prints. Two cats wandered out. I looked for some sign of Jensen's crab, hoping, in fact, that some such rational and concrete explanation could be summoned to explain the ruin. But Filby, alas, had quite simply gone to bits along with his dragon. He'd lost whatever strange inspiration it was that propelled him. His creation lay scattered, not two pieces connected. Wires and fuses were heaped amid unidentifiable crystals, and one twisted bit of elaborate machinery had quite clearly been danced upon and lay now cold and dead, half hidden beneath the bench. Delicate thises and thats sat mired in a puddle of oil that scummed half the floor.

Filby wandered out, adrift, his hair frazzled. He'd received a last letter. There were hints in it of extensive travel, perhaps danger. Silver's visit to the west coast had been delayed again. Filby ran his hand backward through his hair, oblivious to the harrowed result the action effected. He had the look of a nineteenth-century Bedlam lunatic. He muttered something about having a sister in McKinleyville, and seemed almost illuminated when he added, apropos of nothing, that in his sister's town, deeper into the heart of the north coast, stood the tallest totem pole in the world. Two days later he was gone. I locked his garage door for him and made a vow to collect his mail with an eye toward a telling, exotic postmark. But nothing so far has appeared. I've gotten into the habit of spending the evening on the beach with Jensen and his son Bumby, both of whom still hold out hope for the issuance of the last crab. The spring sunsets are unimaginable. Bumby is as fond of them as I am, and can see comparable whorls of color and pattern in the spiral curve of a seashell or in the peculiar green depths of a tidepool.

In fact, when my tomato worm lurched up out of his burrow and unfurled an enormous gauzy pair of mottled brown wings, I took him along to the seaside so that Bumby could watch him set sail, as it were.

The afternoon was cloudless and the ocean sighed on the beach. Perhaps the calm, insisted Jensen, would appeal to the crab. But Bumby by then was indifferent to the fabled crab. He stared into the pickle jar at the half-dozen circles of bright orange dotting the abdomen of the giant sphinx moth that had once crept among my tomato plants in a clever disguise. It was both wonderful and terrible, and held a weird fascination for Bumby, who tapped at the jar, making up and discarding names.

When I unscrewed the lid, the moth fluttered skyward some few feet and looped around in a crazy oval, Bumby charging along in its wake, then racing away in pursuit as the monster hastened south. The picture of it is as clear to me now as rainwater: Bumby running and jumping, kicking up glinting sprays of sand, outlined against the sheer rise of mossy cliffs, and the wonderful moth just out of reach overhead, luring Bumby along the afternoon beach. At last it was impossible to say just what the diminishing speck in the china-blue sky might be—a tiny winged creature silhouetted briefly on the false horizon of our little cove, or some vast flying reptile swooping over the distant ocean where it fell away into the void, off the edge of the flat earth.

Effing the Ineffable

GREGORY BENFORD

Gregory Benford's 1980 novel
Timescape won the Nebula Award, the John W. Campbell
Memorial Award, the Australian Ditmar Award, and the
British Science Fiction Association Award. A Woodrow
Wilson Fellow, Benford is a professor of physics at the
University of California, Irvine. His other novels include
*In the Ocean of Night, The Stars in Shroud, Against Infinity,
Across the Sea of Suns, Artifact,* and his recent collabora-
tion with David Brin, *Heart of the Comet. In Alien Flesh*
collects his best short fiction. He has been compared to
Arthur C. Clarke and to C. P. Snow for his literary gifts
and for his depictions of scientists at work.

The following essay, written especially for this book,
is an insightful, state-of-the-art examination of the alien
in science fiction, and much more.

Their light of pocket-torch, of signal flare,
Licks at the edge of unsuspected places,

While others scan, under an arc-lamp's glare,
Nursery, kitchen sink, or their own faces.
—KINGSLEY AMIS, 1961

There is probably no more fundamental theme in science fiction than the alien. The genre reeks of the desire to embrace the strange, the exotic and unfathomable nature of The Future. Often the science in SF represents *knowledge*—exploring and controlling and semisafe. Aliens balance this desire for certainty with the irreducible unknown.

A lot of the tension in SF arises from such hard certainties *vs.* the enduring, atmospheric mysteries. And while science is quite odd and different to many, it is usually simply used as a reassuring conveyor belt which hauls the alien onstage.

Of course, by *alien* I don't merely mean the familiar ground of alienation which modern literature has made its virtual theme song. Once the province of the intellectuals, alienation is now supermarket stuff. Even MTV knows how commonly we're distanced and estranged from the modern state, or from our relatives, or from the welter of cultural crosscurrents of our times.

Alienation has a spectrum. It can verge into the fantastic simply by being overdrawn, as in Kafka's "The Metamorphosis," which describes a man who wakes up one morning as an enormous insect. Only one step beyond is Rachel Ingalls's recent *Mrs. Caliban*, in which a frogman appears. He simply steps into a kitchen, with minimal differences from ordinary humans. He is merely a puppet representing the Good Male, and in fact can be read as a figment of the protagonist's imagination. The novel isn't about aliens, of course; it's a parable of female angst.

We don't describe our neighbors as alien just because

they drive a Chevy and we have a Renault. What SF does intentionally, abandoning lesser uses to the mainstream, is take us to the extremes of alienness. That, I think, is what makes it most interesting.

I deplore the *Star Trek* view, in which aliens turn out to be benign if you simply talk to them kindly; this is Hubert Humphrey in space. That fits into a larger program of some SF, in which "friendly alien" isn't seen for the inherent contradiction it is. Friendliness is a human category. Describing aliens that way robs them of their true nature, domesticates the strange.

Yet much early SF was permeated with the assumption that aliens *had* to be like us. In *Aelita, or The Decline of Mars,* by Alexei Tolstoi (1922), the intrepid Soviet explorers decide even before landing that Martians must necessarily be manlike, for

> Everywhere life appears, and over life everywhere manlike forms are supreme: it would be impossible to create an animal more perfect than man—the image and similitude of the Master of the Universe.

We've come a long way since such boring certitudes— through the marauding Martians of H. G. Wells, the inventive and Disney-cute Mars of Stanley Weinbaum's 1934 short story "A Martian Odyssey," and into hard SF's meticulously constructed worlds for fantastic creatures. Aliens have been used as stand-in symbols for bad humans, or as trusty native guides, as foils for expansionist empires, etc.

Yet for me the most interesting problem set by the alien is in rendering its alienness. How do you set the ineffable in a frame of scientific concreteness? This is a central problem for SF. Very seldom has it been attempted in full, using the whole artistic and scientific arsenal.

Artful Aliens

Of course, we all know that one cannot depict the *totally* alien. This is less a deep insight than a definition. Stanislaw Lem's *Solaris* asserts that true contact and understanding is impossible. It was a vivid reminder twenty years ago. As a work of genre criticism it seems nowadays ponderously obvious.

Since then its targets—anthropomorphism, the claustrophobic quality of intellectual castles, and cultural relativism—have become rather cold meat. Indeed, everybody now assumes without discussion that in writing about the very strange, we must always gesture toward something known, in order to make analogies or provide signs. So you're careful, because unless you keep reminding the reader that this creature is to be taken literally, it readily becomes (surprise, surprise) a metaphor.

In the mainstream, walk-on aliens come with metaphors and labels worn on the sleeve. How could they not? In "realistic" fiction, aliens can't be real. SF insists that they *are*—and that important issues turn upon admitting alien ways of knowing.

Even in SF, though, I must inveigh against the notion that we make statements about the alien *in the form of a work of art*. Not so. While this reductionist view is useful for inquiring into epistemology or diagnosing contemporary culture or other worthy purposes, it has little to do with what happens when we confront the alien in fiction. Naturally, there are always people who want to put art to use for some purpose—political, social, philosophical, etc. But it is so easy to forget, once you're using art, that it is not only *about* something, it *is* something.

The alien in SF is an *experience*, not a statement or an answer to a question. An artistic—that is, fulfilling, multifaceted, resonant—rendering of the alien is a thing itself in the world, not merely a text or a commentary on the world.

All the deductions we can make from a story about the truly alien give us conceptual knowledge. So does science. But the story should—must—also give us an excitation, captivating and enthralling us. When SF works, it gives us an experience of the style of knowing something. (Or sometimes, as I'll discuss, *not* knowing.)

This means a prime virtue in depicting the truly alien alien is expressiveness, rather than "content"—a buzz-word which provokes the style/substance illusion in criticism. We don't read *The War of the Worlds* for its views on Martian biology or psychology, but for the sensations of *encounter*.

This may well be the most original thing which SF does with the concept of irreducible strangeness. It's worthwhile inquiring into the underlying ideas and the approaches scholars and writers take in pursuit of it.

Science and Sensawonda

Most SF which takes the idea of the alien seriously (though not necessarily solemnly) deploys a simple strategy:

First, use scientifically sound speculative ideas to construct either the background or the actual physical alien. Garnish the strange planet with whatever ecology looks workable, always favoring the more gaudy and spectacular effects.

Next, deploy a logical sequence of deductions about how an alien would evolve in this place. Stick to concepts like Darwinian evolution, or some later modifications ("punctuated equilibria" in evolution, for example). Then make the alien behave in keeping with this world. Present his/her/its actions, getting the maximum effect of the detailed worldview. Only slowly make known how the alien got that way. This guarded unfolding spices the story with mystery.

This usually works well to make a situation strange and intriguing to the reader. Isaac Asimov's *The Gods Themselves* uses speculative physics and well-rendered oceanic imagery to evoke strangeness. Larry Niven and Jerry Pournelle's *The Mote in God's Eye* has three-legged Moties with well-thought-through implications. On the other hand, Hal Clement's classic *Mission of Gravity* uses a gargantuan planet of crushing gravity, yet the aliens come over as more like Midwesterners. (Maybe this was necessary at the time. The planet was so outré, Clement may have used ordinary aliens to keep things manageable.)

An obvious pitfall of this whole class of approach is that the reader—who may be quite technically adept, and can catch the author in a lapse of world-building—may find all this apparatus merely clever and engaging, a fresh kind of problem story. He'll get no sense of strangeness.

What writers are after here is what the fans call sense of wonder—an indefinable rush when beholding something odd and new and perhaps a bit awesome. Dat ole sensawonda is the essential SF experience. No alien should leave home without it.

Beyond this approach there are refinements. Chad Oliver's *The Shores of Another Sea* treats a chilling alien form which is never more than glimpsed, but whose strangeness slowly comes across, through its use of animals in Africa. Some writers have tried to render alien perceptions, grounding their effects in the sciences. Damon Knight's short story "Stranger Station" treats the anguish of a human trying to enter into an alien's way of thinking. The human emerges with a provisional explanation of how a vastly powerful alien society sees us. (There is a strong hint, though, that he has merely projected his own childhood traumas on the huge creature, so this is really another failed attempt at real contact.)

What I find most interesting about this area is the tricky way it can make so many of our cherished ideas disappear up our own assumptions.

Alien Chat

Scientists often say that communication with aliens could proceed because, after all, we both inhabit the same physical universe. We should agree on the basic laws, yes?—gravitation, electromagnetism, stellar evolution, etc.

This is the gospel of the Universal Language. I'm not so sure. After all, we must frame our ideas in theory, or else they're just collections of data. Language can't simply refer to an agreed-upon real world, because we don't know the alien agrees about reality.

There's an old anthropologists' joke about this. In the outback one anthropologist is trying to learn a native's language by just pointing at objects until the native tells what the object is called in the language. He wanders around pointing and gradually getting more excited. He tells a colleague that these people have built into their language the concept that nature is all one essence, because whatever he points to, the native says the same word.

It is a great discovery. Only much later do they discover that the word the native used is the one for finger.

So you can't just rely on raw data. You must somehow convey concepts—which means theory. And in science, theory inevitably leads to mathematics.

Indeed, the standard scenario for communicating by radio with distant civilizations relies on sending interesting *dit-dah-dit* patterns, which the receiving creatures dutifully decompose into pictures. Those sketches show us, our planetary system, some physical constants (like the ratio of the proton mass to the electron mass), and so most confidently on and on.

Let's play with some notions that go against this grain.

Suppose the aliens don't even recognize the importance of *dit-dah-dit*. Why not? Their arithmetic could be nonnumerical. That is, purely comparative, rather than quantitative. They would think solely in terms of whether A was bigger than B, without bothering to break A and B into countable fragments.

How could this arise? Suppose their surroundings have few solid objects or stable structures—say, they are jelly creatures awash in a soupy sea. Indeed, if they were large creatures, requiring a lot of ocean to support their grazing on lesser beasts, they might seldom meet even each other. Seeing smaller fish as mere uncountable swarms—but knowing intuitively which knot of delicious stuff is bigger than the others—they might never evolve the notion of large numbers at all. (This idea isn't crazy even for humans. The artificial intelligence researcher Marvin Minsky told me of a patient he had once seen who could count only up to three. She could not envision six as anything other than two threes.)

For these beings, geometry would be largely topological, reflecting their concern with overall sensed structure rather than with size, shape, or measurement, à la Euclid. Such sea beasts would lack combustion and crystallography, but would begin their science with a deep intuition of fluid mechanics. Bernoulli's Law, which describes simple fluid flows, would be as obvious as gravitation (things fall when you let go) is to us.

Of course, these creatures might never build a radio to listen for us. But even land-based folk might not share our assumptions about what's obvious.

Remember, our concepts are unsuited to scales far removed from those of our everyday experience. Ask what Aristotle would have thought of issues in quantum electrodynamics, and you soon realize that he would have held *no* views, because the subject lies beyond his conceptual grasp. His natural world didn't have quanta or atoms or light waves in it. In a very limited sense, Aristotle was alien.

Perhaps only in the cool corridors of mathematics could there be genuinely translatable ideas. Marvin Minsky takes this view. He believes that any evolved creature—maybe even intelligent whorls of magnetic field, or plasma beings doing their crimson mad dances in the hearts of stars—would have to dream up certain ideas, or else make no progress in surviving, or mathematics, or anything else. He labels these ideas Objects, Causes, and Goals.

Are these fundamental notions any alien must confront and use? We've cast a pale shadow of doubt over Objects, and I wonder about Causes. Causality isn't a crystal-clear notion in even our *own* science. There are puzzles about quantum cats and, as I elaborated in my novel *Timescape*, fundamental worries about the sequence of time, too.

Why should Objects, Causes, and Goals emerge in some otherworldly biosphere? Minsky holds that the ideas of arithmetic and of causal reasoning will emerge eventually because every biosphere is limited. Basically, it's economics—eventually, some inevitable scarcity will crop up. The smart bunny will turn into a fast-track achiever, since he'll get more out of his efforts. Such selection will affect all his later biases. Minsky has framed technical arguments showing that these notions must turn up in any efficient (and, presumably, intelligent) computer.

I have my doubts, but others have gone a long way toward making math alone carry the burden of communication. Hans Freudenthal's LINCOS is a computer language designed to isolate the deepest ideas in logic itself, and build a language around it. It uses binary symbols typed out in lines. LINCOS stands ready the moment we run into something green, slimy, and repulsive, and yet with that restless urge to . . . write.

Math is central to the whole issue of communication

because it allows you to describe "things" accurately and even beautifully without even knowing what they are. Richard Feynman once said, to the horror of some, that "the glory of mathematics is that *we do not have to say what we are talking about*" (emphasis his).

This is quite a threat to the humanists, who often wish scientists would become more verbally fluent. Feynman means that the "stuff" that conveys physical fields, for example, will work whether we call it wave or particle or thingmabob. We don't have to have cozy pictures, so long as we write down the right equations. I'm reasonably comfortable with this idea. As David Politzer of Caltech once remarked, "English is just what we use to fill in between the equations." Maybe scientists are themselves useful models of aliens.

Delving into the artistic pursuit of alienness always brings up the problem of talking. As I've sketched here, there are good reasons to believe some aliens are genuinely unreachable. You must share a *lot* to even recognize aliens as worth talking to—note how long it's taken us to get around to thinking about the whales and dolphins.

But suppose we finesse the communication card for a moment. How does a writer *assume* some chat can occur, and then create the sensation of strangeness?

The Trapdoor Moment

One of my favorite SF stories is Terry Carr's "The Dance of the Changer and the Three," in which a human visiting a world remarks, "I was ambassador to a planetful of things that would tell me with a straight face that two and two are orange." This reminds me of surrealism in its deliberate rejection of logic. Notice, though, that even while it is commenting on the fundamental strangeness of the aliens, this sentence tries to impose a human perspective—why should the natives have a "straight face" at all? Or any face?

The story deals with creatures on the rather ordinary world of Loarra, and their folk legends are shown in loving detail. This takes most of the text, and the unwary reader thinks he is reading a pleasant bit of pseudoanthropology. Then the aliens suddenly kill most of the expedition. Why?

> Their reason for wiping out the mining operation was untranslatable. No, they weren't mad. No, they didn't want us to go away. Yes, we were welcome to the stuff we were taking out of the depths of the Loarran ocean.
>
> And, most importantly: No, they couldn't tell me whether they were likely ever to repeat their attack.

The story concludes two paragraphs later, with the humans unable to decide what to do next. Notice that the use of *mad* can be read here either as colloquial for angry or else as genuinely crazy. And through the aliens' rejection of prediction they deny the very notion of science as we would hold it. This seems to rule out the Universal Language dogma.

I like the story because it strings you along and then drops the trapdoor just as you're lulled into a pleasant sensation of Loarran pseudo-Polynesian simplicity. The ideas revealed this way are startling, but the core of the story is that sideways lurch into the strange.

For contrast, consider one of the most famous stories about alien encounter, Fredric Brown's "Arena" (1944). A man is trapped inside a desert-floored dome and told he must fight it out with an implacable alien foe for mastery of the galaxy. In their struggle, the alien "roller" reaches the man telepathically (avoiding the whole language problem, you'll notice):

He felt sheer horror at the utter *alienness*, the *differentness* of those thoughts. Things that he felt but could not understand and could never express, because no terrestrial language had the words, no terrestrial mind had images to fit them. The mind of a spider, he thought, or the mind of a praying mantis or a Martian sand-serpent, raised to intelligence and put in telepathic rapport with human minds, would be a homely and familiar thing, compared to this.

But if the roller was utterly alien, it would be incomprehensible. As the critic John Huntington has pointed out, it is *understandable* alienness that so horrifies the human. In fact, it is horrible because it stimulates difficult, inexpressible feelings in the man! He understands the alien by reading his own feelings. He can't deal with them, so he attacks their origin.

"Arena" is usually read as a paean to hard-boiled, Campbellian rationality. I think you can read it as covertly pushing unconscious emotionality. This is a completely different program—intellectually and emotionally—from Carr's.

Modernist Aliens

Oscar Wilde remarked that in matters of supreme moment, style is always more important than substance. So, too, here. We cannot know the true deep substance of the totally alien, but we *can* use conscious and conspicuous style to suggest it. Some of the best SF takes this approach. It is quite different from the Hal Clement–style careful scientific explanations.

In Robert Silverberg's short story "Sundance," the text surges back and forth between points of view, changes tenses, and ricochets between objective description and intense personal vision—all to achieve a sense of dislocation, of reality distortion, of fevered intermittent contact that you cannot quite resolve into a clear picture: "It is like falling through many trapdoors, looking for the one room whose floor is not hinged."

The story culminates in rapidly reflecting and refracting visions of the same "reality," seeing slaughtered aliens for one moment as objects, and then experiencing them from the inside. The narrative voices lurch and dive and veer, always pulling the trapdoor from under any definitive view. The story concludes, "And you fall through"— there is no solid ground.

This is one of the best examples of how SF has used styles and approaches developed first in the dawning decades of the twentieth century, in what the critics term modernism. Breaking with the whole nineteenth-century vision, modernism evolved methods to undermine consensual reality and achieve a more personal, dislocated view. In Joycean stream of consciousness, in the Faulknerian wrenchings of *The Sound and the Fury*, literary devices dynamited cozy assumptions.

When science fiction uses such methods, they have different content. This is, I think, one of the most important contributions the genre has made to literature as a whole. Run-on sentences don't merely mean internal hysteria, flooding of the sensorium, runaway *ennui*, etc. Instead, the method suggests genuinely different ways of perceiving the world, emerging not from psychology and sociology, but from evolution, genetics, even physics.

Unnoticed, SF has taken mainstream methods of breaking down traditional narrative and turned them to achieve uniquely SF ends. (I'd almost term it—delving into jargon myself—using modernism to achieve a kind of SF postrealism.) Nor has this ground been fully explored. I believe it is only now being pioneered.

One of the most interesting uses is that, in SF, these techniques can translate as a rendering of the scientifically unknowable—or, at least, unfathomable by humans. The blizzard of strangeness motif is a persistent notion, even among hard science types.

Time and again in SF, encounters with the alien swamp mere humans. In Fred Hoyle's *The Black Cloud*, Chris Kingsley, the eccentric and brilliant scientist-protagonist, is driven into a kind of overloaded insanity when he attempts full contact with a huge, intruding superintelligent cloud. To accommodate the immense flood of new ideas and perceptions, Kingsley "decided to accept the rule that the new should always supersede the old whenever there was trouble between them"—an SF article of faith. But in the end, contradictions are unmanageable. The new information settling into the same neural brain sites makes sanity and life itself impossible. Kingsley (an echo of Kingsley Amis?) dies. Hoyle is no stylist, but I find it significant that he is drawn to the same notion of contact. Others later expanded on this insight.

Thus one underlying message in SF is that the truly alien doesn't just disturb and educate, it *breaks down reality*—often fatally—for us. Here SF departs quite profoundly from the humanist tradition in the arts. Science fiction nowhere more firmly rejects—indeed, explodes—humanism than in treating the alien. Humanist dogma holds that man is the measure of all things, as Shakespeare put it. SF makes a larger rejection of this than did modernism or surrealism, because it even discards the scientists' Universal Language and the mathematicians' faith in Platonic "natural" ideas. SF even says the universe may be unknowable, and its moral structure might forever lie beyond humanity's ken.

This makes Camus and Sartre and nihilism seem like pretty small potatoes. If you're shopping for literary alienation, SF offers the industrial-strength, economy-size stuff. Yet it also contains the symbols of certainty, through science.

I suspect that the long-standing antagonism between

the literary world and the SF community isn't merely the old story of the stylish effetes *vs.* the nerd engineers. Instinctively, without much overt discussion, the two groups dispute the fundamental ideals behind humanism. SF writers take different views of the universe and can't be reconciled by a few favorable notices in the *New York Times Book Review.*

Strange Bedfellows

Writers as diverse as Philip José Farmer ("The Lovers"), James Tiptree, Jr. ("And I Awoke and Found Me Here on a Cold Hill's Side"), and Gardner Dozois (*Strangers*) have dwelled upon the erotic component in the alien. It turns up in such drive-in movie classics as *I Married a Monster from Outer Space.*

Discussing as personal a subject as sex, I might as well drop the convenient cover of dispassionate critic and write about my own work. At least this approach minimizes the number of potential lawsuits.

When I began thinking about the alien in detail, one of the first stories I wrote was "In Alien Flesh." I constructed it more or less unconsciously, piecing the story together from parts written at separate times over a period of months. For a long while I didn't know where the tale was going.

In it, a man named Reginri has been hired to crawl up into a huge, beached, whalelike alien on the shore of an alien sea. Reginri is a ordinary worker, not a scientist. He simply finds sites to plunge sensors directly into the inner reaches of the being, called the Drongheda. Direct contact floods him with images, feelings—that sensual overload. It provokes ineffable thoughts. And he gets trapped inside the beast.

I wrote most of the story, but had no ending. So I retreated, building a frame around the central tale, which makes the main narrative a flashback. In the frame, Reginri is looking back on his nearly fatal encounter with the Drongheda. I put into this part an approaching fog which humans must avoid—a damaging mist of another planet. Only after I wrote the last lines of the story did I suddenly see what the end of the flashback portion had to be:

> There was something ominous about it and something inviting as well. He watched as it engulfed trees nearby. He studied it intently, judging the distance. The looming presence was quite close now. But he was sure it would be all right.

That done—though not understood, at least by me—I quickly retreated to the point where Reginri is smothered in the alien mountain of flesh and in desperation taps directly into the Drongheda's nerves. I started writing again, filling in action without thinking or planning very much.

Shaken by the flood of strange mathematics and sensation he has gotten from the Drongheda, Reginri finds his way out. Standing in the wash of waves as the Drongheda moves off on its inexplicable way, Reginri learns that one of his fellow workers has been crushed by the alien. Looking back, only then does he see that the hole he had used to crawl up into the Drongheda, pushing and worming his way in, was not "something like a welt"—the description I'd written before, and let stand—but in fact is now quite obviously a sexual orifice!

Until I wrote those lines, I had no clue what the story was really about. What a field day for Freudian analysis! A critic's playground! Effing the ineffable . . .

I decided to let the frame stand. Having written the thing by intuition, I didn't dare tinker with it in the cool light of a critical eye. There's always a point in writing when you have to let go, for fear that you'll tinker away all the life in a piece. So, whatever the tale means or says about my own disquieting interior, there it is.

Though I have now applied the reductionist hammer, which I scorned at the beginning of this essay, to one of my own works, I must say that I think postreadings do tell part of the story. Still . . . once you've dissected a salamander, you know more about it, sure—but it's dead.

As for my own way of assembling the story, I prefer this manner of pondering, shuffling back and forth, and by bits and pieces trying to artistically render the alien. Intuitively, not seeking final answers, and with a certain lack of embarrassment as well.

I'll return to my first assertion, too, and maintain that performing the usual critical slice-and-dice on "In Alien Flesh" misses the thrust of it. Rendering the alien, making the reader experience it, is the crucial contribution of SF. Such tales can argue over communication, spring trapdoors, inundate the reader with stylistic riverruns—all to achieve the end of a fresh experience. That's what the alien is really about.

> *What relief at last*
> *To meet in green bulk and stench*
> *The terrors cloaked inside,*
> *Yesterday released only on the analytic couch.*
> *Shaped in strange mud,*
> *Violent forms, chittering*
> *With frantic energy beneath*
> *Pale yellow, quilted skies.*
>
> *A blister on the mind,*
> *This need for darkness. Lanced*
> *By voyages to the coolly distant,*
> *The cozy-weird. But with acrid pincer*
> *The twisted thing cuts quick*
> *To bones unsuspected.*

Science Fiction
Films of 1985

BILL WARREN

It is sometimes difficult to convey to people who have no clear idea of science fiction's history, from Mary Shelley's *Frankenstein* in 1818 to the present, how this creative impulse, international in scope, with so much genius already behind it, has so pervasively entered the cultures of our world, and in so many ways: stories, novels, films, television, poetry, theater, opera, and dance, at every level of quality from the sublime to the ridiculous. Whether expressed as art or science, playing with imaginative possibilities is central to human cultures. Science fiction films, good and bad, reflect our kind of civilization, perhaps more revealingly when they are unconsciously bad or innocent entertainments. Cinema and television were the science fictional dreams of past times. For many of us the very act of watching a science fiction film is, well, doubly science fictional.

Bill Warren's two-volume *Keep Watching the Skies!* is the most thorough, not to mention witty, survey of American science fiction films from 1950 to 1962 ever published. His occasional stories have appeared in *Amazing* and *Worlds of Fantasy*. He has written comic book scripts and worked as a film archivist and researcher. He understands the needs of film and written science fiction, and is sensitive to the successes and failures of SF on the screen.

When books are written on the science fiction movies of the 1980s, 1985 is likely to be described as the year in which most of the carefully planned "teenpix" bombed at the boxoffice. The year brought mostly "high-concept" SF movies, films based on one supposedly surefire idea around which all the publicity and advertising could be geared. This vacuous idea is regarded by some as the most profitable approach of the last few years in Hollywood, but it's the same idea that American International used in the 1950s; *I Was a Teenage Werewolf* is nothing if not a "high-concept" movie.

Because SF movies featuring people twelve to thirty as the leading characters had succeeded in recent years, the summer saw not only several that were targeted at this group, but also a number that had plotlines much like one another: teenagers messing around with superscience. Some non–SF genre movies, including *Fright Night, Silver Bullet, Once Bitten, The Goonies,* and *Teen Wolf,* also dealt with teenagers and fanciful happenings.

Studios were confident these were sure bets, but of the SF films in this category, only *Back to the Future* can be called a hit. Several, including *Weird Science, Explorers,* and *Real Genius,* were financial failures. Hollywood was baffled. They ascribed the success of *Back to the Future* (and *The Goonies*) to the magic name of Steven Spielberg. (When his TV series, *Amazing Stories,* didn't pan out critically or commercially, sages claimed it was because his is not a TV audience.) But the same sages had a more difficult time deciding why the other films, so carefully aimed at their audiences, did not perform up to expectations.

Usually, movie producers have fairly good ideas about who is doing what, and they try to avoid doing similar movies. (At least at the budget level I'm talking about here; get down to a million and below and it is an entirely different story.) But it soon became known that there were several similar films about to be released, so the distributors tried to have theirs out first; as a result, audiences were required to choose from a passel of cookie-cutter movies, and all of them suffered because of it.

Another problem: there's a Hollywood catchphrase, "skewing young." Samuel Z. Arkoff once pointed out that a little kid will sit through anything a big kid will sit through, but the reverse is not true. Misreading the lesson of *E.T.*, Paramount decided that people wanted to see preteens in imaginative stories; *Explorers* and *D.A.R.Y.L.* both had their problems but also had major virtues. Both films did badly: they were "skewed young"—aimed at too young an audience.

Of course, even Hollywood falls back on obvious wisdom at times: although none of them was really a stinker, none of the movies was as good as should be. Critics, on the other hand, seemed to delight in telling us all that these films were uniformly rotten. After such a slew of films aimed at youngsters, the critics became increasingly hostile to any that catered to the same audience, and the films were savaged. If these films had been scattered over a three-year period, not seeming to follow a trend, each would have been greeted more enthusiastically, both by audiences and by critics. But instead, they were jammed into the summer of 1985.

While there were some major disappointments (*Enemy Mine*, *Lifeforce*), a few exceptional films (*The Quiet Earth*, *Brazil*), and no masterpieces, the overall level of SF movies in 1985 was not notably lower than in previous years. The teenpix were highly visible, but the mixture was much the same as in previous years; there were some slasher pictures, a few *Road Warrior* imitations, and some moderately interesting imports. Nonetheless, because of the generally catastrophic boxoffice reception of the teen SF movies, the overall number of SF movies is likely to decline somewhat from mid-1986 through 1987. (A larger number of films didn't get theatrical release and went directly to videotape in 1985, but that's marketing strategy.)

Back to the Future (the Hugo winner) was a ring-tailed wonder of a film, one of the most entertaining American movies of 1985. It was about as thin as a paper pizza, but made with imagination and verve. To an inventive plot that unwinds predictably but absolutely as you want it to, it adds a lively, talented cast and a sweetly satirical point of view.

Marty McFly (Michael J. Fox), a typical 1980s teenager, has a nerd for a father (Crispin Glover), a near-alcoholic for a mother (Lea Thompson), and a mad scientist, Dr. Brown (Christopher Lloyd), for a best friend. Dr. Brown becomes involved with some terrorists and is shot; fleeing the terrorists in the modified De Lorean Brown claims is a time machine, Marty zooms back to 1955. His mother (now, of course, a teenager herself) falls for him, so he frantically has to get her interested in his father, to prevent Marty and his siblings back in 1985 from unexisting. As well as to avoid a bully (Thomas F. Wilson) and help the Dr. Brown of 1955 figure out the mechanism of Dr. Brown of 1985 and get Marty back to the future.

For all of its sassy, silly plot (the script is by director Robert Zemeckis and Bob Gale), much of the greatest pleasure in *Back to the Future* comes from the performances of Michael J. Fox and Christopher Lloyd. Fox shows a real talent for fast-paced farce, and Lloyd is one of the great comic actors of our time, but until this film has been so different and unrecognizable in movie after movie that most who know him at all recall him only as Reverend Jim Ignatowski of TV's *Taxi*. Wisely, the writers here have opted for Dr. Brown to be a little like Jim—warm, affectionate, crazy; Brown is, in fact, like a cross between Jim Ignatowski and Gyro Gearloose.

Back to the Future was, along with the dreadful *Rambo First Blood Part II*, one of the most successful movies of 1985; according to *Variety*'s figures, *Back to the Future* earned $46,723,229—and that's only about 25 percent of its projected actual U.S. earnings. Naturally, a sequel is scheduled.

Another film aimed at kids but which failed at the box-office was Paramount's *D.A.R.Y.L.* It's rare, but sometimes it happens: a good movie can be made from an unpromising premise. I don't know of any in which the gap between concept and result was wider than in *D.A.R.Y.L.*

D.A.R.Y.L. (Data Analyzing Robot Youth Lifeform), or hereafter just Daryl, is a little boy (Barret Oliver) with a robot brain who has been raised in isolation by scientists. One scientist takes pity on the child and frees him; the scientist is killed, but the little boy is still pursued by bad guys. Daryl becomes part of a Typical American Family with cookouts, baseball games, and ice cream. The evil, mean, wicked, bad, and nasty scientists take him back again. The glacial military types order him destroyed. You would be forgiven if you were to think this would be an icky, schmaltzy, glitch of a movie.

But it isn't. It's sleek, sensitive, funny, and touching, a silk purse from a sow's ear if there ever was one. *D.A.R.Y.L.* was written by David Ambrose, Allan Scott, and Jeffrey Ellis. There's hardly a misstep in the dialogue or characterizations, even when they seem highly unpromising. Almost everyone is characterized, from the largest to the smallest roles. Only the soulless general (Ron Frazier) is stereotyped.

This was the first American film by Australian Simon Wincer, and it's not only engrossing, it's emotionally involving throughout because of the direction and the performances. Wincer likes his characters to undergo believable changes: Daryl becomes more human; his adoptive mother (Mary Beth Hurt), at first frightened of the precocious, naive boy, comes to love him; one of the scientists (Josef Sommer) changes from a villain to a hero.

D.A.R.Y.L. is not outstanding, but none of the other kidpix was more satisfying. It is, of course, "just another Hollywood movie," but was done with talent, warmth, and perception. And it failed terribly at the boxoffice because Paramount didn't know how to promote it (nor did they even really try). They were putting all their money behind Joe Dante's *Explorers*.

But that film also failed at the boxoffice, partly because those who initiated the project at Paramount left the studio to become the new team at Disney. Dante warned Paramount that the schedule on which they wanted him to complete the film was not long enough, yet after production began, they cut six more weeks off it. Even though it had a lavish budget and a year's shooting schedule, *Explorers* looks rushed.

It was hard not to be disappointed by the result. Much of the cleverness that enlivened *Gremlins* is present, but so much is missing from the simple storyline, and there's such an abrupt change in tone partway through, that audiences just didn't respond.

Eric Luke's script is muddled; we see young Ben Crandall (Ethan Hawke) receiving messages in his dreams that enable his friend Wolfgang (River Phoenix) to create a kind of maneuverable force-field. However, this is not explained at all well, and many were puzzled as to just what the heck is going on. We see the three boys (including Jason Presson) build a little spaceship and, at last, go exploring. They find a huge, mysterious spaceship, and have various adventures. But Luke has presented Ben as a sweet, starry-eyed dreamer; what the boy finds aboard the spaceship—a media-stuffed alien and the alien's sister—is a dash of cold water on his dreams.

The scene involving the aliens, though for me the best part of the film, even dazzling at times, is oddly protracted without really going anywhere; apparently Dante and his partners became so impressed with Rob Bottin's funny, convincing alien suit and by Robert Picardo's lively performance as the alien Wak, that they just couldn't cut the sequence. I was amused by the cavorting, singing, bug-eyed monster, but I was apparently one of the few.

Despite good direction, talented performers, miraculously good alien costumes, and acceptable special effects, *Explorers* plays like a short version of a longer film: much seems to have been left out. And in fact, ultimately even *more* was left out; for the videotape and cable release, Dante further cut the film, improving it for most people.

Steven Spielberg directed only *The Color Purple* in 1985, far from his usual sort of thing, but his production company released three other movies: *Back to the Future*, *The Goonies*, and, at Christmas, *Young Sherlock Holmes*, which divided audiences and did not do well financially. In *Young Sherlock Holmes*, writer Chris Columbus (*Gremlins*) imagined what might have happened if Holmes and Watson had met when young teenagers at a London school. This is a pleasant idea, and the clever film nicely carries out this premise. It should have been more robust and exciting, but I found it good holiday entertainment.

Though the bizarre plot—including a vengeful Egyptian sect murdering people here and there about London— seems more like Fu Manchu, it isn't too far off from the kind of thing Doyle did in two of his three Holmes novels.

The plotline involves many of the main characters experiencing bizarre hallucinations; these ideas are all imaginative and often funny, but there are too many of them in the film. The hallucinations, though splendidly done (the effects are by Industrial Light & Magic), become repetitious, and that flying machine should have been scratched from the first draft of the script.

But the film, directed by Barry Levinson, is bright and lively; Nicholas Rowe and Alan Cox make a good Holmes and Watson team (though once again Watson is depicted as being more thick-skulled than in the original stories), and their affection is obvious. Anthony Higgins as Rathe, fencing master (and presumably another kind of teacher) at the boys' school, is precisely cast: he looks like the kind of stalwart fellow that young men always become fond of in this kind of boys'-school fiction.

Young Sherlock Holmes plays like an especially antic Holmes story crossed with Dickens and *Tom Brown's School Days*, plunked down into a Christmas-card view of Victorian London. I'm sorry it isn't more stylish, more vivid, but you can't have everything.

Then there were the Clone Wars. The summer brought three films far too much like one another.

John Hughes's *Weird Science* was a stranger and less successful film than his *The Breakfast Club*, released earlier the same year. Anthony Michael Hall as Gary and Ilan Mitchell-Smith as his genius pal Wyatt are hopeless nerds, the object of scorn by teenage girls and contempt by teenage boys. Also, Wyatt is bullied by his monstrous older brother (Bill Paxton), an enthusiastic military school student. So one night, Gary and Wyatt use a computer (but more like magic) to whomp up gorgeous, full-grown Lisa (Kelly LeBrock), who immediately takes over their lives for the better.

The central idea of *Weird Science* has become rather old hat in a short time; it's a lot like *Play It Again, Sam*, in that a fantasy figure straightens out the life of a nerd (or two nerds, as here). It's too bad that Hughes, talented as both writer and director, couldn't have come up with a better storyline than this, because his cast is notably good, and, though too silly, the film is frequently funny.

Hughes used a broad style—more like *Animal House* than *The Breakfast Club*. He gets some of this right, but overall the film just isn't wild *enough*. Despite the sheer fantasy of the premise, Hughes only bends reality; he doesn't make it sing and sizzle, and that's what was called for here. He's intent on making us believe in his characters, even the literal fantasy of Lisa. This works at odds with the material, and we're left dissatisfied, even if we really don't know why.

In some ways, *Real Genius* is an observant, understanding portrait of genuine geniuses. Although set at the fictional Pacific Tech, the setting is clearly supposed to be Cal Tech; the various stunts performed by the brilliant kids who are the center of the story are genuine, except for the popcorn-filled climax. It is also a stinging criticism of the Strategic Defense Initiative: the opening scene shows a low-orbit spacecraft using a powerful laser to kill a person sitting quietly in a chair. A popular TV scientist and college professor has been hired to build the real thing. There're two stories here—the wild hijinks of brilliant youngsters working off tensions, and the revenge on the manipulative professor.

Although *Real Genius* is a comedy, it just isn't all that funny most of the time, partly because it's such a formula film. Writers Neal Israel and Pat Proft, who wrote *Police Academy* and *Bachelor Party*, among others, have a rigid set of characters for their frenetic comedies: a brilliant free spirit, a nerd who learns better, a disciplinarian tyrant the free spirit & pals overcome, and a slimy weasel enslaved to the tyrant. The more talented Peter Torokvei rewrote the film and Martha Coolidge directed it; as a result, we believe in and trust the characters, despite their stereotyped origins. *Real Genius* is too much like other films, but is still an intelligent variation on this tired theme.

My Science Project was Disney/Touchstone Films' entry in the 1985 Teens Involved in Weirdness derby, and except for *Teen Wolf*, was the last of the pack. As these things go, it was okay, with extravagant special effects and a nicely structured plot.

But writer-director Jonathan R. Betuel has a cheap attitude toward teenagers. Everyone in the film is a walking cliché, and that's tiresome. This is another film which flat-out tells us that if you're intelligent, you're a spazz, a geek, a drip, a nerd; you wear glasses, you can't get laid, and you're bitterly jealous of those who can. At least *Real Genius* was on the side of the brains of the world.

The premise of *My Science Project* is based on a supposedly real event. In the 1950s, President Eisenhower was allegedly called away from a golf game to examine the spaceship of a pair of dead aliens. We see this at the beginning, complete with Eisenhower in golf togs. Thirty years later, car-crazy teenager Michael (John Stockwell) finds a device from the ship, which he intends to turn in as his much-needed science project, but after some weirdness, he decides to show it first to ex-hippie science teacher Bob (Dennis Hopper).

The device draws power from any available source, and when juiced up enough, starts sucking in things and people from other time periods, past and future (but mostly past); the high school corridors turn blue and cloudy. At the climax, Michael, his Brooklynite friend Vince (Fisher Stevens, doing a dead-on impersonation of Sal Mineo at his greasiest), and that painful nerd Sherman (Raphael Sbarge) overcome the best fighters of several time periods—including a dinosaur—to reach the device and turn it off before their whole school is sucked into another dimension. For one of the summer of '85 teen/SF movies, *My*

Science Project rates a bit above *Weird Science* in most respects, and a bit below *Real Genius*.

Of course, not all or even a majority of the SF films of 1985 were made for youngsters. There was Ron Howard's ambitious *Cocoon*, with a cast of mostly older actors, and it was also financially successful, grossing well over $20 million. However, *Cocoon* is the kind of science fiction movie made for (and probably by) people who aren't really comfortable with science fiction; it brought no new ideas, no frightening concepts, no satiric intent. It was a warm, comfortable "little" film which attempted to give us a strong and useful message: even if you're old, your life does not have to be over. Although that is the message director Ron Howard and screenwriter Tom Benedek clearly wanted us to receive, unfortunately the one sent was closer to a dreary thought: if you're old and can't find aliens to help you, you might as well drop dead.

The film was, however, embraced by most viewers, and although the undesired message depressed me, I liked the film much more than I disliked it.

Wilford Brimley, Hume Cronyn, and Don Ameche (who won the Supporting Actor Oscar for his role, the first acting Oscar for an SF film in about fifty years) are among the elderly inhabitants of a Florida retirement home who encounter some friendly but secretive aliens. Disguised as human beings, the aliens have taken a lease on a nearby house and are using the swimming pool in an effort to revive the cocoons of the title. These contain other aliens that had to be left behind when the planet was evacuated by the visitors thousands of years ago when Atlantis (no less) sank beneath the waves. The human beings are revitalized by their exposure to whatever means the aliens have to revive their cocooned companions; minor complications set in when the aliens are forced to leave and take many of the old folks with them.

Unfortunately, once the situations are set up, what

happens is predictable; the film has to mark time. Our three leading men and their lady friends (Maureen Stapleton, Gwen Verdon, Jessica Tandy) are revitalized, charter-boat pilot Steve Guttenberg falls for phosphorescent alien Tahnee Welch (daughter of Raquel), and—well, that's about it, until the climax.

The performers are, one and all, excellent. An actor himself, Ron Howard is especially adept at getting performances from his talented casts; the standouts here are Brian Dennehy as the amiable leader of the aliens, Wilford Brimley, and Jack Gilford. *Cocoon* is a pleasant, amiable movie, painless to watch and made with skill and compassion. It is a soft film, however: in all sincerity, it attempts to be kind, understanding, and warm, and largely succeeds— but at the loss of tension, excitement, and a real sense of adventure. A Hugo nominee.

Baby Secret of the Lost Legend, on the other hand, sacrificed story values to a sense of adventure, and the film tried to change from a moderately interesting dinosaurs-are-alive adventure to a vaguely Indiana Jones–like adventure. It was seriously compromised and, though having some moments, ultimately a failure, both artistically and at the boxoffice.

Paleontologist Susan (Sean Young) and her tiresome baseball-player husband George (William Katt) find a family of brontosaurs in the African jungle. After killing one of them, evil paleontologist Dr. Kiviat (Patrick McGoohan) wants to capture the infant brontosaur (the baby of the title), while the other two try to prevent this. A lot of time is wasted on extraneous details, but once the show gets on the road, for a while *Baby* is a bouncy adventure for the undemanding.

The dinosaurs almost work; the miniature sets are splendid. Dinosaur engineers Isidoro Raponi and Roland Tantin have attempted something widely regarded as impossible to achieve (believable people-in-dinosaur-suits), but came close to bringing it off. Although I am very fond of Ray Harryhausen-Jim Danforth-type stop-motion animation, much of what the dinosaurs are required to do in *Baby* might well have been beyond the limits of stop motion.

Baby tried to be something for everyone, and does have some bright spots and a genuinely appealing baby dinosaur, but also a lot of missteps and digressions, as well as a generally hangdog air.

No one could ever accuse *Lifeforce* of having a hangdog air. Based on Colin Wilson's novel *Space Vampires* (a far more fitting title for the movie as well), this was an exuberant, wild-eyed, and silly science fiction spectacle, brisk to the point of being dizzying. And if you can't quite tell what's going on at the climax—I certainly couldn't—the ride is mostly fun anyway.

Inside the coma of Halley's comet (already it's dated) a joint British-U.S. space expedition discovers a spaceship 150 miles long and 2 miles high, containing desiccated space bats, and three nude human beings in suspended animation. They're taken aboard the shuttle, but then things start going wrong. The three are ultimately taken to London where they soon begin draining people of their life forces.

But wait, that's not all. There's also shuttle pilot Steve Railsback (in a too-intense performance), who has some kind of psychic affinity with the woman space vampire (Mathilda May, who spends much of the film spectacularly nude). And the victims, turned to shriveled corpses, revive later and suck life energy out of yet other people, who revive later and on and on like that, until London is full of rioting space vampires and their victims, while a blue beam of stolen souls stabs upward at the spaceship, now unfolded like a colossal umbrella.

Lifeforce is big and bold, with excellent special effects by John Dykstra, and it gets down to the nitty-gritty quickly. The climax, clearly inspired by the superlative *Quatermass* teleplays and films of Nigel Kneale, is an eye-popping phantasmagoria of fire, explosions, winds, stolen souls, panic, and death.

However, *Lifeforce* is also almost overwhelmingly silly. Writers Dan O'Bannon and Don Jakoby may have been trying to emulate Kneale's careful, straight-faced approach to his imaginative SF concepts, but they were dealing with far wilder material than even Kneale ever touched, and they missed his precisely structured introduction of bizarreness. When the actors, including talented performers like Peter Firth, Frank Finlay, and Michael Gothard, start discussing the outlandish events in their tense, jittery performances, the audience starts laughing and never stops. *Lifeforce* would have worked a lot better if the characters (but not the actors) had acted at times as if what was going on was funny. Not a spoof, but a light approach.

Despite a cracking pace and excellent effects, *Lifeforce* became the howler of the summer, and though it made well over $3 million, its cost was so high that it was a financial failure. The same writers and director team tried again in 1986 with *Invaders from Mars*.

Year's end brought what must have been the most expensive SF film of the year, *Enemy Mine*. Because of production problems, the movie may have cost as much as $50 million to make. It began under the direction of Richard Loncraine, shooting on location in Iceland. However, he fell behind schedule and the footage didn't satisfy 20th Century-Fox studio chiefs, so they turned the film over to Wolfgang Petersen (director of *Das Boot*), who started again from scratch. The result was disappointing.

Enemy Mine is a big, elaborate science fiction version of two-man war stories like *Hell in the Pacific*. Dennis Quaid is Will Davidge, a human pilot who crash-lands on an uninhabited planet after a space battle with a Drac, one of a race with whom human beings are warring. The Drac (Louis

Gossett, Jr.), whom Davidge eventually calls Jerry, is a lizardlike hermaphrodite, as shrewd as but more understanding than Davidge. The two have to cooperate to survive, and eventually become friends.

Now, this is good, schmaltzy material for a melodrama about friendship, but something went wrong between Edward Khmara's decent script of Barry Longyear's novella and the actual film. The movie is overblown visually and emotionally cold except for Gossett's exceptional performance through Chris Walas's elaborate makeup. Dennis Quaid, fine in other films (*The Right Stuff*, for example), is strained and hammy.

It's shot in hot oranges and cool, dead grays, seemingly on the same few hundred feet of terrain—almost entirely highly artificial-looking sets, built at great expense in Germany. The main feeling I came away with from *Enemy Mine* is regret for the lost opportunities. After *The Never-Ending Story* and now this operatic but miscalculated epic, I'm beginning to suspect that Petersen isn't really a good director.

As usual, 1985 brought some sequels and remakes. Those who expected *Mad Max Beyond Thunderdome* to be just like *The Road Warrior*, the movie it's a sequel to, are naive. After all, *The Road Warrior* was hardly like *Mad Max*, the film to which *it* was a sequel. Though all three are basically the work of one person, George Miller, he's taken great care to see that each film has its own ideas, its own look; he doesn't simply repeat things.

That being said, it must also be admitted that despite its many outstanding qualities, *Mad Max Beyond Thunderdome* is less compelling and exciting than *The Road Warrior*. It partly compensates for this by a richness of texture, design and idea almost unparalled in sequel history. Miller has created a believable post–atomic holocaust landscape, one of the few in movie history. The culture he presents, part leather-freak, part frontier, part futuristic, seems of a piece and is of a density and intensity that makes it seem like a remembered past.

It's fifteen years after *The Road Warrior*. Max (again Mel Gibson) comes to Bartertown, a settlement "managed" by Aunty Entity (Tina Turner), and becomes a victim of the political intrigues between Aunty and Master (Angelo Rossito). Eventually, Max is abandoned in the desert again, and this time is rescued by a band of children who live in a lush oasis. Moses Max leads the children to Bartertown and back, and the film concludes in a spectacular display of Australian stunt brilliance, this time played for laughs as the rickety, speedy cars and trains smash deafeningly into one another.

Mad Max Beyond Thunderdome was collaboratively directed by Miller and George Ogilvie; Miller produced, and cowrote with Terry Hayes. The film is genuinely epic, a science fiction spectacle of dust, dirt, pig crap, children, and sand. It was one of the best SF films of the year, and although it did significantly less well than *The Road Warrior*, I hope this witty, intelligent film generates at least one more sequel, so poor weary Max can find his own promised land at last. He deserves it. When films like *Enemy Mine* and *Ladyhawke* can get Hugo nominations over *Mad Max Beyond Thunderdome*, I realize I have lost touch with the opinions of SF fans. (*Ladyhawke*, being a fantasy, is not included in this essay.)

Every few years, someone gets the idea of doing a new Frankenstein film; after all, for fifty years, they've been a staple of the movie diet (and the first was made in 1910). 1985 brought the elaborate film of *The Bride*. Although it unquestionably has its faults, it largely lives up to its pretensions.

Columbia Pictures announced that the film, written by Lloyd Fonvielle and directed by Franc Roddam, had nothing to do with James Whale's fabulous classic, *The Bride of*

Frankenstein. But in fact, the opening scenes of *The Bride* recapitulate the closing scenes of the old movie: the Monster (Clancy Brown) is lurking around the tower while Baron Frankenstein (Sting) and his fey assistant (Quentin Crisp) bring the Bride (Jennifer Beals) to life as a mate for the Monster, but she rejects the Monster at once. *The Bride* then intercuts between the adventures of the Monster at large in the world and Frankenstein's educating the Bride, whom he names Eva. The Monster is befriended by a dwarf, Rinaldo (David Rappaport), who names him Viktor. At the end, fate brings the two Frankenstein-made creations together again.

The Bride is a conscious attempt to impose the viewpoints of the 1980s on this story set in the 1830s, with Eva becoming a liberated woman (as was Mary Shelley), while domineering Frankenstein gradually becomes obsessed by her. The film also tries to be a more conventional Frankenstein story as well; Viktor is a good guy here, a big, inarticulate, innocent lamb who wins our sympathy through his friendship with Rinaldo.

The film is too slow, and it didn't please those looking for a blood-and-thunder horror thriller. But it has a valid viewpoint that consistently surprised me. Jennifer Beals is good as Eva, and David Rappaport is outstanding as Rinaldo. Although Clancy Brown comes up to the demands of the script as Viktor/the Monster, he does little to rise above them. Sting is required to be an indolent, brittle nobleman, obsessed by his creation and with controlling her. The role is written in a too-restricted manner; he's more like Peter Cushing than Colin Clive in the role, but lacks the fire of Cushing and the vibrating sensitivity of Clive. He's the worst kind of male chauvinist pig: intensely attractive, brilliant, but still controlling, domineering, unfair.

The Bride attempts to bring a modern outlook to a classic tale. It split moviegoers violently and made little money. But I feel that this slow, imaginative film shows that there are ways of bringing this corpse back to life again and again. It does tend to overintellectualize, but at least it is respectful of the material.

In 1953, Columbia Pictures released a wild-eyed, scaremongering salute to eternal vigilance called *Invasion U.S.A.*, in which Certain Unnamed Powers launched nuclear attacks on the U.S. and then invaded key cities. In 1985, Chuck Norris gave us a brand-new *Invasion U.S.A.* but, alack and alas, it is not a remake of the first outlandish movie. It's outlandish in its own ways, but that's mostly because it's so dumb.

As usual, in *Invasion U.S.A.* Norris kicks, slugs, and shoots mobs of grimacing extras. Only this time they are heavy-duty invading terrorists under the direction of Certain Unnamed Powers. Playing disaffected C.I.A. agent Matt Hunter, literally all by himself Norris brings to a halt what must be a Soviet plan (the chief villain is Mikhail Rostov) of terrorism by shooting the crap out of mobs of terrorists. How he knows where they are going to strike is unexplained and mystifying; we see him interrogate one sniveling hood who really must have been loaded with information, because thereafter whenever terrorists strike— at least in Dade County, Florida—Chuck Norris is right there to stop them.

Joseph Zito directed this dopey script (written by Norris and James Bruner), and has given *Invasion U.S.A.* a lot of zip and zow. The film really is nothing more than an excuse to sew a bunch of action scenes together; at that, it's just fine. But its point of view is deplorable as well as silly: a single good American—*one guy*—can wipe out all opposition.

Warning Sign was a blend of *The Andromeda Strain* and *Night of the Living Dead*. First known as *Biohazard* (see below), it's a technically convincing but unpleasantly tense suspense story set in a germ warfare plant where things get out of control. The script by Hal Barwood and Matthew Robbins was intended to sound a cautionary note about the dangers of such research while remaining a suspenseful thriller. Unfortunately, the plentiful horror stuff seems shoehorned in and detracts from the intended warning. Most of the characters are just sketched-in elements representing types we have seen before. Despite an unusually high-powered cast for one of these things, the actors and first-time director Barwood never convince us these people are real.

The situation is quickly set up: a vial of undoubtedly nasty stuff cracks in a germfree environment, and things get bad very soon. The installation seals itself. Tough government agent Connolly (Yaphet Kotto), soon arriving with a decontamination and containment team, tells worried sheriff Cal Morse (Sam Waterston) that the supposedly peaceful place was really developing deadly germs. And now one of those germs is loose in the building, where only Cal's wife Joanie (Kathleen Quinlan) is apparently immune. Cal enlists the aid of renegade scientist Dan Fairchild (Jeffrey De Munn) to enter the place, rescue Joanie and try to help those trapped within.

A reasonable idea for a thriller. But why did Barwood and Robbins insist that the germ turn those it infects into disfigured, bloodthirsty maniacs? Supposedly, the germ inflames the "rage center" of the brain—but why don't the victims try to kill each other? Instead, they go after only the uninfected.

Warning Sign becomes suffused with a sick, unpleasant tension. We aren't eager to see what comes next, we just want the whole thing to be over as fast as possible. The film sat on the shelf a while, and no wonder. It isn't that it's a terrible movie, it's that there's nothing new in it; it has been given handsome treatment and has some good scares. But *Warning Sign* is mostly not much.

1985 also brought the film that pre-empted the *Biohazard* title, but this silly, cheap, and amateurish film went directly to videotape. The muddled movie uses a setup similar to the old *Terror from the Year 5000* combined with *Scanners* to do yet another imitation of *Alien*. This time, scientists, including psychic Angelique Pettyjohn, are trying to materialize something from another dimension. A tiny monster played by a child (Christopher Ray, son of the director) gets loose and kills a few people and also shreds an *E.T.* poster. In the foggy plot, Pettyjohn turns out to be an alien herself; though the beginning says the advent of the "Bio-Monster" was accidental, it finally insists it was deliberate.

It was produced, directed, and written by energetic horror movie fan Fred Olen Ray, who has made several ultra-low-budget films in the past few years, none of which (as far as I know) got theatrical release. If they are all as primitive as this one, they shouldn't even end up on videotape. Ray seems to be a nice guy and clearly loves SF and horror movies, but making a good film takes more than being a dedicated fan.

Another *Alien* imitation did get theatrical release, but did better on videotape. This was *Creature*, also made by a horror movie fan, Bill Malone. It's better by far than *Biohazard*, but it's still a bad movie, although Malone keeps giving hints that he might be better than his material.

In *Creature*'s near future, the world is apparently ruled by rival corporations. When something unusual is found on Titan (the film was, in fact, originally called *Titan Find*), expeditions are launched. Soon enough, aliens apparently left on Titan eons before begin killing various people. Unfortunately, we never know how many of the aliens there are, or even what they're really up to. The movie is extremely gory, with lots of vomited blood, slime, and a face ripped off in close-up, with the head still screaming.

The incoherent plot mixes *Alien* with touches of *Invasion of the Body Snatchers* (and includes a direct reference in the dialogue to *The Thing from Another World*); it's depressing and monotonous, with an ending out of left field (someone thought dead turns up abruptly and kills the last alien). The photography is fair, the special effects (by Robert Skotak) are excellent for the budget level, and the music is dreadful. The film does feature a funny, raunchy performance by Klaus Kinski, one of the most eccentric actors on or off the screen. When he's around (briefly), *Creature* takes on a semblance of life; after Kinski's departure, the film becomes drained of interest.

Another low-budget film showing only flickers of imagination was *The Dungeonmaster*, an incomprehensible mix of SF and fantasy. Computer expert Jeffrey Byron and his girlfriend Leslie Wing are captured by Mestema (Richard Moll), who seems to be the Devil, and who wants to test his occult powers against Byron's computer abilities (the hero has a gadget strapped to his wrist which [a] computes probabilities and [b] shoots rays, and [c] does damned little else). Byron suddenly gains a superhero costume and is put through some tests in sequences of widely varying quality written and directed by several people.

Rosemarie Turko wrote and directed "Ice Gallery," one of the better sequences; John Buechler's "Demons of the Dead" was merely a showcase of mediocre puppetry and makeup that goes nowhere; Charles Band's "Heavy Metal"—actually sixties-type rock with heavy-metal costumes—is over quickly and thank you; David Allen's "Stone Canyon Giant" features dwarfs and a stop-motion stone statue that for all it does could more easily have been played by a man in a suit. Steve Ford directed and star Byron wrote "Slasher"—merely serial murder stuff in LA, though it's better written than any other sequence even if not directed well; in Peter Manoogian's meaningless "Cave Beast," the hero fights a demon that turns into an angel; Ted Nicolaou's brief, dull "Desert Pursuit" is just another *Road Warrior* clone.

The Dungeonmaster was released by Charles Band's Empire Pictures, which is trying to be the American International of the 1980s, releasing cheap, quickly made genre films aimed at an international and videotape market. So far, only two of their films have shown real quality, and those were *Trancers* and *Re-Animator*.

Despite some serious budget problems, *Trancers* is one of the best SF movies of 1985. It's a tight little thriller with an inventive script, good acting, and an unusual premise. Clearly intended to be similar to *Blade Runner*, it turned out to be something different and, in some ways, superior. However, the trancers themselves—hypnotized slaves of Martin Whistler, an evil mastermind—could easily have been done away with; they add nothing to the story and almost seem to have been ignored by the writers.

Tim Thomerson sardonically plays Jack Deth, a cop of three hundred years hence, who is determined to hunt down trancers. Jack thinks Martin Whistler was killed, but in fact Whistler has gone back in time to December 1985 in Los Angeles and is killing the ancestors of the ruling council of future Angel City. Jack gets an injection, and like Whistler, winds up in the body of an ancestor who's a private eye. Naturally, being a private eye, Jack talks in sharp, clipped tones and becomes involved with a beautiful woman.

The film abounds in small, witty details, including slang of the twenty-third century ("dry hair's for squids"), ancestors turning up in odd places, the Christmas season interfering, Jack watching 1985 TV, jokes on his name, and so on. It has a good sense of location, using little-seen areas of Los Angeles, and even suggests the future society with some degree of skill.

Trancers was written by Danny Eilson and Paul DeMeo and surprisingly well directed by Charles Band, who in no other film has demonstrated the talent he shows here. *Trancers* had a brief theatrical play, then went to videotape;

I recommend you catch it there. For a cheap little movie, it's remarkably good.

As has been usual for the last several years, 1985 brought with it yet more foreign imitations of *The Road Warrior* and other post-holocaust films. Some of these went directly to videotape, such as *Warrior of the Lost World*, a 1983 Italian movie featuring some actors known to the West (among them Robert Ginty, Persis Khambatta, Donald Pleasence, and Fred Williamson). According to the reliable "Lor" in *Variety*, this was "a well-directed action fantasy that might have been a winner with a better script." Set after "radiation wars," the film, says "Lor," is "firmly in the *Mad Max* groove, though visually [writer-director David] Worth aims at a look resembling George Lucas's . . . *THX 1138*."

Desert Warrior, filmed in the Philippines in 1983, was called "Vindicator" and "Wheels of Fire" before release, but apparently is terrible by any name. *Boxoffice* said it was "pretty unsavory stuff" that was "poorly written and badly acted," set in a post-apocalypse desert environment. Hero Trace (Gary Watkins) has to rescue his sister Harley (Lynda Wiesmeier) from a villain called Scourge (actor unidentified). "Jagr" in *Variety* said that it was "poorly played and ridiculous" with clumsily staged action and unconvincing effects. *Desert Warrior* was written by Fredrick Bailey and produced and directed by Cirio Santiago.

I presume it was even worse than *The Exterminators of the Year 3000*, which I did see. This Italian-Spanish coproduction was written by Elisa Briganti, Dardano Sacchetti, and José Truchado Reyes, and directed by the undoubtedly pseudonymous Jules Harrison. Detto Mariano's music imitated the German group Kraftwerk. The cast, as usual, was made up of Italian or Spanish actors under more pseudonyms, and/or American players you never heard of. There were Robert Jannucci, Alicia Moro, Alan Collins, and Luca Ventantini.

In *this* post-holocaust future, nuclear bombs have destroyed the ozone layer and so wiped out water on the face of the earth (although there's plenty of shrubbery). Tommy, about twelve and with a mechanical arm (called "bionic" in the dialogue), wants to find what happened to his father, who went in search of water. He teams up with a Mad Max–like hero called Alien and his girlfriend Trash, and together they battle the Exterminators of the title, who're led by Crazy Bull, as close to an exact duplication of *The Road Warrior*'s Wez as possible. There's a lot of dust-raising activity, finding water and losing it again, before the bad guys are wiped out and, as if that's all it takes, the skies burst open in a torrent of rain.

The film is rife with unexplained elements (strange people in hoods guarding water in what appears to be a pumping station) and absurd dialogue. Alien to Crazy Bull: "Go jump in the lake." Crazy Bull: "Ah, humorous, eh?" Spunky Tommy is referred to at one point as "that sneaky little beaver." The film is boring, ugly, and trivial.

Slightly better is *Escape from the Bronx*, another Italian film, this time trying to rip off *Escape from New York*; it was shot in English with some location work in New York, and may be a sequel to *1990: the Bronx Warriors*. Here, the Bronx has been declared uninhabitable, and most of the population relocated to New Mexico(!). An evil corporation sends roaming bands of silver-clad goons through Da Bronx fricasseeing hangers-on with flame throwers. The hero, who looks like Treat Williams in *Hair*, is named Trash (Mark Gregory). When his parents are burned to death, he plots revenge against the evil corporation chief and his head goon, amusingly played by Henry Silva, who might have written some of his own dialogue. With intrepid woman reporter Moon Gray (who dies) and famous thief Strike (actor unidentified but okay), he travels through the vast, brightly lit catacombs that underlie all of New York City(!).

Although director Enzo G. Castellari, an old hand at

this sort of thing by now, keeps things going, he has a limited idea of style: when someone arrives where there are other people, there are many shots of heads turning to look at the newcomer. He also has a point-of-view shot of a dangling ladder, as if the ladder can see. The ending seems both definitive and inconclusive, as if Castellari wants to do this again. Although the movie is less offensive than most of these things, he shouldn't bother.

Somewhat similar was the American-made *Future-Kill*. Actually, only the title tells us it's set in the future; it was shot in today's Austin, Texas, and except for the *Road Warrior*-style clothing and an apparent cyborg named Splatter, there's really nothing about the film that couldn't take place in the here and now. Some arrogant fraternity types go down to the sleazy part of town to kidnap nuclear war protester punks who live in a colony there. Their chosen victim is the head-honcho punk, who is promptly killed by psychotic Splatter, who also kills a couple of the frat rats before they can flee.

The film oddly makes both Splatter's bunch and the frat rats almost completely unsympathetic, leaving us no one whatever to root for. It is not bad in some ways, not overly graphic in its violence, but ugly, being shot in seedy areas of town. The opening is much worse than what follows (the fraternity "comedy" stuff is loathsome). No acting to speak of, although both Edwin Neal (as Splatter) and Marilyn Burns, in briefly as his former lover, aren't bad. Both were in *The Texas Chainsaw Massacre*, and much was made of this in advertising.

The Canadian-made *Defcon-4* is well directed by Paul Donovan, who also wrote, and the cast, including Tim Choate, Lenore Zann, Kate Lynch, Maury Chaykin, and Kevin King, is above average. It opens on a manned U.S. satellite which is watching for various missile launches and tests; to the horror of the three aboard, they see nuclear war break out on Earth. The satellite expends all but one of its missiles defending itself, then some time later is dragged to Earth. One of the crew is killed, and the others (a man and a woman) eventually fall into the hands of a group of vicious thugs led by a disdainful collegiate youth.

The film is cheap but the effects are mostly very good. Donovan shows much more talent as a director than as a writer, for the major defect of *Defcon-4* is that it is familiar stuff. The first half is superior to the second, which is conventional post-holocaust material. Oddly, the movie ended up on some best-of-the-year lists, as well as on some *worst-of-the-year* lists. It's neither, actually; it's an intelligent, inventive variation on a tired theme and suggests that Paul Donovan is a promising talent.

Yet another post-holocaust film, also American, was *City Limits*, which I have been unable to see—although I wanted to, as it was made by the same writer-director team who made the interesting and entertaining *Android*. However, *City Limits*, though it had a larger budget than the earlier film, was not received as well by reviewers.

According to David Chute in the Los Angeles *Herald Examiner*, the film "depicts roving youth gangs as the sole hope of democracy, arrayed against the fat conglomerate that moves into a blasted Los Angeles to take over and enslave the populace." The film presents comic books as the "Alexandrian library of the new age." Shades of Robert Bloch's story "A Proud and Lonely Thing." Chute liked some of the ideas in the film, that it had "a more positive, anti-nihilist approach to the post-nuke genre," but also thought it was far too mild. "Japa" in *Variety* said the film "should have a cultish following" and praised the score and action scenes and "extraordinary visuals." The Los Angeles *Reader* found the film fragmentary, but still suggested that director Aaron Lipstadt shows talent.

This time writer Don Opper doesn't appear as an actor, but all critics praised most of the cast, particularly Darrell Larson, John Stockwell, Kim Cattrall, and Rae Dawn

Chong. James Earl Jones also appears. Robby Benson was considered improbable as the leader of the villains.

There was yet another postapocalypse movie in 1985, but it was dramatically different from those mentioned already—in concept, style, quality, and country of origin. This was *The Quiet Earth*, a little-seen film from New Zealand, inventively and imaginatively made, with a memorably enigmatic ending. It is, in fact, one of the best SF films of 1985. Even though that may seem like faint praise, this would be an interesting film in any year.

Zac Hobson (Bruno Lawrence) wakes up to find himself apparently not only the only living person in the world, but, except for plants, the only living thing; all other human beings and animals have vanished. He soon discovers that a project he was working on, a mysterious power grid being initiated by the U.S. and New Zealand, simply caused everyone to vanish the instant it was turned on. He wanders through deserted Auckland, playing a saxophone, choosing a car that suits his fancy, and finally setting himself up in a huge mansion. He tries to contact other people to no avail, although he finds the rare corpse or two. In a funny, sad scene, he sets up cutouts of celebrities on the lawn of the mansion, then arranges for himself to be cheered as king of the world by recorded voices.

Eventually he finds two other people, Joanne (Alison Routledge), and Api (Peter Smith), a Maori. Combining their information, they realize that for whatever reason, they survived because at the instant the grid was activated, they were dying. (I found this explanation unsatisfactory, but at the end there's a suggestion that it may not be correct anyway.) There are some sexual and racial tensions among the three, not resolved when they find that the grid is still operating and might wipe them out, too. Zac has to drive an explosives-laden truck into the power source of the grid and perishes in the explosion.

But in the last, haunting scene of *The Quiet Earth*, Zac

awakes on a beach with unusual clouds in the distance; after a moment, a Saturn-like planet rises above the horizon. Zac's sacrifice saved his companions, but has put him—elsewhere. Just where he is (and some have illogically concluded he's on Titan) cannot be explained; it's a mysterious other-where.

The Quiet Earth was written by Bill Baer, Sam Pillsbury, and actor Lawrence and directed by Geoffrey Murphy, from a novel by Craig Henderson. Murphy's films are hard to classify: they're neither dramas nor comedies, but sardonically observed realism. He's a true original who has a strong personal style and a sure grasp of moviemaking techniques. *The Quiet Earth* is fascinating, amusing, and mature. The ending is likely to throw some people for a loop, which is a shame, because it's part and parcel of the odd film that precedes it. Though it runs down toward the end, this is likely to be considered a minor classic in years to come; it's the best last-man-on-Earth movie I have ever seen.

In 1979 the BBC showed Nigel Kneale's *The Quatermass Conclusion* in several parts; the same footage was to be used, with cutting, for theatrical release in the United States. However, though Kneale carefully structured his script for eventual reduction to feature length, the producers cut on other dotted lines than those provided by him, and the resulting film met with no one's satisfaction. It was finally released in the U.S. on videotape in 1985, and virtually everyone who saw it was disappointed. But while it is, unfortunately, the least of the four Quatermass stories, it is still an imaginative, intelligent, and intriguing science fiction thriller, worth anyone's time to watch it.

Perhaps it was an error for Kneale to set the film in the near future, when civilization has begun to fracture and crumble; this bitterly observed future world is story enough without the intercession of one of the most unusual alien menaces in movie history.

Quatermass (John Mills), the rocket expert, has begun

to go a little senile. He is worried about a new joint space project between the U.S. and the U.S.S.R.. Once the leading exponent of space research, he has become hostile to the idea, and has become obsessed with finding his granddaughter, who left him recently. He meets a dashing young radio astronomer (Simon McCorkindale, in the only pleasing performance I've seen from this usually smug actor) and his family. Roaming bands of young people cross the country; calling themselves the Planet People, they have a conviction that they are going to go to another world. En masse, they enter various of the stone rings, like Stonehenge, that dot the English landscape. Once they are there, a beam stabs down from space (destroying, incidentally, the U.S.–U.S.S.R. linkup) and reduces them to a yellowish dust.

This happens all over the world as thousands upon thousands of young people, including McCorkindale's family, are destroyed by beams from space. Quatermass and other elderly scientists eventually find a way to combat this, but at great cost to themselves. This is not idly called *The Quatermass Conclusion*.

Although perhaps the doom-laden, depressing tone of the film is overdone—the skies eventually turn yellow from the powdered remains of children—there's no denying that it is still laden with typical Kneale brilliance. He delights in connecting the past on Earth to alien visitations in novel ways: here, those stone rings were not left *by* aliens, but by our ancestors to warn us to stay away from those spots, where visitors eons ago left devices that cause the beams to focus there. At the end, Quatermass and his fellow scientists create the electronic analogue of thousands of people to attract the destructive harvest beam to them.

Although *The Quatermass Conclusion* is as tightly woven as other Kneale scripts, with a bittersweet ending and yet another novel view of alien visitation, it does disappoint most who see it. I liked it very much myself, although I think that the last Quatermass story should have featured him welcoming the first *friendly* alien visitors. Perhaps the best single line in the film is the anguished outcry of one of the Planet People, echoing the fear and mistrust of science that all too many people have had all through history: "Stop trying to *know* things!"

Cavegirl was a childish, boring comedy rife with bug- and booger-eating jokes, fart jokes, and sex jokes. A nerd (Daniel Roebuck) is the butt of various pranks, justified solely because he *is* a nerd. There's a confusing, perhaps impenetrable relationship between a helicopter, scientists conducting a test, and the nerd exploring a cave. He's sent back to the prehistoric past where he's still the butt of jokes, but a gorgeous cavegirl (Cindy Ann Thompson) falls in love with him. Her unveiling her breasts is a big moment. Even though the film takes pains to establish how the nerd goes back in time, at the end he simply *walks* back to the present, temporarily. There's some faint, momentary inspiration in some of the camera work and an odd, undeveloped glimmer of an idea in having a weird old coot in the present know caveman language. But mostly the film, produced, written, directed, and photographed by David Oliver, is stupid and forgettable.

Likewise stupid and likewise forgettable is *Transylvania 6-5000*. The only clever aspect of this film, written and directed by Rudy DeLuca, is the title, and that comes from a Bugs Bunny cartoon. The feature was shot in Yugoslavia; it should have been shot at sunrise. The storyline involves a couple of reporters looking for Frankenstein's Monster. They find a mad scientist who has helped cure various weirdos, freaks, and sexual psychotics by means that somehow make them look (in some cases temporarily) like famous monsters.

Neither as writer nor director does DeLuca show the slightest trace of ability. The film is so poorly organized that not only do the "monsters" not turn up until the last reel, but there's not even any hint that they are around until then. And talented performers, not just leads Jeff Goldblum and Ed Begley, Jr., but Joseph Bologna, Jeffrey Jones, and Carol Kane are left floundering.

This sloppy, slow, boring mess is the worst horror-film spoof in years—and there are darned few that are good. *Transylvania 6-5000* is neither funny nor scary; it's a labored, obvious waste of talented performers. Don't watch it on cable. Don't rent it on videotape.

The other spoof of the year was less clearly one. It's an extremely odd and gory loose adaptation of H. P. Lovecraft's "Herbert West, Reanimator" stories, written by Dennis Paoli, William J. Norris and Stuart Gordon, and directed by Gordon (his first film). Gordon is a respected and highly talented theatrical director from Chicago, who staged not only *Warp* but also versions of Joe Haldeman's *Forever War* and Kurt Vonnegut's *The Sirens of Titan*. I've seen the latter and consider it one of the most entertaining evenings I have ever spent in a theater. It should have won every SF award in sight but, as it was "merely" a play, hardly anyone saw it.

Gordon made the transition from theater to film with H. P. Lovecraft's Re-Animator, a movie that's both sophisticated and pretty rough on audiences not expecting what they get. It is a cleverly plotted but ultraviolent thriller, such a straight-faced spoof of horror movies that it can easily be taken for the genuine article.

Jeffrey Combs plays Herbert West, a gimlet-eyed zealot, typically cold-blooded and monomaniacal, who has developed a glowing green fluid that brings dead things back to life—eviscerated cats, for instance, or both the decapitated head and body of an enemy. The story opens with a man's eyes exploding and concludes with West being crushed by thirty feet of living intestine. In between, we see such amazing sights as a head giving head . . . .

The photography by Mac Ahlberg and the various

makeup effects are mostly good. On the other hand, Richard Band's score is a virtual copy of Bernard Herrmann's famous *Psycho* score. Band told interviewers that he was trying to spoof Herrmann the way that the movie spoofed other movies, but it simply sounds like a rip-off.

It is such a straight-faced joke that on that level it largely fails until the exuberant climax, with dozens of insane reanimated corpses attacking the living members of the cast. But it's lively and inventive; if Gordon can lift himself out of the grue and violence genre, he could be as fine a movie director as he is a theatrical one.

Morons from Outer Space is, as many people have noticed, not precisely a promising title. Though populated with good performers, produced on a lavish budget, and well directed, the film is so uneven and its targets of satire so widespread and diffuse that it's understandable why Universal was reluctant to handle it in the United States.

Mike Hodges directed. His previous films, including *Pulp*, *Get Carter*, and *Flash Gordon*, didn't give me any clue as to what *Morons from Outer Space* might be like. I was surprised that it's as funny as it is, and disappointed that once all the basic ideas are presented, the film has nowhere else to go. The best the script by Mel Smith (who plays one of the Morons) and Griff Rhys Jones (who plays their Earth friend) can come up with is to dump Bernard, the alien played by Smith, into an unrealistically lush Arizona while the other, even stupider, aliens are having a grand time in England. Bernard has to get across the U.S. to try to rendezvous with Julian (Paul Brown), Dez (Jimmy Nail), and Sandra (Joanne Pearce) in New York, and they aren't anxious to see him.

The first half of the film is distinctly better than the second. There's a spoof of *Close Encounters of the Third Kind* as a French scientist prepares to talk to the aliens when they emerge from their ship (he plays "Born Free" on a big theater Wurlitzer). As the scientists slowly realize that these alien visitors, whom they expected to be far superior to us mentally, are actually dolts, the film has its best moments. Later it takes off on a spoof of celebrity cults that ultimately amounts to nothing.

Still, a science fiction comedy that treats SF ideas with respect as well as affection is unusual, and though the film is about half as funny as it should be, the talented performers and the occasional amusing moments keep things going, if at a low boil. Worth catching on cable.

Unless you are fond of Italian high-style thrillers, you might as well avoid *Creepers*. This was cut by twenty-five minutes from the original version, called *Phenomena*, also available on videotape. As it stands, it is a consistently interesting but disjointed horror thriller with SF elements, set in Switzerland and shot in English. Jennifer Connelly, a beautiful and talented young actress, plays the daughter of a famous movie star, sent to a girls' school in Switzerland. (The location used is Richard Wagner's old villa.) Girls her age have been vanishing from the school. Their corpses are sometimes found crawling with maggots (we're treated to a close-up of a rotting, worm-infested head). Jennifer— her role name as well—can communicate with insects, an odd idea that plays a real part in unraveling the mystery of the phantom killer. Donald Pleasence clearly enjoys his role as John McGregor, a wheelchair-bound Scottish entomologist living in Switzerland, waited on by a doting chimpanzee.

The climax is one of the strangest in recent memory: Jennifer is battling with a fifteen-year-old deformed dwarf (the killer) on a lake when a cloud of insects, attracted by her distress, attacks the dwarf. Covered with biting bugs, he falls into the lake. Spilled fuel ignites the lake, and Jennifer falls in, too. She battles the monster underwater, and he's defeated; on shore, she's attacked by the killer's overprotective mother (last seen up to her neck in a vat of rotting flesh and maggots), but saved by Pleasence's razor-carrying chimpanzee, seeking revenge for Pleasence's death earlier in the film. And they say they don't make them like that any more. Written, produced, and directed by the inventive but obviously lunatic Dario Argento.

Death Warmed Up is the second New Zealand SF film of 1985, this one far below *The Quiet Earth* in quality, although director David Blyth, who cowrote with Michael Heath, shows a lot of promise. The plotline is weirdly convoluted, and at the end, Blyth just keeps lots of action coming at us apparently so we will overlook the fact that nothing is being explained. Nothing *could* be, and we wind up with no idea whatever of why anything we saw occurred.

Mad scientist Dr. Archer Howell (Gary Day) declares that "We are the generation of the end," feeling that immortality is possible now. Somehow in an effort to prove this, he chemically forces young Michael Tucker (Michael Hurst) to kill his own parents. Seven years later, eager for revenge, Michael is released from the booby hatch and together with three friends promptly goes to Howell's island retreat, where he is doing graphically depicted but inexplicable brain operations. (The head of one of his victims explodes.) There's action with previous victims of Howell's operations, leftover World War II ammunition tunnels, and an escape of the mutated surgical victims. There's a lot of excitement, including two people bursting into flame, but no explanations.

The structure is sloppy and disconnected; each scene works reasonably well, but the plot does not satisfactorily explain them. Still, it's nastily witty, with good dialogue, amusingly satiric acting, and well-staged action. But it's ultimately much more confusing than anything else. The director is clearly fond of the movies of David Cronenberg, but he lacks Cronenberg's unifying vision and stringent (if sometimes obscure) logic.

Larry Cohen, an idiosyncratic, distinctive, but sloppy

writer-director, was represented in 1985 by *The Stuff.* Typical Cohen, it was stuffed with imaginative, satiric ideas, but executed as though the vigorous Cohen had to get things over quickly and on to another project. Scenes don't end where they should; connecting material is missing; attempts are made to bolster continuity by overdubbing explanatory dialogue; the visual quality varies so wildly it's as if some of the footage was shot on outdated sixteen-millimeter film. The movie lacks coherent explanation.

Cohen was trying to do a high-tech "blob" movie, but went careening off in other directions as well, so that few of the ideas work satisfactorily. A white substance is found oozing from the ground; when tasted, it's found to be both delicious and addictive. Soon packaged as a dessert, "The Stuff" begins eating into the profits of ice cream manufacturers, who form a cartel to hire a savvy, informal industrial spy (winningly played by Michael Moriarty, often a stiff stick). Meanwhile, a kid whose family are already Stuff junkies discovers a glob of the Stuff crawling around the family refrigerator. The plot heats up with chases around the South. The spy enlists the help of the woman (Andrea Marcovicci) doing "Stuff" commercials—allowing Cohen a brief sway into spoofing TV spots, the kid, a chocolate-chip-cookie king (Garrett Morris), and a right-wing military nut (Paul Sorvino). Eventually it's proved the Stuff is alive, and eats its victims from within.

But there's no consistency: Cohen can't seem to decide if the Stuff is intelligent and whether or why it has planned all this, and never even hints where it comes from. But as usual in a Cohen film, there's a lot of intelligence (if muddled) at work, many good scenes, and generally fine acting. Though *The Stuff* is one of his lesser films, it is unmistakably a Larry Cohen movie.

George Romero was back with the third of his living-dead films, *Day of the Dead.* It was a sequel to *Dawn of the Dead,* itself more or less a sequel to Romero's notorious debut, *Night of the Living Dead*. The drive, wit and energy that made *Dawn of the Dead* so unexpectedly pleasing are almost entirely lacking in *Day of the Dead*. Romero has taken his mad idea far too seriously this time, and insisted on a sick, unrelenting tension that makes the film difficult to sit through.

Romero wrote and directed *Day of the Dead*, set in the near future when the cannibalistic walking corpses have taken over most of the United States (and presumably the world, though this is only hinted at). Unfortunately, this time out Romero has chosen to set his story almost entirely on a few underground sets, among a group of people all of whom seem to hate each other.

They're sitting around shouting at one another, marking time to be a zombie dinner. One scientist (Richard Liberty) has discovered gleamings of intelligence in a captive zombie dubbed Bub (Howard Sherman), but the military goons, led by Rhodes (Joe Pilato), just want to slaughter all zombies they encounter and get the hell away from the subterranean base. This premise makes for a disturbing but ultimately boring movie, intense but oppressive, with an air of desperation and desolation. This cannot be considered a fun flick by even the most rabid Romero fanatics; it's too gloom- and doom-laden for almost anyone, with a slow pace, unparalleled gruesomeness, and a sense that the world is at an end.

Not as gory but promising more gore than *Day of the Dead* was Dan O'Bannon's *The Return of the Living Dead*, strangely enough a *second* sequel to *Night of the Living Dead*. (There are labyrinthine legal complications allowing competing sequels.) Unlike *Day*, O'Bannon's *Living Dead* is a comedy, from the first shot (a notice telling us that what we are about to see is absolutely true and all the real names have been used) to the last, when it is all starting over again. This is O'Bannon's first feature as a director; in his other scripts, including *Alien* and *Blue Thunder*, he has demonstrated a sardonic point of view and an ability to tighten tension, and those are here, in this wild, anarchy-fueled madness.

A bunch of punks and some workers in a medical supplies warehouse are attacked by walking corpses from a neighboring cemetery when gas from some zombies stored in the warehouse is accidentally released. Things keep escalating until the military drops an atom bomb on the whole mess.

Unlike Romero's film, *The Return of the Living Dead* definitely *is* fun, with a fast pace, funny characters, and more imagination than gruesomeness. This time the zombies eat raw brains, and use whatever means necessary to get a fresh supply (including CB radios: a zombie intones, "Send more cops," and the dispatcher does). There's a disturbing, haunting scene in which an incredible half-corpse tells our beleaguered little band how painful it is to be dead and to want to eat brains. The major problems with the movie are a strangely set-bound quality (the comic-book stylization isn't powerful enough to offset a feeling of cheapness) and a lack of really sympathetic characters. I didn't like the punk & new-wave score. And, of course, this kind of thing, however well done, isn't exactly new. But O'Bannon will be back, with bigger and better films—and then this debut film will be sought out and praised.

Only barely science fiction but worthy of note was *Creator*, another film shabbily treated by Universal, as were *Morons from Outer Space* and the unusual, hypnotic *Dreamchild*. Peter O'Toole, in a typical egocentric, eccentric role, plays scientist Harry Wolper, who, for the twenty-five years since her death, has been trying to clone his deeply beloved wife. He becomes involved with graduate student Boris (Vincent Spano) and free-spirit Meli (Mariel Hemingway), who donates her eggs for Harry's experiments. Soon, he apprehensively begins to return her love, but annoys her by constantly talking about his dead wife. Meanwhile,

Boris falls in love with Barbara (Virginia Madsen), and this leads to a near-tragedy.

Harry's rival, the disciplinarian and ambitious Sid Kuhlenbeck (David Ogden Stiers, very good), sabotages Harry's finally successful attempt at cloning, and sees to it that Harry is put out to pasture in a branch of the college reserved for doddering old professors with tenure. But it all works out well for everyone except Kuhlenbeck.

Creator was written by Jeremy Leven from his own novel and directed by Ivan Passer; I don't know who's to blame for the film's uneasy and extreme shifts in tone. It begins as a good, witty comedy about research, grants, and college science-department rivalries, veers into tender romance, then plunges into stark tragedy. It's understandable that some viewers had a hard time keeping their footing.

The biggest monster of all was back in *Godzilla 1985*, a Japanese (of course) film directed by Kohiji Hashimoto, with American scenes inserted by R. J. Kiser. Peculiarly, the film was written as if there had been no Godzilla activities (i.e. sequels) since the first film back in the early fifties. Even Raymond Burr returns as the same reporter he played in American-shot scenes for *that* film, here staring into TV monitors and muttering suggestions that this time Godzilla will win. The Big G is more powerful than before, and the film has a much more serious approach and better special effects. He may still look just like what he is, a guy in a rubber suit, but the suit is better and the miniature cityscapes he trashes are far more elaborate.

Unfortunately, the American distributor, New World, deliberately chose to force a camp aura on the picture, with uncaring dubbing and a spoofy archness in the American-shot scenes. The film would have been hard to take seriously in any event, but this trashing only left it almost impossible to know *how* to take it. The genuine innocence of the Japanese films was allayed with an unpleasant

American smart-ass attitude, and the result was neither fish, fowl, nor real Godzilla.

An Australian movie about a giant monster was also released in 1985, but here the monster was, probably uniquely, a giant pig. *Razorback* is an exercise in powerful visual style, scudding dust, lights piercing the darkness, tumbling metal, and the briefly glimpsed gigantic boar that gives the move its title and menace. Clearly inspired by *Jaws*, director Russell Mulcahy and writer Everett DeRouche still managed to deliver the goods with this witty, eerie, and dusty little film. The acting is above par, and if you can overcome any qualms you have about our hero battling a giant piggy, you may enjoy *Razorback*.

The remainder of the SF films of 1985, with a notable exception I'll get to in a moment, were the usual mix of film-festival entries with little distribution, minor horror movies with an SF gimmick, and the few oddities that always show up. I've seen none of these, but not for want of trying.

Evils of the Night, which features the redoubtable, durable John Carradine as a scientist from outer space, was reviewed from Cannes by *Variety*'s "Strat," who didn't like it. He called it "a tepid blend of teen sex, sci-fi and low-level horror" centering around mysterious goings-on at a lake in the forest. "Strictly formula stuff," according to "Strat," although reasonably well-known people appear in it, including Neville Brand, Aldo Ray, Tina Louise, and Julie Newmar.

Boggy Creek II, also alliteratively titled *The Barbaric Beast of Boggy Creek Part II*, was described by *Variety*'s "Lor" as a "very mild and folksy piece of regional filmmaking in which it is clear that the filmmaker (who doubles as his own leading man) really likes his creatures." Writer-producer-director Charles B. Pierce stars as a University of Arkansas professor who investigates the Bigfoot-like creature supposedly living in the Boggy Creek region of Arkansas. This is a sequel to Pierce's 1972 *The Legend of Boggy Creek* and, according to "Lor," is "painfully short on thrills."

Another film with mostly regional release was the spoofy *Doctor Otto and the Riddle of the Gloom Beam*. Made in Nashville, this movie was the only '85 release I was unable to find any reviews on, so apart from the fact that it stars Jim Varney and a few others and was directed by John Cherry II, who co-wrote with producer Coke Sams, I know only that it's a comedy about a mad scientist trying to take over the world but who, of course, fails.

The 1984 French film by producer, writer, and director Claude Lelouch, *Viva la Vie!* saw some American release in 1985. Sporting major European stars, including Charlotte Rampling, Michel Piccoli, Jean-Louis Trintignant, Charles Aznavour, and Anouk Aimée, Lelouch's film is described as being either an homage to or a sendup of the movies of Jean-Luc Godard. Piccoli and Rampling are two arrogant Parisians abducted by extra-terrestrials. The film is larded with interviews with the other players and Lelouch himself; it apparently ends with a resounding cliché that perhaps Lelouch thought was original. But at the request of Lelouch, the scant reviews, not favorable, don't divulge what is going on in the story. The film did well in France.

A better-liked film was the Danish *The Element of Crime*, shown at the 1985 Filmex in Los Angeles, but receiving few other U.S. screenings to date, though it may have been picked up for distribution here. The plotline of *The Element of Crime* reportedly is the least interesting element: in a devastated future Europe, a police investigator (Michael Elphick), following the ideas of his college professor mentor (Esmond Knight), puts himself in the place of a vicious serial killer in an effort to track him down. What received resounding praise was the style of writer-director Lars von Trier, here making his feature debut. Michael Wilmington in the *Los Angeles Times* said the film is "splendidly bizarre, perverse, idiosyncratic, defiantly unclassifiable, literally arcing and crackling with creative energy." (That I have to see.) *Variety's* "Kell" said it would "stun even the most blasé international audiences," featuring "superior direction of excellent . . . players, . . . evocative imagery and murky poetic-philosophical threads." Despite this hyperbole, *The Element of Crime* sounds like a film to see.

So does the short feature *Futuropolis*. In the *New York Times*, Janet Maslin said the movie "manages to maintain its homemade air without seeming the least bit amateurish. Combining humorous animation . . . with live action that has a speedily antic rhythm, the film manages to send up various science fiction clichés and also parody half a dozen genres along the way." In the *Los Angeles Times*, Michael Wilmington concurred; he considered the forty-minute movie "as pictorially dense as many pictures three times its length and many times its cost. A gimmicky spaceship, the black, star-strewn immensity of space, a city run by a deranged scientist, special effects galore—they're all part of the brief, wild ride." The film was nine years in the making by its writer-producer-director duo, Steve Segal and Phil Trumbo. Wilmington says "it has a nice, jokey, devil-may-care quality and by the second half, when it has picked up steam, the execution matches the imagination." This sounds like an ideal entry for science fiction convention film programs.

Two animated-cartoon SF movies were released in 1985. The lesser of the two, *The Secret of the Sword*, is just a cobbling-together of several episodes of the "She-Ra" TV series, a sequel of sorts to "He-Man and the Masters of the Universe," based on a line of toys by Mattel. Set in a weird sword-and-sorcery universe in which the villains use super-science while the heroes use glowing, magical swords, *The Secret of the Sword* appeals only to children. Charles Solomon in the *Los Angeles Times* pointed out the wretched, limited animation typical of made-for-TV cartoons, and the nonthreatening violence imposed on them by overly strict broadcast standards. Solomon carefully avoided commenting on the quality of the film.

Apparently superior was *Starchaser: the Legend of Orin.* Made in 3-D and animated in Korea, *Starchaser* is reportedly a fast-paced and entertaining film. Several critics commented on the inherent unreality of a 3-D cartoon, in which (as Vincent Canby said) the "resulting images look like those in a child's toy theater in which the cardboard characters can be made to move from side to side but not from front to back." The plotline is blatantly similar to *Star Wars*, with a blonde young hero finding a powerful laser sword; he's befriended by a wise-cracking space smuggler and a princess, and opposed by a gravelly voiced villain. This is all told against the conventional space empire backdrop. The animation is described as being unimpressive, but most critics said the film is pleasantly easy to sit through.

Then finally, at the tail end of the year, came Terry Gilliam's brilliant, fractured *Brazil*, a Hugo nominee. The troubles Gilliam had in getting his cut of the film shown in the United States were covered by all major news services, and presumably the publicity had a hand in forcing Universal to release it in a form approved by Gilliam, albeit shorter than its European version. Whatever it took, it was worth it to see this film in Gilliam's version.

In approach and style, *Brazil* is unique, and there are damned few works of art in any medium that are truly themselves. The most serious problem with the movie, and it *is* serious, is that in terms of content we've seen it before. It's another *1984*-style dystopia, in which a Common Man is ground down by the Machinery of the State; here, however, Gilliam falters, for his State is run by ditzy lunatics and flaming whackos. In *1984*, the reason the State wins is that it is relentless, shrewd, and powerful; in *Brazil*, the reason the State wins is because it is required in the plotline that the State win. These schlemiels can scarcely tie their shoelaces, much less run the world, so their victory seems contrived rather than inevitable. As satire, *Brazil* is a failure, because of familiarity and because you can't see any trace of our world in Gilliam's; he's making a generalized spoof of bureaucracy, not one especially relevant to our times.

But all that being said, it is also true that *Brazil* is one of the best movies of 1985—a dazzling, scintillating, and vivid entertainment. Visually a strange conglomeration of *Metropolis*, *The Wizard of Oz*, and *Blade Runner*, it resembles none and all of them. Highly stylized—there isn't a conventional "realistic" scene in it—*Brazil* confused some audiences and astonished others. Production designer Norman Garwood must have worked closely with director-writer Gilliam, because the movie looks and feels like nothing so much as one of the strange cut-out animations that Gilliam did for "Monty Python."

The film is nearly impossible to describe, as there's nothing to compare it to. It's set in what might as well be an alternate-reality London, perhaps the present day but one in which computers had to be made out of leftover World War II equipment, the state has taken over, and fashion has gone on a bizarre road (women wear shoes on their heads). Jonathan Pryce, looking much like a young Alec Guinness (George Lucas, are you listening?), is an ideal Everyman, struggling against the enmeshing coils of the state which dearly wants him to simply fit in. His old pal Michael Palin, a contented torturer who hums while he works, keeps warning Pryce that things may go wrong. Ian Holm, Bob Hoskins, and Robert De Niro also appear in memorable cameos, and De Niro's "demise" in the film is the strangest I have ever seen: he turns into clutching newspapers and blows away.

Brazil is a film to be seen repeatedly; there's no way you can get all the jokes, lampoons, satirical asides, and references on one viewing, and they're all worth getting.

The elegance, beauty, imagination, and humor of its design and the airy, faery quality of the strange flying scenes also make repeated viewings desirable. This did only moderately well everywhere it played, but it gained powerful fans and staunch supporters. This will be a cult classic at first, and later, in the fullness of time, a true film classic.

One of the staunchest supporters of *Brazil* was Harlan Ellison in his delightful, infuriating, and informative column in *The Magazine of Fantasy and Science Fiction*. Rife with Ellison's usual knowing asides, personal biases and stinging satire, "Harlan Ellison's Watching" may be uneven, but it is the most vital writing on genre films available today, and one of the best current film columns of any sort. Even if after reading his column you end up flinging the magazine across the room, you will still appreciate it and be glad he's being published in this format, on these topics. One reason some find Ellison annoying is that like all the best critics, he writes from steadfast conviction, is a superlative writer, and so is damnably convincing. When reading his reviews, you can find yourself thinking that he *must* be right, even when you completely disagree. Publishers sometimes irritate Harlan, and so he sometimes leaves his columns; I hope to heaven he doesn't do it with this.

As you can see, there aren't any real trends in the SF films of 1985, but there's the hint of one: though several, including *Creator* and *Lifeforce*, are based on published works, only one, *Enemy Mine*, is derived from what we would ordinarily think of as (for want of a better term) "real" science fiction. Since, like *Dune* the year before, *Enemy Mine* failed at the boxoffice, it was just one more way of convincing studio executives—who mostly don't read anything, much less SF—that published science fiction has nothing to offer movies.

Yet the past ten years has seen a boom not only in SF moviemaking but in published SF as well, and this is not a coincidence. While I am not claiming that the big rise in popularity of published SF is due solely to the success of such films as the *Star Wars* and *Star Trek* series, there is definitely a causative connection. Partly because of the immense popularity of these films, written science fiction is big business as literature now. It has become common to see not just books with SF themes on best-seller lists, but also books written by genuine, authentic, SFWA-card-carrying science fiction pros.

But at their peril, movies have not been playing to this growing audience. Certainly most of the audiences for these movies don't read SF—but they don't read anything else, either. But the kids who do read SF read that more than any other literary form, and those readers (as opposed to convention-going, fanzine-publishing fans) make up a large percentage of the moviegoing audience. So where are the films based on Anderson, Heinlein, Asimov, Clarke, Sturgeon, and so forth? Why aren't their books being filmed?

Although science fiction is the most popular movie genre in the world, there really is an upper limit on the grosses they're going to make (except for Lucas and Spielberg films). If a science fiction film costs no more than around $12–15 million, it stands a good chance of making a profit—a better chance, in fact, than most other kinds of films. The movies therefore have to have a certain limit to their budgets, so no matter how popular a book like *Footfall* by Larry Niven and Jerry Pournelle might be, for example, the epic sweep of its story means it's unlikely to be filmed; it would cost more than it's likely to return.

But what about many Heinlein novels? To me, the ideal unfilmed SF novel is *The Puppet Masters*. Now that has everything: monsters from outer space that look truly icky and gooshy, mind-control, nudity, and plenty of action.

Yet apart from a strange little imitation of it made almost thirty years ago, no one has ever gotten *The Puppet Masters* off the ground.

And it isn't the only easily filmable novel; those reading this have their own choices. I have the feeling—I get these sometimes, but I drink a nice cold beer, and the feeling goes away—that somewhere, someone is going to film a major SF novel or novella and make money at it. This change is looming up out there.

Like it or not, science fiction was ultimately helped by movies like *Star Wars*. It's about time for Hollywood to begin filming written science fiction right, not because it is polite but because it is expedient. And this not only must happen, it will happen. Gary Kurtz, who, after all, produced *Star Wars*, is one of the few Hollywood professionals who both knows this and is in a position to do something about it. He has several projects in mind based on well-known SF novels; if he can get the films off the ground, I think this change may be coming sooner than even I expect.

But the change *will* happen because it *must* happen. It is not like the constant presence of mystery novels on book racks the world over. SF is more important than that, and publishers are now giving science fiction novels important positioning in their schedule of publication; the stuff is being read. Moviemakers usually lag several years behind such trends—but sooner or later they catch up with them. I make no promises that these potential films will be good, but they *will be made*. I know this goes back on things I said earlier, but I have changed my mind. Remember, you read it here first. If I'm wrong, be kind.

APPENDIXES

About the Nebula Award

The Nebula Awards are voted on, and presented by, active members of the Science Fiction Writers of America. Founded in 1965 by Damon Knight, the organization's first president, the SFWA began with a charter membership of 78 writers; it now has over 800 members, among them most of the leading writers of science fiction.

Lloyd Biggle, Jr., the SFWA's first Secretary-Treasurer, originally proposed in 1965 that the organization publish an annual anthology of the best stories of the year. This notion, according to Damon Knight in his introduction to *Nebula Award Stories: 1965* (Doubleday, 1966), "rapidly grew into an annual ballot of SFWA's members to choose the best stories, and an annual Awards Banquet." The trophy was designed by Judith Ann Lawrence from a sketch made by Kate Wilhelm; it is a block of lucite in which are embedded a spiral nebula made of metallic glitter and a specimen of rock crystal. The trophies are handmade, and no two are exactly alike.

Since 1965, the Nebula Awards have been given each year for the best novel, novella, novelette, and short story published during the preceding year. An anthology including the winning pieces of short fiction and several runners-up is also published every year. The Nebula Awards banquet, which takes place each spring, is held in alternate years in New York City and on the West Coast; the banquets are attended by many leading writers and editors and are preceded by meetings and panel discussions.

The Grand Master Nebula Award is given to a living author for a lifetime's achievement in science fiction. This award is given no more than six times in a decade. Nominations for the Grand Master Award are made by the President of the SFWA and are then voted on by the past presidents, the current officers, and the current Nebula Awards jury. The Grand Masters, and the years in which they won, are Robert A. Heinlein (1974), Jack Williamson (1975), Clifford D. Simak (1976), L. Sprague de Camp (1978), Fritz Leiber (1981), Andre Norton (1983), and Arthur C. Clarke (1985).

Past Nebula Award Winners

1965

Best Novel: *Dune* by Frank Herbert

Best Novella: "The Saliva Tree" by Brian W. Aldiss

"He Who Shapes" by Roger Zelazny (tie)

Best Novelette: "The Doors of His Face, the Lamps of His Mouth" by Roger Zelazny

Best Short Story: " 'Repent, Harlequin!' Said the Ticktockman" by Harlan Ellison

1966

Best Novel: *Flowers for Algernon* by Daniel Keyes

Babel-17 by Samuel R. Delany (tie)

Best Novella: "The Last Castle" by Jack Vance

Best Novelette: "Call Him Lord" by Gordon
R. Dickson
Best Short Story: "The Secret Place" by Richard
McKenna

1967

Best Novel: *The Einstein Intersection* by
Samuel R. Delany
Best Novella: "Behold the Man" by Michael
Moorcock
Best Novelette: "Gonna Roll the Bones" by
Fritz Leiber
Best Short Story: "Aye, and Gomorrah" by
Samuel R. Delany

1968

Best Novel: *Rite of Passage* by Alexei Pan-
shin
Best Novella: "Dragonrider" by Anne Mc-
Caffrey
Best Novelette: "Mother to the World" by
Richard Wilson
Best Short Story: "The Planners" by Kate Wil-
helm

1969

Best Novel: *The Left Hand of Darkness* by
Ursula K. Le Guin
Best Novella: "A Boy and His Dog" by Har-
lan Ellison
Best Novelette: "Time Considered as a Helix
of Semi-Precious Stones" by
Samuel R. Delany
Best Short Story: "Passengers" by Robert Silver-
berg

1970

Best Novel: *Ringworld* by Larry Niven
Best Novella: "Ill-Met in Lankhmar" by Fritz Leiber
Best Novelette: "Slow Sculpture" by Theodore Sturgeon
Best Short Story: No Award

1971

Best Novel: *A Time of Changes* by Robert Silverberg
Best Novella: "The Missing Man" by Katherine MacLean
Best Novelette: "The Queen of Air and Darkness" by Poul Anderson
Best Short Story: "Good News from the Vatican" by Robert Silverberg

1972

Best Novel: *The Gods Themselves* by Isaac Asimov
Best Novella: "A Meeting with Medusa" by Arthur C. Clarke
Best Novelette: "Goat Song" by Poul Anderson
Best Short Story: "When It Changed" by Joanna Russ

1973

Best Novel: *Rendezvous with Rama* by Arthur C. Clarke
Best Novella: "The Death of Doctor Island" by Gene Wolfe

Best Novelette: "Of Mist, and Grass and Sand"
by Vonda N. McIntyre
Best Short Story: "Love Is the Plan, the Plan Is
Death" by James Tiptree, Jr.
Best Dramatic Presentation: *Soylent Green*

1974

Best Novel: *The Dispossessed* by Ursula K.
Le Guin
Best Novella: "Born with the Dead" by Robert Silverberg
Best Novelette: "If the Stars Are Gods" by
Gordon Eklund and Gregory Benford
Best Short Story: "The Day Before the Revolution" by Ursula K. Le Guin
Best Dramatic Presentation: *Sleeper*
Grand Master: Robert A. Heinlein

1975

Best Novel: *The Forever War* by Joe Haldeman
Best Novella: "Home Is the Hangman" by
Roger Zelazny
Best Novelette: "San Diego Lightfoot Sue" by
Tom Reamy
Best Short Story: "Catch That Zeppelin!" by
Fritz Leiber
Best Dramatic Presentation: *Young Frankenstein*
Grand Master: Jack Williamson

1976

Best Novel: *Man Plus* by Frederik Pohl
Best Novella: "Houston, Houston, Do You
Read?" by James Tiptree, Jr.

Best Novelette: "The Bicentennial Man" by Isaac Asimov
Best Short Story: "A Crowd of Shadows" by Charles L. Grant
Grand Master: Clifford D. Simak

1977

Best Novel: *Gateway* by Frederik Pohl
Best Novella: "Stardance" by Spider and Jeanne Robinson
Best Novelette: "The Screwfly Solution" by Raccoona Sheldon
Best Short Story: "Jeffty Is Five" by Harlan Ellison
Special Award: *Star Wars*

1978

Best Novel: *Dreamsnake* by Vonda N. McIntyre
Best Novella: "The Persistence of Vision" by John Varley
Best Novelette: "A Glow of Candles, a Unicorn's Eye" by Charles L. Grant
Best Short Story: "Stone" by Edward Bryant
Grand Master: L. Sprague de Camp

1979

Best Novel: *The Fountains of Paradise* by Arthur C. Clarke
Best Novella: "Enemy Mine" by Barry Longyear
Best Novelette: "Sandkings" by George R. R. Martin
Best Short Story: "giANTS" by Edward Bryant

1980

Best Novel: *Timescape* by Gregory Benford
Best Novella: "The Unicorn Tapestry" by Suzy McKee Charnas
Best Novelette: "The Ugly Chickens" by Howard Waldrop
Best Short Story: "Grotto of the Dancing Deer" by Clifford D. Simak

1981

Best Novel: *The Claw of the Conciliator* by Gene Wolfe
Best Novella: "The Saturn Game" by Poul Anderson
Best Novelette: "The Quickening" by Michael Bishop
Best Short Story: "The Bone Flute" by Lisa Tuttle*
Grand Master: Fritz Leiber

1982

Best Novel: *No Enemy But Time* by Michael Bishop
Best Novella: "Another Orphan" by John Kessel
Best Novelette: "Fire Watch" by Connie Willis
Best Short Story: "A Letter from the Clearys" by Connie Willis

1983

Best Novel: *Startide Rising* by David Brin
Best Novella: "Hardfought" by Greg Bear
Best Novelette: "Blood Music" by Greg Bear

*This Nebula Award was declined by the author.

Best Short Story: "The Peacemaker" by Gardner
Dozois
Grand Master: Andre Norton

1984

Best Novel: *Neuromancer* by William Gib-
son
Best Novella: "PRESS ENTER█" by John
Varley
Best Novelette: "Bloodchild" by Octavia E.
Butler
Best Short Story: "Morning Child" by Gardner
Dozois

1985

Best Novel: *Ender's Game* by Orson Scott
Card
Best Novella: "Sailing to Byzantium" by
Robert Silverberg
Best Novelette: "Portraits of His Children" by
George R. R. Martin
Best Short Story: "Out of All Them Bright Stars"
by Nancy Kress
Grand Master: Arthur C. Clarke